BEN STEVENS

INVASIVE SPECIES : BOOK TWO

HOSTILE GENUS

aethonbooks.com

1

His hand on the back of Ratt's chair, Jon braced himself against the turbulence and peered out through the viewport.

"Incredible, isn't it?" Ratt asked over his shoulder, keeping his eyes forward.

"You can say that again," Jon mumbled, leaning in closer to admire the sweeping vistas zipping beneath them as they sped through the cloudless blue sky of the southern Far Rough.

"I've been up before, you know," Jon said, "in a Hopper, but somehow, this is… I dunno, different."

"Probably helps that you aren't being shot at," Ratt said with a smirk.

Jon raised his eyebrows, nodding in agreement.

"See that? Up ahead?" Ratt asked, pointing to the horizon.

Squinting, Jon perceived a thin blue line stretching from one end of the horizon to the other.

"That's the Southern Water I was telling you about. I haven't seen it since I was a boy."

"I've never seen it…" Jon muttered, his thoughts turning to the expanse of unimaginably blue water he had seen in the *Wa'ak*

Lum, the dream world where he had learned the truth of things from Maya. *Well, maybe I have.*

"I had no idea it was that close to Home," Jon remarked.

"Close? *Amigo*, it's not close at all. I know it's only been two hours, but this baby is hauling ass." Ratt grinned again, patting his chair's armrest and turning to gauge Jon's reaction.

Jon hadn't considered that, but he supposed it made sense. The new-style transport that they had commandeered was one of only three recently built by the Republic Military. Unlike the comparatively skeletal ships that carried the Heavies into the Rough, like hanging coats on a winged rack, this vessel was thick, smooth, and wingless, from the outside appearing nearly feature-less: a jet-black, stunted cigar. The ship, likely inspired by tech Warbak had obtained from his Harvester masters, seemed to defy gravity, making no sound, while cruising at speeds that made Hoppers seem motionless. The outside of the vessel was armored, and the inside was spacious. All in all, quite an impressive machine.

Turning around, Jon looked at his friends, new and old, and smiled. They sat in the chairs arrayed behind the pilot's area, a smaller, more comfortable space that was probably reserved for a crew. Together with the pilot's chair, they were on a higher level, with the main cargo area in the transport below, significantly larger and longer than the cantilevered upstairs. The main cargo area was a cold, metallic, utilitarian space, designed to house Hopper units and infantry, perhaps even an artillery unit or two, but too small for a Heavy Mech.

Lucy was talking to Maya, but Jon could not hear what was being said over the hum of machinery. Maya, while listening politely to Lucy, locked eyes with Jon and offered a slight smile.

On the other side of the aisle sat his lifelong bud, Rene, known as Carbine. Carbine had eaten a big breakfast before they left, and was slouched over, deep in the embrace of a carb-induced food coma. Jon had spent all his life side by side with his goofball friend and knew his habits well enough to guess that Carbine was undoubtedly sawing logs right now, but as with Lucy and Maya's conversation, the noise was all but drowned out.

Jon returned Maya's smile and looked around at the back of the crew area, his gaze coming to rest on the steep ladder-stairs that led below. Compulsively, he began to visualize the inventory of everything they'd brought along, and soon he was re-living the last few weeks.

The fight to secure even one transport had been fierce.

No one had expected the transition of the Human Republic into its new form to go smoothly, but no one had thought it to work out quite like it had either.

Despite Maya's and Miller's attempts to explain the consequences of Warbak's actions to the citizens of Home, nearly a third of the New Breed and Last Gen could not stomach living side by side with Unpure humans and Invasives, now officially referred to as "the Displaced."

"When one has lived their whole life in the darkness, their vision becomes adjusted to it. So when someone comes along and flips on the light, thinking that they are doing them a favor, the dark dwellers may become resentful, for that flood of alien light is painful and shocking. Their natural reflex is to shriek and turn the light back off, to seek refuge in the familiar comfort of the dark," Maya had explained to a frustrated Jon.

Thankfully, by some miracle, violence had for the most part been avoided. Despite that blessing, peace could not be achieved yet. The differences between the new order and the Old Guard, who, regardless of what they had learned about Warbak and the

Harvesters, refused to accept the Displaced as citizens, simply could not be reconciled.

The leader of those who refused to cooperate was a man named Martin. Jon and Carbine had trained under him in the Academy, but they had never been close. Martin was one of the survivors who went beyond refusing to accept the Displaced as equals in need of help instead of threats to the human race or Earth, even going so far as to deny the wicked intent behind Accoba Warbak's executed plan to transform every New Breed into the robotic killing machines called Spartans. He insisted that Warbak must have had a reason for what he had done, and publicly denounced Maya as an esoterrorist whose lies must not be believed.

Shortly after the cleanup of what came to be known as the Incident—the term given to the transformation of the Spartans and rebel uprising in the Shanty— the Old Guard, outnumbered and outgunned, announced that they would leave Home and take refuge in one of the more prominent enclaves in the Eastern Farmlands, a place called Lincoln. Only force would stop them.

Jon had seen and understood the plight in Maya's eyes. Part of her wanted to stay in Home, to help Miller fight for lasting peace and unity, yet every time she looked at Jon, her determination would cave and shatter, like the orbs Jon had smashed in the battle for the liberation of Home.

For they both knew that if they did not reach the Morning Star, did not finish the race and retrieve the Anvil, Jon was doomed.

The serum that Jon had taken before her rescue from the Ministry had given him great powers, rendering him a veritable super-human, enabling him to go toe-to-toe with Hoppers and Spartans single-handedly. But that power came at a price. The serum was burning him up from the inside out, and if a cure wasn't found in the promise of the Anvil's redemptive power, he would burn out and die before the end of the New Year.

Knowing that a peace had not been reached made it difficult for Maya, as well as everyone else, to leave Home. But leave they must, trusting the fate of Home to Miller and the others.

When Maya and Lucy refused to let the Old Guard take all the military transports for their exodus, violence had almost broken out once more.

"You conquer our city, our Home, and then deny us the opportunity to leave?" Martin had asked. Jon had been there, never leaving Maya's side in the days after the cleanup. Martin's body language and careful wording of questions had set Jon to unease. It seemed to him that this man, one whom he would have called a brother just a month before, was hoping to instigate irreparable damage to the negotiations. The man wanted a fight.

"No one is denying you the chance to go, if that is what you and your people insist on doing," Maya had replied coolly. "However, your choice to leave does not require that we leave ourselves with no means for long-range travel and exploration. In fact," Maya continued, standing as straight and tall as possible, "nothing about your choice requires *anything* from us. It is your choice to leave, not ours to make you go. By allowing you a third of the military equipment, a third of the farmlands, and the majority of the transports, we are being more than generous."

"Generous, you say?" Martin scowled. "How very kind of you." His eyes narrowed, and Jon took a step closer to the goddess, squaring his shoulders and tacitly reminding Martin that he was there. The slits of Martin's eyes turned on Jon.

"You must be very proud of yourself, dethroning our glorious Chairman, only to replace him with this Drop-trash-loving harlot queen."

"That's enough. Take your two transports and get out of here, Martin. We're done."

Later, Miller had expressed his concerns to Jon and Maya about the tenor of the negotiations.

"We may live to regret giving them military equipment."

"While it was their choice to leave Home, we don't want them to die out there. There are still Beasties behind every bush, under every hill, and don't forget, the Harvesters will be back someday."

Jon had hung around and watched with a sinking feeling in his stomach as Martin and the Old Guard packed up a sizeable portion of Home's might and disappeared into the Rough. An unsettling feeling had come over him that he couldn't shake despite his best attempts at optimism.

We haven't seen the last of him.

Later that night, after the sun had set, Jon had met up with his friends and helped pack the last remaining transport for their journey to the Morning Star.

"Hey, c'mon. Don't worry, bud. We'll be back in a couple of days. Everything is going to be okay," Carbine had assured him with a slap on the back.

They'd worked through the evening, loading the supplies for the trip into the cargo hold of the transport, which, as fate or luck would have it, contained four four-wheeled all-terrain vehicles.

These will come in handy later. Jon had run his hand along one's chassis, admiring and inspecting it, unconsciously comparing its make to the Republic Easy Rider that he suddenly realized he missed.

Before long, the bay had been filled with foodstuffs, weapons, medical supplies, and a wide assortment of camp-making and survival gear, as well as what seemed to be most of a machine shop—the last of which Ratt proudly took credit for bringing along.

Maya had wanted to leave immediately. Ratt, on the other hand, argued strongly for sleeping until the next morning. Maya was eager to reach Xibalba, but Ratt countered with the fact that although Jon could see the gold column of light in the distance, he had no way of gauging the actual distance to the light.

"There isn't much point in flying through the night only to have to land somewhere in the morning in order to get some rest. And, if we are over the ocean, we *can't* land and rest. I would say let's take shifts, but I'm the only one here really capable of handling this bad boy." Nobody could refute that with any reasonable argument, and so it had been decided that they would depart in the morning.

The decision had sparked a new idea in Maya. Once they had finished packing and taking inventory, she went to Wyntr and asked the child to show her the golden pillar as well. The girl had happily agreed. Maya easily shaped a Strange that allowed the child not only to take Maya on the same trip as Jon, "seeing" in her mind's eye the location of the Morning Star and its environs, but also to share the girl's story—memories of the child's home, her people, and her long, arduous journey to Home. The goddess had gone to sleep that night deeply satisfied with the way things had developed so far. She shared with her company her thoughts and feelings of the fulfillment of their destinies and the rightness of their course.

The morning had brought with it clear skies and goodbyes.

Jon had joined Maya in saying farewell to Miller, Wyntr, and the rest of the inner circle, promising to return within a week at most. Wyntr, not wanting to be left behind by her savior, cried and clung to Maya's legs.

Lucy had read on their faces their desire to concede to the child's wishes. "This quest is going to be very dangerous, and is not safe for children," she insisted.

"*Feroz Pantera*, we are heading right to her home. Why can we not return her to her people along the way?" Maya implored.

The little girl had looked up at her and smiled hopefully, her brown eyes welling with tears.

"My lady, would it not be better to return her to her people after the Anvil's been recovered and our foes defeated? To take her away from the safety of Home would not only endanger her, but would harm the entire party, as we would have to care for and protect her at all times." Lucy's deathly floral-painted face and eyes were stony, ignoring the heartbreaking look from Wyntr.

Jon had watched the scene unfold and came to Maya and the child, putting his hands on their shoulders to comfort them.

Maya had acquiesced, despite appearing as if a protest might burst from her lips at any moment. Nodding, she knelt down to the girl and hugged her closely, whispering in her ear. Another small tear had trickled its way down the girl's cheek, but she smiled and said, "Okay!", returning Maya's hug. Jon had seen this trick from Maya before and wondered just what the goddess had again told this troubled girl.

After a few more preparations, the five of them—Maya, Lucy, Ratt, Carbine, and Jon— had boarded the loaded transport and taken off into the azure skies in search of their salvation—and that of the world.

"Jon? Earth to Jon!"

"Huh? What?" Jon snapped out of his daydream and turned again to face Ratt in the cockpit.

"I didn't think you'd want to miss this." Ratt gestured at the viewport and what lay beyond.

Stepping deeper into the cockpit and leaning on Ratt's chair, Jon bent forward. His lips parted as silent awe overtook him. There, just beyond what seemed like an arm's reach, was the end of the land and the beginning of the sea. No picture he had ever seen during his upbringing in Home could hold a flame to the real thing. Only the vision Maya had given him came close. It was majestic, vast, seemingly endless, and mysterious. The blue hue of its waters reminded him of liquid sapphires and secret poetry. He watched the solid land disappear beneath them and stared, childlike, out over the ocean that stretched into forever.

"Wow," Jon said softly. "We're really making good time."

"Sure are. Whaddaya think? About time for another course correction check?"

"Yeah," Jon agreed. "Good idea."

Three times already since leaving, he had tried the meditation to check their course. All he had to do was close his eyes and recall the great green-covered hill, and then open his eyes and look. Every time, without fail, it was there: a shaft of golden light, reaching from the vanishing point of the curve of the planet to the heavens above.

This time, as with the last, the pillar of light was there, now slightly to their right: west, as Jon correctly guessed.

"That way, just a little bit." Jon pointed, and Ratt adjusted their flight path accordingly.

"There, right there." Jon gave Ratt a thumbs-up and went back to admiring the view.

They spent a silent hour that way, flying above the blue sea, straight toward the golden light. He was just about to take a break from the view and see how Maya was doing, when all hell broke loose.

2

F aster than anyone could react, the world around Jon and his friends literally unraveled.

A bright flash of brilliant amethyst light filled the viewport for a split second, causing Jon to squint and shield his eyes. Before he could mutter the words, "What in the...?" a second flash occurred. It vanished as abruptly as it had appeared and, in its place, hovering in the sky as if it were a thing in itself, placed by the hand of the Creator, and not simply an absence of thingness, was a tear in space. A growing, yawning portal outlined by a spasmodic perimeter of black and white cubes in various sizes, all flashing and expanding.

A buzzing sound, so loud as to overpower the hum of the transport and the wind outside, instantly cocooned the vessel, and the vibrations shivered through it from stem to stern. Panicked realization hit Jon like the angry, pointed finger of a wrathful god sending lightning to the earth to smite his foes.

"A Drop!"

Jon risked a glance behind him, out of reflex and concern for his friends. Maya's eyes were wide with terror as her gaze met his. Carbine was awakened rudely, while Lucy was already on her feet and making her way to the cockpit.

As his stomach rose into his chest, Jon felt the transport lurch and sway, whether from Ratt jerking on the controls or from some outside force, he could not say. His knees began to buckle and give. He reached out and steadied himself on Ratt's chair, fighting to maintain his balance.

"You can't fly in!" Lucy screamed as she arrived in the cockpit. "You must avoid it!"

"I know!" a panicked Ratt screamed back through gritted teeth, pulling so hard on the dual-handled controls that wiry cords in his thin arms bulged and popped.

The crackling electric rift of blue and purple continued to grow before them, even as Ratt pulled the ship into a steep climb. The expansion of the Drop seemed to keep pace with them, but Ratt climbed higher, and Jon continued to hope.

Paralyzed with awe, Jon stared at the gaping mouth of the Drop. He thought he could see glimpses of stars amongst an infinite backdrop beyond the snapping tendrils of light and flashing cubes that decorated the curtains of the rift's opening.

"Oh my..." The words tumbled out of his mouth like small stones falling from the fading grip of a dying man's hand.

Time dilated, and Jon became aware of one single inward breath that stretched into what felt like a minute or more. The ship continued its sharp climb, higher and higher, yet the snapping eel-like tendrils that ringed the inside of the Drop's opening inched closer and closer, filling up more and more of the viewport until they were all he could see.

The climb had become so steep that Jon fought mightily to keep from falling backward into the hold. Lucy, on the other hand, had no trouble at all, thanks to the magnetic pads in her feet. Jon threw another glance backward. Maya had managed to strap herself into her chair with the heavy-duty shoulder restraints. Carbine was now fully awake, confused and yelling, although Jon could not hear a word he said.

His gaze once again met Maya's. Although he knew he had no control over the outcome of this disaster, Jon bravely nodded at her, trying to assuage some of her fear and worry.

"Oh, shit!" Jon heard Ratt exclaim, and turned around to see what was wrong now.

A massive creature almost twice the size of the transport appeared out of the vast darkness on the other side of the Drop and shot toward the climbing ship.

Jon only caught a glimpse of it. It was totally alien; he had never seen anything like it before. Its body was bell-shaped, its skin, if one could call it that, transparent. Inside its giant, limbless body, Jon spied clusters of crimson threads and assumed they must be the alien's organs. Floating in the center of the diaphanous body was what looked to be a Mech-sized blob of partially cooked egg whites. Dangling beneath this bizarre bell hung a dozen or so vine-like appendages, seemingly as delicate as the rest of the thing's body. Each one flashed with lights and electricity, similar to the arcs produced by the Drop itself.

The speed at which the next events took place prevented any further examination, for although it was surely unintentional, the aim of the Drop-Beastie was spot on. Like a bullet from a sling, the alien creature shot out of the Drop just as they were on the cusp of escaping it and struck the transport head-on.

The already steeply angled ship bucked and heaved, forcing Jon to clutch the chair with both hands to keep from falling back into the bulkhead. A tingling ran through his fingers. Before he could even question the sensation's origin, its intensity raced to vibration, heat, and pain. He hurt, and he sensed the source of his pain was his hands, or perhaps the chair that they were hanging on to. He willed his hands to open and found to his dismay that he could not let go.

The Drop-Beast electrocuted the ship!

Out of the corner of his eye, Jon saw Lucy become detached from the floor and float upward. He quickly realized the ship was frozen somewhere between climbing and falling. Its engines had suddenly cut out, adding another issue to the growing list of disastrous effects of contact with the alien jellyfish. Lucy's levitation act only lasted for a second before being interrupted by the pilot's console exploding in a shower of sparks and steel.

The blast from the console ripped through the cabin, flipping Jon over the chair, which he was still anchored to, like a windsock in a gale storm. Lucy, on the other hand, was flung forcefully back to the rear of the ship, striking a wall above the stairway before tumbling down further into the cargo hold.

A dozen arcs of electricity, identical to the kind seen on the edges of a Drop, shot out of the console and lanced Ratt's body with their forked tongues. They pierced him like skewers, causing him to twitch violently, but one lone tendril missed, shooting past into the passenger cabin, where it struck Maya. Jon heard Maya yelp in surprise, but her voice was quickly drowned out by Ratt's agonized screams. Within seconds, though, he mercifully passed out. Merciful for him, but not so much for everyone else.

A shower of sparks rained down on Maya and Carbine from the ruined console. The lights in the cabin went out, adding to the eldritch glow of the streaming blue Drop light and its shadows. Jon looked back to Maya to make sure she was okay. Carbine—damn him—still hadn't buckled himself and probably wouldn't be able to at this point; his arms were locked in a wrestling match with the two halves of his harness, which dangled out from the sides of the chair. The ship was falling, Jon was sure of it, and beginning to go into a barrel roll. He decided that something must be done, and pulling himself up even with the plane of Ratt's chair, began to climb over it, into the lap of the passed-out kid.

Gotta try to save us! How hard can flying this bucket be?

Trying not to smother or hurt the kid, Jon climbed onto Ratt and took hold of the controls just as the creeping barrel roll came into its own and the ship went full-on upside down, paused for a minute, and then completed its roll straight into a nosedive.

A nosedive right into the Drop.

Oh shit, Jon thought to himself as he surveyed the scene. The controls were shot; there was nothing he could do. He pulled and jockeyed the hand control wheel repeatedly, eliciting no response. The viewport filled again with the dark maw of the Drop and its wreath of electric tentacles and flashing cubes. Jon reflexively braced for an impact that never came, and then as suddenly as the whole episode had begun, their world plunged into darkness.

Zero gravity overcame them. Jon was sure that the ship was still pointed "down" in a nosedive, but that seemed meaningless now. They were in the Drop. The sea of stars he had seen on the other side of the rift before was gone, and now there was nothing but what looked like thick, rolling clouds of darkness. Not clouds *in* the dark, but clouds *of* dark, thick as clay and so close, they sheathed the ship like a coat of paint. Jon felt as if they were flying straight down a smokestack or a pit of quicksand.

The waves of silt-like smoke that rolled against the windows created strange, hypnotic patterns. Jon froze in place and calmed his anxious breathing—which he hadn't even been aware of before—and waited for any sign of impact or further danger, but none came. He concluded that the immediate, life-threatening danger had passed, and sprang back into action, yelling over his shoulder.

"Is everyone all right? Maya?" His voice rang out, loud as the booms had been in the deathly quiet of the cabin.

"We're okay," Maya replied, her words slurred on the edges as if she were drunk. "What about Lucy? Ratt?"

Jon pulled and swung himself out of the chair and off the kid, examining Ratt as best he could in the low light. Not seeing any obvious wounds or bleeding, he pulled himself closer and leaned his ear up to the kid's mouth. Jon released a sigh of relief when he felt Ratt's soft breath against his cheek.

"He's alive!" Jon exclaimed as he came back upright. Just then, Lucy appeared in the stairwell, crawling on all fours. LED flashlights, mounted to the lapels of her new trench coat, cast twin beams, illuminating the cabin with soft cones of blue-white light. Jon could see better now, thanks to Lucy's torches, and glanced over the scene. He needed to visually verify that Maya was indeed okay, as well as his buddy.

"Carbine!" he exclaimed, happy his mate had been lucky enough to remain uninjured in his unbuckled state.

"Right!" Carbine snapped back affirmatively and went straight to work.

Lucy made her way fully into the cabin and pushed off the floor where she had been crawling, hovering in a gentle float toward the center of the room.

"What the hell happened?" she asked no one in particular.

"Something came out of the Drop and hit us. Fried the ship, then we fell in," Jon explained. "Ratt was hit with something, electricity, I think. But it didn't look right."

"I was hit too, but just barely," Maya mumbled groggily as if she had just woken from a deep sleep.

"Are you all right?" Jon asked, scanning her body for any sign of a wound.

"Yeah," she said, rubbing her left temple with her fingertips. "I think so."

"Wait, in? *Into* the Drop?" Carbine's eyes were as wide as full moons.

"Yeah. I think we're on the other side. It's all cloudy or silty out there. I'm not sure which. It's weird," Jon reported.

"No. We can't be on the other side. It doesn't work that way, otherwise, none of the Displaced would be trapped on Earth. No, we are in some place we don't want to be, a bardo of kinds. An in-between," Maya said, her voice wavering with something Jon had seldom heard from her before—fear.

As if cued by the dread in her voice, Jon turned to look out the viewport at the smothering silt-clouds. He started to turn away, but something caught his eye in the swirling patterns. Still holding on to the chair with one hand, Jon pushed himself to float closer to the window.

There!

Something recognizable formed in the swirling patterns of chaos. A gestalt. *A...*

Face!

Jon started, pulling back awkwardly from the glass just as a humanoid face, constructed out of the swirling smoke, pressed itself against the outside of the window and opened its mouth in a silent scream.

Jon's startled cry and sudden, jerky movement caught everyone's attention.

"What is it?" Lucy asked, gliding over to him. Jon recovered from his zero-g tailspin and pointed to the swirling miasma outside.

"There! I saw someone."

Lucy followed the direction of his gesture.

"All I see is cloud-stuff," she said.

"Not someone. Something." Maya's words carried much weight as they fell on the ears of her guardians.

"What do you mean? What was it?" Jon asked.

"They don't have a name in your language. They are the agents of this place—not Earth, but Hell."

"What? Like Harvesters?"

"Yes, but different. These things aren't so much beings *in* Hell. They are a part of Hell itself, part of the actual pocket dimension. A cog in the super-dimensional machinery. Built-in prison wardens. They keep the damned. We need to get out of here."

Maya's tone betrayed her feelings—worry, fear, the need for haste. She leaned forward in her chair, her round eyes wide with apprehension.

Lucy reached the front of the cabin, where Ratt remained strapped into the pilot's seat, Jon floating nearby. She pulled herself into position, straddling Ratt's lap, and began to examine what was left of the controls.

Jon frowned, struggling to comprehend Maya's explanation. Before he could inquire further, the ship lurched once more, and a sound like a torrent of hail on a metal roof filled the cabin. Maya, Jon, and Carbine all flinched. Only Lucy retained her calm demeanor, flicking her eyes toward the window for a second before resuming her examination of the control panel.

"What now?" Carbine said, his tone betraying exhausted annoyance.

Jon looked around the cabin in a vain attempt to track the source of the noise, but it seemed to come from all sides at once: the ominous crashing of a thousand fists knocking into the ship. Gooseflesh rippled across Jon's skin as he looked out into the smoky silt-storm. Shapes of half-men coalesced out of nothing, screaming their rage and beating on the hull before melting back into smoke-stuff.

"They know we are here. Lucy, can you turn the ship around? The Drop might still be open!" The urgency in Maya's voice made Jon feel impotent.

"No, my lady, the systems aren't responding. I am attempting to repair now, or at least reboot the system off my own fusion unit," Lucy shouted back over the *bang, bang, tap* that was growing in intensity.

Dammit! Jon continued to glance around the cabin, frantically looking for something, anything he could do to help. *Useless.*

"What do they want, Maya?" he asked.

"They want us gone, Jon."

Bang! The ship lurched.

"They are a defense mechanism."

Bang! Bang! The ship lurched again.

"They are to this bardo, this place, this…"

Bang! Bang! Bang!

When the ship rocked this time, Jon could hear the ship's frame twisting and groaning under some intense pressure. The hairs on his neck stood at attention as straight as any New Breed soldier ever did.

"They are to this no-place like white blood cells are to your body!"

Bang! Groan! Bang! The sudden shriek of crumpling metal was deafening.

Jon, still listening to Maya and the tumultuous storm of ghost-fists, snapped his head in the direction of the nearest wall, and in shocked awe watched it buckle and collapse inwards as if it were being crushed from the outside in the fist of an enormous Heavy Mech.

Just as quickly, he turned his stare back to Maya.

"They know we're here! And *we* are the foreign body!" She closed her eyes, centering herself. A moment later, she began to sing softly to herself.

Come on! Come and get some! Jon pushed off the wall to shoot across the cabin toward the stairwell. As he passed Carbine, he noticed his friend was loading a magazine into a Lawnmower rifle, retrieved from its storage place beneath the seat. Jon didn't stop his drift or even look back, but hollered back to Carbine as he floated on, "No shooting, bud! Melee weapons only!"

He pushed and pulled his way through the zero-gravity environment with the ease of a seasoned astronaut, though he lacked the grace. This ability was not born from any training, experience, or even natural talent. His ability to get from the cabin to the cargo bay with such speed was simply the result of his serum-heightened reflexes and his body's newfound ability to take quite a punishment, enhanced by a full-blown, panic-induced adrenaline rush. Jon nearly bent the last rail he pull-pushed off of. He bounced and smacked his way down the corridor, leaving a trail of dents in his wake. He felt zero pain. Nothing slowed him down or even caused him to blink, but he was far too preoccupied with the events of the next few minutes to appreciate his new stamina.

The spaciousness of the cargo hold amplified the horrific shrieks of the buckling ship's structure. Focused as he was, Jon didn't pause to look around or stop. He shot straight for the locker he knew contained his hammer and armor. Maybe, just maybe, he could don his armor and helmet, go out the airlock, and ward off these white-blood-cell bastards.

No sooner had he had finished the thought, he stopped as suddenly as if he had impaled himself on an enemy spear or invasive beast's horn. His heart and hopes sank.

There is no airlock. There is just the door…

His carefully aimed last push and drift had brought him to his destination, and he collided with the locker with surprising force, smashing the door partway in.

If I open the door, all our air will leak out into the vacuum. And if I do nothing, then the creatures will break through, and all our air will go out into the vacuum anyway. If only there weren't a vacuum!

Jon punched the locker in frustration, his knuckles nearly

breaking through it. He pulled back a fist and went to swing again.

What if there isn't a vacuum? The thought came from somewhere, he knew not where, but it made sense. Did he actually know that this bardo, this no-place, was a vacuum? Yes, they were floating in what seemed to be zero-gravity, but did that have to mean zero-atmosphere?

Not necessarily! There was still hope, no matter how slight. With that thought, his fist relaxed, and he began to savagely rip and tear open the defunct locker door. A large chunk came off its hinge in Jon's hand. Without looking, he tossed it over his shoulder and reached inside the locker to withdraw his hammer, its stars glowing in all their might and glory. He would protect the goddess or die trying.

When he returned to the cabin, he could see that it had further crumpled in on itself and continued to collapse with every passing second. Carbine had pulled a knife, his other hand gripping his chair, waiting and ready to push off in whatever direction he and his knife might be needed—for all the good it would do.

Maya was still buckled into her chair and harness, her small hands folded across her lap, eyes closed. She continued her invocation song, however hard it was to hear over the noise of the ship imploding. Lucy had unbuttoned her shirt and was frantically ripping, pulling and plugging wires from the ship's control panel into jacks in her breastbone. Other than her working arms and hands, she was as motionless as a statue, and she appeared to be withdrawn inside herself, in some sort of self-induced trance.

Just then, there came a bang with a higher pitch, a different tone, followed by an incredible hissing sound, like high-pressure gas releasing at great speed from a small opening. The hiss became more of a roar, ear-bleedingly loud.

Shit! The air! It is a vacuum! Jon thought, grimacing. He was unable to cover his ears without releasing the hammer, and he would die before he let that happen. His eyes darted around the room. Maya, strangely, seemed unfazed, though Carbine clutched both his ears. His face was awash with agony, his fists open as he palmed the flat of his blade against his head. Lucy, like Maya, seemed unaffected, though this wasn't surprising. Jon was sure she was either mentally elsewhere or was capable of tuning out any noise she wanted. What was a surprise was that the air didn't seem to be leaving the cabin. Despite the deafening roar of high-velocity gas, there was no sign of anything loose being sucked out or moving around, and no breeze—nothing at all except the noise.

Phew. Jon allowed himself a small moment of relief. The bardo was not a vacuum, after all.

Nothing was going out. But something was coming *in*. Jon spied a rent in the ship's hull, through which the silt-smoke was starting to billow.

"They're coming through!" Jon shouted, cocking his hammer back. He wondered how effective his swing would be in a zero-g environment but had no idea what else to do. The rolling smoke poured itself into a large globule in the cabin and began to morph into a humanoid sandstorm. Hazy columns where its legs might have been, maintained an umbilical connection to the sea outside the ship. Looking like the sand genie emerging from the prover-bial bottle, the guardian of the bardo hovered in the air, surveying the room, then screamed.

The scream filled the cabin with an unearthly beast's roar that was unlike anything Jon had ever heard before.

The nervous tension broke Jon's cool, and he returned the animalistic shriek with his own war cry. His attempt to draw the beast's attention worked, the genie launching straight for him. He was ready for it—or so he thought—and swung at the smoke-thing's face. Jon couldn't tell whether his hammer passed straight through his target ineffectively, or whether he'd missed entirely, for as soon as he fired his hammer shot, his body spiraled into a pirouette.

Dammit! Jon had wondered for a second what might happen, but his lack of zero-g experience hadn't prepared him for this much of a blunder. The rapid spinning caused him to lose sight of the creature, as well as his bearings. He released the hammer with one hand, stretching out his arm in the hope of finding something with which to stop the spiral. Before he could locate anything solid, something found him.

It wasn't impact that he felt, more a sort of penetration. A sudden, shocking cold was simply there, where a moment before it had not been. His guts felt beyond ice cold. There was no gradual change in temperature; it was as if someone had teleported dry ice into his chest cavity, or he had been stabbed with an enormous icicle. The spinning stopped, and he realized he was now held fast in the clutches of the smoke. Its thick, rolling substance cocooned him and pierced him. He felt as bound by the silt-smoke as he would have in chains. The cold continued to burn his insides as he struggled to overcome his ethereal restraints.

The umbilical tail that connected the creature to the raging storm outside forked and sent a tentacle-like polyp straight toward Maya, who was still chanting in her chair. Her song ended the second the ghostly appendage reached her. A soft purple glow appeared out of thin air between her and the tendril, interrupting the attack.

The smoky filament smacked into the purple shield that had grown to outline Maya's body and splashed into a dozen directions. The different tributaries of the split smoke-tentacle regrouped in the center of the cabin near the ceiling and began to take the shape of another humanoid.

Jon could feel himself fading, like a sinking swimmer who had already run out of breath and was running on the oxygen fumes left in his blood, his brain slowly shutting down and his vision fading to black. The panicky struggle had passed, and he found himself in a state of almost serene relaxation, of surrender.

He felt his memories slipping from his mind like water through a closed fist. He couldn't grab them. Although his vision had already faded, he closed his eyes and concentrated on one thing. *Maya.* Perhaps if he could not grip that thought, he could cup his hands and try to support it. *Maya. Maya.* To his dismay, he found he couldn't remember what she looked like. *Hold on to the idea, the idea of Maya. Please, please.*

Carbine, who had been clutching his ears in pain from the thunderous noise, found sudden respite when the scream of the storm was somehow muffled. He opened his eyes, examining his hands and arms, then the rest of his body. A soft purple glow covered him and seemed to be shielding him. He glanced up and saw Maya surrounded by the same glow. Then he spotted Jon, above the stairwell near the back of the cabin, gripped by a tornado of smoke. He shouted to Jon, but his words were lost in the roar, and he flinched as a second smoke-man descended on him from above.

Just as it had before, the smoke seemed to strike a plate of glass and spread out before Carbine's face, streaming around him like a river split around a boulder. Carbine recovered from the surprise attack when he realized that the thing could not harm him, but he knew that Jon was not as fortunate. Even through the haze of the whirling smoke, he could see the very image of Jon begin to fade and become slightly transparent as if he were slowly being erased from reality.

Of course, he thought to himself, *they are the white blood cells of this place. They mean to erase us!*

His mind was frantic. He tried not to panic, but what to do?

Carbine knew he couldn't fight it. *Maybe I can cut it off from its source?*

Carbine's intense gaze followed the smoke trail from his friend to the breach in the ship. The scream of the storm was still ringing in his ears as incessantly as the wail of an alarm klaxon, but he steeled his mind against it and focused on how to save Jon.

Carbine searched the cabin for something to cover the tear in the hull through which the smoke poured, but came up empty. Without so much as a silent *Banzai!,* he jumped toward the breach and used his body itself as the dividing barrier, hastily reasoning that if the shield around his body could repel the smoke, then perhaps he could sever the umbilical by flopping on top of it.

His aim was perfect. He pushed off from the chair he had been anchored to, landing belly first directly on top of the smoke creature's umbilicus. The repelling qualities of the shield neatly cut the flow of smoke into two. He smashed through it into the floor of the cabin, and then deftly jammed his knife into the floor to prevent himself from bouncing all the way back. As soon as he recovered from the jolt, he rolled toward the breach, pushing with one hand and maintaining his death-grip on the knife handle with the other. He ended up on his back with his side slightly pressed against the wall.

Try as he might, he could not keep himself still or firmly pressed against the hull to prevent the Wardens from continuing to pour into the cabin. The zero-gravity, coupled with his awkward, feeble purchase and the need to maintain his hold on the knife proved to be too much.

He bounced back and forth between sealing the hull with his body and floating away. He bobbled. Worse still, the tornado that held Jon in its grip of erasure maintained itself autonomously; separation from the storm at large had not slowed it one bit. Jon continued to fade.

Although no one noticed, Lucy's hands had stopped their hectic pulling, punching, and plugging, and shot out to take the ship's controls. Her eyes rolled back from white to their normal forward position as her awareness returned from within itself to the world outside.

The very same instant her slender but strong hands clutched the controls, the cabin lights came back on. Maya's head spun toward the cockpit, and her eyes lit up with hope and nervous excitement. Lucy had done it. Power returned to the listless ship.

"Look for the Drop! Look for the opening!" Maya cried over the tumultuous chaos.

Lucy didn't so much as glance back. She set her jaw and pushed on the sticks, her thumbs simultaneously flicking the thrust.

Carbine lurched up so hard from the pitch of the ship that he nearly lost hold of his knife; Maya's eyes seemed to bulge as she strained against the safety harness; however, the incoming smoke and the tornado with Jon in its clutches seemed completely unaffected by the sudden change of inertia.

Lucy plunged the ship through the bardo-storm at max speed, pushing down and pulling left on the controls, sending it into a sharp turn. Her face wore an expression of coolness. Despite her seemingly aloof demeanor, Carbine knew she was astute enough to know that they were in trouble—real trouble. Maya's shields wouldn't last forever, and even if they could, the Wardens would simply erase the ship instead of the people, damning them to float in this no-place forever.

The ship banked hard and fast, though it was nearly impossible to gauge speed when flying through the endless rolling clouds. Only the rapidity with which the ghost faces flashed by the viewport window gave any indication of how fast they were moving.

"I don't see an opening anywhere!" Lucy yelled over the din, a hint of feverish panic in her normally cool voice.

Please let it still be open, Maya silently prayed as she shifted her frantic gaze back and forth from the viewport to Jon, who, with every passing second, looked more and more like a ghost himself. It positively killed her to watch him fade and do nothing, but there was nothing she could do. She knew that more surely than anyone else here. Unbuckling herself from her chair wouldn't help anything at all… and then it hit her, what Carbine had done. Her shield repelled the smoke. Filled with desperate purpose, she tore at the buckle restraining her and fixed to leap toward Jon.

Freeing herself with a flick of her wrist, Maya slipped out from between the shoulder restraints and threw herself into the tornado. The smoke parted like water around a boat. There was almost no impact when her body collided with what remained of Jon's.

If only I had managed to shape my Strange before the spirit got ahold of Jon, I could've protected him as well!

She wrapped her arms around Jon, like hugging a cloud, as she continued along her trajectory and slammed into the fuselage.

The jolt caused her to exclaim in pain, twisting her body, though she did not release her hold on the wisp that was Jon.

Her face remained scrunched up, but her eyes opened and witnessed with great relief the color and substance begin to return slowly but surely to Jon's form. They floated like that for what seemed like a frozen moment in time. Jon seemed unconscious and was only beginning to return to existence, but all was right in her world despite the raging hell around them. She stared at the look of serenity on his still face like a mother watching her babe sleep, and her heart smiled.

Her victory was short-lived. The Drop-sentinel was not to be defeated. It had been spread across the room by the impact against Maya's shield, but this time, instead of reforming into an anthropomorphic body, it simply began to grow, to multiply itself by way of some alien asexual reproduction. The swirling clouds began to fill the entirety of the cabin's interior. Fear returned as master of Maya's manor of thought; the thing was now erasing the ship.

Maya screamed in helpless frustration as the being returned to cocoon Jon, even though he was still in her arms. The silt poured over and around her form, avoiding her shield by just enough. She began to swat at it, but it was everywhere. Her efforts were as futile as if she were trying to slap away the air itself.

Jon began to fade again, and this time, the ship began to fade with him. Within a minute, the ghosts would have undone all of Lucy's repair work, and the craft would return to a floating free-fall until it finally faded away to nothing. They were doomed… unless Lucy could find the way out.

The smoke wrapped itself around Lucy, and although unable to penetrate her shield, made her continuing search for the Drop extremely difficult. She let go of the sticks with one hand, and, like Maya, waved her shield-shrouded arm back and forth as if shooing a buzzing fly. It helped a little but created a kind of strobe-light effect on her vision. Like rapid blinking, her perceptions altered, but her mind was still able to string the diced-up images together and make a picture of pseudo-continuity. She scanned and scanned.

If Lucy's heart had not been torn out of her chest years ago and replaced with a titanium and carbon-fiber mechanical pump, it would have leapt. Through the raging storm outside and growing thickness of the soul-smog inside, she caught a glimpse of blue-white color not too far off from the port bow of the wounded, dying transport. She shouted a victory yelp as she pulled the ship into a turn that would put it directly into the electric maw of dimensional freedom that was the promise of the Drop.

"I see a Drop! But I don't know if it's the right one!" Her voice was Olympian. Amplified by speakers in her cybernetic body, it overcame the scream of the storm.

It doesn't matter! We have to take the risk! Maya screamed back telepathically through swatting palms and tears of impotent rage as the clouds consumed Jon before her very eyes.

More out of stoic determination than exertion, Lucy gritted her teeth and once again gripped the controls with both hands. Like a kamikaze pilot from Earth's ancient past, she plunged the ship into the Drop without fear or regret as fast as its engines would propel them.

"Here goes."

Lucy wasn't one to knock on wood or cross her fingers, but somewhere deep inside, she crossed the ghost of her human heart. They all knew that if this wasn't the same Drop they had come in through, that they could end up anywhere. Literally.

The second the ship passed the threshold, the ghost sentinels disappeared as thoroughly and suddenly as banished darkness before the glow of electric lights. For the stretch of a blink of an eye, it seemed as though their lives had been saved.

The Drop that delivered them from certain death in the bardo, however, was unlike the one that had brought them to that place; this one was not a rare high-altitude one.

The ship's impact into the earth was abrupt and violent. The nigh-instantaneous destruction it suffered was nearly as complete as the stop it crashed to.

3

Only the faintest wisp of consciousness had returned to Jon when the transport exited the Drop.

The bardo spirit's attack, which had nearly killed him, ended up being Jon's saving grace: his body had not yet returned to a corporeal state when the transport slammed into the earth at top speed. The impact wrenched him free of Maya's embrace, sending him floating and bouncing around like a balloon while everything else in and around the ship made its best impression of a detonating fragmentation grenade.

Having already had the integrity of its hull severely compromised by the ghosts, the transport came apart like so much aluminum foil when it hit. What was left by the time the last bit came to a stop resembled a slug's trail in the sun; a glistening, silver smear across a desert plain. Jon came to as his body finished solidifying. He blinked his eyes several times in rapid succession in an attempt to clear the blur from his vision; he couldn't even begin to describe the dull ache he felt in his... everything.

What the hell happened? The question slowly formed in his mind like a flower coming into bloom. He tasted something on his lips and realized upon reflection that he was lying face down in dry dirt. He licked his lips and spat, pushing himself upright, and slowly drew himself up into standing position. He rubbed his eyes to expedite the blur-removal and looked around.

Desert.

Where are we? Wait... we? He squinted in the bright sunlight that bathed the desert and bounced off the metal bits that used to be the transport. He brought his hand to his brow and continued to survey the scene. Having been unconscious during the wreck, he began to panic as his mind put two and two together. A lump formed in his throat and his chest felt tight. *Where is everybody? Where is Maya?*

The concern erupted into full-blown panic like a strong drug coming on. Jon gave up on trying to figure out what had happened or where he was and started scurrying through the wreckage that stretched behind him for what seemed like a klick. With the frantic intensity of a starving animal digging for food, Jon rummaged through the strewn wreckage, tossing a chunk of fuselage here, flipping over a crate of stowed supplies there, looking for his companions. His mind recited the mantra of those whose growing dread matched their growing awareness of the situation at hand.

No! No, no, no, no, no, please!

He found Lucy and Ratt first. They lay tangled up in each other like two contortionists trying to re-invent the Kama Sutra. He reached down and gently shook them both. Lucy recovered instantly, her presence returning like lightning to her already open eyes. One of her arms shot out as fast as a frog's tongue catching its dinner. Her tanto knife was clutched in the grip of its digits, its blade held a hair's width away from Jon's throat.

"Whoa! Easy there, easy there."

Jon watched with relief as Lucy relaxed, lowered the knife, and said, "Help me with Ratt."

Jon lifted as she pushed, and they gingerly plucked the kid off of her and onto a patch of ground that was relatively clear of debris.

"He is alive but unconscious. Let's find Maya and Carbine," Lucy said, prompting a responsorial nod from Jon.

They leapt into action, splitting up and sifting through the wreckage, each lifting and displacing the larger pieces with the ease of Hercules. Every time Jon had to exert some effort to lift a particularly heavy piece, his body was faintly lit by the same glow that had engulfed him entirely when Lucy had first injected him with the serum. The effect was eerie and made his skin look like a paper lantern.

Before another painfully long two minutes had passed, his efforts paid off. He saw Maya's foot first, sticking out from underneath a large hunk of twisted black metal. His chest felt as if it were once again in the icy clutches of the bardo-spirit. For a cowardly moment, he was too scared to lift the debris, too afraid to look.

The sight of her foot twitching suddenly and the sound of her soft, girlish voice moaning returned life to his dead heart as sure as any defibrillator ever could. He rushed forward and carefully lifted the debris away, making sure not to hurt the prone goddess, and tossed it aside.

Maya lay there, eyes shut and looking more like a drunk that had passed out than someone who had peacefully fallen asleep, her arms and legs twisted and contorted in awkward positions, but otherwise appearing no worse for wear.

Jon dropped to one knee and cradled her head in his hand. "Maya!"

Her eyes fluttered open, like a child waking from a dream. When she saw his face, she smiled.

"You're okay!" she said.

"*Me?*" Jon was incredulous. "I was worried sick about you!"

They both laughed and embraced. He pulled back from their hug and took in the sight of her face. They smiled at each other and Jon leaned forward to hug her once more. Halfway there, some involuntary madness overcame him. His head dipped of its own accord, and he kissed her hard on the lips.

The goddess's eyes widened in mild shock for a heartbeat, then she closed them and returned the kiss. Jon felt wetness on his cheeks and broke off their lip tug-of-war, concern on his face. She was crying, but she was still smiling. A small fleck of saliva lingered on her bottom lip, and she brought her demure hand up to her exquisite mouth, covering it, and laugh-cried. Her other hand reached up and caressed the side of Jon's face.

"I'm fine, guys. Not hurt. But it's cool, go on slobbering on each other."

Stunned and embarrassed, Jon and Maya both spun around to find Carbine standing a few meters away, dusting himself off.

"Carbine! You're okay!" Jon exclaimed, his face contorted with a multitude of emotions.

"We, uh…" Maya mumbled.

"Hey. It's cool," Carbine said with a wink. "Your secret's safe with me. I knew you were concerned about me, even if it didn't look like it." Carbine's grin betrayed his faux hurt.

"Gee, I, uh… I'm sorry, man," Jon stammered, rubbing the back of his head and casting shifting glances at the sandy ground.

"I said it's cool. Everyone else all right?"

Maya turned to look at Jon, clearly curious for the same reason as Carbine.

"Yes. Lucy and Ratt are back that way." Jon pointed behind him to where sand dunes rolled away, littered with chunks of transport and small bushes. "I honestly don't know what Ratt's condition is."

"Let's go find out," Maya said.

"Yeah. But hey," Jon paused and frowned, deep in thought, "somebody want to tell me exactly what happened?"

On their walk back to Lucy and Ratt, Maya explained to Jon what had transpired in the transport, the way the bardo-spirit, the Wardens, had nearly erased Jon, and then the ship itself, from existence. How she had shaped a Strange to protect them from the spirits, how it must not have worked on Jon because the spirit had already penetrated him, and how the protective cocoons she'd shaped on everyone must have saved them from the destructive kinetic energy of the crash.

A few minutes later, they crested the small dune that obscured Ratt from their vision and called out to Lucy, who was nearby and still searching for the survivors.

Another minute later, they had Ratt's shirt off. Lucy went straight to work and began to examine Ratt with a laser wand of some kind, pulled from the kid's gear pouch. After a long minute's silent work, she looked up at the goddess as she continued to run the laser back and forth over Ratt's chest.

"He is alive, but in a coma. Brain and organ activity are normal," Lucy reported. "He doesn't actually appear to be physically hurt at all. A miracle, really. But, that said, I have no idea what's wrong with him."

"Let me see what I can do." Maya knelt down in the sand. She scooted herself up close to the sleeping Ratt, while Lucy pulled back, giving her lady space to work.

A moment later, Jon and the others watched as the goddess did her thing, humming a soft melody and placing her small hands on Ratt's chest, which rose and fell almost imperceptibly.

After a minute, Maya finished her song, scooted back, and stood, brushing grains of clinging sand from her knees.

"I suspect that he was touched by the Drop itself. I am sensing changes deep within his innate Strange. I could be wrong, but I think the Drop, perhaps the pocket-dimension itself, is somehow communicating with him. And, I think…" she added almost as an afterthought, "that he is talking back to it."

Jon frowned, straining to understand the super-dimensional mechanics of Hell and Strange in general, but withheld his questions.

"I will tend to him as best I can, but he may simply need time to return to our world fully," Maya explained.

Jon nodded, then announced to his friends that he would do the meditation of the pillar.

"We need to confirm that we are still even on Earth, and if so, find out how far off course we are."

The pillar of golden light still stood on the horizon like a lighthouse. It offered small relief, though, for they still could not use it to gauge distance. They had no way of knowing whether the base of the beam was just over the small hills in the distance, say maybe a day or two away, or if it burst forth from a place halfway across the globe and entire oceans separated them from it. Still, it was a comfort to know that they had returned from the bardo to the Earth they knew.

"Maya," Jon said, "maybe you should open a door back to Home for us. We have no idea how far away the Morning Star is. I know the Old Guard took all the other transports, but we could set out on wheels, perhaps."

"But we have no way of knowing if that would be faster or slower than finishing the journey on foot," Maya protested. "And we must…" She left the thought unspoken.

"I know, hurry," Jon finished it for her, holding up his hands and flexing them open and closed. Everyone knew that Jon's life-span was a ticking clock, counting down to extinction.

"Maya, Ratt is out, we don't know for how long, or even

what's wrong with him. And our gear..." Jon gestured around, letting the carnage speak for itself. "We simply aren't in any shape to continue on foot. Xibalba could be on the other side of the globe for all we know. We *have* to go back and start over."

He saw the pained look on her face breaking into spoken protest like a wave, cresting at its zenith, about to come crashing down and cut her off with more cold, hard facts.

"It's only been a month, Maya. I have time."

Maya looked at Jon for a long time, her eyes searching him for something. Finally, she broke the awkward silence.

"Very well. We go back, regroup, and start over. We still have time."

The group nodded in agreement and waited for Maya to lead the way via her powerful Strange.

Maya began her shaping exactly as she had before, the last time she had created a Drop-like portal for them to escape from. Only this time, they weren't falling to their deaths in a Ziggurat trash-tube, so it took Jon a second to recognize the melody.

Maya had her back to Jon and the others and was looking out across the desert scrub and the bruised flesh sky that spoke of impending twilight.

She made tiny gestures with her fingers and wrists as if she wore invisible finger-cymbals that made no sound. Her arms and hips swayed gently like one of the spindly limbs of the prolific ocotillo cactus that dotted the plain around them.

The air directly in front of Maya began to shimmer, wavering the very fabric of reality, as if a wall of perfectly clear water had been raised from the ground, and stood vertically, in defiance of the laws of physics.

Then, like a note played off-key, Maya's song was rudely interrupted by a yelp of pain. The goddess instantly ceased her gentle song and her hand shot to her temple as fast as her body dropped to its knees.

The portal, still only half-formed, like a sheet of ripples suspended in the air, oscillated violently before snapping in on itself, reducing in size until it was no bigger than a tea saucer.

A small portal began to fill the now reduced sheet, its aperture starting in the center and growing until it reached the edges, where it abruptly stopped.

Jon rushed forward, wrapping his arms around the pained goddess, demanding to know she was okay.

"I, I, uh… it hurts," Maya said weakly, her left hand still glued to her temple. She looked up through the hood of Jon's embrace and beheld her handiwork.

She had opened a portal to her private chambers in the upper levels of Home, which she had relinquished to To-Kan and Wyntr, yet still remained one of her teleportation anchors. The opening of the portal had been successful, but it was only a hand's width in circumference.

"That's, uh… not good. Right?" Carbine asked.

"No, Rene," Jon snapped without turning around. "That's not good. Maya, what happened?"

"I don't know. My head hurts," she mumbled, her words slurred, and she swayed as if she were hypnotized. A thought lanced Jon's mind, triggering a recent memory.

"Your head. You were rubbing it earlier, in the transport."

"It's, uh… it's where I was hit. By the drop." Maya finished the thought for him, apparently realizing where he was going with his line of thought.

"Whatever put Ratt down, it must've affected me somehow too."

"At least as far as your ability to open doors," Lucy added, appearing at Jon and Maya's side and dropping to one knee. "Let me take a look at you, my lady."

Jon moved aside and switched his concerned gaze from Maya to the grapefruit-sized portal that remained hovering in the air.

"Makes... sense..." Maya mumbled, her speech still struggling to remain coherent. "The Drop... being... the mother... of all... doors... to this... place." The effort having exhausted her, the goddess crumpled into the arms of her oldest guardian and whimpered.

"There, there now. I have you," Lucy soothed, looking up over the petite woman's head to shoot Jon a look of concern.

"We rest here tonight," Jon said, a turn of his head pointing out the setting sun. "Tomorrow, we figure out what to do next, and see what might be salvaged from all this."

Lucy simply nodded in return.

As if having heard Jon's proclamation, the diminutive portal sizzled and then winked out of existence.

Although the sun was fading away, the desert still glowed with the heat of the day, absorbed by the thermal mass of rock and sand, so Jon knew without a doubt that the shiver he felt run down his spine was one of foreboding only.

4

The light of the cold winter day was diffused into a soft, omnipresent glow by the low-lying fog that blanketed the ground and meandered through the gaps in the trees like so many tributaries of a broken river.

The fog brought an uncanny silence yet seemed to amplify every sound that punctuated the stillness of the forest. The crunching of boots on the frost-bitten dead grass created a drumbeat, accentuated now and again by the morbid crowing of carrion birds desperately searching for their next meal.

As the men progressed deeper into the wood, the soft glow of the sun's rays, already concealed by the frost in the air, grew dimmer, further obscured by the tangle of leafless branches that thickened above.

"Your man sure picked a pain-in-the-ass place to meet. Any reason we couldn't have just handled our business in the Shanty?" one of the two men asked the other.

"I would think that would be fairly obvious, Nguyen," the second man said, his tone sharp with irritation.

Truth be told, Martin shared his companion's feelings regarding the remoteness of the rendezvous point, but he hated needless grumbling, especially in a trained soldier. It just sounded like whining. One might think it, but one should never speak it aloud.

When Nguyen failed to respond to the sharp quip, Martin took pity on the kid and elaborated.

"The Provocateur said that extreme care must be taken to ensure that our machinations are not discovered. The Shanty has too many eyes and ears now. It's not like the old days."

"Well, wouldn't it have been the same in the old days? I mean, the Resistance seems to have been there all along. They were way more organized than we thought, right? Otherwise, we'd be kicking it in the Zigg right now, instead of tromping through this forest with the ravens and freezing our butts off."

Martin made a face of disgust, instantly regretting any remorse he'd had for being too hard on the kid.

"Shut up, Nguyen," he said, more irritated than before. "It should be right up ahead. Stay frosty."

"Why? You expect trouble? I thought you said we can trust this guy?" The young soldier prattled on, oblivious to his commanding officer's growing frustration.

"I said shut your cock-holster," Martin grumbled, then added, "Trust no one."

Private Nguyen's nagging questions caused Martin's own reservations to rise to the light of day, with all the rudeness of a cadaver unearthed by an incautious grave-robber. Try as he might, he couldn't force himself to focus on guarding against an ambush, his mind instead drifting back to the events that had led him here. But here he was, away from his beloved command post in the Republic Military, in this frigid, half-dead forest, far to the east of Home.

In the chaos that followed the Incident, the whore-queen of the rebellion and her ilk had seized control of the majority of the Zigg's firepower. The confusion in the ranks of the military's officers had been substantial. People woke up in strange places, naked, and with no memory of how they came to be there. Lily Sapphire, esoterrorist *numero uno*, had spun an elaborate fiction about Warbak. She claimed he had been transforming the New Breed into killing machines, robots called Spartans, and that all the last-gen citizens of Home were being captured by alien devices hidden in the great monuments. But Martin knew this was a lie. What he believed had happened instead made a lot more sense, even though its implications unsettled him deeply.

This Lily and her Unpure army of riff-raff had shaped a powerful Strange, essentially crippling the Republic in one fell swoop. Before anyone knew what was going on, Chairman Warbak and Colonel Taylor had both been murdered. Even Matiaba, the Chairman's most trusted advisor and practical second-in-command of the Republic, had gone missing. Many of the New Breed officers, most notably in the Hopper, Heavy, and Easy-Rider detachments, had also been killed in the coup.

When Martin and the other Old Guard realized this fact, they were sobered in the extreme. If this Lily harlot was powerful enough in Strange not only to cut the heads off of the military beast with ease but also stun and disorient the entire population of the Zigg, then an instant counter-attack would be futile and most certainly spell death for them, and for any hope of survival and dominance the human race had left.

But a counter-attack will happen, Martin thought to himself now as he had then. *We bide our time, plan, and take back what is rightfully ours.*

In a turn of events that had broken his heart as much as it had surprised him, Martin had watched helplessly as more than half of the surviving officers and enlisted men swore their allegiance to the new regime, having swallowed the ludicrous lie about Warbak and his betrayal. *As if he would sell us out to the Harvesters! Inconceivable!*

In those first few hot and frantic days, Martin hadn't known who to trust. Men he had called his friends fell one by one to the so-called goddess and her rebel ideology. Obviously faked and doctored video clips were being shown on the Zigg's holo-vids, detailing the transformation and capture of Home's old and new populations. That the events took place, Martin had no doubt, only he knew in his heart that it was the esoterrorists' doing, not Warbak's.

Waiting for someone else to assemble any sort of organized front to resist the governmental takeover proved to be as impossible as it was essential. Martin had come closer then to despairing than he ever had before. For a brief moment there, it had seemed his only options were submission to the enemy or suicide.

Then it occurred to him that he should be the one who led the loyalists.

In that moment, on the fifth day after the Incident, Martin had presented himself at one of the impromptu "Town Hall" meetings set up by the traitorous Miller and his slut, Lily Sapphire. Equal parts euphoric from impassioned drive and terrified that the esoterrorists would gun him down on the spot, Martin had stood up and addressed the gathered peoples of Home.

Sure, many in the crowd, Shanty folk mostly, had booed him and called him names like fascist and brainwashed; however, a not insignificant portion of former military men had nodded their heads in grave agreement with his concerns.

After his speech, he had been approached by several groups of men, each one like unto a solar system—usually a ranking officer acting as a sun, surrounded by a small cadre of men who orbited him. One by one, Martin had met them, and a plan began to form in his mind to unite these isolated clusters of men into a galaxy.

Everyone he had spoken to shared the same reservations he had regarding the preservation of the Republic, and of the human race. At first, the strong majority of the malcontents did not receive Martin's plan as well as he'd hoped. Many wanted to take action right then, to strike while the enemy was still disorganized. But Martin knew this was folly. Visions of the resulting bloodbath and epic destruction to the Zigg, to Republic property and equipment, had flashed into his mind at each suggestion of acting hastily. Martin understood their urgency, their worry, but he also knew that a chaotic shootout in the Zigg would be a catastrophe. The presence of the sorceress and her inner circle made such an idea even worse than it otherwise would have been. No, they would have to regroup somewhere else, somewhere far away, and wait for a better chance to strike. Either an opportunity would present itself, or he would make one. An opportunity that would allow them to remove the esoterrorist bitch from the equation and even the playing field. An opportunity to retake Home without destroying it, or his men.

Eventually, the disgruntled officers and their men had fallen in line and joined with him. The Old Guard was formed.

And so they confronted Lily Sapphire and the turncoats Jon 310-257 and Master Sergeant Miller, a formally decorated war veteran, more recently serving as a cookie. They performed their bit of theater brilliantly, making their mass exodus from the Zigg, and taking with them a sizeable amount of weaponry and equipment.

They had set up shop in Lincoln, a Republic enclave on the far edges of Home's eastern farmlands, and waited for their chance.

That chance had come much sooner than expected, in the form of contact with a mysterious agent, referring to himself only as "The Provocateur."

The man of mystery had yet to reveal himself—or, as Private Nguyen had so astutely pointed out, prove himself trustworthy. Yet, with his options limited, Martin had taken up the counterinsurgent's offer to meet. *So far, so good. Now we will see if I have made a grave error, or if we are on the path back to rightness.*

The Provocateur—for he refused to give his real name—had contacted Martin on his personal N-tab, no small feat in itself, and informed him that he had a plan for ensuring victory for the Old Guard, and the Republic.

In the days leading up to his journey to the forested rendezvous point, Martin had pondered deeply the identity of this agent. *A remnant of the Ministry, perhaps?*

What a blessing that would prove to be! A Minister on their side would be their best chance at restoring order. But as far as he could tell, every Minister and every Handler—the human half of the Ministry of Social Purity's infamous Scrubber units—had either been killed or rendered powerless in the coup, unable to control their Sniffer counterparts. More fallout from the Incident and whatever Strange blow the so-called goddess had dealt.

Despite his reservations and his concerns regarding the Provocateur's true identity—it could easily be a trap laid by Lily Sapphire and her sycophants—Martin followed the instructions he'd been given.

As Martin and Nguyen trekked farther, the forest around them thickened enough that they had to skirt several clusters of trees, slowing their progress. As well as becoming more numerous, the trees became thicker as they continued. This forest was obviously considerably older, perhaps even pre-Storm in origins. What little light they'd had now grew even dimmer, and the day began to take on the feel of an early night.

"Get out the lantern," Martin ordered. "I nearly tripped just now."

Private Nguyen did as he was ordered without complaint, stopping briefly to take off his ruck and retrieve the battery-powered lantern attached to it.

Now, under the warm orange glow of their electric light, the duo moved into the thickest, darkest part of the ancient forest, closing in on the coordinates they had been given.

"Just up ahead," Nguyen announced.

Martin, in the lead and aware of their position, rolled his eyes for the umpteenth time at the young soldier's greenness. Just what did they teach these kids in Academy anyway?

New Breed, my ass.

"Keep quiet and stay alert. Let me do the talking," Martin snapped.

"Sir! Yes, sir!" the private responded, and Martin heard telltale rustling sounds as the kid sloppily readied his Lawnmower.

Martin gave one last glance down to the N-tab he carried, the one on which he had first been contacted, and confirmed the red dot blinking on its topographical map display was indeed just a few meters in front of him.

Showtime.

The forest floor below them began to slope downward into a grade that beckoned them toward what seemed to be some sort of pit. The canopy of tree branches above became so thick as to completely block out the frosted white light. Martin's mind made cave associations as he and Private Nguyen descended the slope to the edge of a small glade, no larger in circumference than an office in the administrative levels of the Zigg.

Martin's eyes darted back and forth between the blinking dot on his N-tab and the glade, which appeared to be empty of both trees and people. He had come to the right location, but there was no one here.

Entering the clearing itself, Martin and Nguyen instinctively positioned themselves at each other's backs, as they turned in place to survey their surroundings. They were enclosed by thick, gnarled trees on all sides as well as above, so much that Martin could barely see the path he and his ward had taken. Surrounded, but alone.

"It would seem that we have been played for fools," Martin grumbled, his words carried into the frigid air on puffs of steaming breath.

"Great," Nguyen said. Despite the kid's ceaseless grumbling over their three-day journey, Martin did not scold the young man. Their gamble on the promise of help had now proved to be a colossal waste of time. There was much to do in Lincoln. Shelters and defense fortifications needed to be built. A new chain of command had yet to be fully established. If the Old Guard ever wished to realize their dream of re-establishing the Republic, they would first have to survive the winter, waiting for new crops to be planted in spring, and then become as mighty as Home had once been. He had no time for games like this.

"Blast it all to hell," Martin said, scowling. "Let's get out of here. We may yet be able to make it to the Farm road before nightfall."

"I told you to come alone," a voice called out from somewhere in the thick trees.

Martin and Nguyen spun about, alarmed, scanning their surroundings once more.

"Enough games!" Martin shouted, his anger rising. "Show yourself!"

"Relax, Major. I am here," the voice said.

Just to the left of Martin, the air began to shimmer. Realizing immediately that the effect was not simply the refraction of lantern light off of ice crystals suspended in the air, Martin and Nguyen leaped back. Reflexively, Martin's hand shot down to his hip, and with a flick of his thumb, unfastened the nylon strap that bound his sidearm to its holster.

"Jumpy, are we?" the voice said, clearly originating from the shimmer hovering before them.

The scintillation grew in intensity and then appeared to dissolve. An image, no, a true presence of a man appeared in its place.

"Active camouflage!" Martin heard Nguyen gasp.

"I had to know that I was safe first, that I could trust you."

"You?" the major asked, unable to believe his eyes.

"Yes, me. I have been in hiding, watching, ever since," the man said, flashing the soldiers a wry smile.

"We thought you were dead," Martin said.

"And I thought you were going to come alone," came the snappy response.

Martin ignored the jibe and quickly moved to change the subject.

"Well, now that I know who you are, your promise of salvation seems a bit more credible. I came, so you know I'm willing to hear you out. Although I'm not sure why we couldn't have met in a more reasonable location."

"As I said in my communique, secrecy is of the utmost importance. If anyone in Maya's, or rather, Lily Sapphire's circle even so much as gets a whiff of what I am plotting, it will fail. I brought you out here so I could test you, to ascertain your trustworthiness, or to see if the Loyalists need a different leader."

Martin narrowed his eyes and remembered the pistol, still resting in its unfastened holster.

"You know I respect you, I just made that clear. But I do not like your tone. Or your choice of words. That sounded like a threat just now."

"Take it however you will. I care not for your pride or your life. The Republic is much bigger than one man."

Martin could see what he meant, but he still didn't like what had been implied.

"I think you may have things a little backwards," Martin

dared. "You see, I *am* the leader of the Old Guard, and I am here to figure out if *I* can trust *you*."

The Provocateur waved his hand dismissively and smiled. "Whatever helps you sleep at night."

Nguyen shifted uncomfortably, an unconscious gesture that made Martin aware that this banter was fruitless, and besides, it was growing cold.

"Enough of this pissing match. Say what you brought me here for," Martin demanded, relaxing his posture some—a tacit olive branch, but he kept his pistol ready. "Tell me your plan for defeating the insurgents."

"Very well. It is simple. We won't defeat the insurgents."

Martin scowled. *Has he lost his mind? Did the sorceress taint him somehow?* "What nonsense is this?" he growled.

"Listen, Major. *We* won't defeat them. We will arrange for them to defeat themselves."

The electric lamp cast the Provocateur's face in a strange glow, giving him an otherworldly appearance. His widening grin only served to accentuate the unnerving qualities of the man and the situation.

"I'm listening," Martin said, prompting him to continue.

"You see, you are all making the mistake of assuming Maya and her rebels think as we do. That they are military. That their goals are military goals. They are not."

Before Martin could ask what the Provocateur meant by that, he informed them.

"Despite their unthinkable victory over our glorious Chairman, the sorceress and her inner circle of rebels are nothing more than idealists. They aren't actually seeking the power they just took. They truly believe that they are the heroes of this story, and likewise, believe that what they are doing is just; that Invasives are deserving of equal rights and the same protections as humans. They are all, to a one, idealistic fools, like the singing strumpet they follow, putting lofty principles before proven practicalities. I have ways to manipulate them into making an even bigger mess than the one they've already created."

Martin was flabbergasted. His mind strained, trying to understand such naive stupidity.

"We will use this to our advantage and tear them down without having to fire a single bullet. We will grease the wheels, so to speak, and the revolutionary vehicle in which they are riding will accelerate out of their control. They will crash and burn. And when they do, we will step back into the picture to finish them off and take back Home, saving humanity in the process."

"I'll play. How do you plan, exactly, to do this? No more cryptic words. Speak plainly," Martin said, genuinely intrigued.

"Ah yes. I forget that I'm talking to a grunt. A decorated grunt, but a grunt nonetheless. Allow me to elaborate."

Martin ignored the insult and listened as the Provocateur laid out his plan in detail. It was a long con, a masterpiece of conniving manipulation that would, Martin came to see, set the stage for a swift and easy retaking of Home. He stood in silence for a moment, contemplating the plot and its potential.

"As much as it pains me to admit this, I like it. It's a sound plan," Martin said.

"Well, thank you. I learned from the best."

Martin nodded, instantly intimating the man's meaning.

"So it's settled then. We have a trust established?" Martin asked. His mind was beginning to fill with possibility and glory.

"We do."

"I suppose I should count myself lucky that it is so. After all, you are a man of your word. You came alone when I did not." Martin gestured to Private Nguyen.

"When did I say that I came alone?" The Provocateur chuckled, then snapped his fingers.

Like puppets descending onto a stage, suspended from strings above, three blurred objects lowered into the clearing from the tangle of thick tree limbs overhead.

Before Martin could identify the nature of the new arrivals, one reached down with unnaturally long arms, each ending in a six-toed claw, and snatched Nguyen off the ground, pulling him several meters into the air and holding him fast.

The electric lamp fell from the soldier's grip and landed on its side, changing the arc of its orange glow and throwing long shadows over portions of the wooded glade.

Illuminated by the lamp, Martin beheld in shock one of the three creatures as it slipped into view.

Bead-like eyes, small and black, with eerie horizontal lines for pupils, stared back at Martin on either side of an elongated face. The thing's features and head instantly reminded Martin of the skull of a horse, its flesh paper-thin, wrapping its elongated, bony features. Scores of needle teeth, almost as fine as hair, slowly wavered back and forth around the creature's mouth, as if its lipless gums were lined with cilia.

The near-skeletal head was attached to a lanky body, some nightmarish cross between a hairless cat and hairless primate, currently upside down, hanging from the trees above by prehensile feet, identical to the extraordinarily long arms, all of which ended in six long claw-toes.

"What is the meaning of this?" Martin shouted, fetching his pistol from its resting place and pointing it at the Provocateur.

"I would re-holster that weapon if I were you, Major," the Provocateur warned. "The Neal-Laen are ambush predators, preferring to attack from above. They evolved on an arboreal forest world and can be quite swift when moving through trees."

"Not faster than a bullet, I'd wager!" Martin growled back, cocking the hammer back on his pistol to show that he meant business. Above, muffled sounds came from Private Nguyen as he squirmed in the cradling grasp of the hanging creature. A second later, the muffles and the squirming stopped. Only the soft sounds of the winter wind whistling through the trees remained. That, and the pounding of Martin's blood in his ears.

"Squeeze the trigger, and all hope for the Republic is lost. You may or may not kill me, I can't say. But I can guarantee it will be the last thing you ever do."

Keeping his pistol's glow-in-the-dark sights trained on the Provocateur, Martin shifted his eyes enough to see the two Neal-Laen that weren't grappling with Private Nguyen move without making a sound, repositioning themselves within easy striking distance of Martin, to his back left and right respectively.

"Why?" Martin asked, shaking with a volatile mixture of rage and fear. "Why are you doing this?"

"Two reasons. One, I said I needed to test you. Two, I told you to come alone."

A dull thump behind Martin made him jump. He spun, trying and failing to keep the Provocateur threatened with his pistol. On the ground behind him, he found the source of the sound. Nguyen's limp body had been dropped by his captor. Even in the soft glow of the electric torch, Martin could see the kid's face looked shriveled, aged somehow, dried up.

Slowly, with all the grace and self-mastery of a champion gymnast, the Neal-Laen that had killed the boy unfolded itself from the tree canopy, gently turning end over end, until it had grasped the lowest hanging branches with its long arms, and then touched down onto the ground with its mirror-image legs. Once on the ground, the beast came down to stand on all fours, completing its animal appearance. Martin's eyes, wide with horror and disgust, only came to the underside of the beast's belly. He watched, frozen, as a dinner-plate-sized starfish of sorts dislodged itself from the Neal-Laen's neck, crawled to the ground, and then began to go about eating the remains of Private Nguyen's body with an unseen mouth orifice.

"I told you that we would need to work with Drop-trash for this to work. You agreed that was sound. I need to see if it's possible. I need to see your mettle. Sacrifices must be made."

"And that means sacrificing my men?" Martin spun, hating to turn his back on the Simian-Equidae alien, but more strongly wanting to menace the Provocateur with his weapon again.

"Do you have what it takes to see this through, Major? Or do I need to find another confidant? The boy had to go; his blood is on your hands, not mine. I told you to come alone. I told you that secrecy must be maintained at all cost."

Martin wavered back and forth between lowering the gun and pulling the trigger. Finally, cautious wisdom, or perhaps simply self-preservation, won out. He lowered the pistol with a shaky hand and bored into the sinister agent's eye with his stare.

"Fine. I will go along with you. You can count on me to keep our operation a secret. I can handle it. Forget the boy."

"That's the spirit." The Provocateur grinned and waved his hand. The Neal-Laen snatched up Private Nguyen's body and climbed up into the trees, disappearing without so much as the sound of one single twig snapping.

Unable to shake the feeling that he had made a deal with the devil, Martin saw no other option that ended well for him. Then and there, he made a promise to himself and to his fallen soldier that, when the dust had settled, when this was all done and dusted, he would kill the Provocateur. But for now, he would bend the knee.

He holstered his weapon, looked directly into the man's eyes and said, "You had better be right about all this, Matiaba."

5

Morning came without event, though to Jon and Lucy it was just a brighter version of night, neither of them having slept a wink.

Maya appeared no worse for wear. Her headache, if that was what it could be called, was as fully and completely gone as the night's stars above.

"I'd like to try again," she stated to the group matter-of-factly, arms crossed. She had apparently come to them expecting a fight and looked to be in no mood to back down or compromise.

"But, my lady!" Lucy blurted out, beating Jon to the first counter-assault.

"Let me speak!" Maya commanded, causing Lucy's jaw to snap shut instantly. "I know and have reluctantly accepted that I can't open a full-sized door for now, perhaps forever. But I did manage to get that small one formed."

Jon cocked his head and squinted slightly, wondering where she was going with this.

"So I'm going to see if I can easily, and without pain or problem, open a small one."

Jon frowned, crossing his own arms, and judged by the countenances of his companions that they shared his confusion. Naturally, it was Carbine that voiced the obvious question.

"Umm, what good is that going to do?"

Maya's eyes flashed as she spoke. "Find me something to write with."

Before the sun had reached its zenith in the winter sky, they had scoured every bit of debris that lay atop the sand. Having been unsuccessful in their quest to find a proper writing implement, they resorted to a jagged piece of steel, which they could use as an awl to scratch a message into a piece of soft aluminum.

"I guess this will have to do," Maya said, unable to hide her disappointment. "But it should do the trick. Miller will be worried when we don't radio back."

"Or return," Carbine added dourly.

Jon shot him a *"Dude!"* glance and reassured Maya. "It'll work great. What should we say?"

"Send food," Carbine offered, smiling.

"There isn't much room." Maya regarded the flat square of aircraft aluminum, squinting in an attempt to compare its dimensions with her hazy memory of the last night's small window through space. "How about: Ship crashed. All okay. Continuing on foot. Don't worry." Maya looked at her guardians with a hopeful expression.

Jon tried to hide a grimace, while Lucy imitated a statue. Once again, it was Carbine who stated the obvious.

"Isn't that a little misleading? I mean, shouldn't we mention that we're lost? That Ratt is FUBAR. That we have virtually no supplies, and that they should send help?"

Jon hated his buddy's lack of bedside manner, but secretly

agreed with him and couldn't bring himself to protest, even if it meant winning points with Maya.

"What good would that do?" Maya asked Carbine specifically. "Sure, it'd be the truth, but what *good* would it do? We *are* lost, that's true. But that fact is precisely why they can't send help. We can't tell them where to go! All we can do is press on with our quest and give them hope. Let them know we are okay, and to not worry. To hold down the fort until we get back."

"What about Ratt? *He's* not okay?" Carbine persisted.

"I think leaving that out would fall under giving them hope," Jon interjected, evoking a slight nod of affirmation from Maya. "She's right, bud. We don't want them to panic. Let them know we are okay, establish communication. Keep checking in with them. Maybe, once we know where we are, we can tell them and see about getting some help."

"I guess," Carbine said with a shrug. "Just seems like we might regret leaving out those details."

"It's settled," Lucy announced, then took the square from Maya and plopped down into a cross-legged position to go about the scribing.

A moment later, she had finished and offered it back to Maya.

"Hang on to it for a second," Maya said, then stood up, brushed herself off, and nodded to Jon. "Here goes nothing!"

Maya began a repeat of the previous night's performance, although Jon noticed slight variations in both her pitch and volume. Maybe a hand or finger gesture here and there was differ-ent, but he couldn't say with any certainty.

Jon watched with bated breath as Maya began to shape. As before, the goddess gestured and swayed as she sang. He wasn't sure, but Jon felt that the song was going longer than before and felt a splinter of doubt begin to bury itself in his gray matter. He was just about to say something to Maya, like a sane paramedic halting the frantic and futile resuscitation attempts of someone driven by emotion, when a small patch of air in front of Maya began to warble and shimmer.

A blink of an eye later, Maya ended her song with a long note, which cut off abruptly, and the shimmering spot in the air snapped open to reveal a porthole-like window to the Underground garden.

"It worked!" Carbine shouted.

Maya turned around and treated Jon to a triumphant smile.

Gotta make the small victories count, he thought and returned her smile with one of his own.

"No time to waste," Lucy announced. "Here!" she said, offering her lady the message-bearing square of metal.

"Right! I didn't shape it to stay open for very long. That would have taken a lot more Strange." Maya took the square and turned, slowly walking up to the portal, getting as close as possible to it without touching it.

"For luck!" she announced, and with a snap of her wrist, carefully aimed the message through the dimensional window. The square sailed through open air like a ninja's shuriken, disappearing from their vicinity and landing somewhere on the other side.

"There. We'll check back in with them later and try to establish a scheduled time to communicate face to face," Maya said, nodding to herself. Then, stepping back, she waved her arm dismissively, closing the portal until all traces of it were gone and only the desert scrub remained.

"So now what?" Carbine asked the group.

"I guess we play it by ear. Start heading out as soon as Ratt's okay and see what we see. If we get in a bind, like, come to an ocean, perhaps, then we regroup," Jon said, and everyone nodded. In the back of his mind, he knew that meant going the long way around said ocean—if such a long way even existed.

After a bit of awkward silence, Jon and Lucy worked together first to build shelter, if not for a sense of security, then to at least keep the sun off Ratt, which even in the late winter was relentless in this part of the world, wherever that may be.

Ratt remained in his supernatural sleep with Maya watching over him, while Carbine joined Jon and Lucy in their quest for anything of value that might have survived the crash.

They worked until sundown, finally calling it quits when they could no longer see what garbage was versus what was valuable. Lucy wanted to continue, being able to see in the dark, while Carbine had started to suggest that she take a break. Jon placed a hand on his friend's shoulder and advised, "Let her go. She needs to be alone for a bit." Lucy was a very effective warrior and excelled at combat, but she couldn't shield her real self from Jon now. Her metal shell protected her from trauma and damage, from blade and bullet, but was transparent when it came to hiding her fears. Jon knew by now that her tough act was just that.

When Jon and Carbine returned to the lean-to, they found that Maya had built a small fire. It was comforting, as the desert night was beginning to grow cold. They gave her a report of what they had managed to salvage so far: some food, very little of their camping equipment, a hatchet, and their sleeping bags had escaped unscathed; the two Hoppers they had brought had been demolished, but they'd managed to find Carbine's railgun, salvaged from the Mini-Mech he had used during the Battle of Home. They'd even found most of its ammo, the drums scattered across the sandy dirt. While excited that the weapon was found intact, Carbine lamented the fact that he wouldn't be able to use it, the recoil of such a weapon being too much for his human frame to bear.

The greatest disappointment had been the discovery of all four ATVs; crunched, mangled, and deconstructed in every way. They'd also found a wide assortment of bits that they could only assume belonged to the machine shop that Ratt had loaded on board. Jon had found his hammer as well as Carbine's pistol. The rest of what they had packed was lost to them, though they discussed searching for anything else, even broken stuff that might be of value to them, in the morning.

The three of them sat in the dirt around Ratt's sleeping form. Maya gratefully accepted a bottle of water that Jon had found and used it to dampen a bit of cloth—Jon guessed it used to be a seat cushion cover—and dabbed Ratt's forehead with it. She tended to him with the detail and care of a geisha in a tea ceremony, while Jon watched, and Carbine stirred the embers of their fire with a bit of sturdy stick.

Jon had not grown up camping—had never "grown up" in any way other than the rigors of an endless boot camp, with drills replacing childhood, State replacing family—and so he had never really sat around a fire before, under the starlight canopy, and smelled the rich, musky, primordial scent of wood smoke. He liked it; he liked it a lot. There was something about it that was as ancient, natural, and right as the goddess that sat across from him. He was mesmerized both by the gentle curves of her cheekbones and eyes and the dancing lights and shadows that played across them. A flush of blood filled his cheeks as he recalled their spontaneous kiss earlier. Should he bring it up to her later, in private? What was he thinking? Even if they were beginning to develop feelings for each other, Jon was her guardian, her servant. Furthermore, he was one with a very short lifespan. He didn't have time for things like love.

Out in the desert darkness, they could hear the hunting and mating sounds of hundreds of different animals, birds, and insects. A pack of coyotes yipped somewhere off in the direction of the hills they had seen, off in the direction of the golden pillar.

Jon rummaged through the pile of stuff they had gathered and presented a freeze-dried meal to Maya, sheathed in a thick plastic pouch.

"Here, eat."

She looked up from her ministrations, and she smiled at Jon with her eyes, their corners softening at the gesture of kindness. She folded the wet cloth into a small rectangle, placed it on Ratt's forehead, and then took the food offered to her.

"You should eat too, and try to sleep. I know that the serum makes you neither hungry nor tired, but your body is still human, and going without will harm you. It will break you down and…"—she tilted her head slightly sideways and drew closer to him— "and I couldn't bear to watch that happen to you."

"Okay, Maya. I will try. You too, Carbine." Jon dug out two more pouches of food and tossed one to his friend.

"Oh man! Ham omelet. I was hoping for stroganoff," Carbine bemoaned, but eagerly tore into his meal-pouch regardless. The three of them ate in silence, Jon forcing himself to chew and swallow. When they had finished their meal, Jon looked over to Maya and spoke softly.

"I don't think I can sleep, no matter how hard I try. I haven't been able to sleep a wink ever since, you know." Jon held up his hands and waved them slowly side to side.

Maya seemed to think about this for a moment, pursing her lips and twiddling her thumbs. Then a smile appeared on her face as sudden and bright as unexpected lightning in the sky.

"I believe I can help with that!" she exclaimed. She stood up and gestured at the boys. "Okay. Get yourselves comfy. I'm going to sing you to sleep!"

Jon felt a little embarrassed and looked over at Carbine, who had a look on his face that read, *Seriously?*

"Come on, silly," she said to Carbine. "Not that long ago, you would have been pretty excited to have a private show with Lily Sapphire." She winked knowingly at him, and he gulped, eyes wide. Jon and Maya both laughed out loud, melting the awkward ice. They puttered around for a minute, putting away odd bits, reorganizing things, and unrolling their sleeping bags.

Once they were all settled down, they lay together in the fading glow of the slowly dying fire. Having become accustomed to it, Jon could no longer smell the wood smoke or the sage-scented breeze that blew gently over his face and through the lean-to.

Jon and Carbine closed their eyes and lay still, feeling the tension, stress, and fatigue leave their bodies with every deep exhalation. After a spell, Maya began to cast hers. It hadn't occurred to Jon before that she wove her magic web with song, but he realized now that every time she shaped Strange, she sang. It made sense to him. *There is great power in music. It can reach down into deep places inside us that others can seldom find, let alone influence. It can resonate not only with our hearts but with the vibrations of the very universe. It could be said that all vibration is music—the sounds of nature, a babbling brook, the wind, the planet spinning and sailing through its clockwork tour of the heavens.* Jon recalled the insights of Maya's first revelation and remembered that throughout the history of man's rule over the world, many governments and religions had attempted to ban music, so it would seem that even wicked men understood the transformative potential and power that music contained.

Her voice sang its song into the dark, working its magic. She sang in a language alien to Jon. He wondered briefly whether the song would sound as enchanting if he could understand what she was saying. Being unable to, he lay, spellbound by the melody and sound. He felt the familiar, though recently absent, feeling of dullness behind his eyes, eyes whose lids were growing heavy. Before she had finished her song, Jon fell asleep with the world's most serene smile on his face.

The sleeping Strange worked well; almost *too* well. Jon was awakened by Maya vigorously shaking his shoulder and strenuously whispering, "Jon! Jon!" He opened his eyes with a start. He was confused for half a second—*Where am I? Whu*—But then his soldier instincts kicked in. He looked at Maya, propping himself up on one elbow, her dark outline hovering over him like a guardian angel.

"What's happening?" he asked.

"I heard something out there." He couldn't make out her features in the dark but heard the genuine concern in her voice. He sat up and she moved back a little. Clouds had moved in as he slept, obscuring what moonlight there had been, turning the night as dark and silent as the grave. He looked over his sleeping companions. Ratt hadn't moved, and Carbine was out like a light too. Lucy had still not returned from her self-imposed solitary confinement.

"Suppose it's just Lucy?" Jon mused out loud.

"No way," Maya replied instantly. "If it were Lucy, I wouldn't have heard her."

"You've got a point there," Jon admitted. He reached out and squeezed Maya's hand. "Hang tight; I'll take a look around."

Just as Jon peeled back his sleeping bag, he heard it: a low, guttural growling coming from somewhere out in the black, off to his right.

Some kind of animal, most likely... hopefully.

He ceased moving to hear better and felt Maya's hand tighten its grip. The growling stopped, but in its place came the sound of rustling, or scurrying. Jon fumbled in the dark for his hammer, which he had laid next to him before falling asleep. Finding it, he closed his fingers around the haft and stood up, gently releasing Maya's hand. He carefully stepped over her, walked to the edge of their camp, then turned back and whispered, "It's probably nothing."

A figure pounced out of the darkness and hit Jon in the chest like a riot-control bean bag shot, sending him tumbling backward.

Maya screamed, Carbine stirred, and Jon ended up flat on his back with a deranged humanoid on top of him, its eyes glowing crimson in the dark. Jon felt something, sweat or drool, he wasn't sure, drip down from the savage and land on his forehead. The form belched forth a throaty growl and menaced Jon with a display of sharp canines.

It was dark, but mottled moonlight had broken through the heavy clouds above. The smell coming off the man was unreal—somewhere between rancid sweat and two-week-old dead animals in the summer.

Jon fought back the urge to retch as he attempted to wrestle his arms into a better position and throw the man off of him. Its strength surprised him, and he found they were almost evenly matched. Unable to fling the attacker from his chest, he tucked his arms in and around the assailant's legs that squeezed Jon's bucking waist. The savage's growl died, and it opened its barbaric mouth wider, lunging for Jon's throat. Jon tucked his chin and slashed the face of his assailant with his forearm and elbow, unhinging the man's jaw and effectively deflecting the incoming bite.

The stunning blow was just what Jon needed. He popped his waist up into a back bridge, pushing off the ground with his feet while he hooked his hands under the savage's foul armpits and threw it off of him, sending it into a forward somersault.

Without wasting any time, Jon rolled to his side, followed through to his knees, and leapt to his feet, pausing only to pick up his hammer.

The savage, too, had returned to its feet and turned back around to face Jon. It opened its ugly mouth and wiggled its jaw around. Jon heard a horrible popping noise and watched in disgust as the dislocated jaw moved back into place. Jon hefted his hammer into the ready position. It began to glow blue with its star pattern, casting a haunting light over the edge of the camp, illuminating the immediate environs as well as the wild-man.

Jon could now see that his foe was indeed human, or at least appeared human. What must have been clothes at one time were now only a tangled smattering of threads, his ensemble now resembling netting more than shirt and pants. His feet were bare, and his skin, darker than Jon's, was smeared with what looked like years' worth of dirt.

His hair was long, tangled, and disheveled. The glowing red eyes and long, claw-like fingernails told Jon that this wasn't just a homeless vagabond.

The savage spewed out another beastly roar and charged at Jon, its dirty claw-like hands half outstretched. Jon took one long stride forward and lowered his guard, putting himself in the wild-man's range and baiting the attack. Like a hungry fish on its long journey upriver, the brute took the bait and aimed a sloppy haymaker of a swing at Jon's face with its jagged nails.

Jon had been waiting for it, and the savage was doing exactly what he had hoped it would do—swinging high. Jon spun to the right and collapsed down on himself. He continued the spin as he crouched and let the hammer go, the swing timed perfectly.

As Jon completed his low turn, he ducked under the incoming swipe, crouching before the man-beast. The swinging hammer caught up full circle, connecting squarely against the inside of the savage's left knee joint with a loud, wet smack.

Jon continued to spin, rising as he did so. By the time he came to a stop, the man-beast had fallen to one knee, balancing itself with the opposing hand. It snarled at Jon, unable to stand, but not appearing to be in pain. Jon gritted his teeth and grunted back at it, then let fly his hammer again.

A hollow crack echoed through the night as Jon's hammer

crashed into the savage's skull. The hammer cleared and returned to a chambered position as Jon shifted his hips. The savage flew back, groaned, and folded over onto the ground.

Jon stood triumphantly over the fallen enemy, his chest rising and falling, eyes wide, still buzzing with adrenaline. He heard a commotion from the camp and raised his weapon above his head so that his body would not obscure its glow. He saw Carbine stepping out of the lean-to, pistol in hand.

"What's going on?" Carbine asked. Jon could see Maya behind him, peering over his shoulder.

"Some kind of wild-man. Possessed, I think. I don't…" Jon's voice trailed off as he lowered the hammer and examined the body. He leaned in and held the hammer out like a lantern to get a closer look. His blow had completely caved in the side of the wild-man's skull; the long, greasy, tangled mess of hair was dry, though. Jon squinted and focused his eyes, trying to will them to see better in the dim light, yet still found no evidence of blood.

What the…? Jon's eyes narrowed even further as the caved-in skull began to un-cave like a balloon inflating.

"Carbine!" Jon shouted, raising his hammer for another strike. He didn't wait for the savage's regeneration to finish before raining blow after blow down upon the thing's head.

Smack. Smack. Smack.

Before Carbine could trot up to his friend, Jon had pounded the savage's head flat and fully into the ground with his hammer. Still no blood. And again, it began to slowly re-inflate and repair itself.

"Jon, what in the actual—?" Carbine's words were arrested in his throat by the sound of more growls in the night.

Jon tore his gaze from the regenerating man-creature at his feet and turned to look out into the desert. A swarm of glowing red eyes stared back at him.

From out of the edge of darkness and into the glow of the

hammer stepped a pack of savages similar to the first— ragged, dirty, drooling upright beasts of men. Their mouths hung open, showing off extremely large canine teeth that seemed to shine when the hammer-light struck them. They came out of the shadows, forming a loose half-circle around the camp.

Jon looked from one to another as they approached like wolves on the hunt. It occurred to him that their appearance was somewhat wolf-like, these beast men. He shuddered. The goddess and her guardians were in over their heads.

Jon began to step backward slowly, and Carbine followed his lead. They were too exposed and, besides, they needed to protect the goddess first and foremost. Unfortunately, giving ground encouraged the hunters, and they began to tighten their noose around Jon, Carbine, Ratt, and Maya both more quickly and with more brazenness. Jon knew the tipping point was coming, and it was coming fast.

6

The little boy pulled the cupboard door shut behind him and crouched in the dark, cramped space. His breathing sounded as loud to him as the winds of a spring tornado. He gulped a few big gulps and tried to slow his racing heart and heaving chest. He surfed the razor's edge between the fear of being caught and the thrill of the night's adventure to come. He had come into the Paramount earlier when it was open and milled around with the other patrons until the moment was just right. Once old man Allen was occupied, he'd stolen away into the upstairs offices. He'd helped himself inside and found a large cupboard that was mostly empty, certainly empty enough for him to hide inside until past closing, so he could have the ancient theater to himself.

He had wanted to get inside the Paramount for years, but the place had been locked up and protected. He had heard the grownups talk of "preservation" and "time-capsule," but he didn't understand what that meant. He only knew that it was a sanctum of magic, a place that contained all the treasures of the past, of Earth-That-Was. Everything that got him high, that glittered, that brought a touch of the sublime to his otherwise utilitarian, pointless life, was hidden in the Paramount's treasure trove. Ever since he'd seen his first relic, Ratt had been fascinated with the past.

Blessed and cursed with a genius-level IQ, the child found little satisfaction in the company of others, and as he grew, he withdrew more and more into his own little world. That world was a fantasy pieced together with scraps from the past. He consumed anything pre-Storm with the ravenous ferocity of a starving animal. Literature in any shape or form, whether it be a pulp novel or a masterful work of literature or even a takeout menu from a long-gone Thai restaurant mattered not. He read it; read it and treasured it.

Pre-Storm clothes, gadgets, knick-knacks, and anything else under the sun was as gold to him. He daydreamed entire days away, pondering the nature of things he had read references to but couldn't imagine. What were these smartphones that so many people in Earth-That-Was wrote about? What was Tiger Cry beef? Mostly, he wondered what a "TV show" and "movie" looked like. He had read enough bits and pieces to understand what they were —moving pictures—but he had never seen one. Tonight, he would satisfy that burning curiosity. He had learned by listening to the grownups that a vast store of "movies," as well as something called a projector, had been found in the basement of a pre-storm building called The Paramount.

By some wild stroke of luck, this building had survived the Great Storm, the Scrappers recently discovering it while out on one of their missions—an expedition into the thick, dense ruins of what had once been the City Center.

After the Storm, people in the crowded parts of Austin-That-Was suffered the greatest. Food riots, fighting, collapsing and burning buildings, and other forms of brutal savagery had taken care of the majority of the population. Those who had fled and made it out, along with the more self-sufficient residents of the outskirts, had become the survivors. Generations had gone by before the survivors became organized enough to try to reclaim the city.

Two weeks ago, a Scrapper party had come back to report a find of note: a veritable vault of pre-Storm "movies." Ratt had overheard the grownups talking about it and decided to tag along with the older boys who were accompanying the men to the "unveiling" of the find. And so he had, and now sat, trying his hardest not to let the pain of his cramping back overcome him. He could still hear people downstairs; it wouldn't be too much longer.

He awoke suddenly and quickly realized that his butt was numb, his neck was stiff, there was drool smeared all over his hand and left cheek, and he had to pee something fierce.

He looked around and couldn't see his hand in front of his face. No light shone through the cracks outlining the cupboard door. He held his breath and listened as hard as he could, but there was only silence.

Ever cautious, he apprehensively pushed open the hinged wooden door panel. Pitch black. He crawled out and tried to stand up. Pins and needles ran from his ass to his toes. He stumbled like an amateur circus performer trying out stilt-walking for the first time. He careened this way and that on club-like feet, able to tell that something he was dragging was touching the floor, but unable to truly feel it. His right foot came down slightly sideways and rolled, and he lurched forward in a fall, his hands reaching out into the dark in a desperate attempt to find something to cling to.

He felt something and grabbed it, trying to prevent the fall. Whatever it was, it wasn't tied down and came tumbling down with him, showering his fallen form and the floor around him with a volley of unknown objects. The subsequent crashing sounds were so loud, Ratt could have sworn that an Artillery Unit was shelling the theater.

After bouncing his face off the floor, Ratt lay perfectly still. He fought back the urge to cry out or even bring his hands to the bleeding lip his tooth had torn. Like a wild rabbit watching the hunter from under the branches of a tree not five yards away, he was motionless, listening for a reaction to his disastrous attempt at stealth.

With bated breath, he anticipated the raising of the alarm, but it never came. He allowed himself a sigh of relief but remained on high alert. He wiped the blood from his lip. It was swollen, and he could feel the troubled flesh on the inside of his mouth with his tongue. It was bumpy and gross. He slowly stood up and quietly brushed himself off. Although he still couldn't see squat, his eyes were coming around and adjusting slightly. He could now differentiate darker shapes of black in the ambient darkness of the room, allowing him to navigate between the furniture in the office without any more bumps and crashes.

By the time he had crossed the room and reached the office door, feeling had fully returned to his extremities. Itching had replaced numbness, but Ratt ignored the urge and felt out for the door handle. Ratt felt around clumsily until he found the latch. He slowly turned it and pulled the door open. It let out a long creak, causing Ratt to wish he had yanked instead. Again he froze and waited to hear the "Polo!" to his "Marco!", but only silence answered back.

On the other side of the door, he was relieved to find a tad bit of ambient light. The mezzanine here was exposed to the outdoors, a small portion of the far corner having fallen away. Ratt could smell the outside air and hear the cooing of doves in the middle distance. He turned toward the nearest wall, opened his fly, and relieved himself. Next, he made his way to the large fake plant in the corner near the open door. Feeling around behind it, he found the backpack he had stashed there earlier.

Satisfied with the convergence of his plan, he smiled giddily and plopped the bottom of the frame on the floor. He untied the bits of stringy leather that laced the pack's main cavity closed and reached his slender arm inside, feeling around for the torch he knew was there. He was frustrated, for it had settled to the bottom and he was having a heck of a time finding it; he should have taken it out before he even got there and stored it someplace more practical, like his hoodie pouch.

"Yes!" The boy's tiny fingers found the torch and withdrew it from the pack. A flick of his thumb, and the musty theater became semi-illuminated, the torch's cone of light waving through the air. The multitude of dust motes now visible looked like snowflakes in the torch's beam, and Ratt felt like a kid on Christmas morning about to open his presents without first waking his parents.

Able to see where he was going now, he easily made his way down the broad, sweeping stairs to the main theater room. He gazed over the long-abandoned chairs that poked their rectangular stubby frames up into the room like tombstones in an indoor graveyard. His imagination was on fire with questions as he took it all in. With the throng of people now absent, he could see the theater for what it was in all its haunted, anachronistic glory.

He floated down the sloping grade of the auditorium floor to the base of the stage at the forefront of the room. Running his free hand along the edge, he followed the curve to the end, where floor met wall, under an old sign that read "EXIT." A short series of five steps led from the rotten carpet and concrete floor of the auditorium to the warped wooden-slat floor of the stage. Trotting up them with ease, his gaze following the mouldering remains of a thick, heavy black curtain that reached nearly from floor to ceiling, and noticed for the first time the catwalks and the lights.

His gaze lingered on the lights, and he moved the beam of his torch from one to another, pausing for several moments on each one. Every one was a smooth black tube with a square mouth, no, a frame of some kind, fastened to the outside diameter of the tube.

This frame, he could see, was designed to hold a sheet of transparent, colored material, for some of them still did. Ratt quickly surmised that the function of these lights, which in many ways resembled large, fixed and mounted versions of the very torch he held, was to shed different shades of colored light down onto the stage. He imagined how much fun it would be to work up in those lofty stations, pointing the focus of the beam here and there—a subtle but important part of the show.

"We all have our part to play in the illusion," he said to himself, and smiled a musing smile.

As it was in most adventures, he found the real goods behind the curtain. The "Management Only" sign was hanging askew by one rivet, but it still marked the staircase leading down into the basement. Ratt re-shouldered the sagging, heavy pack and made his way downstairs.

He was the proverbial kid in a candy store. The basement storage room was a virtual Library of Alexandria of pre-Storm cinema. And there, on a simple table that to Ratt now looked like an ancient temple's pedestal holding a priceless relic of the past, was the film projector. He had overheard the grownups speak of the tragedy earlier; of what a shame it was that the projector no longer worked, and how wonderful it would be if it did; what secrets they might have gleaned from the past, etcetera, etcetera.

When he had tried to speak up and offer to take a look at it, they hadn't even heard him. He was a child, after all; what could he possibly have of value to offer to the discourse? Well, he would show them. That was when he had hatched his plan to sneak in and fix the damned thing. Then he could learn the secrets of the ancients, and they would respect him and title him a man.

The child went right to setting up shop, taking off his pack and dumping its contents onto the table. He plucked a cloth-wrapped morsel of salted meat, grinding it into a lump along with dried fruit and grain powder. Thoughtfully munching away on it, he walked in a slow circle around the projector, examining and scrutinizing it as if he were a pre-Storm consumer considering the purchase of a car.

By the time he had finished his snack, he knew how to proceed. Ratt went to work, sifting through the bits he had dumped out on the table; he played nurse as well as surgeon, trading one tool for another with fevered intensity. A screwdriver here, a 6-inch adjustable wrench there, and then his fingers mashed up some quick-dry epoxy like teeth to chewing gum.

Pausing only occasionally to wipe the beads of sweat from his furrowed brow, Ratt worked for no less than an hour before he finally stopped, stepped back, and brushed his grubby hands on his pants legs. He crossed his arms and looked his work over.

"Well, I think that'll do her."

He made his way over to the steel racks that ran from floor to ceiling around the perimeter of the room and began to browse through the reels of film.

Where do I even begin? he wondered as he stared at the thousands of titles, completely overwhelmed by the sheer vastness of choice.

"Huh." Ratt stopped when he saw a title that reminded him of his current situation as if it were a meaningful synchronicity.

From Dusk till Dawn, the sticker on the film canister read in old English.

Ratt pulled the canister down from the shelf and brought it over to the table. Like a seasoned professional, he set it up and then produced an object from his pack's pile. It was what was called a power pack—a cell of energy, common to and smuggled out of the war-mongering "Human Republic" of the north. Ratt, being the antique aficionado that he was, had converted it to take pre-Storm, North American 110.

Ratt plugged the antiquated device into the energy cell,

pointed it at a blank wall, and hopped a squat on the floor, ready to unlock the secrets of the ancients.

When the film ended, Ratt sat transfixed until the reel ran its course, sending the screen into blackness and making a *flap flap flap* sound as it spun around and around, slapping its loose end against the body of the projector.

Ratt moved to stand and switch the machine off, his thoughts still hypnotized by the cinematographic marvel he had just witnessed, when the room grew dark. Darker than it should be, darker than he remembered.

Remembered? Wait? This isn't happening, this is a memory.

"*This* is happening, Ratt," said a disembodied voice.

Ratt couldn't argue for once. He recognized his infiltration of the theater and movie viewing as a memory; he also realized that his current situation was not part of that memory.

"Who's there?" The child stood up, glancing furtively about, only to realize that he was no longer a child, but the man-boy he currently was. He was here, in this dreamworld, while also, somehow, distantly aware of his body lying on the sandy ground of a desert, at the feet of the goddess he served.

The dark theater continued to darken until no shapes or distances could be perceived. A second longer and Ratt was in a perfect void of black, yet still able to see his own body as clear as day.

"What's going on? Who are you?" Ratt demanded.

"I'm waiting for you, Ratt. I need you to finish what I've started. To help my *old friend*." The voice came from all around, as if it were a loudspeaker in his skull, making its location in the void impossible to discern. But Ratt was beginning to suspect there wasn't a "body" to this voice anyway. This place, this vision, was outside the pale of a normal Earth-and-physics-bound encounter.

"You cannot perish now. I've pulled this memory from your mind to show you your adversary. It is old, and has been on Earth before. Enki was not the only prisoner kept in Hell, after all."

"Enki? What are you talking about? Why don't you show yourself?"

"I won't be able to maintain a connection with you much longer. Awaken, share your knowledge. Survive. Enter the Labyrinth inside the Engine. My *old friend* needs your help."

"Wait!" Ratt shrieked, throwing his open hands up in a pleading gesture. "I don't understand what you're talking about!"

"You will, Ratt. You will."

"To your right!" Carbine shouted out, and Jon reacted with his hammer before his eyes, swinging the glowing head into a savage that charged in to test the waters while Jon was tangling with another.

The blow sent the foe tumbling into the dust. A moment later, it stood back up, snarling.

Two flat shots rang out from Carbine's pistol, and Jon watched the exit wounds blossom open on the savage's chest. Only the concussive force caused the man-beast to stumble; otherwise, it did not seem hurt at all.

"We can't fight this!" Jon yelled, holding back panic more effectively than he was holding back the pack of beastly thugs. The savage ignored the gaping chest wounds and redoubled its efforts to overtake Jon. Its boldness tipped the scales of caution for the rest of the pack, and they all charged in from the edges of the camp, their half-circle closing around the party like a fist.

Maya perched over the comatose Ratt like a mother bird protecting its young while more flat cracks issued from Carbine's pistol, followed by a series of clicks.

"Reloading!" Carbine shouted.

Jon acknowledged his buddy's alert only mentally; he was too preoccupied with the charging savage. He timed his dodge perfectly, waiting until the last second before rolling to the right, pivoting on his heel and swinging the spiked back of his hammer's head, trailing just behind the passing attacker. The spike sank into the flesh of the thing's back and hooked the shoulder blade. Jon leaned back into his pivot and pulled the savage, swinging it around like a stone on the end of a rope. He was gaining momentum and speed, and not two full revolutions later, a nasty, meaty rip resounded as the blow sundered the savage's torso. Half a rack of ribs and one arm hung from the spiked head of the hammer, while the rest of the man-beast went spiraling out into the dark, crashing to the ground. At this point, Jon was no longer surprised by the lack of blood. He knew they were dealing with lifeless meat puppets, but their exact nature still eluded him. He started to use the bottom of his boot to pry the half-rotten flesh from his hammer's nail, but only got as far as lowering the head before he became aware of yet another rabid man-beast using the cover of the lean-to to covertly gain on Jon.

"Shit!" He flinched, anticipating the pounce he could tell was coming from the creature's stance.

Brrrraapptt came the cavalry call that was the familiar report of Lucy's automatic pistol, the Big Fucking Gun.

Before the savage could pounce on Jon, its left leg disappeared at the hip in a spray of gray, clay-like flesh matter. The savage listed like a sinking ship and went partly to the ground, providing the perfect springboard for Lucy, who was in full cyborg sprint behind it.

"Behind you!" Lucy shouted, leaping onto the back of the fallen savage and jumping from it, flipping into a tight roll in the space above Jon's head. Jon turned in amazement, watching as she unfolded in the air and came down on another savage that had been stalking Jon from behind. She sliced downward diagonally across the creature's chest as she landed. She half-squatted as she landed, bounced right back up, and rolled her hips like a belly dancer as she cross-slashed across the savage twice more, spilling its rotten entrails down its lap and legs. The creature staggered, pausing in its approach. Lucy gritted her teeth and spun in place, whipping her Macuahuitl around and taking the dumbfounded savage's head clean off.

"We may not be able to provide a true death for them, but we can at least slow them the fuck down!" Lucy called out.

Lucy's sudden appearance slowed the advance of the savages; they behaved like hyenas, unsure of how to proceed after watching a lioness—or in this case, a jaguar—slaughter two of their own. It revealed a sort of intelligence, no matter how primitive and animalistic. They made to regroup, back off some, but Lucy gave no quarter, pointing her BFG at one nearby and dumping a volley of explosive rounds into it. The eruptions in its torso served as tracers, allowing her to steer the burst from navel to forehead, causing the undead creature to come apart like a humanoid string of firecrackers.

Inspired by Lucy's triumphant return, Jon kicked the ribcage off his hammer and charged the nearest savage, a female, who was presently giving ground. When she realized that Jon was chasing her, she stopped her retreat and made to scrap. Like the others, this one's clothes had long ago disintegrated, revealing flat, saggy breasts smeared with filth. Jon nearly hesitated to strike a woman, even one as wretched as this one, but her claw-like fingers and glowing red eyes reminded him that if he did not, she would happily murder him and possibly eat him.

She shrieked like some demonic bird of prey and showed her claws in a threatening display, but made no real move to attack. The hesitation would cost her. Jon let fly one blow, then another and another, rolling his elbow and shoulder, dipping to return the hammer quickly over and over again. He could not slice and dismember the way Lucy did, but he could deal enough damage to the she-thing that it would slow her down for at least a few minutes. He stepped away from the crumpled pile of woman and ran over to Maya and Ratt, now unguarded, as Carbine and Lucy gave chase to the routing savages.

"We can't keep this up forever." Maya looked up into Jon's eyes as he approached. She was kneeling on the ground next to Ratt, one hand on his chest.

"I think they're running," Jon said and looked out into the darkness. From where he stood, the starlight from his hammer barely illuminated the silhouettes and shapes of Lucy, Carbine, and the retreating savages.

Lucy seemed happy to chase and cut down every one to the last, but Carbine called her back. "Lucy! They're coming back again!" Lucy paused, her head scanning side to side, searching the periphery of their makeshift camp.

"No, not like that!" Carbine shouted. "These ones are regenerating!"

Jon, hearing his friend's words, turned away from Maya to see that, indeed, several of the fallen ones between him and Lucy were again upright.

The few whose heads Lucy had managed to separate from their bodies only wiggled around on the ground, damaged to the point of preventing regeneration, but still a long way from death. Jon wondered for a moment whether he and Lucy could possibly behead them all, but before he could decide one way or the other, a barbaric rally cry from out in the desert decided for him. He turned and scanned the desert, the dark of the night somehow easier to penetrate than it had been earlier. More were coming. At least two dozen.

"Fall back!" Jon shouted to Lucy, glancing left and right to make sure he had successfully kept track of Maya's and Carbine's whereabouts. Concern bordering on panic covered each of their faces like a mask, but they were as of yet unharmed.

"Form a circle! Back to back!" Lucy yelled as she ran toward Jon and the others. Directly in her path, one of the fallen savages began pushing itself off the hard-pan floor of the desert. It looked up just in time to witness Lucy's charge. It raised one of its arms in a futile defensive gesture, and her Aztec war-club sliced the arm neatly in half before passing on into its neck and beyond, her aim and power unaffected.

Jon watched the balance shift, as slow and persistent as the incoming tide, with growing concern. One of the more daring savages leaped an impossible leap—for a normal man—and landed directly in front of Maya, its legs rooted in the sand to either side of Ratt's prone body.

Jon caught the blur of movement from the corner of his eye and sprang into a counter-attack before Maya's scream of alarm had reached his ears.

He swung high, going for the thing's head and ensuring that he wouldn't accidentally hit Maya, but the savage dipped, just in time to prepare for a lunge at the goddess, and caused Jon's blow to miss by an inch.

Rocking back on his heels and engaging every muscle in his body from head to toe, Jon slowed the hammer swing and regrouped, trying to turn his missed shot into a new opportunity. Releasing the haft with one hand, Jon intercepted the hammer just below its head and jumped forward, landing right up against the back of the savage. Before the man-beast could react, Jon lowered the long haft of his weapon over and in front of the savage and quickly pulled back, effectively pinning the villain against his chest.

The wretched creature struggled mightily against Jon's hold and its foul stench assaulted Jon's senses, but he held fast, preventing the attack that surely would have torn Maya to shreds.

"Run!" Jon growled to Maya through gritted teeth, forgetting that they were surrounded and there was nowhere for the goddess, or her comatose ward, to escape to.

"Jon!" Carbine shouted, and quickly sidestepped the ground they held to get a clean shot at the pinned savage.

Trying his best to stay out of the grasping arms of the grappled creature, Carbine placed the tip of his pistol to its temple and squeezed the trigger. Jon was in perfect synchronization with his life-long battle buddy and pulled his head back to one side, maintaining his iron grip on the hammer that trapped his victim. Rotten brain matter and soupy viscera ejected out the side of the savage's head a split-second later and Jon felt the struggling stop with a jerk and spasm.

"Behind you!" Jon heard Lucy call from off to his right. Releasing his grip on the hammer and letting the half-headless savage slump to the ground to smother Ratt, Jon began to spin in place, but it was too late.

Claws raked across his back, etching deep grooves into him, severing corded muscles and scraping rib bones.

Blood poured down Jon's back like water breaking through a dam. Falling to his knees, he let slip his grip on the hammer and braced his fall on both the slain savage and Ratt.

Lucy yelled something unintelligible and let rip a burst from her BFG, but the volley of rounds was intercepted by a half-dozen more attackers moving in for the kill, clearly inspired by their pack-mate's success.

Grimacing, Jon rolled onto his rear, picking his hammer back up in the process, and feebly turned to face the one that had nearly sundered him. Waves of heat ran through his body, though he was not sure if it was the pain of his coming death, or the serum kicking into overdrive to heal his grievous wounds.

The savage before him grinned with primal glee. It flashed its claws triumphantly before him. They were dripping with Jon's blood, droplets forming little pools in the sand. Sadistically, the lording man-beast raised the slick claws and extended his too-long-to-be-normal tongue, slowly licking one clean.

"I'm still standing, bastard!" Jon hissed, despite the fact that he was, in fact, half kneeling, half sitting, and not, in fact, standing at all.

The savage's eyes widened abruptly, and for a moment, Jon thought that maybe the incoming jaguaress had reached him. Then the thing leaped backward, perfectly maintaining its footing upon landing. It tilted its head back and issued a series of short, bark-like noises.

As suddenly as the leap backward had been, the rest of the savages, the entire pack, froze in place and stopped their assault.

Lucy bridged the gap between herself and her companions with great ease, as some of the beast-men moved out of her way, giving her a wide berth.

Lucy slowed her sprint and cautiously re-joined the others, sweeping her pistol and Macuahuitl, waiting for the attack to resume.

"Why did they stop?" Carbine asked, flicking his pistol back and forth from one target to another, like eyeballs in a stationary skull tracking a fast-moving insect.

"I don't know, and I don't like it," Lucy replied, weapons at the ready, her stance low.

"We don't dare wait and find out if they'll change their minds again. We have to make a run for it," Jon said, slowly rising to his feet.

"Jon! You're hurt!" Maya exclaimed, reaching forward, but stopped short of touching the tears on Jon's back.

"I know, but the pain is subsiding," Jon said without taking his eyes off the blockade. "I think the serum saved my life… again."

"How? How do we escape? I mean, what do we do?" Carbine muttered.

Keeping the pistol aloft, Lucy saddled her war-club and bending down, first rolled the body of the savage off of Ratt, then picked him up and threw him over her shoulder.

"I have one explosive charge. I'll toss it into the crowd. After it goes off, we run in that direction. My lady, you stay between me and Jon. Aim for the head. That seems to work best."

"I'll take the rear," Carbine announced.

Lucy nodded at first, and then, apparently having a second thought, added, "No, you aren't strong enough. You stay with Maya. I'll take the front. Jon, you cover our rear."

"Ten-four," Jon and Carbine said in unison.

"On my count, three, two—"

"No, wait."

It took Jon more than an instant to realize that the speaker wasn't Lucy, or Carbine, or even Maya, and snapped his head around in bewilderment to find Ratt alert and attempting to climb down from Lucy's shoulder.

Jon kept his attention away from the line of savages longer than he intended, as Ratt's visage stunned him. The kid's eyes had two sets of irises and pupils.

"They're vampires. I know what to do."

The vampires hovered just outside the perimeter of the camp. They stood shoulder to shoulder and stared longingly with their red eyes at the potential meals before them, yet they twitched and behaved as if afraid. Pacing, shifting their weight from one foot to another, taking a step forward, only to hesitate, and return to where they started.

"They look like they're holding it," Carbine said.

"I doubt having to use the bathroom is their issue, bud," Jon said dryly, reminding himself to knock some battlefield sense into his friend later if they ever made it out of this.

"I hope this plan works, Ratt," Jon said.

"It will," Ratt answered with calm concentration in his voice. "Just remember. After the beam is established, we need to stand inside of it. We will be safe there until morning."

"I still don't get why they aren't attacking," Carbine said. "They clearly had the upper hand."

"That I don't know. But they will. They will. We want them to, for this to work best," Ratt explained. "But we don't need them to."

"Well, let's get this party started!" Lucy cried as she finished reloading her BFG and took aim at one of the vampire savages' heads.

One squeeze of the trigger later and the head of her target disintegrated and scattered to the wind like a fistful of thrown confetti. This brought a chorus of shrieks and growls from the vampiric host. She took another carefully aimed shot, sending another head to the wind, and with its departure, she brought about the charge they'd hoped for.

Crazed with an insatiable thirst for blood and overcome with a rush of a pack-mentality lynching, the three dozen or so savage vampires charged the party from all directions, screaming, claws outstretched, some galloping like apes on all fours, only adding to their feral, dog-like appearance.

"Hold," Ratt said calmly, but loud enough for everyone to hear over the demons' shrieks and Maya's soft singing. Memories of his dream and of the Tarantino and Rodriguez magicians' work were fresh in his mind and coming alive before his very eyes. He paced and gauged the mob's distance.

"Hold," Ratt repeated himself, this time with more intensity and urgency in his young voice.

The sea of glowing red eyes grew closer and closer like a crimson meteor storm until they were bearing down on the party. Ratt could see their faded human features glow in the light of Jon's hammer and their own fevered eyes, their mouths yawning open, saliva dripping from their fanged teeth.

"Now!" he barked, setting Jon, Carbine, and Lucy into action.

The makeshift poles that held up the lean-to had broken, and Carbine, Jon, and Lucy pushed the roof backward so as to fall away from the party rather than on top of them. The sudden flinging off of the roof caused the mob to pause for a heartbeat, and that was all Maya needed.

She shot her hands up to the sky and spread her palms open wide, her previously silent song ending in a high, beautiful note. A ball of twinkling light shot forth from the little diamond-shaped space between her hands and launched high into the dark and starless night sky.

Like a pyrotechnic effect from a Lily Sapphire show, the twinkling ball exploded into a bright ball of brilliant sunlight. The ball was not *like* sunlight; it *was* sunlight. A small portal had been opened to a place far away, a place near and dear to her, a place where it was already day.

Maya's eyes closed, and her face was bathed in the warmth and glow of a miniature Sol, no more than twenty meters above. The rays of light shot out from the sphere like a spotlight, hitting the savages facing the party like a tsunami and reducing them to falling piles of ash. One could even hear the *whoomp* as if a lit match had just touched down into a large puddle of gasoline.

Taking advantage of the lull in the stunned beast-men's attack, the companions bolted forward, stepping into the beam of sunlight and occupying the space filled by savages just a moment before.

Jon looked here and there, scanning and listening, his mouth slack. He looked over to Carbine, who was doing the same thing, and they exchanged looks of amused relief. Carbine let out a sigh, which tripped, stumbled, then fell into full-out laughter. Even Lucy cracked a grin.

Ratt wore a look of proud satisfaction and gave Maya a thumbs-up.

"That's our little lady."

She shyly returned his smile.

"And now we wait," Ratt added. "Sunrise isn't too far off."

To their sides, the remaining beast-men stood, dumbfounded and impotent, unable to press their attack. A few, either daring or stupid, tried to test the beam, only to pull back with flaming and smoking limbs.

For a short while, none of them, neither Jon nor Maya, nor Carbine or Lucy or Ratt did anything at all. They just stood in amusement and mild awe and admired their handiwork, relieved that it seemed to be over.

They watched as the dark sky slowly but surely grew lighter and lighter until eventually soft blues could be seen on the eastern horizon. One by one, the savages reluctantly slunk away into the desert hills, until at last the wayward companions were alone.

When they felt it was safe, Maya canceled the portal with another wave of her arm.

"It worked!" Carbine exclaimed.

"Yes. I am so tired, though," Maya said quietly.

Ratt, having returned to the company of walking, talking people, explained his dream-vision to them while he constructed a working light out of the salvage they had consolidated near their shelter. He couldn't answer or speculate further as to the origins of the prophetic dream, just that it had happened.

"I was in the presence of something. I'm not sure what. It was intelligent, of that much I'm sure. I may be wrong. But I believe it was the Drop. Or something behind it."

"Something behind it?" Jon asked, puzzled.

"Yeah. Like there is an intelligence of some kind behind the Drops. Their function. Somehow. He spoke of our adversary. Upon awakening, I knew immediately what he was talking about."

"Vampires?" Carbine asked, unfamiliar with the word.

Maya nodded. "I'm familiar with the term, from crypto-mythology from pre-Storm Earth."

"Except it's not just mythology," Ratt said, raising one outstretched index finger to the sky. "Only thing I don't get. The voice, the presence. It was a voice, but I still can't shake the feeling that—"

"Ratt, we get it," Jon interrupted. "The point?"

"Right." Ratt dipped his head and shrugged his shoulders. "He said he—not him, but the adversary—he said he, no, *it*—"

"Ratt!" the whole party shouted.

"Okay! He said that it was old and had been on Earth before. Something about Enki not being the only prisoner in Hell."

At Ratt's words, Jon spied Maya visibly stiffen. She appeared to be trembling, but the morning sun had already begun its preheat setting of the dry land.

"What is it?" Jon asked her.

"I don't know… but I wonder. Things I heard. Stories. A long, long time ago." This time, she shuddered so that no one could miss it, and wrapped her arms around herself.

Jon turned to Maya, hoping she could shed some light of a different kind on the mystery, but her face remained expression-less, although she looked to be deep in thought.

"What's with your eyes?" Carbine asked the other question on everyone's lips.

"My eyes?" Ratt asked, looking up, frowning. His eyes, now quite alien in their appearance, were magnified as usual through the thick lenses of his goggles. "What's wrong with my eyes?"

"They, uh…" Carbine started. "There are two of them."

Ratt looked as if he might say something smart-ass to Carbine, his mouth pulled to one side wryly.

"What he means," Jon interrupted, "is that each of your eyes contains two irises and two pupils. They are overlapped a bit on top of each other. It's uh… a little weird, kiddo."

"Unsettling!" Ratt exclaimed and brought his hands up to his goggles as if they were somehow mirrors that he could use to examine himself.

"I've seen that before, one other time," Maya spoke up, her voice soft and laced with something Jon couldn't quite put his finger on.

"Huh?" They all turned to her.

"Where?" Jon and Ratt asked.

"A long time ago. Someone that I… someone that used to be a friend," Maya said, lowering her gaze to the desert floor.

Jon squinted one eye and thought to press her, but decided against it.

"It's from the Drop. It has to be. From his contact with whatever he met. The other person who, uh, who had eyes like that also came into contact with this place," Maya continued.

"This place?" Carbine asked.

"This place. Hell. The pocket dimension. One of my crew, someone… close to Enki, he uh, he helped us free Enki from this place, just before the Storm. Afterward, his eyes… they… they looked like that."

"I see," Ratt muttered, straightening his goggles and seeming satisfied with the explanation without further detail. "As long as they still work, which they do, I am quite content."

For himself, Jon wasn't so sure, but decided that further information could wait for another time. Maya had said she was tired. It had been a long night for all of them and they had much ground to put between themselves and this place before nightfall. He had no doubt the pack of savages would try their hand a second time.

Without any further questions into the matter, they all chalked it up to a mystery and focused on things they *could* influence, like what to do next. Lucy's temporary absence was never brought up.

They organized into two teams—Lucy and Carbine went out in search of Ratt's hoverboard and the ruined ATVs, one of which Jon and Maya could assist Ratt in repairing and then fabricate a makeshift sled with which they could drag as many supplies and tools as they could fit on it. The decision to leave camp was unanimous. Their destination: the gold pillar of light beyond the hills, calling to them with its destiny song like a candle in a darkened window.

8

"Well? Is it safe?" Carbine asked as he belly-crawled up to his friend.

"I can't tell yet," Jon replied, without taking his eyes from the binoculars.

"I'm sure I don't have to remind you of the farmhouse, and what can happen if we rush in. There is no hurry. Let's just watch and learn."

In the valley below, several klicks from where Jon and the others hid among the rocks and patches of paddle cactus, lay a city.

Surrounding the clearly occupied city was a wall, its footprint somewhat circular in shape.

Along the top of the wall's perimeter, pacing back and forth, walked several dozen armed men and women. From what Jon could see, their weapons were somewhat substandard compared to the plasma launchers and Lawnmowers of Home. They also lacked any uniformity. Like the clothes these sentries wore, it would seem that they used anything at hand. The overall feeling that Jon got was more akin to the East Side Lords of Underground than the armies of the Human Republic.

The wall itself was every bit as ragtag as the people who defended it. Constructed from what Ratt called "urbanite," it was built from the crushed, fragmented, and broken remains of a previous, pre-Storm city's structures. These chunks of a dead city lay stacked into a rough wall, the gaps between them plastered and reinforced with what looked like cement, mud, rebar, wood, clay, and rope.

Ugly or not, Jon surmised that the wall did its job well enough, keeping unwanted people and things out. The sheer height and thickness alone convinced him that anything short of a Mech would have an impossible time breaching it.

Unlike the wall, the rest of the city's construction was new. It was as if the builders had swept up the old city to build the wall and started fresh. The architecture was unlike anything Jon had seen before; the strong majority of the buildings constructed from some red ocher-stained earthen brick, with flat roofs and square windows and doors. Some were one story tall, with others towering several stories. Ratt had told him that it was called adobe and had suggested, based on its presence as well as the climate and vegetation—what little of it there was—that they had come out of the Drop either slightly west, in flying ship relative terms, or south of where they had crossed over the Southern Sea.

Shortly after the run-in with the savages, they'd watched the sun rise and set and cross-referenced its motions with the pillar of gold light. They had concluded that Xibalba must be southeast of their current location, and Ratt had ventured to guess that there would be no sea standing between them, assuming the shapes of the continents hadn't changed too much from the Storm. He had studied pre-Storm maps of Earth-That-Was, and based on their original course as well as the physical appearance of the child Wyntr, had expected their destination to be either in Central or South America, but he also knew that during the Storm, the seas had raged like never before, altering the coastlines forever. Stories abounded in the days of his parents that had told of entire cities like Houston-That-Was being swallowed by the drink. A place once called Panama, might be an issue, if Xibalba were that far south.

For two days and nights, they had followed the direction of the pillar into the rising hills, every step haunted by the worry that they would encounter more of the savages. However, on the morn of the third day, unmolested, they had crested the summit of a small mountain and discovered the city below.

From their vantage point, high up in the hills that embraced and sheltered the valley and city below, Jon, Lucy, and Carbine studied the city. They had diligently performed their duty in shifts, day and night, for the last three days. After trekking through the desert, they welcomed the respite, having picked out a good location with plenty of rocky cover and a few paddle cacti, and set up their stakeout. But now their supplies were running low. Food and water were in short supply. Jon, of course, offered to refrain from eating anything again, but Maya insisted that he keep his body strong, despite his lack of hunger, if only to ward off the growing fire of death that was burning in his blood.

They were running out of time, but all were in agreement that they needed to ascertain the disposition of the city before simply strolling up to its gates. The first night, Carbine had seen what he swore was a glint of glowing red eyes on the face of one of the sentries that patrolled the flat, wide walkways atop the wall. To confirm his suspicions, he'd called Lucy over and asked her to use her robotic eyes to zoom in and switch to thermal vision. Ratt had educated them all as to the ins and outs of the undead during their journey, which was otherwise uneventful. Lucy had confirmed that the sentry was ambient temperature, just like the savages.

The walking dead.

And yet, most of the city was not. An easy nine out of ten of the city's occupants gave off heat signatures, just like normal walking, talking, living humans. Nor did the sentries behave anything like the animalistic savages they had met earlier. It was a puzzler, and it was the source of their prolonged caution.

Over the last two and a half days, they'd watched and studied, and prepared. Carbine assisted Lucy with a deeper analysis by using optics mounted to his railgun. Using these, he was able to see through solid walls and control how "deep" he went by turning a dial on the side of the makeshift scope.

When they weren't using the railgun's scope to make observations, Ratt insisted that he be allowed to modify the weapon so that Carbine might still be able to use it.

"You aren't going to break it, are you?" Carbine asked, offering the weapon to the whiz-kid, but unable to let go of it, prompting a sort of tug-of-war. "I love this pea-shooter."

"Don't be silly. But if I don't change it a bit, it'll rip you in two. You aren't in the Mini-Mech anymore."

Carbine frowned at that thought. In his final battle with Colonel Taylor, the Mechanized Infantry Sniper Suit, or MISS, had been shredded by Taylor's Heavy Mech's guns. Carbine himself had suffered damages from that exchange, damage from which he had nearly bled out, ultimately resulting in his having to receive a prosthetic leg, much like Sgt. Miller's. Ratt had managed to rebuild the power armor once, but the efforts had proven to be in vain, for the sum of his hard work was now a scattered smear of metal on the desert plain, three days' march behind them.

"I'm thinking that if I add a spike here," Ratt gestured to the rifle's underside, "you can drive the gun into the ground, which will not only serve as a uni-pod, but will also absorb some of the recoil."

"Please don't call it a gun..." Carbine muttered, more to himself than to Ratt.

"Then, I will add a hydro-pneumatic recuperator, like Artillery uses. It will further reduce the recoil."

"A what?" Carbine asked.

"If all else fails, I can machine bore a second barrel in the rear and put a single extremely dense projectile on a second firing mechanism and tether it to a heavy-duty spring. The mass of the rear-firing projectile will slow it down considerably. I can buffer the end of the new bore with shock absorbers and the spring will pull the lump back into place... hmm... gonna have to whip up some kind of latching mechanism too. Anyway, the rails in the barrel will help a lot too. If I have the parts, maybe I can extend the darn thing. You see, a chemically powered weapon feels all the kinetic energy of the shot right away, but that process is elongated, slowed down in a rail gun. The electromagnets in the rail speed the projectile up to its full speed *as* it passes down the barrel, not reaching top speed until it leaves! That means a serious reduction in felt recoil. Combine this with the modifications I will make, and you should be able to shoot this again without knocking yourself over."

"Egghead, I have no idea what you just said, but if it works, I'm happy."

Ratt went about performing his work on the rifle while the rest of them continued their reconnaissance.

They observed what for all intents and purposes appeared to be a normal city. There was a market, an oasis, a large plaza where the adobe bricks were made and set out to dry. Livestock, gardens, clean streets. Life appeared to be productive and pleasant. In the central eastern portion of the city stood a palace of ornate splendor, a miniature version of the Ziggurat, its stepped adobe walls whitewashed and its balconies generously graced with flora of every imaginable variety that thrived in this climate. The city, despite the fact that it seemed to be guarded by the undead, looked convincingly like a pearl in the dustbin—a sample of juicy, ripe fruit in an otherwise barren wasteland, as alluring to the hungry and forlorn as a carnivorous plant to a thirsty fly.

There appeared to be no savagery; if the cold, moving humans down there amongst the warm, moving figures were indeed vampires, they behaved very differently from the ones they had already encountered. They needed more information as badly as they needed fresh supplies.

Plagued with indecision, Jon and Carbine watched the comings and goings of the city below until the sun was nearly set and twilight brought the chill of desert night with it.

"I've seen enough," Jon said. "Come on, let's get back to camp."

"I don't like it. Not one little bit," Jon said, his arms crossed in front of his chest.

"Well, I didn't like it when she insisted on being captured by the goddamn Scrubbers. Or that I had to rescue you two twats," Lucy responded, not bothering to even look up from cleaning her pistol.

Maya, who was wrapped in one of the sleeping bags for warmth against the cold night—they couldn't risk a fire, as even at this altitude, its light was sure to be spotted by someone on the wall or in the city it surrounded—shot her senior guardian a disapproving glance. The look was not lost on those whom it had been intended to defend. In the last couple of days, the new moon had come, and the cloud cover had dissipated—both a blessing and a curse.

"This is different," Jon protested.

"Oh yeah? How so?"

"Stop arguing. Please." Maya saved Jon from having to answer Lucy with the inevitable stutter of frustration. Jon and

Lucy had been arguing ever since Maya had proposed her plan for getting into the city.

The guardians had returned from their scouting post with news and shared it. The silent mulling over both the lack of real information and their dwindling supplies had been interrupted when a look of cheerful determination suddenly possessed Maya.

"Ladies and gentlemen, I do believe it's time for Lily Sapphire to perform again," she'd announced.

Now, thirty minutes later, Jon was still protesting.

"Listen here, Maya," he started to explain again.

"For a new guardian, you sure are informal. It's *'my lady'*," Lucy spat at him.

"*No deberías ser tan cruel, mi amiga jaguar lucha.*" Maya looked at Lucy, exhaustion on her face.

"*Me disculpo,*" Lucy responded softly, her eyes cast down.

Jon hesitated a second, watching the two women, then continued. "Maya. I mean no disrespect, and I don't mean to argue with you. But there is no way I'm going to let you waltz into that city where you may be hurt, or worse! I didn't put my life on the line just to watch you throw yours away!" He looked to Carbine for some backup, but his friend had chosen earlier to agree with Lucy, no doubt in the hopes of earning some brownie points. "Lucy, you fought the savages with me. You saw what those things are like, what they are capable of! And we don't even yet understand the dynamic of the city, what it's like down there..." His voice trailed off.

"Oh, Jon." Maya smiled at him in the moonlight. "We have no choice. We only have a few days' worth of food and water left. Only having one ATV and Ratt's hoverboard is slowing our progress down. We need fresh supplies, and maybe horses if we can get them. The longer we wait here, the stronger your fire grows. I will be fine because Lucy will come with me." Her childlike moon face ran the gamut of emotion from deep affection to determination to sympathy to sudden bouncy happiness.

"Wha—?" Jon arched one eyebrow.

"And Ratt too." She beamed.

"Hey, hey wait. What about us?" Carbine said, apparently finally finding the nerve to object. Ratt also looked slightly concerned.

"Well, if my sworn guardians would stop arguing, I will explain my plan."

After going over the details, the team set to work preparing everything they would need. Maya opened another portal to her suite in the Ziggurat, and they delivered a second message to Miller and To-Kan, explaining their situation. She told them of the finding of the city, and their dual hope in both finding supplies where they were, and in establishing a time to initiate a two-way conversation with their friends in Home, hopefully planning out some kind of rescue operation.

At one point during the construction required for the execution of Maya's plan, Carbine had spied Lucy struggling with bent bars intended for the frame of a caravan they meant to build. She was clearly attempting to juggle more things than she had hands to hold.

She's not used to only having the two arms. He paused in his work, secretly watching her for a minute. He couldn't help himself; there was something mesmerizing about the warrior woman. He didn't mean to be a creep about it; he was simply fascinated by her, and furthermore, a small ember of sympathy had begun to smolder within him. *What a cruel, sick joke they played on her.*

After abusing her for years, the brutal men that had broken her body had then aimed to possess it fully, trapping her mind in a robotic shell, a caricature, a sculpted body, a misogynistic mockery of who she was and who they'd wanted her to be. Plainly put, she was unrealistically sexy—a robot fantasy from the perverted mind of a chauvinist; a mechanical playmate crossed with the painted Saint of Death. Carbine didn't have to ask to know that parts of her were non-existent. She had never known, and would never know the bliss of making love by her own choice and free will. Cruel indeed.

Can I blame her for being so angry all the time?

He watched her struggle with her lack of extra limbs and the caravan's frame for a few seconds longer, then threw all caution to the wind. *Screw it.*

He let go of his half of the canopy that he and Jon were stretching—much to Jon's chagrin—and strode over to her with confidence in his step.

"Lucy. Please, let me help."

Her cybernetic eyes flashed with white-hot rage, then narrowed as she snapped her head around to glare at him. Her nostrils flared, revealing the amazing workmanship put into her artificial body.

"Walk away. Walk away now or face my wrath." Lucy's voice trembled.

"I just want to—"

"I will cut your balls off," she hissed.

"Doesn't it get old? Ya know? Don't you get tired of acting like a bitch all the time?" Carbine's pulse quickened when her eyes opened wide in shock and rage.

She released her arms and hands from their designated task and turned on him. He ducked, then caught the two blows intended for his face and head.

"I. AM. NOT. YOUR. ENEMY!" Carbine managed to get out through the sheer exhaustion of keeping Lucy from killing him.

She stared at him, her face a wicked mix of pure loathing and sheer bewilderment. At this point, everyone else in the camp watched, while doing their best impressions of marble statues. You could hear a mouse cough.

Carbine stared back into that painted face, his steely resolve unwavering.

"I just want to be your friend and help you, okay?" And with that, he released her wrists and placed his hands up in the universal gesture of surrender.

The strike never came. Lucy wavered. Her lips parted, and she made like she might say something, but closed her mouth again after a moment. She blinked twice, her eyes softening. She inhaled deeply, then let it out slowly.

"You military guys are thick in the head," she said matter-of-factly, with no hint of defeat or humor in her voice. "Lash these two together while I hold them in place."

Carbine did as bid, and soon, much to everyone's surprise, they had finished the task.

"Carbine," she said flatly. "Thanks."

At this, Carbine almost smiled, but knew better than to push it. "Don't mention it. We're battle-buddies. That's what we do—help each other." And with that, he'd nodded to her and gone back to work, helping Jon with Maya's palanquin.

Now he watched Lucy from afar.

One click forward on the scope, and he saw her long raven hair tied tightly into a knot. He moved the gun slightly to Ratt and saw the kid's lips moving. Three clicks backward and he could take in the whole front gate area, his trio of friends in and on their machines, the guards atop the carefully piled rubble wall, no longer pacing but training their primitive firearms on the newcomers below.

He moved the reticle of the scope to somewhere near the middle of the spread-out sentries. Clicked out as far as he was, he could see all who could see his friends as well as the gate itself. He would have to click forward again to improve his aim if and when the time came, but for now, he needed to see the big picture.

"Just try it, assholes."

———

"Woooooow," Maya said, drawing the word out long and slow. "This wall sure looks bigger up close." She projected her voice as if speaking in a town hall and tucked her tiny chin down toward her breastbone when she spoke, trying to make sure the necklace she wore picked up her voice loud and clear. Jon, a good klick and a half away, flinched a little, as Maya's voice came over extremely loud and garbled.

"Umm, hey, Maya," Ratt meeked out. "I assure you, you don't have to do that. The mic will pick up your voice fine. In fact, it's probably picking up mine fine too."

"Not to mention, you'll give us away and blow our cover. Please, my lady, behave as you would normally. Act casual," Lucy added.

"Oh! Of course!" Maya tittered, blushing slightly.

"With all due respect, my lady, it would seem that the graver a situation is, the more amused you become. I don't care for putting you in danger any more than Jon. The only difference between him and me is that I am somewhat used to it. I see it as nothing more than the changing of one season, one I like, into another, which I loathe. I'm not sure if it's because you are immortal, or what..."

"Let's just call it high wisdom." Maya grinned back at her guardian.

"Call it what you like, but please, my lady, try to recognize the danger we are in and behave appropriately."

At this, Maya stuck her tongue out at Lucy and crossed her arms in mock defiance.

The necklace the goddess wore was the latest gadget created by the ever-resourceful Ratt, who hadn't slept a wink last night, instead opting to help assuage Jon's concerns for the goddess's safety. Digging through the sled of parts they had brought, Ratt had found what he needed to create a one-way radio, a sender and a receiver, but alas, he did not have enough equipment to design it to work both ways. And so, they would have to content themselves with Jon being able to hear what was going on around Maya. Between that and Carbine watching them with his high-powered, see-through-walls scope on the cover-providing railgun, Jon felt somewhat satisfied and at least semi-confident that they could protect Maya, if need be. Plus, Lucy would be there, and Jon had no illusions about her ability to deal death when required to do so.

While Ratt had busied himself with the radio necklace, Jon and the others had cleared the sled and, using the sleeping bags and salvaged tarpaulins, had erected a cover over it. If they wanted to pose as traveling troubadours, it wouldn't do to approach the city on foot or have Maya riding shotgun on Ratt's hoverboard or Lucy's ATV exposed to the elements. The result was more Shanty-chic than Cleopatra, but it would pass.

"Declare su negocio!" a sentry shouted down from the rampart in Spanish. Jon tightened his lips and frowned, wishing he understood what was being said, but trusting his friends below to inform him if things started to go south.

"I speak for my lady, Lily Sapphire. She requests an audience with the rulers of this city," Lucy announced. Through his binoculars, Jon saw her looking up at the sentry, but he quickly shifted his view, for the mid-day sun reflected off some of the rustic blocks of the wall and flashed in his lenses.

"For what reason?" the haughty guard asked.

"To discuss playing here. Miss Sapphire is a traveling performer of great renown."

"I have never heard of her," the guard said as if bragging.

"Nevertheless, every bastion of civilization that we visit, we have left with its citizenry in a much higher spirit than before our arrival. We are sure your leaders would appreciate us performing." Lucy was on her best behavior.

Jon, who had the earpiece that made the other half of Maya's necklace, could hear the whole exchange and was impressed with what he heard, impressed and thankful that Lucy had forced the parley to English. It would seem that Lucy could avoid confrontation when she wanted to after all.

The sentry sneered at Lucy's rebuke and thought for a minute, rubbing his bearded chin.

"Well?" Lucy dared. "What have you?"

"Wait here," the sentry replied— as if they had anywhere else to go.

For the hundredth time, Jon wished he could reach out, if only with his voice, to talk to Maya, for the silence was deafening. The minutes felt like hours. Nearly half an hour went by with no sign of movement down below, on either side. Jon called out to his companion to keep his eyes peeled for any sign of funny business. His nervous, paranoid imagination played out sequences of horror over and over again. Who was to say that the men who posed as soldiers down there wouldn't decide to attack, if only to take whatever wealth Lily Sapphire might possess? Or worse, murder... or rape. Not all marauders were nomadic. They knew next to nothing about this city, nor about those who ruled it.

Then Jon heard thuds, clicks, and clanks, and he and Carbine watched as the gate began to swing open.

"Carbine?" he said.

"I'm on it," the sniper responded, clicking the scope one click forward and tapping the toggle that allowed him to "see through" the gate's material.

"What do you got?" Jon demanded coolly.

"I got four bogies. Right behind the gate. They're armed, but the rifles are slung, Jon. Things look chill."

Jon's shoulders dropped, and he breathed a sigh of relief.

Moving his binoculars back to Lucy, who remained out front of the ATV and caravan, he saw she betrayed no expression or movement as the sentry that had spoken to her from the wall now approached on foot from the open gate.

"*Señor* Don Luis Fernando sends his apologies for having made you wait and bids you welcome to New Puebla." The sentry even bowed. Lucy nodded her head back in a gesture of gratitude. She squeezed the clutch, popped the gear lever down with her toes, and threw a glance over to Ratt. Neither one of them risked a look back at the mountain, nor the watchers they knew were there.

Maya had heard the exchange as well as Jon, and now she whispered aloud, "See, Jon? So far, so good."

Please be careful. Jon put the binoculars down, for now that Maya and company had passed through the gates, they were useless to him.

9

"I still think this is a bad idea," Candice said. Miller didn't miss that she had been picking at her cuticles with her fingernails since he'd arrived.

"Look, Candy, I know you're nervous, but I'll be there. I'll walk you through everything. It'll all be jus' fine." Miller did his best to soothe the former waitress's nerves, resting a meaty paw of a hand on her shoulder.

"It's not just that I'm nervous, Milly," Candice said, biting her lower lip. "It's that I don't belong there! I have absolutely zero qualifications for the job!"

Miller frowned and sat across from her in the cafe's booth. After Miller's injury in the Battle of Texhoma, he had been lost, struggling with his injury and subsequent re-assignment as a cookie. Lost, until he'd found Maya and the Underground Resistance. He had spent many years slinging hash in the very café they now sat in. He knew her, probably better than she knew herself, having spent all those many years side by side with her. Only now, he had to convince her that what he saw in her was real and good.

"Candy," Miller began, his voice rich and dark, like the black coffee customers of Candice's café loved. "That's jus' the thing. You have exactly the kind of qualifications the council needs right now. We want equal representation. A voice for everybody. We already had a stratocracy, and you saw how that worked out. What we need now is someone on the council to represent every diverse group that's in Home."

"And you want me to what? Represent the food workers of the world?" Candy asked, her mouth twisted to one side.

"C'mon, nah," Miller scoffed, "I want you to speak for the former Republic citizens that wasn't in the field. All the people of the Zigg that had support jobs. The ones that never had a voice befo'."

Candice cast Miller a jaundiced look but held her tongue. Seeing her defenses weaken, Miller moved in for the kill.

"We have members from the Shanty, Human and Displaced. We have military, one from every division."

"Well, yeah, that makes sense," Candice said, her voice quiet and full of doubt.

"The point is, not only do you fit that requirement— support — you are one of the most compassionate and caring people I ever met. We could use a touch of that. Please. Don't make me beg, girl."

Candice closed her eyes, sighed, and slowly shook her head.

"Okay, okay. Fine. I guess I could use a break from pouring coffee. Wait! You aren't going to make me pour coffee for the council, are you?"

Miller laughed and stood up. "Perish the thought. You're a bona fide councilwoman now."

"Yikes. That's not helping," Candice said, grimacing.

"C'mon. Let's get up there. Everyone'll be waiting."

Miller and Candice left the café and strolled through the once idyllic corridors of the Zigg's residential sections. Much had changed, but just as much had remained the same. It had only been a few weeks since Warbak's attempted Harvest, the *Purge,* and his fall, and every day of those few weeks, men and women like Miller had worked without rest, trying to hold back the rising tide of chaos. Miraculously, they had managed, just barely, to prevent everything from spiraling into a complete mess. They had organized patrols, managed to keep the water and power on, begun work on a hierarchy, a chain of command, and gathered the best and brightest of those who remained and were now attempting to flesh out their impromptu council, the acting government body of New Home. Unfortunately, most of the officers had left with the Old Guard, and every day, Miller was feeling the loss of that skill and experience. He had the men but lacked leadership. Boys like Quiteke had stepped up, but they just weren't quite ready for what lay ahead.

But they gon' have to be... If only Jon and Maya would return. What's taking them so damn long?

Even if the golden pillar of mystical light and the hidden fortress it marked lay on the other side of the globe, they all had figured Maya and her guardians would be back Home within a week, two at the most. But days had turned to two weeks, and still no sign or word from them. Concern had turned to worry after the first week, and now a low-grade panic was knocking at the door. Miller had sent out tropiscopic radio signals every night, signals that would bounce off the ionosphere and go over the horizon. The transport that Maya had left in was equipped with a working receiver and transmitter, so although Miller was unable to ring them up, they should have received his nigh-continuous loop-broadcast, if they were monitoring, and gotten back to him by now.

The fact that they hadn't meant one of three things—that they had gone farther over the globe than anyone anticipated, that their equipment was broken, or that something worse had befallen them. Miller had even gone so far as to question the foreign girl,

Wyntr, to try to ascertain just how far away this "Morning Star" was. The child's story remained consistent, and the girl insisted that she had walked to Home. Which meant, based on all the old maps of Earth-Before-The-Storm that they had in the Vault, that Maya and crew's destination was in the same hemisphere, if not the same continent, as Home.

Please, be alive. Please hurry back. I can't do this without you. Miller kept his dark thoughts about the goddess and her inner circle close to his chest, but knew that everyone else would notice Maya's absence and figure it out eventually. They would soon have to face the reality that they were alone in this. Hence the call to form and make official the ruling council.

After entering and riding one of the elevators that bordered the open core of the Ziggurat, Miller and Candice stepped out into the upper level, formerly occupied by Warbak's Ministry of Social Purity, now requisitioned as the command center for the Council of New Home.

Ahead of them stood a pair of closed wooden doors, pre-Storm, thick, heavy, and classy. Flanking the doors stood two soldiers, their sex unknown, obscured by full-body armor of the kind worn by the Heavy Infantry. Miller raised a knife-hand in salute and was greeted by brisk salutes back.

"As you were," Miller said, strolling up to them with Candice in tow. The soldiers both silently executed a left and right face respectively and opened the ancient doors.

"General Miller." An elderly woman's voice announced both his arrival and new rank to the room as he and Candice stepped in.

"To-Kan," Miller responded, nodding in the woman's direction. Before showing Candice to her seat and taking his own, he stood for a moment and took in the room and the assembly of councilors in it.

There was To-Kan, matron of the Vault. Long had she been

with the Resistance, and equally long was her memory. At ninety-three, it was remarkable that she was still alive, having spent the majority of her life in the harsh post-Storm conditions, hiding in Underground, dodging Warbak's Scrubbers, Invasive Beasties, and the East Side Lords. Also remarkable, as well as priceless, was her keen memory of what the world had been like prior to the great Storm. Her insights were as sharp as her wit, a trait that many were quick to learn via a good tongue-lashing after misjudging her stooped posture and wrinkled skin.

Sitting next to the wizened woman was a young, skinny black man, darker of skin than Miller, with super-short hair, nearly shaved. Quiteke. Promoted after the battle of the Harvest, and then soon after asked by Miller personally to represent the Easy-Rider division of the New Military. The young soldier had offered Miller the same doubts Candice just had regarding his qualifications, but the truth then, as now, was that Miller lacked skilled officers, nearly all of them having gone with the Old Guard, and he believed that a younger, fresh voice was what New Home needed. He had stood by those convictions minutes ago, when swaying Candice to join the council, but now that he saw the look on the Quiteke's face, and realized just how overwhelmed the kid actually was, Miller began to wonder if he was making a huge mistake.

What choice do I really have?

Filling out the council on the opposite side of the long, rectangular table sat Elena, long-time resistance member and owner of the now destroyed Underground bar and brothel, representing the dispossessed citizens of the Shanty. The rest of the room held almost half a dozen more council members, representing all aspects of the former Republic's military infrastructure, as well as one "Hincit," a Displaced alien who looked quite a bit like a turtle, and had to exist out of water in a self-contained tank of sorts. The tank featured a computer and speakers that both translated the Displaced's words as well as projected them to all with ears to listen.

"Welcome, Miller," Elena said, nodding.

"Back atcha, sweetie." Miller returned the nod as he approached the table. "Council, I present to you Candice. I have asked her to represent the support staff citizens of the Zigg." Miller knew that most at the table already knew Candice in some fashion or another, but wanted to establish some small measure of proper decorum, despite his casual greetings.

"'Tis a pleasure." Elena waved in their direction, freeing a loosely tied-back dreadlock.

Miller pulled a chair back on his side of the table, gestured to Candice, then strolled around to sit between Elena and Quiteke.

"I, uh…" Candice stuttered, "I uh— I am, uh… happy to be here. I will do my best. Thank you."

"You'll do fine," Miller said, sitting down and gesturing for her to do the same. "So what is on the agenda today?"

"Arrangements are being made to barricade off the Tek's lair in Underground," Quiteke announced.

"Da last shipment of food from da east 'as not arrived," Elena blurted out.

Miller held up a hand. "One at a time! Let's try and set an example here. Quiteke, please."

"Okay, boss. So, like I was saying, arrangements have been made to go ahead and quarantine the part of Underground where the Tektonic was reported. We know enough to know that the beast can't leave its lair, and we hope to prevent anyone from coming too close to it. The stockpiles of cement that we procured should be enough to do the trick."

"And signage?" Miller asked.

"Yes, that too."

"Good. Keep me informed, I want me and the Hoppers

present when we execute. Just in case." Miller folded his hands together and pointed two fingers to the young soldier.

"Sure thing. Good call, Sarge, er, I mean, General."

"Okay, moving on. Elena, you said something about the last food shipment not arriving?"

The former bartender leaned forward and opened her mouth to speak but was rudely interrupted by the sudden flinging open of the chamber's double oak doors.

"I'm sorry to just barge in here." It was Captain Juste Wojax, Miller's new second-in-command and ace Hopper pilot, one of the few New Breed to stay on after the Purge.

Exasperated not only at the council meeting's lack of progress, Miller growled at the intrusion.

"What is it, Captain? We have a lot of work to do here and—"

"We have a situation in the Warrens, sir," the young man announced, his face beaded with a sheen of fresh sweat.

A low murmuring erupted from the assembled council, but Miller silenced them with a wave of his hand as he got to his feet. *Now what?*

"A situation? What kind of situation?" he asked, fearing the worst.

"At the Hammered Wombat, sir," the captain stammered. Miller instantly recognized the name of the Shanty's oldest and most notorious drinking establishment, long used by Miller, Maya, and the Resistance in the days of Warbak as both a meeting place and a location where one could trade in secrets and intel.

"Spit it out, Captain! What's going on?"

"It's him, sir. Matiaba," Wojax blurted out.

Miller frowned deeply and stared through his captain, trying to understand.

"Matiaba has been spotted, sir. He is in the Wombat as we speak."

"Ho-ly shit."

"Is he still here?" Miller asked his men, who had remained outside the tavern's main entrance as ordered, trying to look as casual as possible.

"Yes, sir," one of the men, Lieutenant Rayn, reported. He raised one arm to his head and tapped his right ear. "We have a live feed with the men on the inside. The target is still at his table, sir."

"Good, let's move." Miller moved past the two men and pushed open the door to the Hammered Wombat. The men followed close behind, each withdrawing their compact submachine guns from under their rain slicks.

The tavern was unchanged from Miller's memory of it—a hodge-podge of various furnitures and patrons, testifying to the slow growth and long history of the well-loved establishment.

Miller took stock of the room and saw that his men saw him. Besides the two to his back, there were three trusted men, in Shanty-appropriate street clothes, who had positioned themselves in strategic locations throughout the bar, keeping tabs on and preventing Matiaba from escaping out the back.

Matiaba, closest aide and practical second-in-command of the Republic under Chairman Accoba Warbak. A true weasel of a man who had been responsible for the capture and creation of Lucy, Maya's oldest guardian, among many other crimes, including prostitution and torture.

The aide had gone missing during the events of the Purge and it had been assumed that he was dead, although a body had never been recovered. Now, more than three weeks later, here he was, in the flesh, nursing a jar of Belsen's famous hooch and acting as if he hadn't a care in the world.

Miller's men had informed him that they had reached out to Belsen, the pub's proprietor, and informed him what was about to go down. Now Miller looked to the bar and made eye contact with the man, nodding to him.

"Bar is closed!" Belsen shouted, getting every bit of mileage out of his barrel-sized chest and sounding as if he had a megaphone at his disposal. "Clear the room! Now!"

A multitude of confused imbibers glanced around, not understanding. Only one figure remained cool and still —Matiaba.

"I said out! Now!" Belsen retrieved a pump-action pre-Storm shotgun and chambered a round for effect, sending the previously chambered round flying across the room.

Getting the message loud and clear, everyone, human and Displaced alike, abandoned their poison and began filing out toward the door.

Belsen approached Miller near the rear of the herd, a sheepdog to the sheep.

"Try not to make a mess, man," he said.

"I give you my word," Miller replied, placing one huge hand on the equally big man's shoulder.

"Gig's up, Matiaba. We have you surrounded. There is no escape this time," Miller said as he approached the aide from behind. He signaled his men, front and back, and the five of them arranged themselves into a large circle around Miller and the former aide.

"This time? Escape? Whatever are you talking about? I never *escaped* to begin with. I thought we were free now," Matiaba said without turning around. The aide extended one lithe leg under the table and pushed a chair back for Miller.

"We are free, Matiaba. But you, you won't be for long. You need to answer for your crimes." Miller walked around the table to face Matiaba, ignoring the offered chair.

"My crimes?" Matiaba looked up at Miller over the top of his brew. "Pardon me, *General*, but all I did was follow orders.

Surely not every officer in the Republic that wasn't part of your Underground Resistance has been arrested."

Miller stopped, caught off guard, and stared, slack-jawed.

"From what I've seen, every able-bodied man and woman in Home that didn't leave with the Old Guard has been given a new job. Have you asked yourself why I didn't leave with the Schismatics?"

"I—uh… no. I haven't asked myself that," Miller said, collecting himself. "Though *you* should be asking yourself that. We are taking you in, Matiaba."

The former aide stopped smiling and sat up straight, pulling the wrinkles out of his shirt as he did.

"Again, I ask, why am I being treated differently than any other soldier in the former Republic?"

"You know why," Miller said. "For the things you done."

"Things?"

"What you did to Lucy, for starters." Miller signaled to his men and their circle around the table tightened.

"General Miller, I fear you aren't hearing me. The 'things' I did were nothing more than me following orders."

"Nice try," Miller said. "Come on, get up. Don't make me tear this place up."

"No need to be dramatic, I will go with you."

"You… what?" Miller asked.

"You heard me correctly."

Miller glanced up to the faces of the men who now stood behind the table, reading them, hoping somehow to see what they might think of this peculiar and unexpected turn of events.

"At the very least, I would like a fair trial. Allow me to present myself to your council. Allow me to make my defense. Clear my good name. That is why I didn't go with the Old Guard. Clearly, you must see that I had the opportunity?"

Miller found that he couldn't argue with the logic. Matiaba

hadn't been seen or heard of since before the Purge. He could have escaped if escape had been his plan. But what *was* his plan?

Miller caught the scrutinizing glances of his men, no doubt all wondering what he would do. He shifted in place for an uncomfortable minute. Matiaba remained seated and staring at him, but bore no hint of irony or cockiness, yet Miller found himself unable to trust the man.

"Fine. I'll take you to the council. You'll get your fair trial. But you had better not try any funny stuff."

Raising his hands in a conciliatory gesture, Matiaba stood. "You have my word."

10

"Please, allow me," the bellhop said, holding the door open for Maya, now Lily Sapphire. She smiled, curtsied, and walked into the room.

Lucy quickly moved to follow, but the bellhop deftly positioned himself between the two women.

"We have a room prepared for you just downstairs, miss."

The bellhop, a short, weaselly, sweaty man, raised a conciliatory hand to Lucy and motioned to his left, back out into the hallway from which they had just come.

Lucy smiled at this, cocking her head slightly, taking perverse pleasure in the fact that were she of the mind, she could rend the upper half of this man's body from the lower with a roundhouse kick.

"No bother," Maya called out from inside the penthouse suite. "She will be sleeping with me, Mister..."

"Pedro, Miss Sapphire. Pedro Gonzales, at your service." He stepped aside and bowed his head.

"I did not realize that your assistant was *with* you." He leered at Lucy as she walked past him and licked his sweaty lips. Lucy suppressed a shudder like a sick person attempting not to vomit.

"And the boy?" Pedro inquired, his eyebrows arched in a knowing expression.

"Please, I would have him in here as well."

"As you wish, miss." Pedro left to retrieve Ratt and the second load of supplies being unloaded from the sled. They had departed from their impromptu transport and followed an escort up to the lavish palace that stood over the rest of the squat adobe city.

Unable to do any real intel-gathering during their brief jaunt across the city to the palace, the trio had simply done their best to take it all in without looking out of place. What little sightseeing they did manage to do had imparted on them the impression of a typical post-Storm city-state.

It had its unique cultural and geographical character—the adobe buildings, the intoxicating scents wafting from the spice market, goat meat simmering in pepper sauce, woven textiles dyed with local resources and draped over a people of dark bronze skin and black hair. Women beat rugs outside with corn brooms; children tended to livestock and other chores, while men with guns drank tequila, patrolled the streets, and eyed the newcomers with suspicion. While unique in its way, it had its similarities with all the other civilized places, Home's Near Rough Enclaves, Maya had visited before arriving in Home, in that there was a distinct divide between the "haves" and the "have-nots."

This fact was hard to miss. After passing an entire block of low-ceilinged, rough-hewn adobe houses with dirty, barefoot children in the streets outside, skinny mules tied up out front, mangy dogs drinking water out of mud puddles, and the smell of open sewage somewhere—blissfully out of sight—they'd come to a street cut from a different cloth altogether.

The streets were cleaner, the houses much better built— haciendas with lovely, wavy red tiles on the roofs, lush gardens in the front yard, the only smells being those of roses and gardenias. The buildings had windows with actual glass, shutters, and curtains, not just ragged shreds of old cloth. Mechanical vehicles —some with wheels, some more modern with fusion-cell hovering capabilities—were parked out in the place of horses and mules. But what was most odd about this street and the next two they would pass down before reaching the palace was the eerie silence. There were no signs of life in any of the buildings they passed. No women dumping pots off the ornate, wrought-iron-wrapped balconies; no children working or playing in the gated yards. In fact, the only human presence they saw during that three-block journey were well-armed sentries, just like those on the wall and who had escorted them, positioned on the street side of the estates' gates and walls.

Compared to the first district that they had passed through, each house in the "haves" district was a palace. Yet compared to the actual palace in the center of the city, even the mansions had seemed like hovels.

Maya had never seen such splendor on Earth. The palace and its penthouse rivaled anything in Home, even amongst the top levels of the Ziggurat.

Now alone with Lucy, Maya took in the contents of the penthouse suite. Just past the entrance stood a short, round table upon which sat a greeting card, a glass of sparkling wine, and a plate with fresh figs and small baked goods on it. The air in the room smelled of clean linens and a light breeze blew in from the balcony, the doors to which had been left open, with only a pearl white curtain drawn across the opening, rippling slightly in the breeze.

She strolled further into the suite, admiring the pre-Storm art decorating the walls, and then she noticed the bed. Larger than any she had ever seen, it was cornered by thick, dark wooden posts that reached from floor to ceiling, each ornately carved with a Mesoamerican theme. The tops of the posts were joined by a canopy from which hung lavender-tinted draperies, partially obscuring the mattress, sheets, and pillows within. Lucy got to work unpacking the stuff they had brought, procuring her two Macuahuitls comically hidden inside a box labeled *Instruments*. Maya walked past the bed and brushed her fingers across the pleasant textures of the canopy before making her way outside to the balcony.

She gazed out across the city and inhaled deeply. She could almost smell it—the sense that something lay hidden here, between the cracks of the mud buildings, beneath the polished veneer of the palace in all its luxury. Something dark lay sleeping while the tired men, women, and children of New Puebla went about their lives.

Suddenly, there came a knock at the door, and then it opened.

Lucy barely had enough time to cover her war-clubs with a nearby bath towel before Pedro and Ratt entered the suite. Maya noticed with some satisfaction that Ratt had managed to tint his goggles, hiding his new mysterious and alien eyes from the New Puebloans.

"Your manservant and the rest of your luggage, *Señorita* Sapphire," Pedro announced as he eyed Lucy, who stood next to the bed, stiff and awkward.

Maya returned from the balcony and smiled at Pedro.

"Thank you, sir."

"*Señor* Fernando bids you rest some, for he would like to see you after sundown. You are cordially invited to dine with him and his wife. We will send for you when the time comes. For now, is there anything I can get you? Food? Drink?"

"No, thank you, good sir. We are fine. We will rest and await the hour of repast," Maya responded politely and then gave Lucy a slight nod. Lucy moved to the luggage and began to rummage for something.

"No tip necessary, Miss Sapphire. It is our custom here." The sweaty man bowed, turned, and left, shutting the door behind him. The trio all silently counted to ten, then they all relaxed and huddled together to discuss what to do next.

"Okay, guys. We don't know what's really going on here, so stay on your guard. We will go to this dinner tonight and see what we can learn. Let's go ahead and rest if we can," Maya whispered to her friends.

"Totally." Ratt seemed relieved. "I'm exhausted."

"I will stand watch. You two get to bed," Lucy offered and retrieved her sword-clubs from under the towel.

Ratt didn't have to be told twice, having stayed up all night working on the necklace and packing the hoverboard. He peeled off his darkened goggles and hit the mattress as hard as the city's women's pestles coming down on the handful of maize in their mortars.

Maya whispered down into her radio necklace before climbing in beside Ratt. "Get some rest, you two," Maya said to her silent and invisible guardian angels on the mountainside. "If you can, that is. I'm sorry that I'm not there to sing you to sleep."

Far up on the hillside, Jon flicked the safety off the railgun and tracked the incoming outlines down the hallway to the doors of the penthouse suite.

Heads up, Lucy.

Lucy flung the door open so quickly and so suddenly, she completely surprised the trio of young girls on the other side. They stood frozen, like a hare gazing into the eyes of the hunting cat, the lead one's fist raised in mid-air, prepared yet prevented from knocking a second time. Lucy suspected their wide eyes were more from her Santa Muerta appearance than the abrupt answer to their knock, but acted as if nothing was out of place, even knowing what her visage would signify to the Latina girls.

"Yes?" Lucy asked coolly.

The girls were all young and pretty. Each one's dark hair hung over their slender shoulders in a singular loose braid, the spaghetti-strap white gowns they wore contrasting wonderfully with their cinnamon skin. The two behind the knocker carried items, one a neatly folded assembly of clothes, the other a basket filled with bathing salts and scented oils.

"*Señorita*, we are here to prepare Miss Sapphire for *Señor* Fernando," the knocker spoke shyly.

Lucy carefully eyed the girls and the goods in their arms. Satisfied, she slowly stepped back and to the side. "Of course, please come in." She closed the door after the last girl passed through and called out to her lady.

Maya awoke with grace and ease and welcomed the ladies into her chamber. Lucy gave Maya an inquisitive look and Maya signaled her with a slight nod that all was okay and to relax.

"*Señorita* Sapphire," the lead girl said as she bowed. "We are here to prepare you for *Señor* Fernando."

"So I've heard." Maya crawled out from behind the canopy. "Let's go ahead and get to it; I wouldn't want to keep him waiting," she said playfully. She brought her thumbs up to the straps of her nightgown, paused and looked at Ratt.

"Time for you to go, boy," Lucy ordered.

Ratt stood still with a dumb look on his face, his double eyes blinking as if they were petitioning her demand in Morse code.

"Ratt, why don't you put on your glasses and scope out places where we may be able to hold the show?" Maya suggested, winking at him.

Ratt nodded his understanding and grabbed both his tinted goggles and his leather jacket, which he draped over his Dead Kennedys t-shirt as he ducked out of the suite.

Lucy was a watchful ghost while Maya allowed the girls to lead her into the bath chamber, disrobe her, and draw a hot bath. They poured generous amounts of oils, salts, and soaps into the running water, making it smell of honey and flowers. They scrubbed her skin tenderly and washed her hair by hand, massaging her scalp.

Two of the girls stationed themselves behind her, one folding shampoo into her hair, the other tenderly mopping her shoulder with a soaked cloth, while the third sat in front of Maya and asked for her leg. Taking it once it was offered, she raised it out of the tub's water and began to apply a creamy lotion of some kind to Maya's short, slender legs.

The serving girl turned around and squeezed another dollop of lotion into her hands, then leaned back over the tub to apply it to Maya's upper leg. As she leaned over, Maya could see a peculiar marking on the nape of the girl's neck, perhaps a tattoo—a pictographic symbol that she did not recognize.

Before Maya could study it in detail, the serving girl turned around again, wiped her hands on a towel, and then faced her once more, this time with an ivory-handled razor in hand. The girl's bushy ponytail had fallen over the tattoo now, obstructing it from further scrutiny.

Forgetting about it for the time being, Maya watched the young girl carefully pull the razor along the contours of her leg, peeling off her stubble, dead skin, and the lathered lotion. It felt good, invigorating.

The girl, while young, was skilled at her art and never once cut Maya's skin. Maya watched the polished edge of the razor run up her calf and noticed another anomaly on the serving girl: a small, rectangular piece of plastic seemingly embedded in the underside of her forearm.

Cybernetics? Maya wondered and frowned subconsciously.

The girl shaving Maya's leg noticed the frown as she leaned up to wipe clean the blade before another pass.

"Is something wrong, *Señorita* Sapphire?"

"Oh!" Maya's cheeks flushed. "I, um, was noticing your neck tattoo and that, um... Well, what is that on your arm, if I may ask?"

The serving girl looked a mix of amused, confused, and scared. Maya caught one dubious eyebrow raise on the girl's face before she remembered her place and dismissed it. Maya also felt the momentary pause in the scalp massage and shoulder-arm wash from the girls behind her. The girl holding the razor looked over Maya, presumably to read the face of the girl washing Maya's hair. Apparently satisfied at what she saw, she turned her gaze downward to Maya.

"I beg forgiveness, *Señorita*, but I'm not sure what you mean." The girl was clearly trying hard to be polite but was confused. The situation seemed to make her uncomfortable. She behaved as if she were afraid to give offense. Her voice was softer than the squeak of a church mouse.

"Umm." Maya, too, was feeling awkward now, wondering if perhaps she was making a social faux pas. Maya brought her arm out of the hot water, shook the bubbles off as best she could, then pointed at her neck first before touching her fingers to the inside of her arm. Maya watched the dawning of comprehension in the young girl's face, followed by the return of confusion, although the nervous tension seemed to have evaporated into the air like the steam rising from her bath.

"This is my stamp of citizenship." The girl pulled her ringed, loose braid of raven locks aside with her left hand, exposing her neck to Maya's gaze the way a lover would open a blouse. Maya could see the tattoo well now and leaned forward in the tub to get a closer look. It looked to Maya like a shield, a device, a family crest of some kind. Framed by a square no bigger than five square centimeters, there was what looked like a deformed rabbit under a full moon, perched on the ground before some half-buried root.

Then the girl released her fingertips from their duty and turned her arm over. Maya studied the square of plastic that embossed the girl's skin. The plastic was whitish, semi-transparent and had a nipple-like, stunted tube protruding about one centimeter from it at a 15-degree angle.

"What is it?" Maya asked and reached her hand out to touch it. The girls all giggled a bit. The one whose arm Maya was examining shook her head and wrinkled her nose.

"What's so funny?" Maya smiled at her embarrassment.

"You don't have one?" the girl asked, stretching her neck to look over Maya's body.

"No." It was Maya's turn to wrinkle her nose. The girls seemed genuinely confused now.

"You have neither? No Citizen Stamp nor tax connection?" the girl asked.

When Maya shook her head, she may just as well have told them that she didn't have a nose or that she didn't eat food and breathe air.

The girls were clearly confused and taken aback. The girl who had her arm out for Maya to examine recoiled a bit, her sense of place and duty unable to suppress the rising tide of xenophobia within her. Maya knew that something was off, so she played it cool and changed the subject quickly.

"Please, shave my armpits too, when you're done with my legs."

After the bath, the girls dried her off with soft towels that smelled of lemons and anointed her with oils on her neck, wrists, behind her ears, and her breasts. When they went to dab the same oil on the insides of her thighs, she stopped them with a gentle hand and said, "I do not think that is necessary. I have no intention of anyone coming close to that area." She received another look of scared confusion from the serving girls but paid it no mind.

Maya then allowed the girls to dress her in the undergarments and gown they had brought with them. They were opulent and finely crafted, clothing worthy of a goddess indeed. The gown was a rich cream color, more eggnog than white, with sewn-on pearls and lush ruffles flowing down the sides of the princess seams. The raised and regal collar, along with the long, trailing train, gave the dress a formal and expensive appearance. She looked like the mistress of a manor. They brought her jeweled earrings also. When they had finished, Maya presented herself to Lucy, who had been waiting in the suite's foyer.

"What do you think?" Maya asked playfully, executing a pirouette while holding her dress up off the floor.

"Better you than me, my lady." Lucy smiled saucily. The serving girls, having gathered up the dirty towels and their things, politely made their way to the door and bowed out, explaining that Maya could expect an escort to dinner within the hour—a promise that proved to be true.

Her escorts arrived not thirty minutes after the girls' departure, two men in fine suits. Their black hair was slicked back, with golden bracelets adorning their wrists, and tuxedo-style holsters housing pistols under their open jackets. They were polite in demeanor, though Maya could detect an undercurrent, an edge of something sinister, telling her that these guys were toughs and had dealt out their fair share of cruelty in service to their master.

It was what *Lucy* noticed, though, that put her on high alert.

"Neither of them shows heat signatures in my thermal optics," Lucy whispered into Maya's ear.

"Is something wrong?" one of the men asked, his question obviously prompted by the whispering.

"No, nothing at all. Everything is fine. Please, lead the way." Maya, ever the professional performer, maintained a superb poker face and secretly hoped that she knew what she was doing. She assured herself that Lucy was with her, and besides, she could bet that either Jon or Carbine or both had just noticed the same thing as Lucy, and hopefully even now had the goons in their cross-hairs.

Jon had been watching when the serving girls arrived. Carbine had taken Maya's advice to get some rest and was sound asleep. After a quick crash-course from his bud on how to operate the scope, Jon was soon settled in for a long evening of sniper stake-out.

He watched the young girls enter and quickly ascertained that they weren't a threat to the goddess. However, he soon became flustered when Maya began to disrobe.

A battle between the Olympian desire to keep watch over Maya and the titanic desire to be a gentleman and look away, to not watch Maya in the nude, commenced in his mind.

He couldn't make up his mind quickly enough and watched as Maya dropped her nightgown to the floor moments after Ratt had left the room.

His eyes bugged, and his heart skipped a beat. He could feel heat rising, among other things, and his cheeks flushing.

He quickly turned away, cursing himself as he did so.

Shit, shit, shit.

He lay with his back against the rock he had been leaning on and stared up at the black sky, his breath ragged.

This is no time for embarrassment and courtesy, soldier. You need to be watching her, protecting her. But it's just a couple of serving girls. And besides, Lucy is there.

At least a dozen times, Jon went back and forth in his mind, his dual duty as proper man and effective guardian exchanging blows with each other in a savage fight to the death. Finally, his sense of duty overcame his inner gentleman with a knockout punch.

Spinning around, Jon flattened himself back out and thrust his face and eye back up to the oversized scope.

He moved the reticle around the room to find Maya and located her. In one quick glance through the matter-penetrating telescope, he beheld the scene. There was Maya, facing him, sitting in the pool, legs apart, one up and out of the water as a serving girl ran a razor along it, up toward her—

Nope!

As quick as the involuntary gulp in his throat, he pulled his face from the scope and decided that audio monitoring through the earpiece would suffice.

Jon listened to the conversation in the bath, to Maya's uncomfortable situation over her question and her lack of a tax connection and Citizen Stamp—whatever the hell those were—and therefore didn't question the prolonged silence that followed.

He did, however, hear the occasional splash of water or rustling of fabric, and when he eventually didn't even hear that, didn't hear anything for several minutes, he began to wonder.

Not wanting to play the peeping Tom, but knowing he needed to check in, Jon again returned to the scope to investigate the mysterious silence. He returned to the railgun, which had been set up on a bipod as well as having the new modified spike driven into rock. It hadn't moved an inch. Jon peered into the scope, apprehensive, guiltily hoping and yet not hoping to see Maya in the position he'd seen her in earlier, with the tub's water and bubbles only slightly covering the most private bits of her body.

His heart immediately stopped its twitching when an empty porcelain tub greeted his eyes instead of a naked goddess. Panic set in like a flash flood. Jon took the weapon in his hands and pivoted it on the bipod stand, scanning the penthouse suite for any sign of life. Nothing. No one. They were all gone.

Then something glinted off the counter near the tub. Jon zoomed in on it.

The radio necklace.

Oh no.

11

The escorts brought Maya and Lucy through the byzantine palace to a large banquet hall with high, vaulted ceilings from which gaudy chandeliers hung, each bearing the weight of what seemed like a hundred candles, bathing the cavernous chamber in their light and warmth. As soon as they were all past the archway that separated the banquet hall from the hallway proper, the men abruptly turned on the girls, impeding further entry.

Lucy bristled, and her right hand parted her long coat in the fashion of an old western gunslinger. Not wanting to jump the gun, she kept the BFG hidden away inside the speed holster that was her right thigh.

"Your servant girl will wait outside with us," one of the slick men said to Maya.

"The fuck I will," Lucy snapped back instantly. Maya could tell that Lucy's tolerance for pleasantries was quickly coming to an end. The men, for their part, remained unmoved. Maya quickly diffused the situation.

"It's okay, Lucy. I will go on alone. I'm sure our host is as gentle as he is gracious." She smiled at the men and then turned to Lucy. "I will be fine." Her statement sounded like an order.

Lucy stared defiantly into the goddess's eyes.

"Go, now. Find Ratt and wait for me," Maya ordered her friend and then turned back to the men, smiling and nodding.

The men nodded back, one of them adjusting his gold bracelet as he did so, and they showed Lucy out, leaving Maya to enter and explore the hall.

Columns dotted the long sides of the hall, the tops of which were connected by arches, all decorated in Spanish Colonial style and adorned with well-placed flowers and fire baskets. A wooden table of fine artistry ran the length of the rectangular room. Chairs, like guard towers along New Puebla's wall, interrupted the flow and studded the perimeter of the table, while a runner of bright silk ran along the top, spotted here and there by floral arrangements and condiment trays. At the far end of the table, Maya spotted two figures, casually reclined. She made her way down the side of the table and approached them, doing her best to appear as cool and confident as Lucy would. When she was halfway there, she could make out that the two figures were a man and a woman.

The man, a clean-shaven Hispanic fellow with gelled black hair pulled tightly into a long ponytail, sat at the head of the table in the only chair there.

He wore simple but expensive-looking black slacks and a tucked-in button-down white shirt with sharp folded collar flaps. It was a third of the way unbuttoned, presumably to show off his gold chains and not his chest hair, but Maya couldn't guess. The man was reclining deeply in his chair, slouching really, looking relaxed and aloof. A jeweled goblet filled with a deep burgundy wine hung in his limp-wristed hand. He had one of his legs draped over the armrest of his chair. An empty plate and glittering silverware graced the table in front of him. He spoke to the woman to his left as Maya approached from his right.

"Sofia, look, our guest has arrived."

The woman glanced over at Maya, a look of disapproval on her heavily made-up face. Sofia was sitting, legs spread wide in her chair and, like the man, with her chair pulled away from the table. She wore shiny black baggy pants and a matching short-sleeved top that was tight and exposed her copper midriff and diamond-studded navel. Her arms were as smooth as the fabric of her silky pants and ended in a display of long, painted fingernails.

She was well-endowed, her cleavage prominently displayed by the push-up quality of the top. The look was framed by a red and black plaid vest, buttoned at the top and opening in an upside-down V. She wore a chain similar to the man's, but with some fine stone-crusted medallion hanging from it. She had long blond hair —Maya could tell it was dyed—which was piled high in two places, bunched up before being tied down by a black and white paisley decorated bandana, tied on the top, near the crown of her head.

Her eyes were heavy with makeup, but the dark complexion of her skin helped to mitigate the raccoon look. Still, Maya wondered how Sofia's eyelashes didn't stick together when she blinked. Her natural eyebrows were clean-shaven and replaced with sharp drawn-on curves. A solid black teardrop tattoo adorned her cheek. Paisley water drops, bigger versions of the same image printed on her bandana, ran down the side of her right arm. Her lips were painted a red as deep and dark as the wine, and pencil-outlined in a thin black. Dangerously large hoop earrings dangled from her ears, which bounced as she turned her head to study Maya.

Sofia drank from her wine glass without taking her eyes off Maya, watching her as a bird of prey might watch a vole venture from its den. She pulled the cup away, revealing a drop of wine that lingered on her thick lips. She opened her mouth in an over-exaggerated display of animalistic sexuality to lick the drop from the edge of her mouth.

Maya instantly noticed her teeth—clad in solid gold, with long and large imposing canines, curving slightly and ending in needle tips. When Sofia's eyes flashed bright red for a single absent heartbeat, Maya knew that the display wasn't simply a queen hen displaying her sexuality, but that Maya was *meant* to see the teeth, *meant* to see the eyes and the demonic power behind them. She was meant to be scared, or captivated, or both.

"Yes, lover. I wonder if she is as hungry as I am," Sofia said, her voice dripping with cruel humor. Maya knew well what Sofia was, and what she was hungry for. The man pulled his drooped leg back from over the armrest and stood, extending his goblet out in toast-like gesture.

"Please. Although it is unforgivably tardy, allow me to personally welcome you to New Puebla, *Señorita* Sapphire. I am Don Luis Fernando, the father of this city, and this is my wife, Sofia."

Maya closed the distance and stopped just short of the corner, now standing opposite the table from Sofia. She curtsied and thanked him.

"I accept your welcome most happily, *Señor* Fernando. Thank you."

"Please, call me Don Luis."

Maya could feel Sofia's eyes burning holes in her, but pretended not to notice.

"We would be so very happy if the famous singer Lily Sapphire joined us for dinner. Wouldn't we, dear?" Don Luis said as he placed his goblet on the table and walked over to the chair closest to Maya, pulling it out from the table.

"Delighted," Sofia retorted.

Maya ignored the tone and smiled as she sat down in the chair she was offered.

"Thank you, Don Luis." Then she added, "Sofia" with a polite nod.

"Care for a drink?" Sofia inquired and played her extraordinarily long nails around the rim of her wine glass. Maya's eyes were drawn to the vessel and now, being much closer, she was able to see and then realize with certainty that it was not wine they were drinking. She swallowed involuntarily, her nerves beginning to rattle. It was also then that she realized that she had forgotten to put her radio necklace back on after the bath.

Oh dear. And Lucy is not here either. She knew that things were not going as planned, that she had possibly bitten off more than she could chew. There was nothing to do now but continue the charade and hope that something good would come from all this, hopefully with no one near and dear to her getting hurt in the process—including herself.

"Water, please," she squeaked out.

Then Don Luis reached his hand up and snapped his fingers.

"Of course, *Señorita*." A female figure, until now unseen in the shadows of the dining hall's arches, came forward with a decorated vase. The servant girl filled the empty glass at Maya's setting, and Maya noticed the same plastic square embedded in her arm as the girls who had bathed and dressed her.

Maya realized that her eyes were lingering too long. She snapped her gaze back up straight into the curious and watchful eyes of Don Luis, who had resumed his seat. She knew she had been caught, and her cheeks burned. Her host looked to his goblet and picked it back up, taking a sip from it. He placed it back down, licking his lips, and then let out a satisfied sigh.

"Something tells me you are aware of what we are. And yet, you came, not only to our city, but to this table, willingly." Don Luis studied Maya for a tell. Behind her, the servant girl returned with a plate of delicacies—fruit, cheese, and the like—for Maya to dine on.

"I am familiar with your kind. I encountered several out in the desert on my way here." Maya steadied herself against the faintness she was feeling, as well as against her heart, which was pounding in her chest, threatening to cause her hands to shake.

"Are you now? Did you now?" Don Luis seemed cruelly amused. "And just what is my 'kind'?" He sipped again from his goblet. Sofia scoffed and rolled her heavily made-up eyes.

"I know that's not wine in your cups, *Señor* Fernando," Maya said coyly and plucked a ripe strawberry from her plate.

"I told you, call me Don Luis." He smiled at Maya's boldness. "But you must understand, *Señorita* Sapphire, we are not monsters. We are not like the wild dogs that you say you encountered."

"Since when do we explain ourselves to our food, lover?" Sofia interrupted.

Don Luis shot a look at his wife. Maya saw his eyes flash red.

"As I was saying." He turned back to Maya. "Here in *my* city, we have established a true civilization. An equilibrium."

"I admit I haven't seen any sign of the savagery I witnessed in the desert," Maya conceded. "Except for the obvious dichotomy between the upper and lower classes." Another strawberry and a small wedge of cheese disappeared from Maya's plate.

"I see." Don Luis's demeanor showed a sudden gentleness.

He raised his right hand and shrugged. "What can I say? One's material worth is a reflection of one's value and one's contribution to one's society. The humans are lazy, wretched, and simple-minded and care not to improve their lot. Without us to guide and protect them, they surely would degenerate to the level of dogs, eating what scraps they can find, copulating in the street, and licking their own asses."

Maya heard Sofia chortle quietly in her cup of blood.

"My most gracious host." Maya raised her head, looking as regal as she could. "Have you forgotten that I am one of the lazy, wretched, simple-minded ones you speak of?"

"*I* sure as fuck haven't," Sofia mumbled.

Don Luis bolted up onto his feet and slammed his palms on the table. The dishes and candelabras rattled, and the flowers in their vases swayed as if in a gentle breeze, but no soft wind came from the enraged Don.

"Must I banish you to your chamber as if you were no more than a disobedient bitch that sneaks meat from its master's table?" His eyes glowed bright red, and he attempted in no way to hide his anger. Maya thought that, in his mind, he must be an imposing sight, but to her, he looked no different than any other bully she had ever seen. A Latin vampiric Warbak, and nothing more.

Sofia slowly opened her mouth, the light from the room's hundred candles gleaming off her golden teeth. She hissed so quietly, Maya could barely hear it. After a moment, Sofia closed her mouth and lowered her eyes and slowly stood up.

"Sit back down," Don Luis ordered. Sofia, still looking down, hesitated.

"Must I stay and suffer insult while you treat this meat as our equal?" Sofia asked, the trembling edge of hate clear in her voice.

Don Luis seemed to consider his options, rapping his fingers on the surface of the table. Then, when the silence was beginning to make Maya feel like a little worm on a big hook, he spoke.

"No, go ahead and leave, Sofia. Your insulting behavior to our guest disgusts and embarrasses me. Leave now, while you still can." His voice had returned to a normal volume, but the cruelty in it no longer rang with amusement, but instead dripped with ice, giving Maya the chills.

Sofia did as bidden, but not without first locking eyes with Maya. There was a promise in those red eyes, heavy with makeup and framed by the sharp swoops of drawn eyebrows—a promise of pain to come. Maya played it off coolly, doing her best to channel Lucy.

Don Luis watched his wife walk away and visibly calmed himself as he once again tried to pour on the faux charm.

"I apologize for that outburst. I simply cannot abide by Sofia's behavior. Her blatant racism would make us out no better than the wild ones you say you met on the way here. I prefer a higher standard of conduct. We have a good relationship with the humans here." He paused as he sat back down, seeming to suddenly have a thought that derailed his current train of thought.

"I must ask—and I beg your pardon—but you say you witnessed savagery in the desert from the wild ones?" He rested his left hand on his chin and looked at Maya. "It is my understanding that the wild ones never willingly pass up the chance to eat. How exactly did a traveling musician and her tiny troupe come to avoid this grim fate while still being in close enough proximity to know the savages for what they were?"

Maya instantly regretted having said anything, and shifted uncomfortably in her seat as she slowly chewed on a grape, using the food to buy her a little time to fabricate a response.

"We were fortunate to have come across them mere moments before dawn. They left us before they could overtake us in fear of the sun's rays. We put a good distance between us during the day. The four-wheeled machine and the hoverboard can go fairly fast when they need to." Maya looked into Don Luis's eyes—which had stopped glowing—as she spoke.

Believe it. Believe it.

"Fortunate indeed." Don Luis smiled and sipped from his goblet once more, tipping it back and finishing it.

"Have you eaten enough, *Señorita?* I would take the air with you, if it pleases you." He offered his hand as he rose.

"Yes, I am satisfied, and I would be delighted to join you." Relieved that her deception remained intact, Maya decided to play interested, to use Don Luis's arrogance to her advantage. She had learned some about the nature of this city, but she needed to learn more. It was already becoming clear that she might not be able to simply procure supplies and move on after her performance, and furthermore, if there were humans suffering here, she felt driven to do something about it.

Apparently pleased with her response, Don Luis took her hand in his and held it up in the air at a comfortable height for her, escorting her out of the banquet hall through a door opposite from the one she had entered. It was not lost on Maya that Lucy would not know she was leaving with Don Luis, but it was too late to do anything about that.

They left the banquet hall and entered an antechamber with passages leading both upstairs and downstairs, as well as outside. Maya looked at the stone stairs that disappeared into the reaches of the palace and wondered where Sofia had gotten to but knew better than to bring her up. They continued and stepped out onto a balcony. The night air was musky and thick with the dried dung fires warming the houses in the human districts, though the homes of the resident vampires didn't require such fetters.

Don Luis, still supporting Maya's hand, guided her to the railing of the balcony. She could see that the nightlife of the city took on a different character from the tedium of the daily human life-sustaining activities. Those who enjoyed life at the top of the social pyramid, as well as the food chain, were out in the streets playing. Maya could see roving packs of vampires—their red eyes gave them away—making their way to and fro, from impromptu outdoor discotheques to what looked to Maya like Elena's bar back in the Shanty.

What she *didn't* see, though, was what surprised her. There was no murder. No chasing. No hunting.

Perhaps he doesn't tell all lies...

"You say you have a higher standard, a rule of law, an equilibrium." Maya turned from the rail and gazed upon Don Luis's face. She smiled and arched one eyebrow. "Please, good sir, do elaborate."

"Very well, with pleasure." Don Luis turned out toward the city, scanning for something. When he found it, he pointed his finger. "Do you see there, that farm?"

"Yes, I think so." Maya squinted into the black. Her eyesight was not as good in the dark as his. It appeared to be a small industrial farm; even in the dark, Maya could make out the pen that framed the lot adjacent to the building and what appeared to be sleeping cows dotting the muddy yard.

"It's one of New Puebla's dairy farms," Don Luis said. "Do you see that adobe house next to it?"

"Yes."

"That is where the man who manages the farm lives. Do you see any difference between his house and the cows' dwellings?"

Maya, believing he had made his point, frowned with disappointment.

Maya turned on him. "So you *do* feel the same way about humans as your wife?"

"Relax, pussycat. I mean no insult. Yes, I cannot deny that my kind is superior, but please allow me to continue to explain."

"Very well, go on."

"While the farmer is clearly superior in nature to the cow, he needs the cows to survive, no? But unlike the coyote of the desert, he does not slaughter the cows in a savage manner. No, he shelters them, feeds them, heals them when they are sick, presuming that the cow can still produce milk. He protects them from themselves by erecting the fence to keep them from wandering off and encountering danger that they are too stupid even to recognize, let alone avoid or deal with. The wild ones you met on your way here, they are like the coyote, while I," he paused for dramatic effect, "am like the farmer. No human here dies before his time.

Only the incurably sick, the old, those who no longer impart anything of value to the greater good. I saw you notice the tax connection on the serving girl's arm a minute ago at dinner. That is how we collect our tax; that is how we withdraw our sustenance from our herd. There is no slaughter in the streets, no savagery; we are not barbaric brigands, my dear."

He paused again, looking at Maya with a zealot's passion in his eyes. Her eyelids fluttered, like a grounded butterfly taking to the sky. She forced a smile and nodded her understanding.

"When a human is born, the child is registered, and the intravenous port is installed; they get a new one every year, with care, so as not to infect the host. The same goes for those wishing to immigrate to our fair city and take respite from the howling madness of the world at large and whatever else the Drops might bring."

Maya remained as calm as she could, setting her lips into a hard line and doing her best to soothe her reflexively flaring nostrils.

"Everyone benefits, Lily—can I call you Lily?"

She nodded.

"They get everything they need, while I and my kind get everything *we* need. It's the perfect arrangement. The tax is fair and monitored, and we never bleed anyone dry. Why would we? Were we to do that, we would soon find ourselves starving like the wild ones. We collect only enough to sustain us, and they, the humans, heal and regenerate what we take. It's an ideal tax-farm. It doesn't even hurt them. My people are happy here. By submitting to the social contract, by paying their blood-tax and letting the true sovereign class make the ruling decisions for them, they have more leisure time to pursue their interests in life. Where else can they go to find shelter and protection in this hellish world? If they were to strike out on their own, they would struggle daily and surely die before long. The world outside these walls of protection is savage and brutal, as I'm sure you well know."

"And the neck tattoos?" Maya asked.

"What rancher doesn't brand his herd?" Don Luis asked with sick amusement. When he saw Maya wince a little, he hurriedly added, "It's for their own good, Lily. When they receive the brand, what we prefer to call the Citizen Stamp, they have proof of identification. Each one receives a unique number, and my captains, lieutenants, and their men can use this number to make sure that each citizen gets their allotment of foodstuffs and necessary items from us in exchange for their blood tax, which is also kept well track of. Not only that, but the mark, which is near the source of the easiest blood flow, a source that the wild ones go for nine times out of ten, the mark is seen by their would-be attacker. This saves their lives, you see? It is a message, a message that they as citizens of New Puebla are under my protection. If harm comes to them, then their attackers have to answer to me."

"It all sounds very civilized," Maya lied. "And I suppose that allowing me into your city, wanting me to perform, has nothing to do with the bread-and-circus tactics of keeping your *cattle* distracted from the tedium of daily life?" Maya smiled at Don Luis in a way that let him know she was playing.

Don Luis smiled back. "You are too smart, *Señorita*. And your beauty surpasses your intelligence. You belong here with me, by my side."

"And I suppose I could if I only consent to receive my Citizen Stamp and pay my 'taxes'?" Maya smirked.

"While for most, those are the terms of our social contract, for you, it would be different."

"Different?"

"Come, walk with me. I will show you the future," Don Luis said dramatically. Inside, Maya was simultaneously amused at both how ridiculous he sounded and just how much he believed in his own bullshit. She played along exceptionally well, a true Lily Sapphire performance, gazing into his eyes and allowing her breathing to intensify, causing her lace-wreathed chest to rise and fall theatrically. She took his hand in hers and allowed herself to be carried away into the city night. They strolled along the parapets and ramparts of the palace's outer perimeter, taking in the sights. It was the time of the vampire. They saw many of them down below in the streets, and Maya's escort asked her if she would like to go down to the street level and join them before he showed her his surprise. She smiled and nodded her consent.

They went a short way farther and came to a low-grade ramp that switchbacked down the side of the palace. Large square planting beds decorated the intersections, with several electric light lamp posts illuminating the way down.

Despite having only minutes earlier likened her race to cattle, Don Luis was very gentlemanly as he guided her down the ramps, pausing only momentarily to pluck a rose from one of the square beds. He handed her the rose, yellow in color, by its thorned stem and she squinted her eyes in a smile as she took it. She made a sound, somewhere between a gasp and a squeak, and flinched as she took the rose from him.

Having feigned carelessness perfectly, Maya pricked her fingertip on a thorn when she wrapped her delicate fingers around its stem.

A teardrop of bright blood began to trickle down her hand. Don Luis quickened at the sight of it, and he opened his mouth to let escape a quiet moan. She pulled her hand away from the rose, leaving Don Luis to hold it, and she held her bleeding hand in her other, hovering close to and in front of her chest. She studied his eyes and saw that they were locked on to her hand. She knew what to do.

Maya stepped close into Don Luis and turned her hand, with its small trickle of blood running down and around the curve of her palm, its path now having reached her wrist, up toward his mouth.

"Go ahead; I want you to taste me," she said in a paradoxically shy and confident voice. He dropped the rose like a thing forgotten and cradled her slender tan arm in his hands. Another slight moan escaped his lips. He brought her hand close, and, beginning at her fingertip, closed his lips around her digit and began sucking the blood flow only slightly. He pulled away slightly and kissed his way down her finger, palm, and wrist, cleaning the trail of drying blood as he went. Both the puncture on her finger-tip and the trail itself were just enough to give him a taste, the tiniest little tease. He was becoming drunk on the urge, though—Maya could see it—like growing arousal, sexual and primal. You could put a tiger in a dress suit and teach it to walk upright, but it would remain a tiger. He pulled his lips away from her wrist, and Maya watched in horrific apprehension as his canine teeth stretched, elongated, and formed into points as fine as the rose's thorns.

Don Luis's eyes now glowed red, and his face wore an expression of animalistic ecstasy, the quintessence of need, desire, and lust. With sudden and surprising strength, she yanked her arm away from him. In a flash, the beginnings of rage played across his face, and Maya saw there in him the genesis of rape and murder. She acted immediately, determined to shut off and stem the flow of whatever storm might be brewing in the most primitive parts of his brain.

"Ah, ah, ah. Just a taste. If you want more, I want it to be *my* way. I am not one of your cows."

Don Luis looked nearly panicked, fighting back his urges to take her right here on the palace ramp. "State your price!" he nearly gasped.

"I want you to drink me in front of everyone. I want them all to see it." Maya breathed heavily. The panic of Don Luis's face turned to confusion.

"I want you to drink me at the finale of my concert and then take me as yours, make me your second wife… I want you to *turn* me."

When he smiled, with his eyes red and his fangs grown, Maya knew for sure what the devil looked like, and she also knew without a doubt that she had him.

12

"How long is this dinner supposed to last?" Lucy asked the two thugs guarding the hall's doors.

"Until it's finished," one of the two men said, smirking, causing the other to laugh.

Lucy smiled back, though not at the joke. She was smiling at the mental image she had of ripping the man into pieces. Her painted eyes fluttered, and her smile widened.

"Charming," she said.

"Annoying is more like it. Why don't you go have a seat over there?" The tough scowled at her and pointed with a finger.

I'd like to rip that finger off and stick it up your ass.

"I will continue to remain here and be annoying until you tell me how much longer it's going to be."

"*Vete a la mierda, niñita.* Or I will make you. We ain't gonna interrupt the king's dinner date for nothing." The tough stepped away from the wall where he had been leaning and stood up as straight as he could, puffing out his chest.

Lucy did not back down, but altered her smile to show her teeth.

"You can either interrupt his date by simply peeking in and

letting me know what is taking so long, or I will interrupt from out here by making so much noise that you will wish you had. I start screaming in three, two, one—"

"Okay, okay! *Esta bien!*" the tough said, shaking his head. "Be right back."

"*Muchas gracias,*" Lucy replied, her smile vanishing in an instant.

She watched the man disappear into the dining hall and heard some muffled conversation on the other side of the door. A short minute later, the man returned.

"Well?" she asked.

"They aren't there," the tough reported.

"*¿Qué?*" Lucy felt her enhanced nervous system switch into battle mode. She had to restrain herself from launching her BFG into her waiting hand and releasing the dogs of war on these two, and the whole city if need be.

"Relax, *chica.* They went for a walk. Your friend will meet you back in your room. You can go now." The man smiled and crossed his tree trunk arms in front of his chest.

Lucy wasn't one to panic, but she came close. She knew well the monstrous nature of the people they were dealing with, and the idea of her lady being off with one, unprotected, rattled her to her machine core. Every bit of her programming wanted to spring into action, to find and rescue Maya, but part of her restrained herself. If she laid into these guys now and went tearing through the palace, they could forget any chance they had of re-supplying. Not to mention, she might inadvertently put them all in such danger as to make escape from the city impossible. As much as she hated it, she would have to hope that Maya was not in danger, or, if she was, that she would be able to take care of herself.

Damn it all!

The least she could do was find Ratt, and then together maybe they could track down Maya and get the hell out of this city. Jon had been right. Coming here was proving to be a big mistake. No amount of transportation or food would be worth it if they themselves ended up on the menu.

Lucy made for the exit and, finding it, stood on the threshold, looking out over New Puebla by night. Not for the first time since being reborn at the hands of Warbak's top man, Matiaba, she hated her embellished appearance. Her ghastly visage was known, known and feared in the Shanty, but here? How would the average citizen react to seeing her? She cursed again, lamenting the lack of even a hood to hide her painted face, and stepped out into the streets.

Now where did the little twerp get himself to?

Lucy wandered the streets like a ghost haunting a place not its own. She tried not to look panicked or otherwise draw attention to herself, but failed at every turn. Human and vampire alike cast strange glances at her whenever they came near, no doubt wondering who she was, why she looked like painted death, and why she didn't smell of blood.

This is no good, she thought, avoiding the confused stares of the undead, and looked for an alley or dimmer path that she could navigate, hoping the darkness would help obscure her unusual appearance.

She found just such a street before long and ducked into it, instantly wondering what she was thinking. The street was only dimly lit by the glow of cook fires in the windows of the hovels that lined it, and was devoid of foot traffic, which in turn meant devoid of Ratt.

This is pointless. Maybe the best thing to do is just to go back to our suite and wait. Her thoughts and the futility of her situation pained her, but she didn't see many other options. If she kept wandering the city, it was probably only a matter of time before someone questioned her, or accosted her, and then she would have no choice but to show them what she was really made of.

She was about to turn around and head back to the main thoroughfare, when she rounded a sharp corner and startled two children who were busying themselves picking through a pile of garbage.

"Santa Muerta!" one of the children gasped, bolting upright and freezing in place before Lucy like a prisoner in front of a firing squad.

"Hey, easy there. I won't hurt you," Lucy said as softly as possible. In her mind's eye, the dirty children before her transformed and became the children of Underground, pickers, the ones that Home forgot, trying to eke out a small measure of survival by sifting through the refuse of the Ziggurat. Without even knowing their story, Lucy pitied the pair of waifs before her every bit as much as she had pitied the children who lived in the buried ghost city of Denver-That-Was.

"Eres el diablo?" the second child asked, also frozen in place, hands full of rotten produce and trembling.

"Am I the devil?" Lucy repeated the question, the child's words breaking her phantom heart. It pained her to see fear in the children's dirty faces. In a better world, ones as tender as these should be innocent and full of joy, not covered in filth, starving, and afraid of the devil.

"No, sweet one. I am a friend. *Amiga.*" She touched one hand to her chest and smiled at them. *"Mi nombre es Lucy."*

"Eres humana?" the first child asked, her body language showing that she was on the cusp of relaxing a little.

"Yes, little one. I am a human." *In a manner of speaking.*

Lucy crouched down to the two girls' level.

"Aren't you afraid of the curfew?" the second girl asked. Lucy could see now that she was the older of the two. Big sister, most likely. Lucy squinted, curious to know more, so tried her hand at prompting further conversation.

"Curfew?" she asked the girls.

"Humans can't be out this late. It's the rules," they explained.

"Well, you two are out," Lucy pointed out and instantly regretted it, seeing fear return to their young faces.

"Are you *policía?*" the older girl asked. "Will you report us?"

"No, *niña.* Your secret is safe with me. You're not going to report *me*, are you? I know I've been naughty too." Lucy deftly turned the tables on the girls and caused them to laugh a little.

"What are your names?" she asked, quickly changing the subject.

"Camila," the younger said.

"Maria," the older said.

"It's nice to meet you both." Lucy smiled. A thought flashed in her mind. She plucked both of her lapel-mounted LED flashlights from her trench coat and flicked them on. The girls' eyes lit up with delight at the soft but strong blue-white lights.

"These are special. They have very strong batteries, *muy fuerte,* yeah? They will last for many, many moons. Here, you can have them." Lucy gave the girls one each and watched with joy as the children turned them off and on again, clearly impressed.

"Do you two live around here?" Lucy asked, happy that the kids were happy.

"*Si!*" they replied in unison. "Just around the corner," Maria added.

"That's great!" Lucy said. "I'm not from here. I'm visiting."

The girls both stopped in their playful examinations of the flashlights and looked at Lucy in puzzlement.

"Vis-eh-teen?" Camila asked, joining the word's syllables together slowly as if she had never heard it before.

"Yeah, I'm a visitor. A *desconocido.* Do you understand?"

The girl's heads nodded in the affirmative, but their eyes told a different story.

Lucy almost asked them if they knew where she could trade for some food, but then remembered how she had just found them, digging in a trash midden, hands full of shriveled and bruised tubers.

"You two enjoy those flashlights and stay safe, okay? Run along home now," she said, standing back upright.

"*Si Claro!*" the girls said. Then, "Wait, Miss Lucy?" Maria asked.

Lucy turned to the oldest girl, impressed with the child's manners.

"Yes, Maria?"

"May I please ask you a question?"

Lucy tried not to laugh at the sheer adorableness of the child. "Of course."

"Why do you look like that?"

Lucy smiled at the girl, masking the pain the question brought. She thought for a minute about how to proceed, and then told the girl a story.

"Well, you know the *Sante Muerta* is only scary-*looking*, right?"

The girls nodded vigorously.

"Okay, well, you see, I am just like her. I look scary because I punish the bad people. I'm only scary to them, not to good little girls like you. I help the good people."

"You punish the bad men?" Camila asked, her eyes lighting up.

"Yes, little one. I go around and scare them and make them not do bad things anymore."

"Maria!" Camila nearly shouted. "She does what Eduardo wants to do!"

Maria's face paled and her eyes shot daggers at her little sister. Lucy watched them both carefully, thinking she knew what was going on. Being a soldier in an underground resistance taught you things.

"Who is Eduardo?" Lucy asked, trying to sound kind and innocent. *And why does he want to stop bad men?*

"He—uh… he is our… *Hermano mayor*," Maria said, looking down, actively avoiding eye contact with Lucy.

"Older brother, huh? Hey, it's okay. You can trust me." Lucy stepped forward and squatted back down. The girl still wouldn't look up.

"Maybe I can help him stop the bad men. Would you let me help?" Lucy asked softly and reached out to brush away a raven lock of the girl's hair from her grubby face. *"Por favor?"*

As much as it pained Lucy to see the girl trust a stranger so easily, she was relieved when Maria lifted her eyes and looked back up at Lucy.

"Okay," Maria said.

Lucy smiled big and moved her hand to stroke the girl's cheek. "Thank you."

Lucy followed the girls down the dark alley, making small talk the whole way, assuring them that they were safe and that she could be trusted.

Before departing, Lucy had helped to gather up as many edibles from the trash pile as possible and wished to herself that she had some foodstuffs with her, but what little they had were back up the mountain with Jon and Carbine.

Thoughts of Jon and Carbine led her to thoughts of Ratt and Maya. She was still worried about their safety but saw in this a mystery that might prove worth solving. They were here, after all, to obtain as much intel on the city and its ways and means as possible. Lucy had a strong suspicion that this Eduardo might represent a source for vital information, and perhaps an ally.

Eventually, the girls led her to a small home, no bigger than the crew cabin in the transport had been. The house appeared to be hand-built from sun-dried bricks, which peeked through worn gaps in the outer layer of clay-like plaster, all of which bore a deep russet color. A simple doorway and several small windows broke up the flowing, organic-looking curves of the structure, none of which had anything more than a tattered cloth covering them.

"Tu casa?" she asked the girls, a question to which they both nodded yes.

"It's lovely," Lucy said, sincerely meaning it, despite the apparent poverty of the dwelling.

Camila disappeared behind the entrance's curtain, while Maria stood back, beckoning to Lucy with a wave of her hand.

"Mamá!" Maria called out as she led Lucy into her home. "We brought a friend!"

Lucy stepped into a plain, open-floor-style home and was met by the astonished stares of a young man, perhaps around Ratt's age, and a heavy-set older woman who until that moment had been bent over a large, shallow frying pan.

That Lucy's appearance was unusual was an understatement, and Lucy knew this, so she didn't waste a second in attempting to assuage any fear or alarm the home's tenants may be feeling.

"No se alarmes, I am a friend," Lucy said, both hands in the air. "Your lovely daughters invited me to join them. I am a stranger to the city and did not know about the curfew."

The young man had been perched on a stool near the woman, whom Lucy assumed was the mother of all three children. He rose to his feet, fists clenched. Neither of them said a word and only continued to stare at Lucy in shock.

"Please, I mean no harm. I have some questions if you would be so kind." Lucy could practically feel the apprehension in the room, so redoubled her efforts to calm them.

"I know my visage, my *apariencia* is unsettling, but I assure you, I harbor no bad intentions to you or your family."

"What do you want?" the boy, presumably Eduardo, asked.

"Maria and Camila here mentioned something when I told them what I do."

At this, Maria shifted in place and once more cast her eyes down.

"What you do?" Eduardo asked, clearly confused.

"I told them that I stop bad men." Taking a risk, Lucy decided to command her right thigh to open, revealing her hidden pistol. She saw both pairs of eyes, Eduardo's and his mother's, flick to the weapon. Keeping her hands up where they could see them, she nodded to them, tacitly telling them all they needed to know, and then commanded her thigh-compartment to close back up with a thought.

"I see," Eduardo said, eyes narrowing.

The mother's face transformed as suddenly as Lucy's thigh had, morphing into a pained expression: one part hope, one part merciful begging.

"Our prayers are answered! *La Virgen de Guadalupe* has sent the *Sante Muerte* to save us!"

Now it was Lucy's turn to look shocked. Recovering as quickly as possible, she cocked her head slightly and narrowed her eyes.

"What goes on in this city? Save you from whom? The vampires?"

"*Si, Los Vampiros,*" Eduardo said. "They are devils. They keep us small, you see? My father stood up to them and now he is gone."

"Gone?" Lucy asked, watching the mother for a reaction as Eduardo spoke.

"Gone. They took him. They take many of us. People disappear. Never come back. Especially people who can do *mágico*."

So people down here can shape Strange too, huh? Interesting.

"Why don't you all leave if you are in danger? Just pack up and go? Why do you stay submissive to the *Vampiros* if they harm you?"

At this question, the mother made a sound, like a cry, cut off and stifled. She shook her head slowly as Eduardo's eyes, too old for his teenaged face, bore into Lucy with impassioned anger.

"Señora," he said, his voice as flat and laced with as much danger as the sides of Lucy's war-clubs, "they won't let us leave."

13

After being ejected from the suite, Ratt found his way out of the palace and onto the streets that they had ridden through on their way in. On foot, he could see more, smell more, and hear more. Up close and personal, the city was more real, more tangible. He noticed strange tattoos on the human citizenry's necks as well as the intravenous ports installed on their arms, which reminded him of field medicine techniques he had seen employed during the war with Home when he was a child.

He wondered at the tattoos but didn't ask anyone. He passed some old women with a child sitting on inverted rusty buckets next to what looked like an over-sized frying pan set over a small fire of white ash and red coals. He watched them reach into the pan with simple wooden tongs and flip several small, flat yellow circles—corn tortillas. Even coming from as far to the north as Home, no Latino boy worthy of the name would fail to recognize a corn tortilla when he saw one. This familiar food brought a smile to Ratt's face, and he waved at the multi-generational group of women. The child stared at him as if he were an alien and the old women scowled.

Friendly neighborhood. Ratt rolled his eyes, hidden behind his tinted lenses, and moved on. He strolled through the night, unmolested for little over an hour, passing homes of such poverty that they would have fit in perfectly in the Shanty or Underground before he stumbled upon the answer to the mystery of the ubiquitous neck tattoos.

Not twenty yards ahead, on the other side of a well-worn, hard-packed mud street, was a line of people stretching off into the distance and around the end of the block. How much longer the line was after that, Ratt could not say. Having illegally read as many books and studied as many pre-Storm films as he could find, Ratt was familiar with pre-Storm history. The scene in front of him evoked memories of images he had seen in an old compilation of ancient *magazines*.

Ghostly images of a bygone era, all in black and white, of things called "gulag," "concentration camp," and "Soviet bread lines." Every person in this line was human, of that Ratt was sure —no glowing red eyes, no fangs—and every single one of them came equipped with the IV port and neck tattoo. The only people present who didn't have those accoutrements were the armored soldier-looking types at the front of the line. They were not part of the line but were instead facing the queue, receiving the people in the line, one at a time.

Ratt slid from the street-alley intersection where he had been standing to a position where most of his profile was obscured by a light post with a trash bin at its base. Trying not to draw attention to himself, Ratt reached into his pants pocket, brushing aside the pre-Storm vintage skater chain that dangled there, and withdrew a hand-sized clear plastic bag. He casually dumped the bag on the lid of the trash bin and opened it with nimble fingers. He proceeded to drag out the motions of rolling a cigarette while he studied the bread line, attempting to look as aloof and indifferent as possible.

What he saw there disturbed his freedom-loving sensibilities, but it wasn't necessarily hellish or horrific by any means. He watched in mild disgust as each human citizen at the front of the line offered up their arm to the vampiric tenders of the process, tilting their heads to allow their neck tattoo to be inspected and scanned in, like a barcode upon a pre-Storm grocery shop's inventory.

The tenders took the offered arms without so much as a word and plugged a large catheter-like needle into the citizen's port; the blood tax paid. Quick and painless, and Ratt only saw a few dozen people faint from dizziness, while the majority simply finished paying their toll and received a small bag of maize and a bottle of milk for their trouble and were sent on their way.

So that's how things work around here, huh? Blood for food. Freedom for security. Well, I think I've seen enough of my fellow humans treated like a commodity. Time to head back to the palace.

Ratt popped his freshly rolled cigarette between his lips and, cupping his hands, lit it up.

He took one last lingering look at the blood-line, then, turning to leave, exhaled a cloud of blue-tinged smoke into the night air.

He arrived back at the palace's front entrance without any further adventure and was allowed in by the same pair of human guards who had let him out earlier.

Sheesh. These guys not only roll over for, but also serve and protect their overlords. Makes me sick, man.

As he wandered through the darkened corridors, lit here and there by decorative Colonial-style wall sconces, he began to ponder if there were any citizens whatsoever who weren't so willing to give up their blood to a class that lived at such a higher standard than them, especially when the lower class seemed to be doing all the work.

From what Ratt had seen, it was the humans that made repairs to the roads the vampires provided. They were granted space to make their dwellings, but only the most basic of raw materials were available to them, while all the fine stone and lumber—those materials more rare in this post-Storm world—were saved for the vampires, who then used human labor to build the mansions and human labor to guard the same by daylight.

It was the humans that toiled in the garden plots, the humans that grew and then harvested the maize with which they were paid. The land was within the walls of the vampire-ruled, vampire-owned, and vampire-protected city, and so it was accepted as fair. As he continued to ponder, it seemed more and more to him that the entire system was based on and supported by acceptance alone. Acceptance and belief in the "rightness" and "fairness" of the ruling class and working class. On the surface, it would seem that despite having access to the means of production, and in actuality being the ones who produced the food and maintained the infrastructure, the thought of turning against the ruling class that lived in luxury was as alien to these people as anything that ever crawled from a Drop.

Maybe they accept the situation because they get protection from whatever might come from those Drops...

But what lies on the surface and what probes the depths of men's dreams are two different things entirely. Ratt pondered this deeply, no longer paying attention to where he was going, but simply walking along the palace corridors, lost in his musings.

Surely they must resent their situation but feel too scared to act... Surely some among them wish to avoid this blood tax and better their lives... but maybe not. Maybe, as ugly as it is, we need to leave these people to sleep in the bed they've made? Bending the knee to the bloodsuckers may seem abhorrent, but in this broken world, full of potentially worse monsters, say, Harvesters for example, perhaps living under the yoke of the vamps is worth the protection they receive...

Lost in his thoughts, Ratt failed to recognize that his steps had gone awry three turns ago, and he was nowhere near the suite. He had also failed to notice that the ornate sconces no longer decorated the walls. In their places were ancient, medieval-looking torches in iron brackets, burning loudly with snaps and pops, dripping small flaming bits of tallow to the stone floor.

It wasn't until he reached the end of the hallway that he realized he was in the wrong place.

Uh-oh. Way to not pay attention, Ratt. Where did I get to?

Where he had expected to find the stairs that led up to the suite, he instead found a set of older, sinister-looking stone steps that curved downward, not upward. They bent toward his right as they disappeared into darkness, the path appearing to be swallowed by shadows. He felt a wave of cool air rising from below, a too-chilly-to-be-refreshing draft.

He was then suddenly struck with that familiar feeling one gets when doing something they shouldn't or being somewhere they shouldn't. Ratt glanced over his shoulders, first left, then right. He was alone.

"How did this happen?" he wondered out loud, his spoken voice giving a tactile quality to his circumstances.

For a moment, he thought it best that he turn around, seek out the suite, and apologize to any vampire he might accidentally come across—for it was wise, he thought, to be polite to the wolves when you were the new sheep in town. And turn around he almost did, until he heard a woman's sobs from down below, the absolute and complete terror in the sound causing goosebumps to rise all over his body.

Silence.

No, he could now hear the crackling of the torches behind him. And his breathing.

The deathly stillness of the hall was interrupted by another scream, the kind of scream that was all too familiar to him. This time, the scream was a word—no, two words.

"No! Please!"

Ratt froze, his mind and body suddenly possessed by the ghost of slaughters past. He had heard those same two words screamed by a woman before. It was the last two things his mother had uttered on this Earth before being gunned down by soldiers from the Human Republic. In the silence between that plea for mercy and the next scream, Ratt relived the terror and trauma of watching his family die at the hands of men who'd thought it their right to rule over others, to squash independence in order to consolidate natural resources and establish a new, *fair* order, a government that would do what it must for the *greater good*. War was war, they said, and rape and murder and "collateral damage" was bound to happen. Deal with it, kid. You should be grateful that we're here to protect you from the Drops, from Strange, from Beasties, from Drop-trash. Your parents were terrorists. Ad nauseum.

"Enough!" Ratt exclaimed, probably louder than he should have. All thoughts of self-preservation were banished by those words, and upon hearing the third scream, Ratt snapped out of his possessed reverie and bolted down the stairs recklessly. The way quickly became dark, but he dared not slow his descent. He was, however, forced to pull his goggles up onto his forehead so he could see a tad better. Like a blind man, he put one hand out in front of him, probing the black before him, the other hand flat against the wall for stability as he spiraled down the steps in a run, praying not to roll an ankle or trip, should he land wrong, as he skipped several steps with each run-jump down.

Just as the last vestiges of the light above and behind him faded fully, forcing him to slow his run to a walk, light from ahead and farther down began to creep into the edges of the shadows. Another full turn down the long, winding staircase and solid enough torchlight had returned.

The next scream was louder, and more sounds echoed down

here—growling, snapping, wicked laughter. Even knowing he was unarmed, Ratt did not slow his run or make any attempt at stealth. He was mad, driven by the memory of his dying mother.

Tears began to blur his vision, making polychromatic snowflakes out of the torchlight when he, at last, came to the final step and beheld a large chamber. He blinked hard, pushing the teardrops away, then took in the scene.

The room itself was vast; it seemed to take up the entire footprint of the palace above it. Were he not distracted by what he saw, Ratt would have surmised that this was the basement or dungeon. The room had an arena-like quality to it: a large, ovoid lower-part of open space surrounded by a high wall and landing, complete with seating that was broken up here and there with structural support walls and pylons obviously holding up the enormous palace above them.

The air was damp and musty, fitting for an underground crypt or ossuary, and a cold draft blew through it, the origin of which eluded Ratt's quick assessment. The stairs that he'd taken down ended on the upper landing that wrapped around the lower arena space. It was onto this landing that Ratt stepped and saw just a short distance beneath him a woman clutching a bundle of rags. Her hair was messy, and she looked as though she had just woken up from a long and restless sleep.

Despite the coolness of the room, her forehead was covered in a collage of sweat drops. Her face was as pale as cream and her eyes as wide and round as saucers. Her clothes were as ragged as her hair, and dirty.

She clutched the bundle of rags tightly to her bosom as if her very life depended on it, yet she slowly removed one trembling hand from the bundle and pointed left of Ratt. Her mouth opened to speak, but only the cool, damp breeze moaned its woeful song.

He felt it before he could see it—that sensation that had been a hallmark of the ancient cinema that Ratt loved so much. A common line from some of his favorite movies popped into his mind. *They are right behind me, aren't they?*

Ratt's armored wall of adrenaline-fueled vigor faltered and his senses crept back in, bringing with them familiar friends such as self-preservation and caution. He gently closed his eyes and exhaled as if to mime "Fuck me" and made to spring into action, but it was too late.

A clammy hand gripped the back of his neck, as cold as the gusts that issued from the unknown depths of the dungeon and rippled across his face. He could feel a thumbnail, as stout as the stone beneath his feet and as sharp as the regret he felt for rushing in, push into his neck flesh and puncture skin. It hurt, and the strength in this hand reminded him of Lucy's raw power. Ratt knew there would be no overpowering the owner of this stern grip. He relaxed, his legs turning to water.

"Well, well, look, Sofia, more meat to play with," a low male voice dripped into Ratt's ears. It spoke in Spanish; a language that Ratt knew and expected. The vise-like hand on the back of his neck turned him around as easily as if he were one of the burros he had seen on the streets above, fitted with bridle and reins.

"Is that true, meat? Did you come down here to play with us?" A woman stood before him, next to the man who held him fast. The woman smiled mischievously, revealing a set of gold-clad teeth and fangs. She wore an outfit that was paradoxically made of high-quality materials but designed to look like the lower-class gangsters of Earth's past. "Hmmm," she purred. "Are you a *bruja?* Why do your eyes look like that?"

He could also see now, in his peripheral vision, the man who held him fast by the neck. Ratt couldn't see much, but he had the impression that his captor was similarly dressed to the many palace guards he had seen coming and going all night. Ratt's mind was a maelstrom of conflicting emotions: fear, audacity, courage, terror.

Continuing to smile, the woman playfully bit her bottom lip with a sharp, golden canine. The light from the torches caught the gold and glinted in Ratt's double eyes.

"The queen asked you a question, meat!" the man barked and tightened his superhuman grip. Ratt heard his neck pop and felt a trickle of warm blood running down the side of his neck, under his shirt collar, and down his chest. The cold breeze felt cooler against the warmth of his blood. He made an involuntary whimpering sound, and the man relaxed his grip slightly, not as much as before, but less than the excruciating crush that he'd felt for a moment. The man noticed the crimson rivulet running down Ratt's neck and announced, "This one is ripe!"

"I'm not a witch. I, I just got too close to a Drop," Ratt grunted.

"And why are you down here, meat?" Sofia pressed closer and ran her tongue over the pointed tips of her gold-clad canines.

"I got lost, I heard screams," Ratt tried to explain, unable to keep the fear inside from raising the pitch of his voice higher than normal.

"Awww. You got wost." Sofia mocked Ratt with feigned sympathy, tilting her chin and pouting her plump lips, causing their deep red tint and black outline to stand out all the more. She stepped toward him slowly with a gait he had seen before, and it made him tremble with fear.

It was the way Lucy walked. It was the way a jaguar walked when approaching its prey. It was simultaneously alluring and frightening. She tapped at her lip with one of her impossibly long, lacquered fingernails. Ratt secretly thanked the gods that it wasn't her nails digging into the side of his neck. She stepped as close as one could get. She smelled like expensive perfume. Her manicured hand disappeared from Ratt's line of sight, and he felt her cup his balls. Ratt inhaled sharply from shock.

"You didn't answer the question, meat. Do you want to play with us? Eating makes me so horny," she whispered lustily into his ear, and nibbled on his earlobe. The sensation was pleasurable at first, but then she bit down hard, turning his ear flesh into a torn, bloody flap.

"Ahh!" Ratt exclaimed, despite his attempt to hold back the pain and appear tough.

He wasn't sure if *playing with them* meant getting laid or getting eaten, but he knew he wasn't interested in either option. He hesitated to answer and wiggled uncomfortably in the grip of the vampire duo. Sofia signaled her impatience by tightening her claw-like hold on his nuts. The pain was extraordinarily unique and mighty. Ratt moaned as a sickness rose through his lower abdomen up into chest. He squirmed and would have collapsed to the cold floor if the vampire behind him were not holding him up by the neck.

His moan turned to a high-pitched shriek as her nails came closer together. He was sure that his skin was punctured in more than one place, and his groin felt wet, like he had pissed himself. His mind became plagued with unwanted, white-hot images of cherry tomatoes and grapes sliding onto a kabob skewer.

As if by some blessed act of providence, her sadistic game stopped suddenly, and she all but brushed Ratt aside, her attention caught but something urgent.

"Raphael! They are getting away!" she shrieked, releasing Ratt's traumatized scrotum and running past him.

The man, Raphael, also released his grip on Ratt and ran after Sofia.

Cursing himself for not being strong like Lucy, or the new guys, Jon and Carbine, Ratt slumped to the ground like a tired canvas bag filled with ground maize.

They? he wondered as he lay there. He rolled over, turning his gaze out to the arena, and watched in helpless grief as Sofia and Raphael leapt down from the landing onto the ground below and ran down the fleeing woman and her bundle of rags, which had begun to make sounds horrifyingly like the cries of a human baby.

Oh God, no.

Ratt hated himself. He was the helpless child who stood by and watched his family shot down like dogs in the street all over again.

The human woman, clutching her child, tried to run, but Raphael sprang into the air and landed in front of her, cutting her off. The vampire thug turned and spread his arms out wide, shimmying to the left and then the right as the terrified mother tried in vain to dart around him.

In the time it took for the mother's panicked heart to pulse a single beat more, Sofia was upon her.

The queen of New Puebla grabbed her human ward from behind by the hair and pulled her to the ground. The mother spun around so fast her feet left the ground, and she was thrown several meters when Sofia released her grip. The mother hit the ground and slid across the dirt floor.

Somehow, she'd managed to maintain her grip on the crying baby through the spin and slide. Her screams for mercy joined the wails of her child, but she remained on the ground.

Ratt could take no more and willed his fear and pain away. He pushed himself up and staggered to the edge of the landing just as Raphael and Sofia pounced on the mother and child like two cats springing onto a trapped mouse.

"Stop it, you animals!" Ratt yelled. Both vampires heard him and, surprisingly, stopped what they were doing to look up at him. Even from this distance and with only the light of the wavering torch flame to illuminate the scene, Ratt could see that both Raphael and Sofia had bloody maws. They looked the way a toddler did on its first birthday, with the remains of cake smeared all over its mouth, cheeks, and chin; but the ghastly mess on their faces was not cake, and their victim would surely never have a birthday again.

The killers studied Ratt for an absent heartbeat and then returned to their meal. Ratt could still hear the cries of the infant, so he pulled himself over the rail on the edge of the landing and dropped down to the sandy ground below. His feet hit the soft sand, which gave way more than he had anticipated. With a sharp pain, his right ankle rolled, and he fell to his side hard. Ignoring the pain that stuck to his ankle like glue, he pushed himself up, spat out a glob of sand-flecked saliva, and yelled once again at the monsters, who ignored him as they savaged the woman.

"I said leave them alone, you bastards!" Armed with nothing more than his fists and his sense of chivalry, he charged the grue-some scene before him, tears streaking down the sides of his face.

Ratt was nearly upon them, when, at the very last second, Raphael acknowledged his threat, such as it was, and sprang to his feet, delivering a spinning backhand to Ratt's face. Ratt heard his teeth clack and saw a bright flash of white light as the rest of the world faded to black.

He crumpled to the ground, knocked out for a second or two, but quickly returned to consciousness. As his eyes fluttered open, brushing sand away from his eyeball as they did, Ratt struggled for a full second to remember where he was and what he was doing.

Raphael sat down on his back and pinned Ratt's arms with his knees, just as the direness of the situation returned to him.

Ratt tried to struggle, but he may as well have tried to convince the entire vampire population of New Puebla to go vegan; it was futile. The fight, sadly, was over. Ratt wept, hating himself for being so weak and helpless. He heard and felt his neck pop again as Raphael reached down and grabbed his chin and forehead to yank his head to the side, exposing the tender flesh of his neck. He felt naked, overpowered, violated, and beyond frustrated.

Raphael leaned in, and Ratt braced himself for the bite, but it never came. His assailant sat back up and called out to Sofia.

"It doesn't have a stamp." Raphael sounded genuinely confused.

Sofia stopped feasting on the dying woman, left the crying baby still held in the woman's arms, and stepped over to Ratt and Raphael. She squatted down and examined Ratt's naked neck. She reached down and took Ratt's chin in a strong grip and turned his face up to hers. His neck screamed with the pain of such an awkward manipulation. He grimaced through the tears as she studied him.

"How the fuck did you get in here, *puto*?" Sofia hissed.

Through the fog of rage and grief, Ratt saw a light and made for it.

"I was invited here by the ruler of the city, Don Luis Fernando." Ratt caught the glance between the two of them; though he couldn't see the man, he knew he was looking back at Sofia, could see it in her eyes. Knowing that he was on the right track, Ratt continued.

"I am with Lily Sapphire. A guest of the king. I am Miss Sapphire's lighting technician." With that small handful of statements, Ratt may as well have shaped a powerful Strange on his assailants, for their demeanors both changed instantly and dramatically.

He saw the look of sadistic playfulness drain from Sofia's face as she removed her hand from his chin. She stood up and stepped back. Then, looking at Raphael, she spat, "This one lives."

Ratt exhaled.

"For now," she added.

Concern returned to Ratt's brow.

"Tell your employer what you saw here tonight. Tell her I am not pleased with her home-wrecking intrusion into my city and that after she does her little whore song and dance, I will show her, and you, the real hospitality of New Puebla. My husband be damned." Sofia turned her back on Ratt and stepped back over to the now dead woman and the crying baby.

Sofia squatted down, pried the swaddled baby from its dead mother's arms, and carried it back over to Ratt and Raphael. Ratt winced in fresh pain as the weight holding him down shifted deeper into the knees that pinched and pressed down into his arms.

While still pinning him effectively, Raphael came up off Ratt's back and met Sofia's approach.

"Watch closely, *puto*," Sofia said, the dark, sadistically playful quality having fully returned to her voice. She held the baby up. Its rags tumbled free from its shivering, naked body.

"No, please," Ratt grunted. The duo ignored him. Raphael took hold of the child's legs, and Sofia moved her grip from the babe's underarms to its tiny forearms. She took a half step back and pulled the baby back into a horizontal position, drawn up by its four limbs, held aloft by the two murderous vampires.

Sofia smiled cruelly down at the pinned Ratt, her heavily made-up eyes wide with bloodlust and demonic joy.

"Make a wish."

14

Don Luis took Maya by the arm and hurried her along, back into the palace. His sudden urgency alarmed Maya, and she wondered for a minute whether the vampire lord would be able to restrain himself until tomorrow night, and whether or not she might have just gotten herself in the kind of trouble she didn't want to be in without her guardians. Maya had put on a spectacular show in convincing Don Luis of her desire to join him, but if he called her bluff before she was ready, she wasn't sure she would be able to deal with him alone. Sure, she could shape a Strange to open a small window to the other side of the planet, the side where the sun was out and shining, but would he stand idle while she sang her incantation?

"Where are you taking me, my lord?" Maya asked. Her escort stopped abruptly and turned to face her, still cradling her hand in his.

"Please, as I said before, call me Don Luis. Soon you will be my wife. There is no need for such formalities." He gave her a wide grin. "I am going to show you the source of all this wonder, the Being that made this possible. I want to show you your new god."

It seemed to Maya that he wasn't speaking cryptically on purpose, but that he was drunk on the idea of turning and marrying her. He spoke like a poet who had become consumed by his muse. But while the exact meaning of his statement still eluded her, Maya felt that something important was about to happen, so she took a deep breath, bravely calmed her beating heart, and smiled back, knowing that she needed to be paying attention and be on her guard.

"Sounds fascinating. Please, Don Luis, lead on."

He did just that, guiding her into the very depths of the palace, past dozens of guards both vampiric and human. She feigned giddiness and fascination as they went.

"But first, we need to stop and get something," he explained, as though she would know any different.

"Whatever you say, good sir."

He led her down a dead-end hallway, where a ceiling-high ornate wooden cabinet stood towering like a night's watchman. Floral patterns, first etched, then painted, decorated both doors of the enormous cabinet. Maya decided that although décor in a monster's castle, it was admittedly beautiful, and was a testament to fine craftsmanship.

"What is this all about?" Maya inquired, trying to sound casual.

"A little protection, just in case," Don Luis said with a wink. Then, turning, he reached inside the wide opening of his shirt and fished out a thin string of leather, worn like a necklace. He pulled the loop off his head and Maya noticed that a small brass key dangled from it.

"Behold, one of my most prized possessions," Don Luis said as he used the key to unlock and then open the cabinet doors.

On the other side of the curio's double doors rested a pistol of a design Maya had never seen before. Highly polished, clad in chrome, the weapon was mounted in an open-faced shadowbox picture frame, the back of which was fitted with a deep purple crushed velvet.

Don Luis gently plucked the pistol from its mounting hooks and turned it over in his hand, admiring it.

"This was a prototype. A weapon in its infancy, developed by the American military right before the Storm. It belonged to the Cartel Don whom I worked for," he explained, never taking his glowing eyes off the instrument.

"I'm not much of a weapons enthusiast, but it's quite lovely," Maya said, wondering nervously where this was headed, and what he needed a pistol for. "What, um… caliber is it?" she asked.

"It doesn't have one. This, my dear Lily, is a laser pistol. The only one left of its kind, I'm sure."

Maya widened her eyes in a combination of feigned and real interest but said nothing.

"It fires a single beam that can travel far straighter and far longer than any conventional bullet. When it finds its target, the super-charged electrons excite and combust whatever material it encounters, almost instantly. Had the Storm not occurred, I have no doubt this bad boy would have gone into mass production and eventually replaced most conventional weapons. Sadly, the beam has the same effect on the air it passes through, so the range is limited, for the beam will burn itself out eventually. It's my favorite toy."

"Why do we need it right now?" Maya asked, hoping she didn't sound as nervous as she felt.

"As I said, it's an insurance policy."

"For what?"

"You'll see. Come, follow me to the heart of my palace." Keeping the precious technological relic in his grip, Don Luis led her back out of the dead-end and deeper into the catacombs.

The air down in the catacombs of the palace was cool and wet and smelled of decay. As they walked on, Don Luis began to tell a tale, a tale of the hell that was Earth after the Great Storm, a tale of life after death, and of how both he and New Puebla had come to be.

"I haven't told you how old I am, Lily," Don Luis began. "But when I tell you that I was the same age that I appear to be now when the Great Storm happened, I am not lying. Back then, before the Storm, I lived in Old Puebla, or just 'Puebla,' as it was called then. I wasn't always a king, a ruler, you know. Does that surprise you?" He smirked at his queen-to-be. She smiled back coyly. "I know that is hard to believe—the suit fits me so well, you would think I were born into it—but no. I saw my chance at destiny and seized it." He slowed his walk for a second and reached behind Maya, placing his hand on her buttocks, and squeezed halfway between gentle and firm.

"Just as you are doing now, my dear." Ever the performer, Maya as Lily swallowed her disgust and instead bounced her eyebrows up and down and purred. Don Luis removed his hand, and they walked on.

"Tell me more."

"Before the Storm, I grew up a poor child. At the age of seven, my father was killed. Complications from dealings with the cartels. My mother was left to take care of my three younger siblings and me. This I could not abide. I swallowed my pride and turned my back on my childhood. I went to see the very men responsible for my father's execution. I'm not sure if this amused them or impressed them, but they took me in and gave me work. I started out as a courier, but I soon worked my way up to soldier, and by the time I should have been graduating high school in another world, I was running a crew and making boatloads of cold, hard cash. My mother and siblings never went without anything. I provided for them in all ways, but I had to do so from a distance. My mother hated me for working for the cartel. Can you believe that? She never once said thank you for all the things

I did for her and the children! I *killed* for her! And she never—!" Don Luis caught himself starting to go off, stopped, and collected himself.

As Maya listened, she began to form an understanding of this man. He was too far down the road for her to truly sympathize with him, but she did begin to see the link between who he had been then and who he was now.

"Many people despised the cartel for its methods, but what they failed to understand is that it provided a type of order. Its methods were in reality no more brutal than any government of the world; sometimes, people need killing for the order to be maintained, for the money to flow. And it always flows uphill. It's easy to hate a cartel and love a state. But what cartel ever killed as many people as any of the world's wars? The dons always gave back to their community and protected those who knew their place and didn't cause trouble. Now that I look back on it, those days growing up is where I studied and learned my methods. I run this city on the same principles, and everyone here, every single man, woman, and child, is infinitely better off under my wing than on their own, out in the chaos of the world. That is a truth that everyone in Old Puebla learned when the Storm came."

They reached an intersection of stairs, one leading up and the other down. Don Luis gestured to the set leading down, and Maya nodded her understanding, keeping silent to allow him to continue his soliloquy.

"You see, the people never saw the actual order and stability that the cartel brought to the city until it was gone. When the Storm came, and the east coast was flooded, and the ground broke open from all the earthquakes, the seams of the system began to unravel. The head of the cartel, a man named Garcia, died along with his inner circle in the first quake. A gas main ruptured and caused an explosion that took out all the upper management in one instant. Ambitious lieutenants and rivals took advantage of the missing, dead, and distracted leaders of the cartel. War broke out nearly overnight. Food and clean water shortages caused the common people to turn on each other. The cartels were broken and weren't able to maintain order in the common population, and so chaos ensued." Don Luis paused, both in speech and walk, and turned to look at Maya. A fire smoldered in his undead eyes.

"Then the Drops happened. What was left of the cartel's soldiers tried to fight off the first wave of monsters, but without their leadership, they soon degenerated into small gangs. Before a month had passed, it was all just a memory. There was no civilization left. If Garcia had lived, he could have maintained order and things would have been different. Without him at the helm, the people, the *masses*," Don Luis nearly spat the word, his voice dripping with disdain, "the useless feeders who always bemoaned their status under the cartel, were finally free to run the show themselves, and just look at how they handled it. Not even a month to go from their stable lives to complete barbarism." Don Luis laughed at this.

Maya wondered at the mind that could think and believe such a spin on the story of the Fall. They walked down one last flight of stone steps and came to a large, circular slab of rock that served as a door.

"My mother and siblings all died shortly after the world dipped into madness. They say nature abhors a vacuum and I believe it. Without a ruler, without the cartel, my people were lost. No better off than animals. *This* changed all that." Don Luis let go of Maya's hand, stepped up to the door-slab, and placed his hands on it.

Even in the dim light cast by the torches now some distance above, Maya could see that the round slab was not featureless. Every square inch of it was covered in an Aztec motif, much like the ubiquitous tattoos that decorated the necks of every human in the city. The carvings were raised, embossed, and she could see what looked like a primitive depiction of what could only be described as a demon's face in the center of the slab. It had several fanged mouths and many eyes. It was monstrous, alien, and non-mammalian. Even in her guise as a vampire-enthralled Lily Sapphire, Maya was unable to suppress the slight cold shiver that ran up and down her spine, causing a wave of goosebumps. Her soft arm and neck hairs stood up as if being drawn toward something on the other side of the slab, as if by the pull of a dark star.

She watched as Don Luis slid his hands into two of the door-demon's mouths. He hissed in masochistic pleasure and then removed his hands, now bleeding. It looked like he had reached his hands into a bucket of gore.

Maya began to wonder about the nature of the door's mouth and the source of the blood on Don Luis's hands, but then watched as the red streams dried up and vanished like a pond in a drought.

That was his blood. But why? What is this?

Tiny trickles of blood leaked from the stone demon's mouth, and then the slab began to roll to the side, opening the way to the chamber beyond. The light from the torches did not penetrate the room; it was as if the darkness, normally a simple lack of light, were an actual curtain here, blanketing the chamber beyond. The smell of death emanating from the blackness was overpowering, and Maya winced, fighting back the compulsion to cover her mouth and nose.

Don Luis stepped up close behind Maya and placed one hand on her elbow, the other on the small of her back. An involuntary shudder ran down her spine. He nudged her forward. She told herself that Don Luis hadn't brought her this far, talked to and gushed over her this much just to lead her into a death trap. He could have killed her ages ago if he'd wanted—or at least tried to—and so she collected herself and took a hesitant step forward.

Her foot pierced the curtain of dark as if it were nothing, yet her toes, then foot, then shin disappeared so fully from her sight, she looked like an amputee.

She felt a cold creeping up her leg and felt Don Luis nudge her again. She set her one foot down on the other side and stepped forward with her other, bringing the black to her face like a handful of cupped water from a pool.

Cold. Darkness and cold. Then she opened her eyes on the other side of the curtain in a small, round chamber of stone. Don Luis was beside her, plucking an unlit torch from the inner chamber's wall and lighting it. It turned out that the room was the source of the stench, not the curtain of black, and thanks to the flickering torchlight, Maya was able to see what caused it.

There, in the center of the round chamber, chained to the floor in a dozen places, sat a living creature the likes of which Maya had never seen in all her long years.

It was the size of Carbine's old Mini-Mech and resembled an emaciated sea urchin with noodle-like, prehensile spines, each ending in a tubular mouth or sucker instead of a sharp point. The creature appeared near death, or extremely tired, for the spine tubes that protruded from the upper hemisphere of the thing's body all drooped limply across its mass and reached as far as the floor.

It looked defeated and deflated. Maya saw it try to writhe, even managing to weakly lift a few of its spine tubes off the floor and point them in their direction. The alien appendages probed the air and behaved as if they were sniffing. The mouths at the end of the spine tubes opened and closed rhythmically, like a fish scenting the water.

Maya couldn't see well in the dim, fluctuating torchlight, but her eyes caught the blur of rapid movement every time a tube mouth gaped open. Her eyes narrowed, and she leaned forward unconsciously to get a closer look. She noticed a long, skinny, needle-like probe shoot in and out of the nearest mouth nearly as fast as a hummingbird's wings.

The flashing needle in the spine's mouth added to the sniffing quality of the creature's behavior; each tentacle-like appendage looked like a large snake with a stiletto for a tongue. They behaved autonomously, yet were connected, like a pack of wolves working together to hunt prey.

Maya wondered how this creature would look and behave if it were at its peak strength, and shuddered, banishing the thought from her imagination. The creature was the very definition, the anthropomorphic manifestation, of hungry. It seemed to possess a hundred mouths and nearly nothing else.

"What *is* it?" she dared to ask, her voice muffling the slithering sounds of both the needles rapidly sheathing and unsheathing and the wiggling of the tentacles themselves.

"This is our Progenitor. The Hunger. It's not every man that gets to meet his maker." Don Luis stepped forward, away from Maya and toward the creature.

The limp, tired appendages that only a moment before had seemed on death's door now leapt off the floor and snapped at Don Luis, the torchlight flashing off their needle-probes in the dark. Maya gasped.

"A bit more common is the man who kills his maker. God is dead, so they say. And while I haven't killed my god—*can't* kill my god—I have dominated it and surpassed it."

Maya listened to Don Luis gloat and wondered at what he meant by "can't kill my god." She decided it best not to ask too many questions, lest he realize his slip of the tongue.

"As you can see, it is a little angry over this fact." Don Luis waved his torch at the reaching spine tubes, and they recoiled from the heat.

"I was dying, like the rest of the rabble that survived the Storm, eking out a miserable existence in what was left of the world. Between the bandits, the Drop-trash, and then the advent of the Harvesters, my prospects for longevity were not good. Not good, that is, until I stumbled upon this thing before you. I had been crossing an open bled of desert when a sandstorm began to rise just east of me. It looked bad; it looked like it was growing, and it looked like there was a very good chance that it would soon be coming my way. It would have killed me for sure. I was already malnourished and weak. *Dame Fortuna* would smile on me that day, as she has every night since, for not far from where I was lay a small outcropping of rock, an archipelago of stony hills; a good place to seek shelter, for it was probable that I would find a cave or at least a crevasse in which to hide." Don Luis stared ahead into the room, through and past the creature bound there, reliving in his mind's eye the events that he related to Maya.

"I made it to the rocks just minutes before the sandstorm made it to me, and a cave I did find. I crept into its darkness without regard for my safety. To remain outside would have surely meant death by exposure. What I found inside I thought worse, at first…"

Maya allowed herself to look as intrigued, as she actually was. Don Luis continued his monologue.

"From the darkness came the stings. I felt molten pain in several places over my body at once. I could hear the slithering and sucking of a hundred mouths. I screamed, and my cries of pain echoed off the cave walls, driving me mad. It was a nightmare, and I thought for sure that I was just another victim of the Drops, another post-Storm casualty, that my life was finally over and had meant nothing in the end. It bound me in its vast array of tentacles and fed on me until the darkness of the cave was replaced by the darker black of unconsciousness." Don Luis opened and closed his hand, making several fists as he recalled his torture at the hands of the Drop-Beastie.

"After some time, I have no idea how long, I awoke. There

was no pain and my first thought was that I was in Heaven or Hell. A leftover from my early childhood; my poor mama was a simple-minded Catholic woman, but it's not her fault, for it was part of our culture before the Storm and the Drops. Now, even the most innocent child knows the only god is he who takes and makes for himself. As I have." His eyes glowed with self-righteous pride as he spoke. Maya felt a chill run down her back as she attempted to digest this man's misguided way of thinking.

"Soon I realized that I was still on this Earth—the cold dirt floor of the cave gave it away, though I wasn't keen to the fact that I was not quite alive." At this, he grinned like a spoiled child who got the toy he felt he deserved. "I was attacked, but not killed... or so I thought. I knew not where the stinging tubes were, and I didn't want to stick around to find out. To this day, I have wondered deeply as to the exact nature, the mechanism of this thing, and the vampiric, immortal qualities it bestows on its victims. Are they a side-effect of this being's eating habits? Its alien biological needs? Or is it simply how it breeds? Sure, that sounds crazy, but who are we to question the mechanics of alien and human interaction? I call what I am "vampire," but what does that mean? That is a human word, from ancient mythology, yet here I stand, bitten—well, stung, rather—eaten and killed by an alien, yet now immortal, superhuman. Truly born again. Fire and sunlight kill me, and I need blood to survive. The shoe fits, and I care not to ponder semantics."

"It's as good as a description as any," Maya agreed, looking back and forth from the alien urchin to Don Luis.

"I left the cave in a weakened state, having been killed and not yet having fed. I was in a fever, a dream state, and I remember not where I wandered. The last thing I remember is the night sky beginning to turn lavender with the promise of dawn soon to be, and collapsing on the desert floor, the weight of the sky pressing me down. A band of human survivors came across me; they must have. I only remember vague images as I floated in and out of consciousness. Men and women, inheritors of pre-Storm military equipment and weapons, carving out a meager, post-apocalyptic life. I remember the noise of their vehicles, the old kind that still ran on fossil fuels, and their voices. They just happened to be on the move, and their paths crossed mine that fateful night. Good for me, bad for them. I faded in and out over the next day and a half. Maybe longer. They must have put me in the back of one of their large trucks and assigned someone to care for me. I don't know how it all played out... I never got the chance to ask them..." Don Luis waxed nostalgic and smiled.

The urchin lunged for him again with a volley of outstretched tentacles. They fell short, unable to reach him. Their vain attempt snapped him out of his reverie, and he spun on them, striking one with the torch. Maya blinked as the torch left a comet's tail tracer through the chamber's darkness and blinked again when she heard the flat, wet smack of the tentacle being hit. The spine tubes withdrew again, like a beaten dog, and attempted to bite Don Luis no more.

"It must have been days now that I think about it, but at one point, I was back, only it wasn't the old me. It was the new me. I awoke in the back of a truck on a bed that my saviors had prepared for me. I could hear the cicadas of the night blanketing all the other sounds, but what I remember most is the *hunger*. Like this thing here," Don Luis pointed at the urchin with his torch, "I was possessed by an insatiable hunger, the likes of which I had never experienced, even as a starving, malnourished youth, hustling in the streets of Old Puebla, back before the dons took me in. I remember then, for the first time, I could smell my cure. I could smell the blood that lay trapped inside the bodies of every man and woman in that caravan's camp. Back then, that first time, it felt like I had no control. It wasn't until after, when I had had my fill, that I saw a better way. I tore through that camp the way the tidal waves and hurricanes from the Great Storm had torn through the coastal towns of my country. Nothing could stop me. *Nothing.* I was a force of nature." Don Luis's eyes glinted red, and his voice rose in volume as he told his tale.

"Toward the end there, some tried to stop me. They shot me full of bullets, which I squeezed out of my body by simply thinking about it. The ease with which I slaughtered them, all thirty-something of them, is probably what made it click in my head later that night. The idea, the notion, the *truth*, that I was not an animal, but a *god.* A wolf amongst dogs was an understatement.

"I was not content to live like a savage and hunt my prey in the wilds the way those who attacked you did. I had a much grander vision, and so I set out on a quest. I sought out and approached the *banditos* that roamed the countryside and made them offers. Offers of immortality and power. Offers they couldn't refuse. Those who did became my dinner. Those who didn't became the soldiers in my new army; the lieutenants in my new cartel. We organized, we grew, we built. Before long, we took human slaves and kept them in pens, kept them alive and used them as our never-fail, always-available food source. One thing led to another. I rewarded the most obedient humans with privileges of comfort and some manner of freedom, and soon my cartel had loyal foot soldiers that could serve and protect me during the daylight hours. The system of reciprocation I showed you tonight developed. This city was built. This kingdom was born. The rest, as they say, is history."

Maya listened intently, and, encouraged by the candid nature of Don Luis's tale, she continued to stare longingly into his dark eyes, continuing her charade of excitement and arousal. She would have done any actress from Ratt's old cinema movies proud. Don Luis, excited by Maya's show of interest, continued his tale without reservation.

"The world was my oyster, or so the saying goes, but one thing loomed over my shoulders, one thought troubled my daily torpor. It was the same, age-old question that has haunted every man since time began. Being essentially immortal did not make this ponderous conundrum go away."

"What was it?" Maya asked huskily between heavy breaths.

"Where did I come from? Or, more precisely, who made me?" Don Luis's eyes flashed like fire. "The question turned from a mildly amusing riddle to a burning need, an obsession as strong as my thirst for blood. Especially one night after I observed a peculiar phenomenon." Don Luis stared off at the blank walls of the chamber as he recalled the event that had changed his afterlife.

"A few years after New Puebla had become the functional society that it is today, I was betrayed and bitterly disappointed by one of my top lieutenants. The man, a cousin of my Sofia, disobeyed a direct order I had given him. It's been so many years now that I can't remember exactly what the order was anymore..." Don Luis trailed off; then his eyes flashed again.

"It had something to do with taking the cattle, er, humans in public. Yes, yes, that was it! I told my men that they couldn't do that. It would create fear and dissent. It was the same reason that a rancher removed the animal to be slaughtered from the animals that were to remain alive. If you kill one in front of the others, they tend to... freak out, and things don't work as smoothly anymore." Maya got the clear and distinct message that it wasn't the rape and murder itself that Don Luis had outlawed, just the location. *Just don't do it in public.*

"Anyway, the man had done just that, and there was blowback. The humans rioted, and many had to be put down before order was restored. I was extremely angry with my fiancée's cousin for disobeying me and costing me a good percentage of my stock, not to mention the headache that all the PR would most assuredly give me. I chose to have this man executed in public the day before I married Sofia, cousin or no.

"Death by sun. It was easy; it was clean, not messy. It sent a strong message. The other vampires would learn to obey. The humans would be placated, feeling that justice had been served, that their king was fair and benevolent. Sofia would also learn that queen or no, cousin or no, *I* was the boss and *not* to be trifled with. It would set the stage for a healthy and proper marriage."

"*I* would never question your authority, my lord." Maya leaned in close to Don Luis and rubbed her body against his. He smiled at her and continued his tale.

"Still, it didn't quite work out the way I had envisioned. I had this man tied to a stake in the city square in the late hours of the evening. The humans had woken early, for all wanted to be there and witness the rising sun of justice, the King's Law. The vampires of the city, myself included, retired, of course, just before the first rays of dawn peeked over the horizon. We would come back at dusk to sweep away the ashes of our fallen comrade and take stock. And that is exactly what we did, but when it was over, the inventory was off, the numbers didn't add up. The lieutenant burned, all right, and according to loyal human testimony, it was a glorious torch. It gladdened the hearts of those who had lost friends and family during the brief uprising to witness some vampire death for once, and I was happy to provide it. I could not abide anyone disobeying my laws. But something revealed itself slowly as the night went on. A good number of my men seemed to be missing, most of them belonging to the contingent that the now-crispy lieutenant had commanded. At first, I thought, incredulously, that the lieutenant's men had been so loyal that they had left New Puebla in some sort of protest or tacit rebellion against my justice, but a quick search of their assigned domiciles revealed the truth of the situation." He paused. "They had burned in their sleep."

Honestly intrigued and no longer acting, Maya cocked her head a bit and squinted at Don Luis.

"At first, it was a mystery, but a clue fell into my lap in the form of a report from one of my close advisers. Every one of the vampires who had spontaneously combusted had been sired by the executed lieutenant. In fact, no one he had sired still lived. Every human ever turned by him had burned in their beds when he burned at the stake. I took this information from the adviser in secret and promptly killed him to silence him. Until now, no one else had ever found out the truth." He gripped Maya tightly, his lust for her burning in those unearthly eyes.

"Kill the headwaters of the river, and you kill the river." Maya's eyes widened with fevered interest and a ray of optimistic treason, though to Don Luis, her expression was one of horror and shock.

"This revelation sent stark terror into my heart. How could I be the undisputed ruler of this burgeoning kingdom if my Achilles' heel lay somewhere out there in the wilderness, just waiting to be found and exploited? I tackled this new quest with ten times more urgency, more fury and more resources than I had the building of this city-state. I led an army out into the desert hills where I had stumbled across the thing that had turned me. Although my recollection of that fateful night was blurry at best, I found the creature after only three weeks of tireless searching. Having to bring portable shelter and set up a hermetically sealed camp every morning slowed things down and made the expedition a little tough; capturing and subduing the demon urchin once we found it was more so. I lost nearly half my men to the urchin when they battled it, but my numbers and persistence paid off.

"I watched the creature as we battled it, I watched how it behaved. It seemed to grow stronger with every one of my men that it killed. I watched how it sucked them dry with its needle-mouth-tentacles and turned them from herculean immortals into something more resembling a dried-up maize husk. I quickly realized that it grew strong with the blood of its victims the same way I do, the same way all vampires do. And why not? It was what made us. I was sure of it. This thing…" Don Luis gestured to the limp and exhausted demon urchin chained in cold iron to the chamber floor.

"This thing was the original vampire. As much as I am loath to admit it. I am nothing more than the spawn of a creature from the Drops. I still don't have any way of proving it, but somehow, I know, from a whisper in my mind, that all the bloodlines can be traced to this creature, and I felt that it had been here on Earth before. Later, I proved that theory to be true. It had been here before, though how, and for how long, I cannot say."

Maya wondered what he meant by this and recalled the cryptic message that Ratt had received from the intelligence behind the Drop.

"I ordered my men to fall back, and instead, we surrounded the creature's lair and starved it. Anytime the thing attempted to leave its lair and do battle with us, we chased it back into the cave with arrows of fire. I learned early on of the thing's fear of flame. Hence the need for this insurance policy." Don Luis raised the laser pistol and waved it for Maya to see.

"Our perimeter was so tight that not even a small field rodent could get into the cave and provide sustenance to the thing. I had outsmarted it, for, despite all its power, it was simply an animal. Yes! *I* had outsmarted it, and I meant to outlast it. We fed first on the humans that we had brought with us to help watch over us during the day. It was risky, but everything that I had witnessed thus far led me to believe that the creature could no more wade into the sunlight than its creations could.

"While I couldn't control any small animal possibly getting into the cave during the day, the payoff was worth it. My vampires and I fed well and grew strong, while the strength of the demon-thing waned with the passing of each day. Besides, the chance of any creature of a substantial size just wandering in was remote. I had the beast to the wall, so to speak. We tested the waters for two days after the last human in our party had been drained dry. The beast was still beyond us, so we made a hasty retreat. I decided that my top officers and I would feed on the lesser foot-soldier vampires in the party. My regiment shrank in size but grew in power and, within another week, the beast was near starved. When we finally entered the cave, we found it in a condition much as you see here. Using fire and steel, we corralled and caged the beast. We performed bloodletting on it and brought it to the edge of death, but I dared not let it die and even had to resort to sacrificing one of my officers to it on the journey home. That was nearly a disaster..." Don Luis glanced down at Maya and then wrapped up his tale.

"Let's just say that the trip home was arduous and harrowing and even once here, it took me quite a while and cost me quite a bit of manpower before I could find the right balance between life and death at which to keep this thing. But balance I did find, and now I am nigh-unstoppable. I keep my god in chains, in the depths of my palace, and no one, save you and me, knows the value of it." He smiled a self-satisfied smile. "Once you are my wife, you will be as powerful and safe from harm as anyone ever was or could be. We will rule over the masses forever!" He was drunk on his lust, he was mad, and Maya smiled.

"You mentioned that it has been on Earth before?" she asked, wanting to seize the chance to possibly illuminate Ratt's mysterious message.

"Oh, yes," Don Luis gloated. "To say that I became obsessed with my god is an understatement, my dear. For the last sixty years, I have sent my agents into the lands of Mexico-That-Was. To hunt down any clue that might help me to understand what I had become. After many long decades, the search paid off."

"What? What did you find?" Maya asked, pressing herself closer to him, gazing longingly into his eyes. "I want to know everything!"

"Come, let me show you."

***

"Behold, the evidence," Don Luis said, gesturing to a large book, propped open with care in an ornate wrought-iron easel that adorned his bedroom's largest oak table.

Maya slowly approached the book. Even from across the room, she could make out faded illuminations, the kind she had not seen firsthand in well over a thousand years.

"Written and illustrated proof that our maker has been with us for some time," Don Luis said from behind her, hanging back.

The book looked heavy. Heavy and old. As she came to it, she cautiously extended two fingers and brushed their tips across the rough and crackled edges of the painted and time-stained pages. Handwritten text in the patient style of calligraphers past filled the majority of both pages currently on display. The ink appeared to be made with actual silver and gold, as it was radiant, too radiant for its age. She recognized the language instantly, although the nuances of the dialect were older than Don Luis Fernando ten times over.

Spanish. Old Spanish.

Besides the ancient text, the top half of the right page was filled by an illustration, illuminated in the way of countless religious frescos and manuscripts.

When Maya leaned in and studied the depiction closer, she gasped.

"Stunning, isn't it?" Don Luis asked softly, his approaching footfalls punctuating the space between Maya's accelerated breaths. "The iconographers captured its likeness perfectly."

On the open page, a hand-drawn simulacrum of the Demon Urchin stared at Maya with open, fanged sucker-mouths at the end of its multitude of tentacles.

"H-how?" Maya asked, honestly puzzled. She had existed on Earth for millennia and hadn't seen a single interstellar being walk, or slither, on its surface since the first imprisonment of her late husband, Enki.

Having reached her side, Don Luis gestured to the book. "This," he began, "is the Codex Sitis Autem Sanguis. Compiled by religious brothers in my country's first Dominican monastery. Its founders, the very calligraphers and iconographers that wrote this book, were among some of the first priests brought to the new world at the request of Cortez, a man I admire, a man who knew how to achieve his goals. A kindred spirit."

Maya looked into Don Luis's eyes and could see that he was telling the truth. And why should she doubt him? The proof was staring her in the face. She turned back to the book and allowed her gaze to loiter on the icon. There was no mistaking it; it was the urchin. Her gazed drifted over the calligraphy. Words jumped out at her: blood, fire, devil, Lucifer, sunlight. She shivered.

"The conquistadors of Spain came to this new world in search of gold. Instead, they found the devil himself."

"So it has been here since before the Storm. Before the Drops," Maya stated, more of a proclamation than a question.

"We aren't actually sure. It may be that it merely visited somehow."

Maya spun on him and studied him, her face begging the unspoken question.

"See here?" he said, and stepped in closer, reaching past her and carefully flipping the thick, stiff pages of the Codex one at a time. "Ah, yes, right here." He pointed to a long passage of hand-writing, the only illustrations the decorative frame around the letters and a crucifix on the bottom of the second page.

"The brothers tell here of having met with Juan de Zumárraga, the first Bishop of my country, and his Franciscans. They discuss here their knowledge of the demon's weakness. See?" Don Luis ran his finger across the strings of letters.

"They accompanied the soldiers and Cortez himself to the devil's lair, prepared to do battle with fire 'with God on our side,' they say. But when they arrived, the beast disappeared before their eyes, never to be seen again. They report strange colors in the sky, and what can only be an earthquake. 'The land itself shook with the wrath of the Lord, crumbling stone, and toppling trees. The earth broke open and swallowed the unwary. The heavens parted, and we beheld the glory of our Lord, flashes of *relámpago*, lightning, and a host of angels filled the night sky. When we arrived at the lair of Lucifer, we watched in disbelief as he faded from our eyes, surrounded by flashing cubes. God himself had done the work for us, blessed be his name, Jesu Christo, nuestro Dios.'"

"Incredible," Maya said, not sure what else to say. Her mind was aflood with questions, however, questions that she couldn't ask without revealing to her host that she was older than he and possessed a deeper understanding of the world's history than a traveling troubadour ought to.

"Do you think it could happen again?" she asked, genuinely wanting to know.

"Perhaps. But I certainly hope not. Without me to protect it, my fate would be uncertain. And I, my bride-to-be, am in no hurry to die."

"Man, I am starving!" Carbine said, rubbing his belly to emphasize his spoken lament. "What I wouldn't give to be down there in Ratt's place and get me some real tacos."

"We still have three tubes of ration paste left, bud," Jon reminded him.

"Oh. Boy. Ration paste. My favorite," Carbine said in a monotone voice and went about digging the tube out of his ruck.

"Jon? Boys?" a voice in Jon's ear called.

When Jon heard Maya speak his name into the necklace radio, he nearly fell down the mountain, first springing upright, then stumbling over the rocks that jutted out of the earth like speed bumps, and finally crashing down onto the boulder upon which the railgun sat.

"What's gotten into you?" Carbine asked. "You hungry too?"

"It's Maya! She's back!" Jon shouted as he wiggled down next to the mounted rifle and scope. He wished more than anything that he could answer Maya, tell her how good it was to know she was all right. But he could not, so he settled for allowing tears of joyful relief to fall down his face. He struggled to maintain his vision through bleary eyes that searched through the railgun's scope for the visual counterpart to Maya's heavenly voice.

He had to see her to know that he was not just having auditory hallucinations.

There she was, with Lucy and Ratt, all three of them back in the room together, without a hair on their heads harmed, except for Ratt, who looked like he had been through the wringer. He laugh-cried as all the stress and anxiety of the past evening washed out of him in strong, emotional waves.

"I am so sorry for forgetting the necklace earlier. You guys must have been pretty worried," Maya said.

"It's okay. I'm just glad you're all right," Jon replied, knowing that she couldn't hear him.

"Well, I don't know if you saw me or not, but I know you didn't hear what happened, so I'm going to give you my report anyway. Listen up, guys, 'cause we have some serious news for you."

Jon listened to Maya's recounting of the night's events as dawn's fingers began to reach out over the landscape, probing the darkness like a fumbling but insistent lover.

Jon listened as Maya related the story of her pampering in the bath—some of which Jon was already embarrassingly familiar with—and her dinner with Don Luis and Sofia, Sofia's hostility toward her, and her walk with Don Luis into the evening air.

She told Jon of Don Luis's vision for a civilized society of vampire masters and human cattle who were cared for and protected in exchange for a blood tax and their lawful obedience. It boggled Jon's mind that the system not only worked, but worked so well.

It would seem at a glance that none of the humans who dwelt inside the protective wall of New Puebla considered themselves slaves or captives. Like the cows of Don Luis's parable, the humans had seemingly grown one hundred percent dependent on their masters. They not only gave up their blood and their freedom willingly, but they also went so far as to police each other in the name of and for the sake of the vampires.

It was also clear that the humans outnumbered the vampires twenty to one, yet every morning, as today, the vampires slept soundly in their crypt-like homes, safe and sound, with peace of mind. Despite the fact that their dwellings were neither secret nor hidden, the notion that the humans might turn against the vampires and murder them in their sleep was not even dreamed of.

Or so it seemed.

"Truth is, guys," Maya explained, "as distasteful as it may seem to us at first, to have monsters ruling over humans, the system works. I was convinced for a bit that the best thing for us to do, at least for now—that is, until we recover the Anvil—was to leave these people to live in peace. I thought that if we were to try and take out the vampires and free them, it would only expose these simple people to other threats, the obvious being things from the Drops that aren't as accommodating."

As Jon related to Carbine what Maya had told him, Carbine and Jon were both quick to judge the human citizens harshly for their willingness to give up and become domesticated slaves of a blood-tax farm. Jon was puzzled and felt ashamed for the people in the valley below, but when Carbine gave voice to their shared incredulity, Jon realized that he was in no position to criticize. Maya was right; it would be immoral of them to impose freedom on these people.

Although the exact details of the circumstances differed, had not he and other citizens of Home been guilty of the same craven, unquestionable submissiveness to Accoba Warbak? So much so that they had no longer been aware that they had even submitted? It had become a gestalt, an institution. Complete obedience to the state and compliance with its draconian pogrom against the Displaced had been the law of the land for generations.

Were those who willingly gave up their blood to the rulers and accepted their lower standard of living as a law of nature any more shameful and cowardly than those who'd believed without question the orders from their State? Were the citizens of New Puebla any different from those who'd never questioned the rule not to read? Who'd never questioned the State, and stood by as "illegal aliens" were slaughtered? Who were even complicit in the terrifying witch hunts conducted by the Ministry of Social Purity against the neighbors and children of Home who had been born with the ability to shape Strange, or had dared to read a book?

No, Jon himself had been just as guilty of lying down as the people of New Puebla. They thought that this was just how things were. Jon hadn't realized the nature of his transgressions either. He had believed every lie ever told by the State, until someone had opened his eyes, freed him, and shown him the truth. And, considering the protection these people gained in exchange for the paltry price of blood that would refresh itself, he realized that he would make the same choices as the citizens of New Puebla. At least with the vampires present, New Puebla stood a fighting chance should the Harvesters ever happen this way.

"But what does she mean by *at first*?" Carbine asked. Curious, Jon shrugged and went back to listening to the goddess's report.

Maya now related to Jon and Carbine what Ratt had seen while he'd wandered the city on his own. Ratt had witnessed something horrible that put everything else and their possible courses of action into perspective.

"You see?" Maya went on. "After spending the whole night with Don Luis, even after seeing the urchin demon, I couldn't shake the feeling that the lesser of two evils was to just try and get out of here during the day, slipping away from Don Luis Fernando, and leaving the sleeping dogs to lie. I hate the idea of allowing such a demonic entity to exist, but everything actually seemed to be fairly decent here, by post-Storm standards. Then, after Ratt came stumbling back in, and Lucy returned, and they told me what transpired, what they had each experienced, I realized that things may not be as they appear.

"They killed a human baby, Jon. For sport. And its mother. They made Ratt watch. There is evil here. It may be slow and hard to see, but it's here. Last night, Lucy encountered a poor family who had their father taken from them. The oldest child of this family told Lucy that no one is allowed to leave the city, that they are viewed as property, possessions. He also told her that he and many others are wanting to form some kind of resistance, but don't know where to start. Later this morning, Lucy went among the people, after the vampires had gone to sleep, and she collected many, many tales of people going missing. Especially anyone that can shape Strange. Sound familiar? They don't go missing so frequently as to lower the population noticeably, but enough to keep the population right where it is. Everyone here pays in blood, but some more than others."

Jon listened, but in the back of his mind, he was dreaming of revolution, freedom, liberty, revenge, and a spark of an idea began to form in his mind. Something that had happened to them out in the desert a week ago. He wasn't one hundred percent positive that his hunch was correct, but he quickly became willing to bet on it.

The brew of revolution was a heady one, and as his mind sipped on it, the sips turned to gulps, and before Maya had finished her tale, he was drunk on it.

Reeling, possessed, riveted. What Ratt had seen and experienced made their path clear. The people, the human people of New Puebla, had to be freed. It was Jon's duty to open the eyes and minds of the unconscious slaves who suffered, sometimes in a subtle way and sometimes overtly at the hands of blood-drinking monsters who killed mothers and babies for sport.

It might come at a steep cost, and the burden of self-responsibility was a heavy one, but the people of New Puebla would have to learn how to defend themselves from the chaos, without serving darkness.

The vampires all needed to die.

And Jon believed he knew exactly how to do that now.

15

Miller rapped his thick metal fingers on the table over and over again.

"Hey," Candice said, waving her hand in front of Miller's thousand-yard stare. "Can you please stop that? You're making *me* nervous."

"Huh? Oh, sorry," Miller said, stopping his subconscious finger-drumming and pulling his hand back from the table. He flashed Candice an unenthusiastic, wry half-smile and looked around the council chambers. Nearly everyone who was supposed to be here had arrived and was going about the business of giving and receiving greeting pleasantries, organizing papers in front of their seats, and dodging aides that were making sure the council members wouldn't want for coffee, tea, or water.

"Almost everyone is here," Candice said. Miller shifted his eyes to her. She had followed his gaze across the room and read his mind correctly. They should have started by now, a fact that only added to the palpable anxiety Miller wrestled with.

"Yeah..." he mumbled, rubbing his chin. "Everyone except To-Kan."

Another long minute passed. Miller watched the present

council members settle into their seats and make small talk with their neighbors as they waited. Despite the assurances he had given everyone, most notably and recently Candice, Miller began to wonder if he was making a mistake in trusting the fate of the New Republic to such a diverse and rag-tag group of people.

Nah, man. That's just the old Army training talking. We want, no, need *people up in here. Not jus' soldiers.*

"Are you trying to rub the stubble out? They make these things called razors, you know."

Miller found Candice staring at him again, a plea written on her freckled face.

"Huh? Oh. Sorry. Again," Miller said and took his hand from his face, where his chin-rubbing had replaced his finger-drumming and had almost reached neurotic levels. "I'm just nervous. Something didn't sit right in my craw, ya know? And To-Kan being late is killing me. I want to get this show on the road."

"I know, I know. But don't worry. Everything's going to be just fine." Candice smiled and patted the big man's hand. "Hey, speak of the devil!" she said and together with Miller turned to the set of double doors as they opened, revealing councilwoman To-Kan with a child in tow.

"What the—?" Miller asked out loud, but quietly enough that only he and Candice heard it.

Regardless, To-Kan seemed to know exactly what was on Miller's mind, and probably everyone else's as well and rushed to explain herself before she was barraged with a volley of questions.

"My apologies to the council," To-Kan began. Her breathing was labored and her wrinkled face slightly red. Suddenly, Miller felt a twang of guilt for being upset at the senior woman's tardiness.

"Councilwoman To-Kan," Miller said loudly, hushing the murmuring room as he stood up and leaned on the table. "You know you have nothing but our respect, but the chambers are not the place for a child."

The child in question was Wyntr, the foreign girl who had come to Home and who knew the resting place of the Morning Star, the very place Maya and Jon and the others had set out for weeks ago. The place where they hoped to find the Anvil, the secret weapon of the gods that would enable them to defeat the Harvesters and maybe even stop the Drops.

Wyntr had appeared in the Shanty and on the Underground's radar at the exact same time she appeared on that of the Ministry of Social Purity. Captured and imprisoned, Maya had allowed herself to be arrested so she could get close to the girl, betting everything on guardians she hadn't even met yet.

The plan had worked even better than expected, as Maya had discovered the secret truth behind the Chairman's Purge. That knowledge had given her and the Underground just enough of a head start that they were able to not only stop the enslavement of every man, woman, and child in Home, but also defeat and over-throw Warbak.

And now here they were, struggling to form, let alone maintain, some semblance of order.

"I know, General Miller. I apologize. The babysitter did not show. I tried to find another, but, well, it's a sensitive matter, trust, and the girl... You know what I mean," To-Kan explained.

Miller did know what she meant. Wyntr was a special child, the only person left in Home who knew where Xibalba, resting place of the Morning Star was; where Maya had gone. And now that Maya and her guardians had gone radio silent, overdue by at least a week, Miller feared that the child's secret would soon have to be passed on to another group of intrepid heroes. No, To-Kan was correct, the child could not be cared for by just anyone.

Sighing, Miller nodded his head to the sagely woman and gestured to her seat.

"Very well. Thank you all and welcome back to the second meeting of the New Republic council, and uh… daycare." Although he did not find the situation or his own comments to be funny, Miller heard his remarks prompt more than one chuckle from the group.

"I've called you all back here for two reasons. Two reasons, yet they are one and the same. Our previous meeting was cut short with the news that Chairman Accoba Warbak's aide, the man known as Matiaba, had been spotted in the Shanty. I'm happy to report that that was not only true but that the villain has been apprehended. I made the arrest personally."

"Villain? Villain, you say?" a voice spoke up over the approving murmurs that followed on the heels of Miller's announcement.

A well-dressed man stood up from the table. Miller had seen the man somewhere before, but couldn't place him or recall his name. He certainly wasn't a member of the council. Then again, many in the room were not. Some were members of the newly formed Free-Press Guild, while others, like Captain Wojax, were active military men, positioned in the room to act as guards. Then there was Wyntr… *but who was this man?*

"I was under the impression that my client would receive a fair trial, and yet here you are, *General*, already trying to sway the council with your unguarded and obviously biased words."

Lawyer, then. When did we get lawyers?

"Honorable members of the council, I am Libis. I am representing Matiaba in the trial," the well-dressed man said. He was slightly overweight, with slicked back hair, and wore a pair of glasses that matched his suit nicely. He gestured to Miller and then to the room at large, saying, "I suggest you keep your opinions of my client's character to yourself or hold them for the trial, and even then only when you are asked."

Oh boy. Here we go.

"Fine by me," Miller said, scowling. Then, as he sat back down, he added, "Let's get this circus started."

"You see, ladies and gentlemen?" Libis asked the room. "General Miller here seems to have made up his mind before the trial has even begun."

No one said anything, but a few members shot Miller some worried glances across the table.

"Hey. Take it easy," Candice whispered to Miller, once again patting the back of his giant metal hand.

Miller sighed. He hated lawyers. He hated trials. He was beginning to regret agreeing to this fiasco.

"Fine, fine," Miller said. "Bring him in."

Captain Wojax raised a knife-hand and saluted Miller, then turned to leave the room. A short minute later, he returned, joined by two more soldiers, each in Inner-Zigg attire, armed with pistols, and flanking a handcuffed Matiaba.

Miller nodded to his captain and made a rolling wheel gesture with a finger. The young officer saluted once more and escorted Matiaba to an empty seat at the table.

"Are the handcuffs necessary?" Libis asked no one in particular.

Heads snapped and looked to Miller, either wondering what he would say or waiting for his command. Miller tried to read their faces; confusion and uncertainty was the look *du jour*.

"Fine," Miller said with a tired and audible sigh. "Captain, remove the cuffs."

"Sir, yes sir," Wojax chirped and rushed to remove the manacles from the former aide.

"Thank you," Matiaba said, shaking and rubbing his now free wrists dramatically before sitting down.

Miller waited a moment for Matiaba to get situated and then began.

"Matiaba. You stand accused of war crimes, conspiracy, torture, and murder. How do you plead?"

What a colossal waste of time, Miller thought as he announced the accusations. *Why drag out the inevitable?* He tried not to look bored or roll his eyes as he reached for his cup of tea and took a sip.

"Why, not guilty, of course," Matiaba said calmly.

Miller almost spat out his tea, instead opting to choke on it as he covered his mouth.

"Do you think this is a joke?" Miller asked after he managed to cough the tea from his lungs.

"Not at all," Matiaba said.

"You see, General, I will prove that my client, much like you and many others here, was simply doing his job, and is not guilty of any of the crimes that he has been accused of," Libis said, standing.

"Give me a break!" Miller roared. "You expect me to believe that this man was only following orders when he took Lucy from the Shanty and cut her up? Turned her into a killing machine?"

Neither Libis nor Matiaba showed a sign of emotion at Miller's rage. They looked at each other expressionlessly and then turned back to Miller.

"That is precisely what I expect you to believe, General. For that is the truth."

The council room fell silent as concerned glances shot back and forth.

"If I may?" Libis asked, holding his hand aloft as if an invisible object rested within it.

"Fine," Miller said, almost growling. "Make your case."

"Excellent. First, let's look at the details of the accusations. What was the first on the list? War crimes?"

"Yes," Miller mumbled, frowning.

"I see. And what exactly is the nature of the so-called war crime?" Libis asked, smiling slightly.

"How about the transformation of every New Breed soldier into those demonic robots and the capture of every other man, woman, and child into those Harvester spheres?" Miller snapped, his patience with this charade already long gone.

"I see," Libis said, his small smile now slightly turned downward in a frown of contemplation. "And the conspiracy charges?"

"I think I just made that clear. Did you miss the part about the Harvester spheres?"

"Oh. I see." Libis's smile returned. "Honorable council members, I ask you a simple question. Who do you see here on trial?"

The room was silent. Confused glances came to Miller from nearly everyone in the room.

"You don't need to take your lines from the good general here. I assure you, you can all think and answer for yourselves. It's not a trick question. Who do you see here on trial?"

"Uh... Matiaba?" Quiteke broke the silence, his answer sounding more like a question of its own.

"That is correct, sir. Matiaba. Not Chairman Warbak."

Miller watched in frustration as understanding dawned on his peers' faces. *So that's your game, eh?*

"You see, ladies and gentlemen, my client here was an aide, not a leader. Like everyone in the Ziggurat, he had orders to follow. Matiaba had no choice but to do his job. We should remember all too well the late Ministry of Social Purity, and the consequences for not following orders."

Heads around the room nodded gravely. Miller seethed.

"Would you care to make a statement?" Libis said to Matiaba.

The former aide nodded and stood, looking around the room, pausing briefly to make eye contact with every member of the council.

"I swear on Home, and all it stands for, that I was not aware of Chairman Warbak's intention to transform the New Breed into Spartans, or of his intent to capture the citizens of Home. Furthermore, I had no idea that he was working with Umbra and the Harvesters," Matiaba said.

"And," Libis continued, "please tell the council what you would have done if you had known."

"I would have attempted to stop him."

"What a load of bullshit!" Miller shouted, rising again to his feet and slamming a palm on the table, causing many a cup of tea and water to spill. "You're as guilty as Warbak!"

"General, please," Libis said calmly. Matiaba looked his way, but still bore no sign of agitation or fear.

"On what grounds do you say such things? What evidence do you present? I assumed this council would be founded on the principles of liberty, notions such as *innocent until proven guilty*, or have you simply removed one despot and taken his place yourselves?"

Miller practically shook with rage. He stole glances at his fellow council members and saw to his dismay that they were almost all looking at him with concern, even Candy. Only Elena looked unconvinced.

"And where is your proof that he is innocent?" Miller asked through clenched teeth.

"The burden of proof falls on the accuser, not the accused," Libis said, eyes narrowing with triumphant glee. "Ladies and gentlemen. Allow me to digress for a minute. I assure you, there is a point."

"Very well," To-Kan said. Miller wondered if she'd decided to take over because of his emotional outburst, or if it was merely a coincidence. He curled his palm into a fist and sat back down.

The child, Wyntr, was restless, climbing off To-Kan's lap and playing with the edge of the table. The play caught Miller's attention, and when he looked, he found the girl staring at him, though most of her face was obscured by the table.

Oh, to be that innocent, Miller thought. *Though, for her sake, and countless others like her, I'll be damned if I let Matiaba walk!*

"General Miller," Libis began again, "were you or were you not present during the Battle of Texhoma?"

"What the crap?" Miller barked in answer. "Who's on trial here?"

"Forgive me, ladies and gentlemen, but if the good General won't even—"

"Miller, please," To-Kan said.

"Fine. Yes. Yes, I was present," Miller said, crossing his massive arms in silent protest.

"And during that battle—or slaughter, really—how many people, human and Displaced, did you kill?"

"Why you—!" Miller bolted back upright so fast and hard that his chair shot out from under him, striking the wall behind him and causing many in the room to gasp. He was shaking and had lost any control he had left of his temper. "I should have gunned you down in the Wombat," he said, but not to Libis. His bloodshot eyes drilled holes into the former aide to the Chairman. More gasps, followed by silence.

"Interesting…" Libis mumbled, gently stroking the frames of his glasses with a fingertip.

"I mean…" Miller tried to correct himself, realizing that everyone in the room was staring at him in aghast disbelief.

"You don't have to answer the question, sir." Libis quickly turned the tone of the inquiry as deftly as a master duelist parried the incoming tip of an opponent's rapier. "The question was not meant to bring you shame. We all know that you were decorated by Warbak for your actions in the war of reclamation. Surely you took no joy in the slaughter of your fellow man. You did what you had to do as a soldier in the Republic. You followed your orders."

Miller said nothing. He could feel his massive metal-clad chest heaving with every breath. *Damn him to hell.*

"You've made your point, counselor," To-Kan said, prompting several nods from the other council members. Wyntr pushed herself up into the air off the edge of the table and shouted in mimicry.

"Bang! Bang! You followed orders!"

"To-Kan, control that child!" Miller shouted. Wyntr flashed him a hurt look and disappeared under the table, burying her face in the elderly councilwoman's lap.

"Miller…" Candice said from beside him, almost a whisper. "What's going on with you?"

"Council, if I may continue on to the other charges?" Libis asked. Matiaba stared at Miller. The veteran could swear the former aide smirked, but when he looked again, the man's face was as stoic as a statue.

"Yes, please. The next charge was…" To-Kan drifted off as she studied a paper in front of her with one hand while petting Wyntr's hair with the other. "Torture."

"Torture?" Libis repeated the word as a question.

"Yes. According to the reports given by Maya, Jon, Rene, Ratt, and Lucy, several victims of torture and experimentation were found in the Chairman's pagoda."

"The *Chairman's* pagoda?" Libis asked, giving the room a knowing look.

"We don' need ta hear da same round'bout story, Olsen," Elena said, raising a scolding finger. "I knows dat he was in charge of findin' doz gurls. I was there when he came to my place. I saw him take Lucy back den. I knows what kinda man he really is."

"My client—"

"Libis, please," Matiaba said, raising a hand in objection. "I would like to speak for myself on this matter. And the one to follow."

Heads cocked, studying the former aide. Miller remained unimpressed. As far as he was concerned, this was all part of the man's grand theater. He dared not object, however, for he knew he would, at this point, only be helping the weasel.

"Dearest Councilwoman Elena, please believe me when I tell you that I had no idea what Chairman Warbak was doing with those poor girls. I had my suspicions, but had to guard them very, very carefully. I'm sure you have all heard by now that Accoba Warbak was a telepath. He could shape Strange with the best of them. It was his power alone that gave the Ministers and Handlers their abilities to read minds and control those hellhounds they called Sniffers. Can you *imagine* working at his side? Being in intimate proximity to him day in and day out, whilst sheltering doubts, fears, and concerns? Ladies and gentlemen of the council, please hear me when I tell you that I lived in terror every day of my life, always afraid that today would be the day I thought the wrong thought about Warbak's iron-fisted rule. I shudder at the memory. Apparently, he had been trying to perfect what would become those Spartans for some time. My heart breaks for the people he experimented on. I grieve for their suffering, and yet I am deeply ashamed to tell you that I stand here today, thankful and grateful I never knew the truth, the extent of his sickness. That I never accidentally stumbled across one of his 'experiments'." Matiaba made air quotes around this last word, and then paused, taking the time to make eye contact with everyone in the room again. His face was a kabuki mask of sorrow, and Miller burned, knowing that his peers were falling for it hook, line, and sinker. "I am thankful, because, if I had known, I fear there would've been no way for me to guard the sheer and utter revulsion for Warbak that I feel this very moment, just thinking about it. I beg your forgiveness, members of the council. I was a bliss-fully ignorant coward."

For a minute, no one said anything. Everyone appeared to be in quiet reflection. Even Libis looked to be shaken and made no attempt to regain his position as mouthpiece for the accused.

"A sad story. But what about Lucy? I was 'dere when you took 'er," Elena said.

"It's true, Madam," Matiaba said, looking directly at her. "I did take her away. I had been informed by her pimp at the time that she was sick and would die. I only meant to save her life. I had no idea what Warbak would do to her, or with her. I assure you, I meant no harm."

Elena scoffed. "I wonder what Lucy would say to that. She told me that when you were her client you were particularly cruel and twisted."

"I suppose I should be used to these attacks on my character by now, councilwoman, yet I assure you, they still hurt. It's true that I am guilty of soliciting prostitution. As guilty as you are for promoting it, *mamasan*."

Miller saw Elena flinch at that, but before she could counter-attack, Matiaba went off the offensive and returned to his sob story.

"My frequenting of your brothel is but one sin that I hope to atone for. But for the moment, I do not believe I'm on trial for seeking the company of working girls."

"*Girls* is right," Miller interrupted. "Lucy was just a child then. She told me what you used to do to her." Looks of disgust replaced the sympathetic expressions on the council's faces.

"Lies and hearsay. If that is how it must be, then for my client's sake, I suggest we hear testimony from Lucy herself," Libis quickly countered.

Miller bristled. He glanced around and caught Candice looking at him, concern written on her face.

Dammit, man. I just put myself in a corner.

"Lucy isn't available," Miller mumbled, almost too quiet for anyone to hear.

"I'm sorry?" Libis asked, cupping his hand to his ear, obviously for dramatic effect. "Could you please repeat that?"

"Lucy isn't here, dammit!" Miller growled, frowning deeply.

"Here? As in Home?" Libis continued to press, almost gloating.

"That's correct," Miller admitted to the room. Several council members, the ones he wasn't close to, looked to be somewhere between alarmed and confused. They turned to each other and the room buzzed with the hum of several muffled conversations. "But that doesn't cha—"

"Isn't this Lucy, infamous warrior of the former Underground Resistance, off on an errand with Lily Sapphire, aka Maya? The leader of the rebellion?" Libis said, cutting him off.

"Yes, but—"

"And is the New Breed officer, Jon 310-257, with them also?"

How does he know this? Their mission was a secret!

"Along with another New Breed, Rene, as well as the scientist called Ratt?" Libis asked, not letting up.

"None of this has to do with Matiaba's crimes!" Miller shouted, trying to stem the flow of the rising tide.

"Please, General. Answer the question," Libis said, cocking one eyebrow up over the rim of his glasses, his arms crossed aloofly.

"Yes. They are all together," Miller admitted.

"*Are* together? Or *were* together?" Libis asked. Miller squinted at the lawyer.

"What do you mean?"

"You see, ladies and gentlemen," Libis said, turning his attention from Miller to the room at large. "What not everyone here is aware of is that the people I just mentioned, the very core of the rebellion that overthrew Warbak, are all gone on a secret mission. A mission that you, the acting governmental body of Home, were not considered important enough to be given the details of."

Stifled gasps and hushed murmurs rippled through the room like waves in a pond, issuing out from the metaphorical stone Libis had just tossed.

"General Miller, is this true?" Councilman Monroe asked.

"Yes. You were not told for a good reason," Miller said, trying to collect himself. *I may still be able to salvage this train wreck.* "To put it simply, we didn't know if the Old Guard, or Umbra and the Harvesters, for that matter, had spies in our ranks. We didn't, and still don't know who besides Warbak himself was in on the conspiracy. And clearly, we were right." Miller pointed at Matiaba and Libis.

"And what is the nature of this mission?" Councilperson Hincit, the only genderless and Displaced member of the body asked.

Miller regarded the turtle-like councilperson and spoke plainly, hoping that honesty at this point might repair the damage Matiaba and his lawyer had wrought. "Maya and her guardians are searching for a secret weapon. A weapon of great power. We believe that this weapon will enable us to defeat the Harvesters when they return to Home."

"Unbelievable!" Libis blurted out over the hushed conversations re-erupting through the room. "General Miller knows of an attempt to locate a super-weapon and didn't feel that he needed to share this information with the council. I say."

"We haven't had a chance yet!" Miller said, almost pleading at this point, feeling with every spoken exchange the favor of his peers falling further from him. "We are just forming this government!"

"I see, I see," Libis said, running his fingers down the sides of his glasses again. "Forgive me."

"I would like to get this tribunal back on track if you don't mind," Miller grumbled.

"One more thing," Libis said. When no one objected, he continued. "When are Maya and her guardians due back from retrieving this super-weapon?"

Miller sat in silence, wishing the question away.

"General Miller?" Councilman Monroe asked.

"They were already expected back. We have lost contact with them…" he conceded, hanging his head.

"I see. Well then, I think that fact leads nicely into my client's closing statements, then. That is, of course, unless you actually have some evidence to present regarding the last charge. Murder, was it?"

"Mister Libis raises a good point, General. Do you have any evidence at all? For the charge of murder or anything else?" Monroe continued, now seemingly fully caught in the web that Libis and Matiaba had spun.

Miller didn't say a word, but only continued to look down. He was too tired to rage and fight anymore. He had lost the day.

"No," Libis answered for Miller. "He does not. Not one shred of actual evidence. Only hate and discontent. Libel. And would you all like to know why you've been subjected to this farce? Why my client has been forced to deal with all this? Because it was Mister Matiaba here who, when acting as chief aide to Chairman Warbak, removed then-Sergeant Miller from active duty in the Army and put him into public service, into the kitchens."

Miller's head shot up and he stared, slack-jawed, at the lawyer.

What is this? And just when I thought this couldn't get any worse!

"It's true, ladies and gentlemen. Miller blames my client for what he sees as his humiliation, a change of assignment that General Miller here has never been able to forgive or forget."

"General Miller? Is this true?" Monroe asked.

"I swear," Miller said, sounding tired, "I had no idea."

"Of course you didn't." Libis smirked and plucked a stack of documents off the table and began passing them out to the council. "What you are looking at are copies of the official Republic document recommending Sgt. Miller for re-assignment. Please note the name of the document's author."

"Chief Aide Matiaba…" Hincit read aloud.

"I think that after hearing my client's closing statements, we are done here," Libis concluded.

After an excruciating minute, Matiaba stood, straightened out his suit jacket and addressed the room.

"Good people of the council. While I am clearly not guilty of the crimes which I have been accused of, I am guilty. Guilty of looking the other way for too long. Guilty of not trying harder to contact the Resistance when I could have, *should* have. Guilty of putting my own life before the lives of those who suffered under Chairman Warbak. Guilty of cowardice."

The room was as still as a graveyard. Everyone, even Elena, To-Kan, and Candice, watched and listened in rapt attention.

These punks are good, Miller thought to himself, knowing he had lost. Matiaba would walk.

"I know there is no way for me to redeem myself for these crimes, no way to take back the loss of innocent life that Warbak's regime caused. But there is a way I can try if you will allow it."

"We are listening," Monroe said, gesturing for Matiaba to go on.

"As Chief Aide to Warbak, I was tasked with the lion's share of the day-to-day operational tasks. While Warbak plotted with demons and tortured people, it was I who actually oversaw the fundamental operations. It was I who actually kept the Ziggurat running."

Miller, who had given up and had been stewing in his morose defeat, suddenly perked back up. He felt as if his cybernetic parts were malfunctioning and sending jolts of electricity into his flesh.

No. No way. He can't be serious!

"What is your point, sir?" Monroe asked.

"My point, ladies and gentlemen, is this. If you would allow it, I would like to volunteer my services to you as a fellow council member. I can help you get this city back to running. It would be my honor. It would be my penance."

Miller sat frozen, knowing that any objection he made at this point would fall on deaf ears. Hating every second of it, wishing to everything in the universe that this was all a bad dream, he watched as Monroe called for a spontaneous vote. Words were spoken, hands were raised. More words spoken, more hands raised. The council voted to make Matiaba a member of the ruling body of Home, six to four.

Maya, if you're alive, please hurry home!

16

New Puebla was abuzz with rumors and excited preparation. News hawkers and gossipmongers worked to intrigue and titillate the population as tirelessly as the laborers who had been assigned to construct the stage in the town center that would accommodate Lily Sapphire's first concert in New Puebla. Between the certain knowledge of Lily's show two days hence and its attendant anticipation, as well as the whispers that New Puebla's king, Don Luis Fernando, would be taking a new wife, nobody in the city could talk about much else.

Like the proverbial circus that accompanied the bread in countless civilizations before it, pop music and celebrity relationships filled the imaginations and conversations of every tired soul in the city-state, giving every one of them a mental respite from their otherwise bleak existence of repetitive labor and flat futures.

Among the more hushed whispers traded in the human and vampire circles of New Puebla were ones centered on King Fernando's current wife, Sofia. What was going to happen to her? What did *she* think of all this? Was she being replaced, or would she have a higher position as wife *numero uno*? Was Lily going to be a wife or more of a mistress? If mistress, was she *Señor*

Fernando's alone? Or was Sofia the type of girl to enjoy having a female plaything too? Many suspected she was. And on and on. If there was a variation of the scenario one could imagine, then it was being speculated about over the daily tilling of garden beds, the grinding of maize, the breastfeeding of babies, the quaffing of cerveza and mescal, and the construction of the stage.

As for Don Luis Fernando, he could barely restrain himself. After proposing to Maya and showing her his deepest, darkest secret in the catacombs of his palace, he had escorted her back to her suite and reluctantly parted ways, for dawn was quickly approaching.

Rather than send for her, he returned to her suite the following dusk. Ratt and Lucy kept their distance and did their best to behave like the slave chattel that Don Luis would assuredly see them as while Maya received their host.

He behaved as though possessed with an urgent need. He wanted to turn her then and there, demanded even, and then, having been rejected, resorted to begging.

Maya played him like a pro and told him again to wait until the next night; that she wanted to be taken in front of the whole populace, at the climax of her show.

For a brief moment, Maya wondered if Don Luis's animal urges would overcome his gentlemanly restraint and force her hand. Even with Lucy at her side, she did not think they could easily make their escape from the heart of the city in the dark should they be able to take him, or at the very least, stun him.

And force her hand it would, there was no doubt about it. Luckily for her, Don Luis conceded defeat and promised to abide by her wishes, waiting until the next night.

The two days and nights following Maya's tour of the city were frantic and busy for Maya and every one of her guardians. Ratt was the busiest of them all. He did his best and proved to be worthy of his position as guardian. Maya occupied the attention of Don Luis while Ratt and Lucy worked tirelessly to "prepare for the concert."

Jon and Carbine, too, prepared for their role in the grand finale of Lily's show, though most of their time was filled with the creeping dread-like frustration that comes with waiting for the inevitable. Brave they were, but nervous too. Carbine tried to hide it behind stupid remarks and jokes, but Jon knew his friend too well. On the side of a small mountain overlooking the desert valley and city within, Jon existed in a state of near meditation, trying his best to lull the butterflies in his stomach to sleep with the rhythmic sounds of his deep, slow breaths.

Being unable to communicate back to Maya was the most excruciating part of the entire ordeal. Jon was stressed out, that was for sure, but he could only imagine the trepidation that Maya, Lucy, and Ratt were feeling—wondering, hoping that Jon and Carbine had not only heard their report, subsequent plans, and periodic check-ins, but were prepared to act when the time came to do their part. For if Jon and Carbine dropped the ball, then all would surely be lost, and the show scheduled for the next night would be the last performance Lily Sapphire would ever give, goddess or not.

And so, the time ticked by as uncomfortably as the siesta-inducing heat of a New Puebla summer day.

<hr>

Of all the different variations of rumors concerning Sofia and her opinion on the king's taking of a second wife, very few lips whispered anything close to the truth.

Sofia, for all her perversions and hedonistic ways, did not like the situation one bit.

It wasn't so much that she minded the idea of sharing her man with another woman—they already had done that together many times. She had, as well, without the presence or permission of her husband, taken many playthings to bed, a kinky pastime that most often ended in the deaths of her new friends as well as the sating of her animal appetites. What irritated her was Lily herself. There was just something about her. Sofia hated her. Loathed her. She despised her for being human.

How could a human seduce my husband without even trying?

This was no lust or sexual play, with which Sofia would have been fine. No, this was something else. This pop-tart bitch had captured her man's heart, it would seem. In this, Sofia found a special edge to her hate.

Sofia hadn't been happy in a long time, hadn't ever been happy—not really. But this insult to her queenly pride was too much to bear. She would not suffer the slight. She would dare her imbecile husband to strike her, to retaliate, and then she would make him pay.

Like her husband, she, too, had a vision for New Puebla. One where vampires weren't executed by sun for the raping and killing of a human. Humans were food and toys, nothing more. A wolf might dominate the sheep, only taking what it needed and allowing the herd to continue, but a cat... A cat played with its food. A cat killed for fun and sport. Cats had been *worshiped* before, and they would be again. Sofia thought it was time for the ruling of New Puebla to benefit from a woman's touch.

It was the time of the queen.

Let him drink his little bitch on stage.

She had her loyal men. She would put on a show that would rival Lily Sapphire's.

A show that no one would ever forget.

"*Señorita* Sapphire?" the young female assistant asked timidly as she peeked her head into the lavishly ornate green room that Don Luis had built for Maya.

"Yes? Come in," Maya said into the mirror, continuing to apply her makeup. She was already familiar with the girl and her voice. After his previous rejection in her suite, Don Luis had assigned one of the girls who had bathed her the night before to be Maya's assistant.

The girl had been tasked with helping to procure and provide anything and everything that "*Señorita* Sapphire" might need or want.

The girl, whose name was Rose, had been given a royal decree to carry around and present to the various merchants in the city. It gave her great authority and allowed her to speak for the king, at least in regard to her assigned task of assisting *Señorita* Sapphire. The girl had been overwhelmed with her sudden promotion, her chest swelled with obvious pride, and she performed her job well. Taking into account her current state of mind and her previously shy disposition, Maya saw in her a boon of opportunity. Rose offered no opposition or inquiry into anything that Maya requested, and so she had Ratt put together a shopping list of things they would need for the big surprise finale of Lily Sapphire's greatest concert. Lucy, for her part, revisited the home of Eduardo, his sisters, and their mother. Without going into too much detail, Lucy explained to Eduardo that the time for revolution would be during the Lily Sapphire show and that he should carefully gather all his like-minded friends and be ready to help out once the dust settled.

The resulting machinations and preparations of Maya's plan proved to be as smooth as the polished obsidian that decorated the columns inside her royal suite.

"*Señorita* Sapphire, they are, um... I mean, I have been instructed by *Señor* Fernando that we are ready for you." The girl squeaked it out in the manner of a curious, approaching animal, not sure whether the food being offered was merely a trick that would result in its death.

Impatient little man, thought Maya to herself and rolled her eyes. She couldn't imagine how things must be for Sofia, or what they would be like for her should Maya's ruse become reality. To be married to such a man, to be owned and dangled, like a piece of jewelry. Even with Maya, she was certain he would be kind only as long as the novelty remained, and then he would grow bored, and with boredom would come the inevitable cruelty.

"Of course. Five more minutes, please," Maya said in her kindest, most ladylike voice. She observed Rose's reflection in the mirror and felt sure that Rose had missed the eye-roll, as the timid little thing was staring at her own feet, only halfway through the door of the room. When the girl neither spoke nor moved, Maya added, "In private. Please tell my fiancé that the show will start when I am fully ready, and not a moment sooner." Maya tried to sound gentle but firm.

She saw Rose's eyes flicker to the mirror and quickly back down, as was befitting not only her character but her class. The glance had been as fleeting as the affections of Don Luis were sure to be, but Maya had caught the look of terror on the girl's face and recognized it for what it truly was. She instantly regretted her choice of words and realized what a precarious position it would put poor Rose in. Don Luis was as likely to kill the girl in his outrage at Maya's brazenness as he was to laugh it off and become aroused by his new wife's sauciness.

"No, not that, Rose. Just tell my *Señor* Fernando that the show will start in about five minutes. Please tell him that I need to be perfect for him." Rose looked back up into the mirror with gratitude in her eyes. This gaze into the mirror lingered longer than the first had, and when she saw Maya's look of affection waiting for her, she smiled and nearly blushed.

"As you wish, *Señorita*, thank you." Rose made a quick, jerky, polite bow and left the dressing room, pulling the door shut behind her.

As soon as the door closed, Maya exhaled, and her smile deflated along with her lungs.

Exhausting. Exhausting and nerve-wracking. It will all be over soon, for better or for worse.

She looked at herself in the mirror, looked at the girl behind the makeup and thought about Jon, and also about her late husband. She sat motionless for a solid minute and then finally took a breath as deep as her silent musings. She let it out forcefully through pursed lips.

Well, here goes. We are doing the right thing, aren't we? It's worth the risk. Both to us, and the people of New Puebla. It must be done; otherwise, what is the point of any of this?

She gingerly reached down and touched the necklace Ratt had made, hanging around her neck like the mantle of responsibility she and her guardians had taken up two days ago. She ran her fingers along the contours of the inlaid jewel and sent out a wordless prayer.

Then she clutched it and raised it to her mouth.

"Okay, boys. It's showtime." Another prayer. She had trusted so much to fate before.

Please let Jon be listening and watching. And please protect him now more than ever.

A knock came at her door, and it opened before she could speak. Lucy.

"My lady, we are ready."

Maya wondered to herself if Lucy's heart was as wild as hers. Lucy had always oozed cool, but was that chilly exterior just a defense?

Maya knew this to be true, had seen into the girl's heart the day they'd met, the day she had freed her the way that they would free the people of New Puebla together tonight. But did Lucy have the same reservations about their plan? Did she worry for Carbine as Maya worried for Jon? Maya knew that Lucy was prepared to die if need be, but Maya wished not to if it was at all possible, and if death was their fate, would Lucy think it had been worth it, as Maya did? Some questions were better left unasked. Maya had only to look into her guardian's eyes to know that Lucy was content—no, more than that—she was fulfilled to simply serve her lady.

"Feroz Pantera." Maya turned away from the mirror, spinning in her chair to gaze upon Lucy. "I love you."

Lucy nodded her head almost imperceptibly, stepped to the side, and held the door open for Maya.

"I love you too, my lady."

Was there a more perfect place for a goddess than on a stage, in front of thousands of screaming fans? Were the audience's rabid adorations not some kind of worship? Did the masses not idolize their celebrities? The arrangement was perfect and very befitting of gods and men. Or in this case, goddess and vampire.

Maya was thrilled to be in the limelight again. The sounds of the roaring cheers, the blissed-out looks of fans in the front rows, the constellations of lighters in the dark, the light-show production, the smells coming from the food court and writhing sea of humanity. And above it all, she was there in the center, on the pedestal, being worshiped.

Maya was a goddess of song, always had been, and always would be. She was its living embodiment. She used song to shape Strange. As she strung a melody together, she was capable of voicing an incantation that moved the spheres of the cosmos as well as touched the hearts and minds of men. She was a musician, a performer, and performers needed an audience like... well, like a god needs worshipers.

Add to all that her persona as Lily Sapphire and the doors that it opened. They were the perfect front for a prominent leader in the Resistance and a situation that was as perfect for Maya as she hoped tonight's plan would be.

Each show was like a living thing. It had its own flavor, its own personality. Like the varying cuisines of the different regions within a nation or culture, the shows she performed could be similar in many ways, but each had its certain uniqueness. The undercurrent of excitement running through the ether this night was strong, and its scent carried a top note of nervousness. She hadn't felt nearly this skittish when she had walked onto that stage in Home, knowing full well that she was going to be arrested and imprisoned by the Ministry of Social Purity. She had been calm then, confident in the manifestation of her destiny. She'd known without a shadow of a doubt that Lucy would find Jon, and all would work out as it did.

Tonight, however... Tonight was different. This hadn't been in the big plan. This was a segue, an impromptu *pièce de résistance*, a spontaneous *coup d'état*. Something didn't sit right with her, though she couldn't put her finger on it. Something kept reminding her of her late husband.

What is it? she had thought as she'd walked, not even realizing she had finished her stroll up the back ramp from the green room area and reached the zenith of the stage. Ratt had noticed, however, and had lit her up with his floodlights, provoking a cheer from the crowd and snapping her out of her troubled daydream.

The show must go on.

Ratt had killed the spotlights as quickly as he had turned them on. A few beats of darkness, its black void filled with the cheers, applause, and whistles of the crowd, and then a dizzying array of colorful lights had sprayed across the city center as Ratt dropped the beat. With that, the show had kicked off.

Maya gave as good as she got. Her performance for the vampires and their human slaves was every bit the equal to the show she'd put on back in Home. Like any great stage performer, she did not attempt to stymie the bubbling kettle of nervous fear inside her. Instead, she channeled it into her act, using it as fuel. She moved like the music itself and brought every member of her audience along for the ride as one song bled into the next.

Ratt maintained his position up in the recently constructed catwalks above the stage, working the lights and preparing for the grand finale.

Lucy was in the DJ booth, waiting, pretending to be working.

In actuality, the whole show came from Maya's Strange—the sounds, the music, everything. The music itself was, for all intents and purposes, a type of spirit that she channeled. It was archetypal, archaic. She was the goddess of song and drew her musical accompaniment from the collective subconscious of humankind. She functioned as a medium for the music and directed its flow like a conductor. It was no wonder that her persona, Lily Sapphire, was the most popular act in the land. Every bit of her show was drawn from the desires and dream-pleasure centers of the listeners. Her music touched them each deeply. All were delighted by her showmanship and eternal beauty as well as her spell.

As she summoned, channeled, and directed the music, Maya as Lily pranced, danced, pouted, and captivated. All were enchanted. All were completely oblivious to the fact that she was slowly working an enchantment of a different kind throughout the show. A grand ritual was being pieced together slowly but surely.

17

J on and Carbine could hear the music in the city from their position up the small mountain almost as well as if it had been coming from within their camp. They had been watching the stage with great anticipation since Maya's last transmission from the green room.

"Okay, boys… it's showtime," she had said, and with that, Jon had set himself into motion. He double-checked the clasps and buckles on his body armor, re-tightened the laces on his side-zips, and lifted his hammer. Its textured grip felt good in his hands and soothed his nerves.

Carbine got into the most comfortable position he could and sat, railgun at the ready, hood up to block out any wind, dust, or distraction from his sniper focus.

The second after the music bounced up the canyon and landed in their ears, the two friends spoke their farewells.

"Good luck, buddy," Carbine said from under his hood.

"Same to you," Jon said, ignoring the sense of dread in his mind after speaking, and hoping the mods Ratt had made to Carbine's rifle before departing did the trick.

If the plan failed and everything went to shit, it was very

likely that Carbine would be the only one of them to survive, given the distance between him and New Puebla, but how long he would survive on his own, Jon could not say.

"Don't worry, Jon. I've got your back," Carbine said again from under the sniper's hood, his eyes never leaving the scope of the railgun. There was a hint of uncharacteristic seriousness in his voice.

"You always have."

In between the spoken words lay a silent "Thank you" and "You're my best friend."

Jon didn't have to say it. He knew Carbine knew it. Without another word, Jon was sprinting down the side of the mountain, leaping over small boulders and swathes of prickle-bush. His heightened strength and reflexes made him every bit as agile as a mountain cat, every bit as strong as a mountain bear. He felt invincible and god-like, every bit the equal of the vampiric titans in the city below. He felt alive.

Between the cover of darkness and the distraction of the concert, Jon was not worried about being spotted as he traversed his way down the slope and then across the valley floor. He didn't even attempt to be stealthy. Time was of the essence. He had to make it to the city gates before the finale, hopefully before. With every step in his long stride, he grew more exhilarated. The voice, that voice he'd first heard the day after graduation, the voice that had changed his life, sang to him through his earpiece and called him to the city like a siren. He would not fail her. Not tonight, not ever.

Jon ran on through the darkness, with Maya providing the soundtrack to his sneak attack. As he approached the city, he could see the outlines of the sentries up on the wall.

Far fewer than normal, Jon noted, happy that they had correctly guessed that the Lily Sapphire concert would draw many away from their responsibilities. Jon continued his run, only slightly slower as he crouched down some, rolling his back and doing his best to reduce his profile. He changed his straight-line approach to a strategic zig-zag, moving from one scraggly bush to the next. When he came to the last bunch of branches before the one-hundred-yard open space around the city walls, he paused. Even in the dark, he could see the sentries.

He slowly scanned the ridge-line of the wall. There were at least four that were in a position to spot him; the others were too far away. There may be more, perhaps sitting down, he had no way of knowing for sure, but he and Carbine had done a preliminary scan with the railgun's scope before Maya had started the show. That search had revealed no surprises behind the ramparts or rudimentary guard shacks that dotted the perimeter of the city like fence posts along a cattle pen. He could only hope that things remained the same now as then, and if they had changed, he could hope that Carbine would notice them before they noticed Jon.

Jon squinted into the night and studied the two sentries closest to his location.

Can it be? Jon was amazed at their luck. Perhaps the masters of New Puebla had grown lax from years of success and survival. There were few beasts from the Drops stupid enough to attack a fortified city head-on, and few beasts conniving enough to attempt infiltration. Whatever the reason, Jon didn't care; he only smiled to himself and gave thanks.

The two guards closest to him had their backs to the expanse. From their vantage point on the wall, they could see the concert that they had not been allowed to attend, and they were every bit as entranced by it as the citizens who had been.

Satisfied with his surveillance and good fortune, Jon left the cover of his scrub and sprinted toward the base of the city wall as fast as his burning body would go. If the soldiers on the wall had been even remotely doing their job, Jon's ninja charge would have been undone.

He found, much to his chagrin, that when he pushed his body to the limits of its capability, the fire that burned within him grew stronger and brighter.

At first, he didn't notice; he was focused on running, and running fast. He reached top speed the moment before he noticed his glow and surely would have made the wild horses of the scrub proud. He moved like a force of nature, a trail of dust billowing in his wake, semi-obscured by the blanket of night. But he shone like a beacon in that darkness, causing both himself and the dust trail to resemble a comet of some kind, streaking across the dark, straight toward the city.

It was his glowing fingertips that alerted him to his folly as they pumped in and out of his peripheral vision with each amazing stride. He slowed instantly and broke his focus, looking down at himself. Most of his body was covered by his torso armor, cargo pants, and boots, but the remaining exposed skin was more than enough to betray his location to anyone looking. His neck, face, and hands burned like the sun itself were just beneath his skin, which in the eerie light looked paper-thin.

His run slowed to a walk; then, three steps later, he stopped entirely. He stared at his hands in amazement, his eyes tracing the rivers of his arteries and their capillary tributaries. Cold realization in contrast to his body's heat came crashing down over his head like a bucket of ice water, and he realized that he was standing, glowing, out in the open, halfway between cover and the city wall. Eyes quickened with fear glanced up to the top of the wall. Four sentries still, bobbing their heads to the relentless beat thumping from the city center square.

Run, you idiot!

Jon chided himself and snapped out of his paralysis, making a break for the wall. It was too late to do anything about the fire within him. It would most likely take several minutes to cool down, and that would leave him standing out in the open and darkness. If any of the guards just happened to turn their heads to glance in the direction of their duty...

He ran, albeit not as fast as before, his eyes darting from one sentry to the next, his heart pounding more from a feeling of dread certitude that he would be spotted than the effort of sprinting.

C'mon... C'mon!

At last, with a sense of bewildered surprise, he made it to the base of the city wall. He flattened his form against the cold stones and slowed his breathing, using the mindfulness in athletics technique he'd been taught in the Academy. Base of the wall or not, the glow coming off his body cast a lantern's shine out into the scrub and surely could catch the eye of a sentry, who would, more likely than not, take him for a small fire; he had to cool down fast.

He waited there, still as the stones he leaned against, breathing and listening to his slowing heartbeat form an irregular rhythm with the Lily Sapphire concert in his earpiece. He watched the fire behind his skin fade to soft pink, and then slowly disappear like the headlights of an automobile with a dying battery. His hands pressed against the wall, and he began to study it with them.

If the irresponsible guards on the wall inspired a theory that the ruling class of New Puebla had grown cocky in their so far very successful battle for survival, then the construction of the city's walls proved that theory. Technically, the wall was a wall, but it was hardly defensive. Sure, it might be thick and heavy and would probably hold up great against a charging Drop-Beastie. It would likely perform very well against incoming gunfire and the various sorts of exploding ordnance available to the survivors, freedom fighters, and *banditos* of the post-Storm world. But against an infiltrator, it was more of a *help* than a hindrance.

No effort whatsoever had been made to shape the urbanite or even make the edges flush. The result was a spectacular gift-horse display of footholds and handholds that would rival any pre-

Storm climbing gym. Once again, Jon gave thanks for his fortune and then slung his hammer across his back, grateful also for the leather sling he had built from scrap while Ratt had built the palanquin. Hand over hand, foot over foot, Jon began to climb the wall.

He reached the top without complication and pulled himself up, chin-up style, to recon his surroundings. He had, as hoped, come to the top of the wall extremely close to one of the sentries. The man still had his back to the scrub and Jon and was watching the concert, his head bobbing softly. He sat with one butt cheek on a rusty drum, its label long eroded, and dangled one leg, his heel bouncing off the drum now and again. Jon, maintaining his chin-up with ease, turned his head farther to the left to look down the wall past the man on the drum and saw another sentry. This man was also watching the concert and stood on one leg as he leaned against a guard shack post. Making his best impression of a submarine's periscope, Jon rotated his head now to the right and scanned for the two sentries that he knew would be there.

The one closest to him sat fully on the edge of the wall, his back completely to the scrub, and grinned at the show in the distance like a simpleton. Jon could see the man's face clearly (the first one of the bunch so far) and saw no red eyes. Furthermore, he saw the edges of the man's Citizen Stamp peeking out from under the collar of his shirt.

Humans. Of course the ruling class would have the privilege of attending the concert, while the humans, even the vampire sympathizers, would have to pull duty.

The thought brought mixed feelings. If the guards that Jon needed to get past were all human soldiers, it would undoubtedly make his infiltration infinitely easier, but at the same time, it just meant that there were more vampires in close proximity to Maya, more right there to try to deal with her once she attempted to deal with them. It also meant potentially having to kill humans—a prospect that unsettled him. He was here to free them, not slay them. If there was any way possible to succeed in his mission without forcing a human citizen, even one that served the darkness, to pay the ultimate price, Jon was determined to find it.

He lowered himself back down below the edge of the wall and found a foothold that enabled him to more or less rest. He paused and listened intently to Maya's singing. She was about halfway through the Moon Song; she had told him that this set would mimic the set from the Home show. She didn't need to remind him what that set was—Jon had it memorized, every note, every step of every dance, every expression on her face. It had been burned into his mind forever. It had been, after all, his first encounter with divinity.

After the Moon Song comes... Jon thought and then began to do some mental math.

I've got about ten minutes till the finale... perfect. Jon dropped down to the foothold beneath the one he was resting on and then began to make his way to his right, horizontally across the wall to the guard who was sitting on the edge, pacing himself with the Moon Song.

"My Queen, it has begun."

"Excellent. Rise. Thank you, Raphael," Sofia said and smiled wickedly. Her right-hand man, Raphael, would make a fine mate when this was all over. A new moon had risen over New Puebla. Soon her husband and his brood would be dead. Sofia would feast on half the city to celebrate and then force the other half to build her an armored transport, something that could roam the reaches of the Earth while protecting her and her loyalists from the harmful rays of the daylight sun. Nothing would be able to stop them. They would bring the Hunger with them, spread over the land, creating an army and feeding on whomever they pleased. It was good to be queen.

Raphael rose from his knee and stood before her, matching her smile with a satisfied smirk of his own.

"Did my dear husband receive the tip?" she inquired.

"Most assuredly, Queen. My spies informed him of a plot against his new pet. He still thinks that he cannot be harmed, that after the execution of your cousin, and the revelations that came from it, that you wouldn't dare to attack him. He was overheard saying as much."

"He is truly an idiot if he thinks that after what happened, after what he did, putting food before us, I wouldn't find out about his imprisoned god." Sofia laughed and traced a lacquered fingernail across the bespoke suit that enshrouded Raphael's broad chest. "He has no idea that we have all made trips downstairs; our secret rendezvous with the Hunger. We, my lovely Raphael, are no longer under the yoke of his siredom." Her smile doubled in size as her wandering fingertip inched lower and lower, going past Raphael's belt buckle before twirling around in concentric circles, causing him to grow.

The henchman half closed his eyes and gently thrust his pelvis forward, clearly enjoying the attention.

"I look forward to our celebration, my Queen."

"As do I, as do I." She flashed her eyes playfully and abruptly stopped her sexual torture of her right-hand man. "Despite his ignorance, he is still a formidable foe. I'm not sure we could best him head on." Her smile vanished, and she looked deeply into Raphael's eyes, wanting further reassurance that her plan would succeed.

"Fear not, Queen. The fool knows he couldn't prevent you from wrecking his pet from where he plans to be, in his VIP booth. I have it on good authority that he is packing his ray-gun."

"Perrrrfect," Sofia purred and leaned forward to embrace Raphael in a deep kiss.

After getting her fill, Sofia broke off the kiss and spun around, facing the room filled with twenty-something loyalists, vampire men and women who had all secretly sworn their immortal lives to the Queen of New Puebla. Each one of them had, for their service, been allowed to drink from Sofia, ensuring that none of them would die if something happened to Don Luis Fernando.

"The stage is set, in more ways than one." Sofia laughed, prompting her private militia to do likewise. She beheld her grand plan: the two dozen loyal soldiers all held in front of them large, rectangular riot-control tower shields. At the moment, each shield was covered by dark burlap bags. Bags that could be flung off quickly and easily. Behind those bags was the real *coup de grace,* for each shield was in actuality a mirror.

I will provoke him to the point where he will try to kill me with his fancy little pistol, and then I will get the last laugh!

On the stage, Maya performed, and Maya shaped. The shaping of Strange could be compared to the weaving of a tapestry.

If one had a keen eye, one might be able to detect the weaving itself, although in Maya's case, it was cleverly disguised as song and dance. Very few indeed could see the big picture. The tapestry just looked a mess until the very end, when the picture revealed itself. Isolated, the parts of the tapestry were only bits of colored string. Together, interwoven and bound, the bits of colored string became a vision made manifest. And so it goes with Strange.

Those who knew little about the shaping of Strange were under the false assumption that a Shaper was restricted to one spell or effect at a time, that Strange worked in a linear, cause-and-effect kind of way.

This was undoubtedly a result of trying to apply Newtonian thinking to a very, *very* un-Newtonian type of phenomenon. A Shaper could, if he or she were so inclined, shape a simple cantrip, a one-invocation, one-effect Strange, much in the way a single piece of colored string could be used to make the simplest of pictures on a contrasting color backdrop.

But the more grandiose pictures took time to weave and time to reveal themselves and often formed a picture that was, in actuality, many pictures. A scene-scape. The result, when the art was channeled through a talented artist, was more often than not utterly breathtaking.

To say that Maya was merely talented when it came to shaping Strange would be the equivalent of saying that Leonardo da Vinci had known how to draw. Sure, there were tactical disadvantages to having to sing an entire song in order to make her magic manifest, but Maya was a goddess of song, not a goddess of war. Besides, you couldn't rush perfection; good things come to those who wait, and all that.

When doing the show in Home, Maya had stuck to conventional—that is to say, non-Strange, singing and dancing—until the return from the intermission. Then, and only then had she shaped an invocation of fate, calling down the forces of destiny and revealing to her the whereabouts and identity of Jon, her star-crossed guardian. Once she had found her man, she had returned to a conventional performance.

This show was different. The set—the songs and the music —were the same, yet *different*. A tiny gesture here, a flick of the wrist there, the focus of intent, channeled into and through her voice. That was the difference. Without the focus of intent, what was the difference between a song sung with love and gusto and a chant, an invocation sung to the universe, to whatever gods had set one's mind, heart, and soul afire with cosmic power?

The difference was subtle, except in the mind and will of the Shaper.

This show, unlike the one at Home, was filled in its entirety with intent. Each movement and each note were a separate piece of colored string that Maya was masterfully weaving together to form a picture of many pictures. It had to be perfect, or she and her friends' efforts would be thwarted. It all had to come together at just the same time, in perfect unison, in perfect power and glory. Yet no beads of sweat born from frustrated concentration marched across Maya's brow; she was as gentle and exquisite as a swan gliding across the placid mirror surface of a spring lake on a calm day.

The strings grew short, their ends approaching. Somewhere in the back of her mind, behind the consciousness that directed her voice and body and the higher levels that directed her intent and will into the physical universe, Maya hoped.

Get ready, everyone. Here we go.

From her vantage, Maya could see the entire audience. She turned her gaze to a particular spot in the crowd where she had made a point of letting her eyes linger much throughout the show: the royal box, the VIP section, lifted higher above the masses, in the perfect center of the stadium, providing the best view of the Lily Sapphire show to those within it—specifically to Don Luis Fernando and his entourage.

Don Luis was dressed in his best finery, a dark, smooth suit cut to his body, made from pre-Storm materials no longer available in today's intra-city market. He wore a black fedora that looked positively ridiculous, trimmed with a narrow band of white cloth and, although seated, he held in his hand the polished, orb-shaped pommel of a walking cane, which seemed only to be supporting his arm, and served as a decoration.

He was joined by a half-dozen toughs, also dressed to kill. They sat slightly behind and around him in a semi-circle. If they expected trouble, it was clear that they expected it from any direction besides the stage. To the left of Don Luis was an empty chair. Sofia was nowhere to be seen—no surprise there. The queen's absence worried Maya slightly, yet she didn't hesitate in wrapping up the final bits of her masterwork tapestry.

The show must go on.

Don Luis smiled at her in a way that made her think of a wolf grinning before it consumed its meal of sheep. His eyes burned with a possessive lust that made her shiver. He also knew the end of the show was nearing and seemed ready to spring up from his seat any second and make his way to the stage, where he would drink her life's blood and feed his back to her in front of the vampiric population of New Puebla. Although that time had not yet come, and his fangs remained on the friendly side of her neck's skin, the way he looked at her already made her feel violated. It was unnerving.

She batted her eyes at him and gave him a subtle, seductive smile, the corners of her mouth turning ever so slightly up into her roundish moon cheeks. Don Luis's eyes flashed as he received the message loud and clear. Maya's skin crawled.

The song ended. The audience roared with cheers. Ratt killed the lights and cued up the soft blue floor light installed in the stage behind Maya. Its brilliant rays spread out from the floor to the sky like a peacock plume in full strutting glory. Although she could no longer see him, she knew that Don Luis was still staring at her, molesting her with his wolf eyes, and that his hands remained on the armrest of the chair and walking cane respectively, while everyone else's clapped violently for more. In her mind's eye, Maya gathered the last little bits of the spell strings and began to tie them together, tucked away and trimmed, thereby completing the tapestry.

Her voice sang out *a cappella* across the darkness and hushed the applause like a tsunami spreading out over the masses. The blue light silhouetted her and only added to the mystical ambiance of her last song. She sounded like an angel in mourning, and waves of gooseflesh erupted over the skin of undead and alive alike, sweeping out and over the city in the wake of the silencing tsunami. Her voice went higher and higher until her spell song culminated in a beautiful soprano note that sounded like the glory of Heaven, of the Celestial Court itself, and then all the lights came back on.

Her Strange complete, the lens of every light in the catwalk dissolved away, replaced by perfect miniature portals, a dozen mini-Drop-like windows to the other side of the globe, to a place near and dear to her, the homeland of Enki.

In an instant, the city center square flooded in brilliant, natural, yellow-white sunlight.

And the vampires burned.

18

E ven from his position halfway up the small mountain, Carbine could hear the screams of the burning vampires.

Here we go. Hurry, Jon! The girls and Ratt are going to be under attack any second.

Through the telescopic sights, Carbine watched as Jon pulled himself back up into a chin-up position, this time directly behind the guard who had been sitting on the waist-high edge of the rampart railing. Just moments before, the guard had witnessed what Carbine and Jon could hear. Maya's trap had been sprung, and the dozen spotlights up in the concert's rigging were now waving beams of lethal sunlight back and forth across the city square.

Carbine watched the guard sit in stunned disbelief, his jaw slack, and just as he was snapping out of it and rising to his feet, he was grabbed from behind by Jon and flung off the wall.

Jon kicked his legs over the wall and came to a low stance, reaching behind him to unsling his hammer just as the two closest guards, left and right respectively, turned their heads from the spectacle of pyrotechnic death in the plaza to see why their companion had just screamed.

Carbine was as quick as he was accurate. He didn't wait for Jon to let fly the hammer; he only had to see the direction Jon was looking in to know that he and his railgun had to look the other.

A slight shift of the barrel to the right and, *freeze, squeeze.*

The sentry to the right and slightly behind Jon had his head atomized by a super-sonic slug of depleted uranium before he could even take the safety off his rifle.

The boom echoed down through the canyon and swept over the city, but Carbine didn't worry about anyone noticing. The rulers of New Puebla and their servants had other, bigger concerns at the moment. A slight shift back to the left, just a hair farther, and Carbine found Jon, retrieving his hammer from the crushed rib cage of the other guard. Jon made a quick look back over his shoulder in Carbine's direction, nodded, and then jumped over the wall into the city.

"Egghead, remind me to thank you for your fine work," Carbine said to himself. The rifle kicked considerably more than the Lawnmower he had grown up and trained with, but thanks to the egghead's modifications, it was bearable. Forgetting his relief and gratitude for the moment, Carbine returned his attention to the task at hand.

He could have switched on the railgun's scope to phase through the layer of stone that now separated Jon from his view and even follow him with his gun all the way to Jon's destination and beyond, perhaps, but as previously agreed, Carbine wished Jon good luck and moved his sights to the city square to cover Maya.

If Jon failed, Carbine was to provide cover for Maya to escape. Above all, Maya must live to continue her campaign against the Harvesters. As grim as the thought was, guardians were replaceable, while goddesses were not.

Whoa. I knew things would be intense, but this...

The city was ablaze. Human-shaped pillars of flame ran

amok, crashing into each other and buildings alike, spreading the fire everywhere as they went. Some writhed on the floor, and others had already become nothing more than smoking piles of ash. The initial shock of the surprise attack hadn't worn off yet and nobody, neither human nor vampire, was making any move to launch a counterattack on Maya.

Carbine spun the knob on his scope back two clicks and took in a broader view of the plaza. He instantly spotted Ratt up in the catwalks, operating the twelve spotlights from a control panel, causing each of them to swivel like a machine gun turret, sweeping their beams of light over huge swathes of fleeing vampires.

The effect made Carbine think of a fire-fighter's water cannon or a flamethrower with an incredible range. He also spotted Lucy, who had sprung up and out of the DJ booth and was now upstaging Maya, a Macuahuitl at the ready, and taking pot shots into the crowd with her BFG at any vamp not on fire.

Carbine decided to join Lucy in her endeavors and clicked in three turns.

Freeze, squeeze, repeat.

Maya opened her eyes the very second she had finished the high note. She watched the sea of darkness, flecked like stars with the glowing red eyes of her vampire audience, as it became white-washed with the brightness of sunlight when the dozen spotlights turned on.

Her eyes locked into Don Luis's gaze and she watched his expression change from lust and greed into one of confusion and pain.

Ratt had maneuvered one of the spotlights into a straight line to the VIP booth during the last few seconds of the song, as they hoped to take the head off the wolf in the first few seconds of the attack. The plan was sound, and Ratt's aim was true, but what they didn't count on was Don Luis's constitution. Perhaps by dint of his great age, or maybe because he had been turned by the demon-urchin itself, Don Luis Fernando seemed to be more powerful than his peers. Whatever the reason, he was not instantly vaporized by the beam of sunlight the way the savages had been last week, the way his retinue of bodyguards burned around him.

Maya watched with morbid disappointment as the beam illuminated Don Luis's face, blackening it into a rough, cracked, leathery affair, which seemed to steam or smoke but didn't burst into the consuming flames of purification she had hoped for. His charred face contrasted his ivory fangs, exposed to the light as his lips were pulled back entirely in a sneer of rage and suffering.

Surprised and wounded, Don Luis still had his survival instincts; they were, after all, his strongest character trait next to greed and selfishness. He reflexively pulled his hands to his face and the shiny, polished silver chrome pommel of the cane he had been holding diffused the incoming beam like a disco ball, splashing the burning rays out and away from him, effectively saving him for the moment.

That brief moment turned out to be all he needed to survive longer.

His hand burned, but his face was shielded enough for him to see a bodyguard who was writhing in his seat, only an arm's reach away. Don Luis ruthlessly grabbed the man and pulled him up, holding him out and in front of himself as he dropped the cane. The bodyguard performed admirably as a protector of the city's king, though not for very long.

Don Luis had only been holding the man for a few short

seconds before the body-turned-shield began to burn like the tallow-dipped torches of the palace catacombs. It was long enough, however, for Don Luis to make his getaway.

He leapt out of the VIP booth, using the dying bodyguard as a tower shield, and dashed to a short stone wall that was part of a raised garden bed, one of several that decorated the city square and had existed long before anyone had thought of turning the plaza into concert grounds. He held the man-torch in his hands until he reached the garden bed, his hands burning from the flames.

When he reached it, he tossed the man up and over and ducked down, effectively disappearing from the immediate threat of the sunbeams. Don Luis noticed that immediately after switching from decorative stage lights to lethal beams of sunlight, something he didn't quite understand, the beams began to move, eliminating survivors of the initial assault the way a side-door gunman in a helicopter would mow down fleeing infantry.

He watched in horror as beams of light chased down his fleeing kin and burned them to ash. The city seemed aglow, sounds of screams echoing everywhere.

"How could this have happened? We are *gods*! We must fight back and destroy this witch. I was such a fool! Sofia was right! *Sofia!*" His mind raced, and he searched the crowd for signs of his wife. He had casually noticed that she had not joined him in the VIP booth; in fact, he had not seen her since last night. They had fought again briefly after his short visit to Lily Sapphire's chambers. He had not even listened to what she'd said—something about Lily's assistant wandering through the palace where he didn't belong the night before, something about how she would show him. He'd cared nothing for the rambling gripes coming from his wife. *I should have listened*, he thought now. Perhaps Sofia knew something. *Where* is *she?*

Sofia stared in shock as her city burned.

My husband is a bigger fool than I thought! He has invited a bruja *into our city!*

Besides the light of day, there was only one other thing that Don Luis Fernando and Sofia feared. *Mágico.* Strange. And those who could shape it. Early on in the first days of New Puebla, they had discovered some of their human cattle began to spontaneously alter reality in mystical ways. One, in particular, could light fires from nothing, even going so far as to become a living inferno, seemingly invulnerable to its own conjured flames. That was enough, then and there, for them both to agree that no such talent, no matter how harmless it may have seemed at the time, would ever be allowed in their city. Since then, any Puebloan citizen demonstrating paranormal abilities was swiftly and thoroughly taken care of, without prejudice.

"Now look what your lust and stupidity have wrought us!" Sofia screamed to the night.

She and her men had marched to the plaza from their covert meeting place and entered the plaza from the north, coming at Don Luis's VIP booth from the side. The plan had been simple, if risky: keeping their distance from the VIP booth, they would attack the singing slut from the side of the stage, provoking Don Luis into shooting at Sofia with his laser pistol. Her loyalists would be ready, and form a veritable shield wall phalanx, using their mirrors to reflect the lethal beam directly back to Don Luis. If the initial shot did not kill him outright, then they would move in, like an armored tortoise, until they could get close enough to overpower Don Luis and rip him to shreds. He never would expect it, or even defend against it, because he truly believed that no one would kill him, lest they die themselves.

Now it seemed that perhaps her dirty work had been done for

her, but not in the way she'd expected, wanted, or appreciated. If steps weren't taken immediately, she and her men wouldn't have a city to feed on and rule over, but worse still, and seeming more likely by the second, she and her men would follow Don Luis into a fiery grave.

Good thing we all happen to be carrying giant mirrors.

"The attack is coming from the stage lights! Use your shields to reflect the beams and shoot those *pinche* lights down!"

Sofia withdrew the *pistola* she carried, and thought with perverse pleasure that she would still be able to use it for its original purpose—to kill Lily Sapphire. She pulled the slide back, chambering a round, and called for Raphael to follow her in the attack.

They turned to the stage and began their charge, shields up and guns blazing.

"Come mierda y muere!" Sofia screamed at the top of her lungs. The counter-attack had begun.

Maya found Sofia before Don Luis did. She'd watched as the beam scorched Don Luis and watched as he'd deflected his death with his cane first, and the bodyguard second. She knew that he had ended up behind the meter-high concrete square with the tree growing out of the center and was deciding how best to proceed. Should she try and get Ratt's attention, and if she did, would Ratt be too focused on Don Luis and his cover instead of moving the spotlights where they were needed to maximize vampire carnage? She decided she would keep an eye on the tree bed herself and warn Lucy to prepare for a counterattack.

The counterattack came, but not from Don Luis. Maya had already heard several loud booms echo through the night as

Carbine's railgun entered the fray and picked off fleeing vampires, their heads disappearing in red clouds.

But then she heard a closer, quieter crack. Not a distant, cannon-like sonic boom, but something more like a typical pre-Storm small-arms report.

First one, then two, then a volley. Several of the spotlights went out. One crashed to the stage, its mount to the catwalk railing broken clean in two.

Lucy also picked up on what was going on after nearly being hit by the falling spotlight.

Both women looked around in alarm, now fully comprehending that they were taking fire and quickly losing their "big gun."

There, in the back of the plaza, where the open courtyard met the first block of adobe buildings and was bisected by a road, stood Sofia, flanked by loyal men holding polished metal riot shields and a solid platoon of human guards, as unafraid of the sunlight as the plants of the earth that fed on it.

"Lucy!" Maya blurted out and pointed an outstretched finger in their direction.

"I see them," Lucy replied coolly and flipped off the stage, landing in a perfect crouch before taking off, sprinting toward the new threat, her bladed club already in motion to clear the way.

Ratt was taking heavy fire and attempted to defend himself by retaliating with the sun-spotlights, a reflexive gesture that was as ineffectual as hurling an insult at them.

When the spotlight in his hands exploded from a direct hit and another conventional bullet grazed his shoulder, causing him to half-spin and collapse against the railing of the catwalk behind him, he knew he was done for and made to retreat.

Clutching his bleeding right shoulder with his hand, Ratt shambled over to the scaffolding ladder that was clamped onto the catwalk and ran straight down to the back of the stage below. He climbed on, and as soon as his weight was fully off the grating and onto the ladder, he realized the shot he'd taken might be more than a graze.

His shoulder sizzled and pumped out a fresh squirt of blood. Its rapidly cooling warmth ran down around both sides of his shoulder and met up again below his armpit, creeping further down to his waist, soaking his shirt in the process.

His right arm failed him, and he dropped a rung, nearly falling completely off.

"Ungh!"

His left arm shot up and hooked through the space between two rungs of the simple metal ladder and he caught himself, his legs flailing. He bounced his shins off another rung somewhere below. Wincing, he gritted his teeth and hissed. The adrenaline rush that came from his near fall helped stave off the wave of creeping unconsciousness that was threatening to overtake him. The pain in his shoulder was excruciating.

He heard the gunfire continue as well as the zings of ricochets bouncing nearby. Even from his awkward position up on the ladder, he could see that only a handful of sun-spotlights remained intact. The portals that Maya had summoned remained open, of course, but with their housings destroyed, they remained stationary, while some had fallen to the stage as well, their destructive beams no more than immobile, though dangerous, columns of death that could be avoided with ease by the regrouping vampires.

We're in trouble...

Maya saw it too. Even as Lucy waded into the crowd to take out Sofia and her human gunmen, she was met by the first wave of vampires who had either overcome their initial shock at the sprung trap or had realized the spotlights were no longer moving and now posed only a mild threat.

Lucy, while as talented at death as any grim reaper, was right back to where she had been out in the scrub against the savages. None of them were a match for her, even when the odds were thirty to one, but she couldn't keep them down, and it was only a matter of time before the numbers simply became too many for her to contend with.

Already some were slipping past her, confident that she was occupied enough not to stop them, and they made their way toward the stage.

Maya's eyes grew with fright as she realized that she and her guardians' hand had been played; that their opponent had called their bluff.

She was now a very legitimate target, and Lucy was not there to protect her.

One vampire leapt from his spot in the plaza and flew through the air as if he had been lifted by an invisible wire. His legs bent in a way that enhanced the perception that he was more beast than man—hands up, fingers spread, claws flashing in the ambient firelight that surrounded them. He landed on the stage two meters from Maya, who stumbled backward a step, falling into an instinctual defensive stance, like a mouse when cornered by a cat.

He roared his rage at her, revealing his cuspidate fangs, and made a small dip backward before springing toward her, like the pulling of a slingshot.

Maya yelped and flinched, her petite hands rising to shield her face and neck from the coming assault. She felt a wet spray across her face and the rush of wind across her neck. When she heard the sonic boom catch up with the slug, she opened her eyes and saw her assailant separated into a half-dozen pieces that now lay spread across the stage and had already begun the slow but sure process of growing themselves back together. She thanked Carbine in her mind and rushed forward, flipping her back foot out and connecting it with a large chunk of the vampire's head, sending it flying out into the plaza.

There would be more where he came from, and in short order. Maya found her resolve and began to sing again.

Hurry, Jon.

19

Jon heard the sonic boom a second after he let go of his hammer and watched it crash into the sentry's chest. The blow lifted the man up off his feet and sent him crashing through the support post that he had been leaning against the moment before he spotted Jon throwing his colleague to his death.

Whoa. I still don't know my own strength. Better rein it in a bit. I almost sent that guy flying. Don't want to alert everyone.

Worried that he had been spotted, Jon ducked and spun around, half expecting the fourth guard to be training his rifle sights on him and half expecting the man to be no more. The latter expectation proved to be true.

Good job, Carbine.

Many things had changed over the last month, but Carbine's sharpshooting skill was not one of them. Jon turned back around and retrieved his hammer from the man he had smitten, then glanced up at the hillside and threw a nod and a salute in Carbine's general direction before hopping off the landing to the city below.

He landed on the ground with a thud, kicking up a cloud of dust and surprising the hell out of a human passing by. The man froze and stared at Jon blankly. Jon rose out of his squat and chambered his hammer for a swing.

"Friend or foe?" Jon asked in the common language of Home.

The man, dressed in simple farmer's clothes worn nearly bare, only blinked. In the background, Jon could hear screaming and hollering coming from the city square as well as the broken beat of the repeated but random sonic booms issuing forth from Carbine's railgun. There was no time to waste; Jon repeated his question in different words.

"Look, I'm here to liberate you. I'm a friend." Then, taking one hand off the hammer's handle and placing it on his armor-clad chest, *"Me amigo."* The man said nothing, nor moved at all. Frustrated with the language barrier, Jon rolled his eyes, then turned to go, leaving the dumbstruck citizen behind and making his way to the palace.

Jon heard the crack of a small-arms pistol, then felt first its impact, and second the wave of disappointment.

The bullet that struck him between the shoulder blades was the last thing he had expected from a slave he was working so hard to free.

Jon turned and frowned at the man, who held a pre-Storm 9mm pistol in his shaking hands.

Sheesh. Old-gen pistol like that has no chance of penetrating my armor. I should count myself lucky that this guy's knowledge of armor and ballistics are about as simple as his wardrobe.

Upon seeing Jon's display of invincibility, the man dropped his tiny pistol and ran. Jon let him go, shaking his head and giving thanks that he hadn't been forced to kill another human. He was here to slay vampires and free the humans, and meeting violent resistance from humans who had pledged their service to the very power that oppressed them made his job morally difficult. Revolution was dirty, ugly work.

Jon watched the man disappear and then checked his surroundings for threats and opportunities. There, hanging on a clothesline that stretched across a bleak commons area in the center of an assembly of rough, poorly built adobe hovels, came a great opportunity in the form of laundry.

Jon snatched the poncho off the line and quickly donned it. Despite the chaos that had erupted across the city, he was a *gringo* and would stand out; he needed every edge he could get. Jon secured his hammer under the folds of his new garb and peered across the darkened skyline of the city.

Even from his location at street level, he could see the tip of the palace jutting up into the starry night, its smooth, blocky surfaces periodically flashing reflections of the sunbeams dancing below in the central plaza. Jon began to dash through the streets toward the palace and what was hidden deep inside it, glancing left and right as he went.

Every three or four strides, he could hear the sonic report of Carbine's railgun, and he hoped that Maya was faring well. The closer he got to the palace and the city square, the more crowded and chaotic the scene became. Here, a small pack of vampires fled from the center, some screaming, others cursing, all running straight past Jon without so much as a glance; there, a vampire made of sterner stuff was organizing a counterattack party of human loyalists. Coming or going, all were blessedly far too occupied with the threat in the plaza to notice a poncho-clad gringo in the dark, who, by running through the street with urgency, fit into the scene perfectly.

By the time he reached the palace grounds, Jon could distinctly make out only a small fraction of the dozen-plus sunbeam rays that his friends had started with. He knew the tides were turning against Maya.

Shit, he cursed silently. *Hang on just a little longer, guys.*

With that final hopeful thought, he began to climb the steps that led to the front door of the palace. The plan and the subsequent mess it had unleashed was working exactly the way Maya had hoped; it just wasn't lasting as long as they had wanted.

Hopefully, it was long enough.

Jon made it to the top of the steps and was pleased to see that the front doors were unguarded. Maya's plan had worked, so far. The finale ambush had drawn all the guards away from the palace, clearing the way for him. He tried not to look like he was out of place as he stood there, glancing around.

I'm overthinking it. Just do it.

He stopped only long enough to look back toward the city center. He could see the plaza in the distance; there was a straight road that stretched from the edge of the palace grounds to the city center. He could see the stage and Maya upon it. She seemed to be surrounded by a globe of glowing light, and Ratt was beside her, but he couldn't make out Lucy. There was a throng of people in front of the stage. It looked like either a mosh pit or a melee battle. Jon knew it was the latter. He could see only two sunbeams left, and they were now stationary, making their rays of death easy to avoid.

I'd better hurry.

Turning toward the palace entrance, he drew his hammer and swallowed.

Okay. It was the first left, a stairway at the end of the hall... Jon concentrated on remembering the order of the directions given to him by Maya when they'd hatched the plan.

Upon hearing Ratt's tale, the goddess had determined that slaying the vampires and liberating the humans was their only course of action. Once decided, she had related all she could to Jon and Carbine, hoping they were listening. Entering into a semi-hypnotic trance, she'd recalled the entire evening that she had spent with Don Luis Fernando. She'd watched herself in her mind's eye as she was escorted through the palace by the king after their stroll through the streets. She could pause, rewind, and slow the play-by-play of the night's events. She glossed over the bits regarding his pompous, long-winded, and megalomaniacal speech, only just mentioning them, and instead chose to focus her attention to the details of every turn they'd made, every doorway they'd entered, every step they'd taken on the way down into the depths of the palace's heart to witness the secret that dwelled within.

Now it was Jon who had to muster his mental acuity and remember every twist and turn of Maya's dark journey, while simultaneously keeping watch for anyone else who might be keeping watch for him.

Jon intended to find and kill the demon-urchin. He wanted this—no, *needed* this—more than anything right now, for if it did not die, then Maya surely would. If he screwed up, if he misremembered just one of Maya's directions, then he could become lost in the palace, sacrificing time that none of them had to spare. He had to focus on what she had said yet remain aware enough not to stumble into hostiles unawares.

Suddenly, after what seemed like seconds, though surely must have been minutes, Jon found himself standing before the black door with the small circular opening in it. He was amazed both at the fact that he had made it to the door without running into any guards and at the fact that despite his attempts to maintain situational awareness, he had been in the same semi-hypnotic trance that Maya had been in when she'd recalled the directions to him, acting nearly on rote alone. Quickly deciding not to question his good fortune, Jon shrugged off the trance with a quick shake of his head and made to reach his hands into the yawning circles of hungry darkness that were the mouths on the door.

Wait a second... Will the door even accept my blood? I can't play my hand too soon now... What if it's attuned only to Don Luis?

Knowing that there was no way to know, Jon found himself eyeing the stone of the decorated slab. Could he smash it with his hammer? Would it alert guards? Only one way to know. In this case, brute force seemed the safest bet.

Knock! Knock!

Boom!

Boom!

Jon cocked back for a third blow just as the hairline fractures from the first two began first to appear, then grow, bisecting the dozen mouths and grinning demon face carved into the half-meter-thick stone slab.

BOOM!

The third time proved to be the proverbial charm. As the head of Jon's hammer bounced off the door, fist-sized bits of it followed, spilling out onto the ground. The fissures now more closely resembled yawning gaps. Jon spun the hammer in his grip and used the war-nail to hook and pry. His skin again began to glow with the power of the serum. He felt his body temperature spike. He grunted with the effort as he placed the bottom of his boot against the door for more leverage. When a torso-sized chunk of slab broke free, he nearly lost his balance and had to hop back twice before he regained his footing.

The wave of decay hit his nose before the dust from the crumbling door had even cleared, carrying along with it a palpable sense of dread and persistent, maddening hunger. Jon felt cold wrap itself around his burning body like an ice bath. Every strand of modified DNA in his body was firing the Morse code SOS for fight or flight, and a cold sweat broke out across his dusty skin. He spun the hammer back into its smackdown position.

From beyond the pitch-black veil obscuring the room beyond the door, Jon could hear a dragging slipper-on-pavement sound— the slithering sound of the hundred mouths with their flashing needles. Somebody was awake, hungry, and very pissed off.

Lucy tore into the crowd like a half-dozen tornadoes touching down in the Shanty. Limbs and bits, human and vampire alike, sailed through the plaza like comets, streaming tails of blood and viscera in their wake. Being a cyborg, she had the advantage over normal humans of never tiring, of having machine precision in all her moves. Although it was the only part of her that was still human, even her brain had been enhanced with inorganic circuitry, allowing her to block fear and pain, control and regulate her body's peptides and hormones and, as in the case of the present moment, multitask in a way that only a computer could, executing four different killing blows, to different targets, simultaneously, while perfectly timing a side-step so minuscule as to escape death by a fraction of an inch without flinching.

With all the steadfastness of the ocean's incoming tide, wave after wave of attackers poured into the plaza to break over Lucy's blades and gun. Despite her best efforts, however, for every four that she killed, at least one would indeed slip by to threaten Maya and Ratt. Part of her was aware of this, yet she was unable to do anything about it. It wasn't that she preferred to fight the ones that she was fighting; it was that she was overwhelmed by them and any hesitation or alteration in her dance of death would result in her being wounded first, then slowed down, then killed. And dead guardians meant a dead goddess. Even though she was spinning, ducking, and lunging like an entire troupe of acrobats rolled into one, she had spotted, locked on to, and was tracking the location of one Sofia Fernando, and inch by bloody inch, she was getting closer to her. Knowing that she had waded too far out into this hostile sea to turn around and stand by her lady, Lucy and her war-clubs were now banking on the hope that if Sofia were to fall, the New Puebla counterattack would rout.

Sofia stood at the edge of the bloodbath, continuing to bark orders, rally her human sympathizers and otherwise organize the counterattack, which, despite the massive losses at the hands of Lucy and Carbine, was slowly turning the tide. Nearly all of the deadly floodlights had been shot out, and close to two dozen vampires were now at the stage, clawing at a glowing bubble that seemed to be protecting the traitorous Lily Sapphire.

First I need to get through this ninja bitch, then I will have you, you little skank.

Sofia relished the thought of killing Lily slowly and redoubled her efforts at getting past the cyclone of death that was Lucy. She glanced around for her husband. *Where is he?*

It was not concern for him that she felt, of course, but a desire to kill him herself. He didn't know it, but she had years ago visited his little secret in the catacombs. He thought he was invincible; that no vampire would dare oppose him after the revelations that came to light when he had her cousin executed. He would be cocky, would not defend himself. He would be quintessentially himself. And then she would show him who was really boss.

She didn't see him, which meant one of two things: either he had died from the initial blasts of sunlight, his body now ash, or he had escaped and still lived. He was coward enough to hide. Not a real man at all.

As her eyes scanned the plaza, she caught a glimpse of one of her men, a human sentry, running from the eye of the Lucy storm. It would seem that the lady of death had killed a comrade of his, for this man was dragging the top half of another to the edge of the plaza. Sofia watched as the sentry noticed the web of dirty, torn entrails where his friend's legs should be and screamed. Her eyes narrowed with hate as she watched this sentry of hers release his comrade's underarms, clutch his face in horror, glance up at the bloody melee, and then turn to run.

Coward!

Sofia bolted from her square of ground and intercepted the fleeing man, coming in from the side, entering his peripheral vision at the same time that her smooth, polished-nail-clad hands clutched him by the throat and lifted him a half-meter off the ground, his legs and feet still trying to run. The sentry's hands instinctively went to his throat and clawed feebly at Sofia's fingers. He looked like he wanted to say something, to scream perhaps, or maybe beg for mercy, but not even the sound of escaping air could breach the collapsed tunnel of his throat.

"Mama had a baby and its head popped off." Sofia's eyes lit up with wicked glee. Her nostrils flared, and her lips peeled back in a sneer. Her fingers closed into a fist, and the sentry's head rolled to one side and hung there, still attached by flaps of skin to the body that now drooped from below Sofia's clenched fist. She glowered at her ragtag army.

"Immortality to those who bring me their heads! Death to all cowards! Death to the families of cowards! I will fucking kill every last one of you! *Me cago en todo lo que se menea!*"

That seemed to do the trick. The attention of her men lingered on her only long enough to watch her relax her grip on the sack of skin that used to be the man's neck and then throw his ragdoll body to the ground.

Fully in the grip of bloodlust, Sofia launched herself into the throng, gunning for Lucy instead of standing back and encouraging her men to make the best use of their small-arms fire and spray the painted bitch with a sea of bullets.

Sofia headed straight toward Lucy, wading through the sea of men like a Lily Sapphire concert-goer attempting to rush the front row. The painted cyborg appeared not to notice her, not altering the rhythm of parry, dodge, riposte, slash, tuck, roll, shoot, rinse and repeat that she had going.

Pushing her way forward, Sofia drew closer and closer, circling behind her prey, until she was nearly within arm's reach.

Ratt fell hard. His vision, along with his knowledge of who and where he was and what he was doing, faded in and out in throbbing waves of darkness. He wanted to cry uncle, to give up, but he found something inside himself—that same something that had gotten him this far, that helped him when his parents fell in the battle of Texhoma.

Ratt may not have been, and never would be, a big, strong warrior-type like Jon, but he was no coward. Tears of pain, rage, and frustration burned down his cheeks, the weight of impotence nearly crushing him. He struggled under the whole sum of it all. The world, the loss, the horror, and tragedy; it was almost too much to bear. Throw in the nerve-splitting pain of first a gunshot wound, then a five-meter drop to a hard floor, and the levee of well-meaning bravado had just plain burst.

Somehow, without even knowing what was going on or who he was, he breathed through it. In breath—ragged, shaky. Out breath—smoother, smoother.

There ya go, bud.

In times like this, in the thick of battle, under intense duress and pain, there comes a phenomenon. To one that has never experienced it before and been able to look back and reflect on it, it may seem like one is losing oneself. Of course, the opposite is true.

In situations like the one that Ratt presently found himself in, one doesn't lose oneself; one *finds* oneself. One only loses the identity that one has built up, the identity fettered to the circumstances of one's life, the experiences, memories, ego.

What one finds in the space left behind in the ego's swift departure is one's authentic self. The you who was before you were named.

"Ratt" was gone, driven out by pain and fury. What was there now was the fox caught in the trap's steel jaws, the seal twisting in the waters just ahead of the orca's jagged tooth, the cybernetic angel of death who dips into the oncoming blade rather than shy away.

It could be argued by people cut from the same cloth as Lucy that, in times such as this, one is more "at one" with the universe than any other time in one's life. It could not be denied that one is fully in the present when experiencing this phenomenon. It is the golden rush that athletes speak of, the frenzy of orgasm, the meat-over-mind.

Somewhere in that primordial no-self of now, the boy with no name just breathed and breathed until, slowly, the boy called Ratt returned, opened his eyelids, and saw through the dull blur of tears that he had fallen onto the stage and landed only a few feet from the goddess of song and Strange.

Even from his distorted vantage, he could see that he and Maya were both in trouble. There was no sign of Lucy, and many people were rushing the stage. His loyalty combined with adrenaline made him temporarily forget about the gunshot wound. He rolled over to his front and attempted to push himself into a standing position. He was maybe an inch off the ground when he quickly and painfully became re-acquainted with the shoulder injury as well as met some new friends—*Hello, broken leg; nice to meet you, broken hip. Sprained ankle? Come on in!* Ratt tried to curse his luck but only managed a muffled "Murghrpoh!" as he collapsed back down onto himself and the floor, his face mashing into the stage, drool and blood spilling out of his mouth and wetting his cheek.

Without breaking her song or even looking at him, Maya side-stepped a few paces to get closer to him, bringing her circle of light with her. Ratt felt the warmth wash over his body. Its comforting energy brought back long-forgotten feelings of safety, as well as subconscious, locked-away memories of being a swaddled babe in his mother's arms. Unlike the sunlight that poured from the dozens of mini portals that Maya had opened in the stage lights, this light was not harmful to attacking vampires; it was a protective globe that prevented vampire and human, as well as their projectiles, from getting too close to Maya—and now Ratt.

Ratt watched with mounting relief as incoming bullets ricocheted off the sphere. A vampire, screaming with rage, leapt and clawed at the light, only to be repelled and pushed back a few inches. Maya's Strange was strong, but her face showed strain from the effort. She sang non-stop and gestured with her arms, hands, and fingers, doing some interpretive dance, looking like a child making a cat's cradle with invisible string.

How much longer can she keep this up?

As he studied the crowds surging and being repelled, he was likewise relieved to see that their "eye in the sky," Carbine, was focusing his attention on them. Here and there, a vampire or human would explode in a cloud of red mist, followed by the familiar sonic boom a second later. Despite pulling a trigger as fast as he could, getting off a shot every two seconds, it seemed that Carbine's efforts were a drop in the bucket. The human sympathizers would never get back up, but the vampires' bodies began to regenerate before all the spray had even landed. Still, enough drops fall into a bucket, and the bucket will eventually overflow.

Ratt willed himself to roll back over onto his back. Above him and through the golden hue of Maya's Strange circle, he could see the catwalk from which he'd fallen. He remembered now trying to climb down the ladder, the jolt of fire that had shot through his shoulder... but the rest was a blank.

It was then that he remembered his hoverboard.

He raised his wrist to his face and punched a few buttons on his bracelet with a trembling, bloody finger. A few moments passed, the space between command and execution filled by the animal sounds of the vampire mob and Maya's protection song, its lovely melody tainted by the edge of worry and fatigue in her voice. Then, in the split second before the board began to crack skulls and part the Red Sea, so to speak, Ratt took a deep inhalation and summoned a sound of his own.

"Maya!" he cried to the sky as loud as he could, overcoming the cacophony of scream and song.

Maya heard the boy's cry and thought perhaps Ratt was calling for her out of fear, or because of his injuries. Then she saw one of the heads belonging to the wall of monsters that clawed at the edges of her sphere dip forward in a sudden and violent motion. Replacing it and coming straight toward her was Ratt's oversized hoverboard.

A flash lit up her eyes, one part comprehension, two parts relief. Down the hatch went a shot of optimism, followed by a chaser of doubt that scrunched up her brow.

The shield! A double realization that hit as hard as any bullet slammed Maya's mind. The board couldn't penetrate the shield, meaning she would have to stop shaping Strange to allow it in, which would also allow the vampires to reach her. She took another two steps closer to Ratt, standing directly over him. She closed her eyes for a heartbeat, wished Lucy and Jon well, then all at once quit the song and swept down to pick Ratt up.

"Come on, Ratt!" she squeaked as she tried to lift him up. The board was on them in a second and promptly lowered itself down to a height appropriate for its pre-programmed operator to easily be able to step onto it, were he standing. The incoming assailants were tripping over themselves to be the first to get at her. They were mad with rage, desperate for revenge for the slain, as well as to garner their queen's favor. Maya knew that if they reached her and Ratt, their end would come. It would come messy, and it would come bloody, and it would come fast.

Ratt took her by the elbow even as her hands clutched the lapels of his leather jacket, pushing her off the ground with his other arm. His legs came alive underneath him, and he sat up halfway, rolling onto the obedient remote-controlled board.

The board began to ascend vertically the second Ratt was on it. Maya felt the fingernails of the vampire mob scratch down the flesh of her calf and tear at the edges of her clothes as she stepped onto the board and rose into the sky. Suddenly, the board's ascension hesitated. Maya panicked, knowing she and Ratt were seconds away from being torn to shreds like a hunk of steak thrown into a pack of hungry dogs.

Glancing around to see the source of the problem, Maya noticed the arm of the big vampire that had lunged and caught the edge of the board. A chain of other vampires clung to him and were now working together to pull the rising board back down to their level.

Maya lifted her foot and brought it down on the vampire's fingers as hard as she could. Nothing. She tried again, this time keeping her foot there and twisting it back and forth. Still nothing.

Then, as suddenly as the board had stopped rising, it lurched again and began floating up like a released balloon. Maya felt for and realized that the muscled vampire's hand was still under her foot. Confused, she leaned over the edge of the board to see whether the chain of clutching vampires had broken and instead saw the severed arm hanging from beneath the board, pinned in place only by her foot. That was when the next sonic boom reached her ears.

She first glanced off in the direction of the foothills she knew were there in the darkness, overlooking and cradling the city, then she looked down into the faces and saw nothing but a sea of animals. *No, they are below animals; animals kill only when hungry.* Don Luis Fernando had tried to paint a picture of civilization here, tried to make her believe his delusion, that he and his kind were simply the ruling class and behaved with civility toward their flock, not even killing, but "milking," as it were, taking just enough to sustain them, while keeping everyone alive.

Animals? No, not by a long shot.

Maya stared at a sea of gibbering, howling monsters, and shuddered.

If Don Luis Fernando was to sit down with himself and have a serious, nakedly honest chat about the attribute that he would most credit for his survival and rise to power, it would be his ability to identify an opportunity and seize it.

It was much like the opportunity you might seize when waiting for a person to bend down to tie their boot laces before you slip a poisoned dagger into their ribs from behind.

Cunning? Maybe. Daring? Not really. Don Luis was all about survival at any cost. Running to live and fight another day was the norm, but every norm has its exceptions. Capturing and enslaving the Drop-Beastie that had made him had been one of those exceptions. Leaving the relative safety of cover to take out Lucy instead of fleeing was another.

From his sheltered crouch, he watched Lucy leap over him and sprint into the crowds at the edge of the plaza. He realized with growing dread that she had transformed from Lily Sapphire's assistant and sound booth operator into a whirling dervish of perfect death, becoming, in reality, the Santa Muerta that she so resembled.

More than once, he'd thought about bolting for it, just running, but his fear kept him frozen in place. This hesitation had turned to a glimmer of wicked hope. He'd remained crouched behind the stone retaining wall, hidden from Lily Sapphire and her sunbeams. From there he'd watched as Sofia, his wife—his poor, estranged wife—led the counterattack. He'd watched as the sunbeams blinked out of existence one at a time, like the fading stars of dawn's approach.

When this is over, I should honor my queen and raise her up... or maybe I'll kill her in her sleep so that she can't lord my error in judgment over me...

At one point, he'd dared to turn and peek over the wall to glimpse the stage. He had watched from the shadows as dozens of his vampires rushed the starlet-turned-sorceress, and his curiosity had gotten the better of him.

Good. She is trapped. Soon, then. Don Luis had smiled inwardly, and ducked back down behind cover, satisfied with what he'd seen—a flickering globe of golden light, protecting her and her whelp from the tooth and claw of New Puebla's justice. He needn't be a sorcerer himself to know that her shield wouldn't last for much longer.

Now then... This other one...

She appeared not to notice him, but then again, she appeared not to notice *anyone*. Her eyes were locked in a thousand-yard stare, and the decorated skull of her face was as devoid of expression and effort as the desert was of rain, only reinforcing that appearance. She looked as one lost in thought, in a daydream, yet no one touched her. She deftly dodged claw, fist, and bullet equally, as if she and her combatants had practiced every day for a year to dazzle judges at some synchronized death-dance competition.

There is no way I'm going anywhere near that. The thought had just crossed his mind when he saw his wife squeeze the head off a fleeing soldier and then proceed to push her way through the troops to get herself a piece of lady Death.

She'll get herself killed... The prospect of seeing his wife slashed apart frightened him as much as it amused him. The mental image of her bloody head rolling across the ground, coming to a stop and then looking up at him as he watched her life force evaporate like spilled water on the hardpan plain flashed across his mind's eye. He realized that he was hard.

Yet... There would be no glory or satisfaction. Sofia was a good deal stronger than any man out there, but if she fell to this painted one, then the odds of him following his wife into the forever-sleep increased dramatically. In one of his rare moments of opportune brazenness, Don Luis Fernando saw something in the midst of the chaos that everyone had missed.

He realized what he must do, and leapt from his hiding place into the thick.

It was too late for Sofia. In her passion, she had lost all sense of tactics and timing. She raged at the men in her way and shoved them aside. The cyborg bitch didn't seem to notice her. Hungry lust flashed across her eyes, and she waited just a second as Lucy turned her back to deal with another kamikaze sentry and then lunged... right into the tip of Lucy's Macuahuitl.

A small gasp, more of surprise than pain, escaped Sofia's mouth. Lucy looked coolly over her shoulder into Sofia's face. The melee seemed to freeze for a second, the vampires and men around them not sure what to do with their leader incapacitated.

Sofia could see the light from the nearby scattered fires reflected in Lucy's eyes. For the first time since the night's combat had begun, a hint of emotion rippled across the placid sea that was Lucy's face. Sofia didn't miss it, even though it was barely there —the genesis of a smile at the far corners of her full lips.

"You are as much of a killer as I am... A wolf like me..." Sofia managed to hiss out, the surprise in her voice there for all to hear.

"Not a wolf. A jaguar," Lucy whispered just loudly enough to reach Sofia's supernatural ears, and then she spun in a tight circle, pulling her obsidian-bladed club from Sofia's stomach and bringing her second one to bear at the queen's neckline.

Lucy waited a moment longer than she should have and watched with barely hidden satisfaction as Sofia's head sailed into the crowd of stunned onlookers. She brought her war-clubs into a defensive cross guard and eyed the crowd, testing them, daring them. *Will they rally toward me again, or has the fight gone out of them?* she wondered, and then the electricity hit her in the small of her back like a punch from a Heavy Mech.

Running across the entire length of the plaza from the outside perimeter to the stage was a thick braid of power cords covered by a small wooden ramp to prevent tripping. Don Luis had had it built to provide power to the impromptu stage. This *Día De Los Muertos* witch-woman was damn near straddling it as she stood there, pretending first not to see, then stabbing his wife in the belly.

This was his one chance. He moved with preternatural speed, nothing more than a blur that zig-zagged across the blood-soaked pavers, with only an imperceptible pause as he stooped mid-stride to rip and tear the electric braid free from the wooden half-hex that covered it and bound it to the ground. Like a bolt of lightning that streaks across the sky, making its jagged way from cloud to ground, Don Luis moved through the survivors of the melee and connected with Lucy. She didn't even have time to hear the snapping and sizzling of the live braid, nor did she detect the subtle shift in the air currents as the king of New Puebla raced toward her. She had erred and let her emotions come out to play. Although it lasted only a mere second or two, her pause to take in the victory against one as evil as Sofia, and to allow the throng of hostile humans to back down, had cost her everything.

Don Luis appeared at her side and back like a tango dancer, and where his right hand should have caressed the curve of her back had they been dancing, he stabbed her cybernetic spine with a fistful of severed, snapping, live electrical wires.

Her cybernetic body never felt pain, though it was designed to send reports of damage and malfunction to her brain, so her internal computers and servos could re-direct power and react accordingly. This time, however, the signal that she had been hit didn't even make it up the channels to her brain. The electricity had done its job most effectively, resulting in nothing less than a full and complete short-circuit. No messages were going anywhere, up or down the channels.

She was in what she called full S-Dep, total sensory deprivation, completely cut off from the world outside her consciousness. Still, Lucy knew something bad had happened. She was still aware, still conscious, though her body had shut down, taking with it her vision, her tactile sense, and her hearing, all fully cybernetic. She still had some sense of smell, the nose-olfactory combo being the only sense organ that was linked directly to the brain, allowing it to bypass the backed-up traffic and circuitous byways of the nervous system. But her lungs were nothing more than mechanical intakes that filtered the air in the environment and delivered the oxygen that her organic brain still needed oh-so-badly, and they'd gone down with the rest of her systems.

Shit, was the only distracting thought that ran through Lucy's mind, and then with no more effort than it would take a fully organic human to act on the decision to get up and move, Lucy sent signal after signal in vain to her absentee body in an attempt to get her emergency systems back up and running. She could survive without breathing for thirty minutes, for her body always stored oxygen in its reserves and was ahead of the curve when it came to filtering in the oxygen. But if the motors and servos that powered her reserve system were shorted out too, then her brain would die from oxygen starvation, and soon…

"What a lovely sight!" Don Luis Fernando laughed aloud and tossed the electric anaconda to the side. He looked down at the helpless cyborg and smiled. One of the vampires at the edge of the mob moved in fast, his body language revealing his intention to rip Lucy apart. King Fernando crouched over his kill and bared his fangs, hissing. He was the alpha wolf; this prey was his. The other stopped in his tracks and, lowering his head, began to take steps backward away from his king. Satisfied that his pack knew their place, he returned his affections to Lucy. He kicked her clubs away with a brisk brush of his boot and smiled, his lips pulling back over his elongated canines as he bent down and picked up her BFG.

"Oh, *mami*. I like. It's *mucho grande*. Like me." He grabbed at himself obscenely as he mocked, holding the massive pistol up and turning it from side to side. "But I like mine better," he added, putting Lucy's sidearm into the waistband of his pants, then withdrawing his antique chrome laser pistol from his hip holster. His informants had done him a solid by reporting to him his wife's intention to betray him, though now he would be using the weapon to burn the new wife, and not the old.

"You see, the Aztec club thing? I don't get it. It doesn't do it for me," he explained to himself, not knowing that Lucy couldn't hear him. "Honorable and traditional. What a bunch of crap. Granted, I love being close to my prey when I kill them. I want them to see it in my face, the triumph. I want them to see *me*. Do you see me, bitch?" He squatted back down and got close enough to kiss her. His left hand grabbed her chin and rolled her head back so he was looking directly into her face.

"Now a good gun, on the other hand…" He licked his fangs and brought the pistol flush against Lucy's forehead. "It's like a strong hard cock, no?" Don Luis duck-walked back two steps and probed down Lucy's prone body with the muzzle of the pistol in his right hand, tearing away her black battle fatigues with his left. "Fucking cyborg bitch. Why would you go and remove your only useful part?" He sneered in disappointment and stood back up.

"When I have the gun, you know that I have the power. When I have the power, you respect me. You fucking disrespect me, I teach you a lesson." Don Luis continued like this, his brief thoughts of rape already forgotten. This was his favorite part. This was why he'd worked for the same cartel that had killed his father. This was why he had sold his soul to the devil. This was why he had crowned himself king. He loved the feeling he got when people needed him, or feared him, or otherwise acknowledged and lent credibility to his notion that he was better, richer and more powerful than them. He was a born leader.

Don Luis quit his ranting and again crouched down near Lucy, this time sitting on her chest. He held his left hand out and willed his nails to grow into sharp claws. Even over the chaos of whatever was happening behind him on the stage—the Lily Sapphire bitch would be next; she wasn't going anywhere soon—he could hear the creak of the transformation. He reached out and dragged the pointy tips of his dagger-like nails down Lucy's cheek with just enough pressure to snag and tear open the skin. Her skin was organic and fed with artificial blood, but stretched over an armored exoskeleton, jaw included, that now showed through the pool of blood behind her flayed cheek meat.

"This is gonna be fun. Too bad you're not here to see it, Sofi. See? I can play with my food too."

Lucy couldn't feel the cut or hear his taunts, but she knew a threat was there. Alone, with her consciousness floating in the void of true sensory deprivation, she calmly waited, as warriors oft do, for her emergency protocol to activate fully.

"Boss!" a voice shouted from the crowd. "King Fernando!"

"*What?*" He looked up from his new toy, a scowl of angry impatience smeared across his face.

"They are getting away!" the oaf said and pointed toward the stage. Don Luis turned fully, coming to his feet over the fallen Lucy, and beheld the one he knew as Lily Sapphire, with that nerdy boy of hers, lifting above the crowd on some kind of oversized surfboard. The golden bubble had vanished, and his wife-to-be turned traitor was indeed getting away. The look of impatience melted into disgust and hatred.

"Someone is *always* trying to ruin my fun," Don Luis spat, frowning. He raised the pistol and aimed.

A bright red beam of superheated light exploded into the night. The beam ripped from its muzzle at near the speed of light and lanced Ratt's hoverboard. One second, it was there, structurally sound, and the next, it seemed to come apart as if the very molecules that constituted it became suddenly and instantly magnetically opposed to each other. Maya cried out like a bird shot on the wing as a piece of flaming hoverboard burst forth and punctured her ankle. Ratt, too, was hit with shrapnel from the exploding board, but he was too exhausted to scream in pain; he simply cried and moaned, and then both of them were falling to the ground and the crowd below.

Belly-laughing, Don Luis watched them fall into the mess of people and again summoned his dark powers to project his voice out over the plaza. Silence followed his wolf roar. No one moved. His subjects, human and vampire alike, turned to look at him. Even though half his face and his hands were black and cracked from the damage of the surprise attack, they could see why he was their king. Power and defiance personified stood before them. In his charred hand, his prized pistol, a single shot from which would ignite and destroy any vampire as surely as sunlight. At his feet, the fallen enemy, she who had single-handedly slain at least three dozen of New Puebla's best. He looked in the direction of those closest to where Lily and her boy had fallen.

"Bring them to me."

Don Luis turned back to Lucy. Knowing that he had a better toy on the way, he decided to end this quickly.

"Now…" He let his voice linger in the air like the smell of the burning vampires scattered throughout the plaza. "How does one kill a cyborg, exactly?" he sneered in a mocking tone, knowing full well that her brain was all that remained of her organic organs. And with that, he squatted over her once more, bringing the tip of his pistol against her left temple. He grinned into her expressionless face and said, "Bitch."

BOOM!

Maya screamed bloody murder and would have fallen to her knees were she not being held aloft by two of Fernando's thugs.

But the shot hadn't come from the laser gun.

Don Luis's right arm separated from his torso in a fine mist of deep crimson, and the stone paver just upstream of Lucy's head exploded.

High up on the mountain, Carbine grinned behind the cowl of his sniper hood.

Carbine's grin disappeared as quickly as his railgun's victims. There one second, gone the next. Through the sights of his rifle, he watched Don Luis Fernando's arm fly off. He had been aiming for the torso and missed, but he would take this consolation prize; it had, after all, saved Lucy. Then, as he reached up to chamber another round, a round that was intended to finish the job—as much as was possible anyway, the vampires' regeneration being a factor—he watched in stunned shock as Don Luis sprang forward off of Lucy, fast enough to become blurry, following the chrome laser pistol as it skipped across the pavers. The vampire king moved like a demon possessed, seemingly as much immune to pain as Lucy was, and displaying the same tightly tuned reflexes that she possessed as well.

By the time Carbine realized what was happening, it was too late. His heart thumped in his chest as he fumbled the bolt handle in an attempt to re-chamber his rifle. Don Luis ducked into a roll, grabbing up the pistol mid-roll with his left hand, and turned to face the sniper as he came up on one knee and squeezed off an impossible shot, drawing on his supernatural senses to perfectly re-trace the trajectory of the shot that had severed his arm.

A line of crimson light sliced through the night, tracing its way from Don Luis straight to and up the barrel of Carbine's railgun, igniting the air in its wake. The high-powered rifle exploded in Carbine's hands. He rolled backward from the explosion, pain racking his body. He hit a rock outcropping and tumbled down to the left and below his encampment.

His face broke the roll. He spat dry, dusty dirt out of his mouth, his saliva flecked with blood and mud, and then pushed himself up to his feet. Herculean levels of adrenaline surged through his body. Carbine surveyed the carnage. The railgun was no more, just a pile of scrap; his hands were charred, numb, and bruised bloody. Small dots of bright red seeped out his pores, forming constellations of crimson against the black, burnt, and mud-caked skin. He took a step forward and winced, stopping mid-stride. He quickly found it was difficult to walk when he had an orange-sized chunk of rifle protruding from his hip. His hand reflexively reached down to the source of his pain and felt the embedded foreign object, surrounded by wet fabric.

That's my blood...

He knew he had to do something. He took his hand away, and even in the dark of night, he could see the river of black pouring down his leg.

"That's a lot of blood. Why couldn't it hit me in the... metal one?" Carbine clamped his hand over the wound and tried to apply pressure, but the area was too big, the chunk of rifle too irregular. "Have to... make it to the supplies, have to... find a torch or..." Carbine willed himself to finish the step he started, but fell to the sloped ground below. He nearly passed out then, but managed to summon his deeply-ingrained soldier spirit and began to crawl, pulling his burnt and battered body over the mountain's jagged rocks. He had to get just a few yards up the hill to the stash of supplies they had left when Maya, Lucy, and Ratt had departed down the hill for the city. He was pretty sure Ratt had a laser torch in there somewhere, but would it be enough to stop the bleeding?

"Someone bring whoever that was to me." Don Luis Fernando stood and studied his serfs. A quiet had settled over the city. The battle was over. Don Luis looked down to his still mostly missing arm and watched it regrow before his eyes. He set his jaw firmly and puffed his chest up.

"No one fucks with me and gets away with it!" As he finished this proclamation, he mentally noted to find out who had conveniently been missing, only to show up with his traitorous wife. Her failed betrayal ended up being his saving grace, but the intent to mutiny was still there. They would be made examples of. But all in due time.

A dozen or so of the surviving vampires broke off from the crowd and made for the city gate. Don Luis knew that the lower creatures—the ones he'd made, as opposed to himself, made by the demon-urchin—lacked the level of powers he possessed. It might take them longer to find and capture the sniper, whoever he was, but that didn't matter. Don Luis had seen the target get hit with his preternatural vision and knew he had nothing to fear from that one any longer. His thoughts were interrupted by a parting of the crowd. Don Luis looked up into the face of Lily Sapphire, and he grinned like a wolf licking blood off its teeth.

"You little slut." He gestured for the men carrying her to bring her to him as he waltzed over to Lucy's still, prone body.

"I'm gonna make you watch as I tear this one's brains out."

Maya made a face and whimpered, struggling in vain against her captors' grip.

"And then I think I will give you your little wish. What was it, to be taken by me in front of everyone? Yeah, that was it. *Wasn't it?*"

Maya knew that nothing she said would soothe his rage. She had already played her hand. The time for games was over. This was it. A flash of thoughts and emotions raced through her mind while she watched in slow motion as Don Luis first leered at, then bent down to Lucy. Thoughts swirled of their mission, of the little girl Wyntr, of her poor doomed guardians, Lucy, Ratt, Carbine, and Jon, the Morning Star, the Harvesters, Umbra, her late husband whom she never spoke of. *Her husband... her husband...*

Jon stood in place and recognized his fear. He knew he was in the presence of something truly evil, on the level of the Harvesters for sure. He focused his mind and in turn seized control of his body, as one would slowly yet confidently approach a wild horse to calm it, soothing its flight instincts, cooing to it, stroking its neck and then gently placing a bridle and reins on it. *I am in charge,* Jon thought to himself, *and I can do this.*

His meditative focus was of the little girl who had first enchanted him back in Home, had driven him to commit treason against his State, had brought him here and was even now up top risking her life to allow Jon unfettered access to the palace depths. She was no little girl, Jon reflected; she was a *goddess*. And he believed that he was falling in love with her.

Please, please let this work.

With that, Jon loosened his grip on the hammer's haft and let it slip down to the floor. He took one step into the darkness and could hear the hungry slithering of the needles as they shot in and out of the tubular mouths crowning the tips of each of the urchin's hundred tentacles. He stopped where he was and removed first the poncho, then his Republic body armor, and finally his form-fitting shirt, tossing them to the side of the chamber as if he would never need them again.

If this doesn't work the way we think it will, I won't *ever need them again.*

Jon took two more determined steps. His eyes began to adjust, allowing him to see the tired, starving demon rise in anticipation of its next, much-needed meal. Jon assumed that the creature must take him for a fool and appeared in no way to be suspicious.

Perhaps, he thought, *there were religious fanatics that have been here before and offered themselves so easily and willingly to this thing.*

As he took one more slow step closer, the beast nearly tore some of its appendages off as it snapped at Jon, straining against the chains that bound it.

Or maybe it's just really, really hungry.

Jon paused, as the next step would put him in range of the creature's bite. He held his hands out to his sides, opening his chest up and creating an inviting gesture. A mass of tentacles writhed and reached as hard as they could, their mouths opening and closing in a dying, gasping-for-air kind of way.

Jon steadied his face and pulled it back slightly as one does who is repulsed by what they see. The flashing needles blurred in and out of the gasping circular tube mouths, nearly pricking Jon's skin, so close were they. The slithering sound coming from the hundred mouths was nearly deafening at this range. Jon's heart began to race again. A bead of salty, nervous sweat rolled down and over his flaring nostril.

"You want this, you son of a bitch? Huh? You *want* this?" Jon taunted, more to help stave off his nervous tension than out of bravado. If the urchin heard or understood him, it gave no sign. It simply continued to pull against the chains and flash its hundred needles in Jon's face. Jon closed his eyes and time seemed to stop. He lifted his head up to the dark ceiling, opening his core up more to the urchin and hoping to avoid any needles in the eyes. One last deep breath, and then Jon took a half step forward, placing himself into the sea of hungry tentacles.

They accepted his flesh ravenously. The tube mouths latched on to him all over his body and lifted him off the ground. Fortunately for him, the saliva in the tube mouths acted as a mild neurotoxin and numbed Jon's flesh to the needles' rapid and repeated penetration. Once each mouth-spot had been pierced a couple of dozen times—which took a matter of seconds—and the blood was good and flowing, the tubes began to suck the life out of Jon's body, which was *exactly* what he wanted.

Feeling no pain, only a high-like sensation that increased moment by moment, Jon maintained his arms-wide-open, head-held-high pose and let the urchin drink him. He only hoped that it wouldn't drink him dry before…

Due to the numbing effect, Jon couldn't feel the flow of blood slow as the creature quit sucking and only held him there, his blood flowing naturally from the needle wounds, but he did notice the growing euphoric sensation stabilize. He kept his eyes closed but did exhale a half laugh and mutter, "Got you, bloodsucker." The demon-urchin more spat him out than threw him. He found his body to be considerably weaker than usual as he crashed into the stone bricks of the chamber's interior walls and then fell limply to the floor.

He lay there and chuckled weakly. He couldn't stand up if he'd wanted to, but he did manage to roll his head up and watched as the demon-urchin begin to glow with the now rapidly reproducing serum-enhanced blood cells in its alien body.

"Burn, baby, burn."

Unable to watch what was sure to come next, Maya closed her eyes just as Don Luis Fernando grabbed the side of Lucy's expressionless face.

We've failed! To come this far—Warbak, Home—only to fail now! It's not right!

The plaza had grown so quiet, the goddess could hear the sound of her heart breaking. She wondered for a second about Carbine. Would he get away? She wondered a second longer about Jon. Had he already met the fate that was about to befall Lucy, with Ratt and herself soon to follow?

Interrupting the measured beats of her pounding heart and ringing ears, Maya heard a gasp.

Afraid of what she knew she would see, yet moving like a marionette, she opened her eyes.

"It worked! Our plan worked! Jon did it!" Ratt called out.

A second gasp, smaller than the first, full of surprise and hope, leapt from Maya's tight throat.

Don Luis had relaxed his grip on Lucy's head and taken a step backward. He held both of his hands palm up and was studying them. Then, with a jerking spasm, he turned his surprised gaze to Maya.

She saw in his pale red eyes complete and utter bewilderment, which twisted and melted into dread understanding, followed by panic.

"You have played me!" he screeched, his voice cracking.

A light, not dissimilar to the one that had glowed beneath Jon's skin when pushed to his limits, began to grow within Don Luis.

He held his hands back up to his face and studied the growing glow inside his doomed body.

Then, like the crucial piece of burning kindling carefully

placed under the tinder, his glow seemed to spread to the other vampires in the plaza—for while the urchin was his progenitor, he was, in turn, the father of all New Puebla's privileged class.

Maya didn't even flinch when he began to scream. The heat and brightness coming from within him was so intense at this moment that she couldn't even make out the outline of his body, only light, as bright, blinding, and hot as the sun. The same thing was happening to the other vampires in the plaza for only a second, and then the light became so bright as to blind her completely.

Relieved, knowing that they had beaten the devil, Maya succumbed to her exhaustion, drained from the trauma of the night's events and from pushing herself beyond her normal Strange-shaping abilities. She crumpled to the ground and passed out before her head came to a stop.

A moment later, Don Luis Fernando, along with every single vampire in New Puebla, was no more than ashes drifting through the night on a slight breeze.

When Jon limped into the plaza, dragging his hammer behind him, the human population of New Puebla was still in shock, doing nothing more than standing around and mumbling to each other. No one moved to help or harm Lucy and Maya, both of whom lay on the stone floor amidst small piles of ash and black scorch marks. Likewise, no one accosted, questioned, or other-wise did anything to Jon except step out of his way and stare at him.

He looked as much of a mess as the stage and plaza. His wounds had stopped bleeding—the serum brought rapid cell regeneration along with its death sentence—but he was shirtless and dirty, his flesh caked with dried blood from head to toe, his dark fatigues and boots obscuring his lower wounds. He looked tired, yet still menacing enough to cause even the surviving human sentries to grant him a wide berth. Jon looked over them with his head drooping low, his eyes peering up from under his brow.

"It worked, Jon. It worked." Ratt sounded more surprised than happy. Jon glanced at him and saw that he had been wounded badly in the shoulder and ankle. The kid's jacket was torn, and half his torso was wet with dark blood. He stood mostly on one foot, the other held up like a cat's paw.

"Lucy," Jon muttered.

Ratt swallowed hard and nodded, half shuffling, half jumping over to the fallen warrior's body. Jon dropped the handle of his hammer and fell to his knees. He reached down and gathered Maya into his arms. In his embrace, she looked like no more than a sleeping child, at peace. A fear deeper than that he had experienced in the dungeons of the palace penetrated his heart.

Please, no.

Jon held his breath, choking back the flood of emotion threatening to drown him.

Then, appearing to him like a lighthouse beacon to a lost and storm-harried ship, Jon saw Maya's eyelids flutter to life.

He raised her small frame closer to his massive one, crushing her in an embrace. Through a few tears of joy, he smiled over to Ratt and saw the boy had opened a storage compartment in Lucy's thigh and was injecting himself with a hypodermic shot of medical nanobots.

The surviving citizens of New Puebla, who had either not been in the plaza or had run from it when the shit hit the fan, began to return out of curiosity and concern, and soon a crowd had gathered around the goddess and her guardians.

A couple of brave ones had stepped in a little closer than the others with the clear intent of approaching Jon and Maya, when

Lucy came alive and sprang to her feet. Ratt smiled and leaned back on his haunches, satisfied that he had executed a successful full reboot of the ninja girl, and shut down the dreadful sequence she had been running out of desperation.

"Not a step closer, *hombre*," Lucy menaced.

Even without her Macuahuitls or pistol, she was an intimidating figure. Many of the gathered humans present, including the two currently probing the strangers' personal space, had seen what the cyborg had done, what she could do, and with Sofia and Don Fernando gone, they wanted no part of that. Nevertheless, she quickly located and picked up her BFG and then strode into the gathered crowd. With each step forward she took, the crowd took two back. Within seconds, she had found the resting place of her sword-club, picked it up, and sheathed it.

Maya was regaining consciousness and groaned into Jon's chest. He relaxed his grip and smiled down at her. She blinked her eyes open, saw him, and frowned a little.

"Did it work?" she asked cautiously.

"Yeah, it worked. The serum worked its magic right after the thing began drinking my blood. I guess we were right about the vampires' hyper-metabolism. The same power that allowed them to regenerate from our attacks caused the serum to work a hell of a lot faster than a year. The whole cycle from ingestion to 'flame-on' took less than a minute."

Maya smiled. "And our theory about the demon had been right too."

Jon nodded. Don Luis had inadvertently revealed his greatest weakness to Maya when he had slipped up and said that he "couldn't kill" the demon-urchin. Later that night, after hearing the horrors that Ratt had witnessed, Maya had decided that they needed to do something about the evil that ruled New Puebla. Jon and Carbine had suffered through a grueling one-way conversation, listening to Maya, Ratt, and Lucy hypothesize as to what Don Luis Fernando had meant by his slip-up.

Did it mean the creature was literally and truly immortal? Or did it mean what they'd ended up gambling on: that the Drop-Beastie was the progenitor of the tainted line of victims, conveniently referred to as vampires, and that, if destroyed, then all those who carried its taint would also be destroyed?

It had been a heated discussion and Jon had been beyond frustrated that he couldn't offer his opinion. What would it have mattered anyway? Deep down, he'd suspected that Ratt, the one who had made the first stab at what turned out to be the correct guess, was right. He hadn't liked the plan because Maya would be, essentially, bait. But somehow, she'd survived; they had all survived, and the gambit had paid off.

Lucy snapped him out of his reverie when she placed her hand on his naked shoulder.

"The crowd is getting restless. It's time."

"Do you see Eduardo?" Maya asked.

"No, not yet," Lucy replied.

Jon's gaze left Maya's smiling countenance and scanned the gathered crowd. They were anxious, yes, but not in a dangerous way. Some stared questioningly at him and his companions; some muttered to each other behind raised hands, obscuring their mouths. Some stood on tiptoes, trying to see what was going on. Some frowned. Some cried. Most looked confused and scared, like children, lost without their mothers and fathers.

"It's okay. I'm okay," Maya said quietly to Jon. "Help me up, please."

He hesitated for a second, looked back down to her face, and, seeing all he needed there, nodded. He stood up, lifting her with him and releasing her once she was on her feet. She began to brush herself off. Jon reached a hand out to Ratt and helped him get to his feet as well.

"Come on," Maya said to her guardians and began to slowly walk toward the ruined stage, still towering above the rest of the plaza. The sea of onlookers parted for them easily enough. Maya reached for and squeezed Jon's hand before letting go of it. "It's good to see you again." She looked back over her shoulder, smiled, and winked at him.

"Likewise," Jon said.

Maya walked onto the stage, Jon and Lucy flanking her. Ratt stayed on the steps.

Maya faced the crowd, just as she had done hours earlier. Then, they had been screaming with joy. Seeing a Lily Sapphire show would most likely be the highlight of the decade, if not their entire lives. Now she was greeted by hurt, confusion, worry, concern. Many humans had died in that battle—men who had families, wives, children; men who were needed at their homes and farms. Maya had never anticipated just how many people —*human* people—would fight to the death to protect their oppressors. She looked into the crowds across the plaza, women and men alike, and saw old and young crying over the bodies of human sentries that had met their fates on the edge of Lucy's Macuahuitl. There was not enough left of those who had fallen to her pistol to identify, and this accounted for at least a percentage of the citizens walking around aimlessly, crying and confused.

Maya found herself momentarily at a loss for words. The sight of this suffering confused and frightened her.

"This wasn't how it was supposed to be at all," she mumbled to herself, her resolve evaporating. She opened her mouth to say something and stammered. A tidal wave of raw emotion came crashing in from nowhere, and she found herself choking up. A single burning hot tear blazed its way down her face and fell from her dirty chin to dampen her dress. Just as she was about to turn and run, she felt Jon's hand take hers and squeeze again. She jerked her head and looked at him.

"It's okay," Jon said, gently nodding his head. "They need to hear from you, from Lily Sapphire." She squeezed her eyes shut tight as Jon was squeezing her hand, pushing the tears that welled there out and down her cheeks—a wave of homesteaders following the first trailblazer.

Jon relaxed his grip, gave her one last little squeeze, and then released her hand. She was ready. Again she turned to face the free and broken people of the city-state.

"People of New Puebla. Please hear me." Her voice came out amplified as if she was using a microphone. "You are now free. The monsters that have enslaved you have all been destroyed."

Silence, at first. Confused silence. Then,

"Did we *look* enslaved?"

The question hit her like a slug of DU from Carbine's railgun. She felt as if the air were knocked out of her lungs. Confusion followed the impact of the question, like the shockwave that followed the bullet. Jon glanced over at Maya, then to Lucy, looking as if he hadn't heard the question correctly.

"Wha…what?" Maya managed, scanning the crowd, trying to find the asker of the question.

"I asked you if we looked enslaved. You killed the monsters, as you call them. Those so-called monsters were our government. Our protection, our military." Maya now saw the speaker: a simple-looking farmer man, not a sentry. From the corner of her eye, she saw Lucy's hands drift to the handles of her saddled war-clubs. Her *Feroz Pantera* would, of course, be more concerned with crowd control and her lady's safety, and not the moral crisis developing here.

"What about Eduardo? The Munez family? Their father was

murdered. They told us you couldn't leave! That people disappear!"

"Ricardo Munez was a drunk!" someone shouted back.

"He probably abandoned them!" another voice cried.

Maya turned to Lucy, feeling sick to her stomach.

"Do you see them?" she asked. Lucy scanned the crowd, and with apprehension on her face, turned back to Maya and shook her head slowly side to side.

"I can't believe what I'm hearing!" Jon exclaimed. "We risked our lives for you people!" He stepped forward and stood side by side with Maya. "Surely you people don't think that you were better off with the vampires?" His brow creased, and his eyes flashed. Both of his hands turned palm-up in a demanding gesture.

The old farmer didn't let up. "They were fair. Good rulers. Never hurt no one," the old man shouted, this time louder. All four of the companions saw with trepidation the nods of approval that came from all corners of the gathered crowd. Jon squinted in revulsion and confusion.

Maya shook her head and blurted out, "But the blood tax?"

"Everyone has to pay tax."

"It's no big deal."

"It's for the greater good!"

New voices began to pop up here and there, bringing with them some scattered exclamations of "Yeah" and "That's right."

"No!" Maya's confusion turned to hurt anger. "They *eat* you. They *murder* you. We've seen it!" She clenched her fists and stamped her foot down on the stage.

"Prove it!"

"Lies!"

Then came the worst one yet. From the old farmer, naturally, he who had clearly given up freedom for comfort long ago. "Even if that's true, the ones they occasionally take is nothing compared to what would happen to all of us if they weren't here to protect us from what comes out of the Drops!"

"The real monsters are out there! Demons!" shouted one.

"People like you! You killed my son!" shouted another.

"You killed my husband!" Now there were fists pumping the night air. Lucy flexed and crouched almost imperceptibly, ready for what might come next.

"That couldn't be helped!" Maya cried, her tears making an encore performance. "Our fight was only with the creatures that enslaved you. We never meant to harm you. I'm sorry."

"You're *sorry*?" one haggard and very angry woman shouted as she stood over the top half of a fallen man's body. The questions melted away into a mess of shouts. The crowd had turned into a mob in the blink of an eye.

"Don't you see?" Maya's voice, cracking with sorrow and tears, still boomed magically over the crowd's roar. "You say the vampires provided you with a nice life, but you can still have that nice life without having to die or kneel or work twice as hard! Without them stealing and killing you! No more blood tax! You're free!"

Maybe, in another time, under different circumstances, Maya would have been able to explain to them what she meant when she said they'd still be able to have the same life they'd already had, except better. Maybe. The city was still there, it had its basic infrastructure, and it had the defensive wall. From where Maya stood, the only "service" the ruling class had ever provided was direction—someone to tell them what to do, as it was the human populace that in fact did everything in the city. The rulers had simply supped on the fruits on their serfs' labors and drunk from the chalice of stolen blood. But with each shouted accusation, Maya began to slowly realize that she, and her guardians, had forced their own vision of morality onto an unwilling population.

Somehow, she had become the villain. She had become what she despised.

Cries of "Killers!" and "Terrorists!" and shouted questions such as "Who will maintain the wall?" and "Who will protect us from the Drop-Beasts?" surged and threatened to drown out Maya's pleas, magically enhanced or no.

Stunned, Maya's shouts turned to murmurs, and she lowered her gaze to the ground.

"But... but you're free now. You could protect yourselves; you could govern yourselves... cooperatively, without slavery or violence..." Her words trailed off. Her revolutionary fire had gone out. A cold realization came over her as if she was being wrapped in a wet blanket.

"You people disgust me!" Lacking Maya's Strange, Lucy relied on her cybernetic body to make her voice loud enough for all to hear. Only some of the people near the front of the surging mob heard her. It made no difference—no significant one anyway. "How can you sell your souls to a gang of devils that suck the very life from your veins? Then when we risk our lives to bring you freedom, you cry foul and want to know who will protect you from the creatures of the night? The monsters from the Drops? You bent your very knees and broke your very backs to slave away for *monsters from the Drops*! How can you serve one demon and claim it protects you from another? You're mad! All of you!" Lucy's fury raged like a storm as she continued to scream her lecture at the mob, but her words were as impactful as a storm's winds against stone mountains.

"You have all traded your freedom as men and women of the earth in exchange for some weak promise of security, yet your sons and husbands lie dead before you now because they had to do the fighting to protect their overlords... their... their *owners*! What sort of man would die to protect the ones that rule over him, lie to him, steal from and slowly kill him?"

"We've heard enough of your extremist bullshit!" Maya heard one call over the yelling.

"You've lost nothing today that you can't and already don't do for yourselves!" Maya heard Lucy say, but she knew, too late now, that the villagers were right.

Lost nothing except the dead, Lucy, except the dead. The dead and their security.

"You idiots! Can't you see that she is right?" Lucy held out an open hand at the now silent and diminutive-looking Maya, still weeping. "You did it all, and the vampires just took. That's all they do, the rulers: they take! You've just had someone doing all the thinking for you for so long, you don't know how to think for yourselves anymore!"

Seeing their faces all twisted in hate for her and her friends made Maya feel slightly ill. Seeing the people hold up pieces of their fallen loved ones made her sick to her stomach.

We've failed here. It's hopeless. The thought was like a needle; her self-righteous principles, a balloon. Deflated and defeated, Maya just stood there, weeping and shaking her head.

"Stop it, Lucy," Maya said, just loud enough for her guardian to hear. "They are right. We erred."

Lucy turned and studied Maya's face. Her rage faded, grim understanding slowly colonizing her painted features.

"We want justice!" The crowd surged again, and this time, first one, then three, then many raced for the stage. Some were unarmed, others carried rifles and knives, and still others only carried household and farm implements: cattle prods, shovels, rakes, and the like. Ratt quickly bounced up the stairs to the stage platform proper.

"That's enough!" Lucy's left arm became a blur as it reached for her hip, which had equally as fast popped open and dispensed something into the receiving hand. The carrying hand whipped and threw a small grenade at the base of the stage, just meters before the incoming lynch mob.

There was a bright flash followed by a high-pitched whine. The onrushers stopped dead in their tracks and attempted in vain to cover both their eyes and ears at the same time. When the light faded, Maya could see many of them on their knees or hunched over, vomiting on the ground. Other than that, no one seemed to be hurt— no one new, that is. The shouting and screaming had been hushed, and now that the grenade's whine had faded fully, the plaza was again quiet as the grave, save for the ringing in people's ears.

"This is what's going to happen." Lucy stepped forward now, a good three strides in front of Maya and Jon, her toes nearly touching the edge of the stage. Her arms criss crossed her lithe metallic body, hands resting on the grips of her Macuahuitls.

Her legs opened into a slightly wider than shoulder-width stance, and she turned her head from side to side, making sure that she could see everyone and, more importantly, that they could see her. She continued to use her built-in amplifiers to address the free people of New Puebla.

"Every one of you will turn away from this stage, collect your dead, and return to your miserable lives in your miserable mud homes. You will not dally or hesitate. You have five minutes to clear this plaza, or I will clear it." Maya's tears instantly stopped, and her head snapped up, jaw open as she stared at her jaguar.

"Maya, don't," Jon whispered loud enough for Maya to hear. She looked at him. The expression he gave told her that he felt as she did, but that nothing could be done about it now. It was time for them to depart and suffer their shame elsewhere.

"If even *one* of you obstructs or interferes with me and mine when we walk out this godforsaken shit-hole of a city, I will return and kill all of you." Lucy hesitated and cast a quick sideways glance at Maya.

Maya wanted to tell her that she had gone too far, but she knew that Lucy both knew that and yet still meant what she said. The creeping certainty that she had become the villain today poured deeper into Maya's soul, cement filling the cracks.

"If you are too dumb to tell friend from foe, darkness from light, then you deserve what you get. I won't fucking hesitate."

Maya watched in speechless horror as Lucy studied the crowd, looking for signs that she was getting through to them, that they understood. When the crowd fell into silence, the cyborg continued.

"Now. Tomorrow, you can greet the dawn, mourn your dead, and then take my lady's advice here." She nodded her head back slightly in Maya's general direction. "You can rebuild, work together. Form a militia of volunteers to man that wall and protect your families and your crops from bandits and worse. You could make something here. You could put a touch of humanity back on the map. Move forward. Make your own way." No one moved. No one said a thing. A hundred sets of eyes stared at Lucy in something halfway between fear and shame.

"Or..." She paused for dramatic impact. "You can kowtow to the next vile piece-of-shit that strolls in here and promises you protection in exchange for a slice of your soul. You miserable nothings. Pray that your children grow up in a different world than this and never come to know of your cowardice, your dishonor... your revolting, boot-licking shame."

Silence and stillness.

Then, before any of them could be so stupid as to say something, Lucy stepped back and said, "Your five minutes start now." And for an added touch, she drew both of her weapons.

The people did as they were told, naturally, and cleared the dead from the plaza, scurrying off into the night. Weapons were left on the stone floor to mark the ash and blood stains. Jon collected Maya and put an arm over her shoulders, comforting her as best he could.

Ratt broke the silence, mentioning that they should go rendezvous with Carbine, as he had no way to communicate, not even having fired his railgun into the air to let them know he was okay. Lucy nodded her approval and led the way to the main street, where they had entered the city when they first came to its dark palace.

No one said another word to each other as they walked out of the city.

Only Maya turned to look back.

Wisps of steam rose from the heated water like flames into the air, a thousand licking tongues probing, exploring. A splash echoed. Ripples bounced from the center of the pool to the edges and back. Condensation coalesced on the tiled walls and ran, first as solitary spies, then entire battalions to the slick floor below.

Having reached the shallow edge, a figure rose from the water, naked and glistening.

The man stepped up and out of the pool, and made his way, dripping, to the wooden bench against the wall and the fresh linens piled there.

Reaching down, he plucked up one towel and tied it around his slender waist. Once the first towel was secured in place, he retrieved a second one and fastened it around his long lavender hair.

He stretched his arms and chest, enjoying the tautness in his muscles from the vigorous swim, and he sighed.

"I swear, I shall die of boredom, waiting," he said aloud, mild annoyance lacing his voice.

Umbra slipped his feet into a pair of sandals that lay tucked under the bench and made his way across the room to a recessed vanity in the far wall.

Admiring himself in the embedded mirror, he smiled wryly and went about pouring himself a tall measure of herb-infused wine in a crystal goblet.

He drank deeply, closing his eyes and inhaling, savoring the refreshing flavor. Setting the goblet back down, he retrieved a small glass orb from an ornate golden tripod and held it aloft.

Peering into it with aloofness, he spoke.

"Glyer, I want you."

"Right away, my lord," a voice from the sphere responded.

A minute later, a wretched half-man came crawling into the pool-house. His warped and misshapen head hung low.

Umbra reclined on a cushion, wine in hand, and beheld his advisor.

The man slithered his way into the room and toward his lord. Where his legs should have been, a robotic, serpentine appendage twisted and writhed, gliding snake-like across the floor. On his back, bolted into his flesh, a metal frame supported his otherwise weak torso. His face was disfigured and only wisps of greasy hair lay strewn over his pockmarked skull.

"Why haven't we heard anything yet, Glyer?" Umbra asked the spineless snake-man.

The advisor shuddered and made a face as if a sneeze were trapped in his nose. Slurping up his liberal drool, eyes still downcast, he forced his report.

"Our agent has not yet reported their arrival, my lord."

"They should have already been there. They departed *weeks* ago," Umbra said, his face darkening.

"Yes, my lord," the toady agreed.

"Yes? Yes, what? Yes does nothing for me. Have you been in communication with the agent? Or are you simply waiting for her to report?"

"I will make inquiries, my lord." Glyer shuddered again as if racked by a chill.

"See that you do. You're running out of body parts for me to replace." The threat smothered the conversation like the oppressive humidity in the room.

"Yes, yes, my lord." Glyer bowed deeply.

"In other matters: have there been any developments with the Engine?"

Glyer hesitated and seemed to curl in on himself, twisting in place, appearing to shrink, even as his snake-tail grew fatter.

"I asked you a question, Glyer. I would appreciate an answer." Umbra poured himself a second glass of the spiced wine.

"I'm sorry, my lord. The news is not good."

"When is it ever?" Umbra asked, more to himself than to Glyer, and sipped again from the goblet. "Well? Out with it."

"With the losses we accrued in Home, the souls we failed to harvest, our Strange reserves are at an all-time low. We lack the quintessence needed to power the experimental mecha. Furthermore, all attempts to correct the malfunction have failed."

Umbra sighed and closed his double-irised eyes. Setting the half-drunk goblet down, he stood and stretched his neck. Taking over the universe was such tedious business, but even on a bad day, it was far better to rule in Hell than to serve in Heaven.

He had expected the news about the Engine to be as such. Losing the harvest of Home had been a great setback. He needed those souls to power the second wave of his long-term plan. But even if he had managed to collect, what good would an army do him in Hell, if he was as trapped in it like everyone else?

"How did you do it, dear brother?" he muttered out loud.

Glyer looked up to him from his coiled position on the floor, just for a second, and then snapped his gaze back to the floor when Umbra turned to him.

"I'm beginning to grow concerned, Glyer. If the faux goddess does not bring him to the Morning Star safe and sound, then we are back to square one."

Without vocalizing his agreement, Glyer nodded his head slowly.

"Contact our agent, remind her how important it is that she be honest with us. Send out the drones, scour the land. Find Maya and her ship. If they haven't arrived yet, then something must have happened to them. Find them, and report back. If we have to, we will take them and bring them there ourselves."

"As you command, my lord," Glyer said, and rose, making to depart.

"I have not dismissed you, fool. There is more. I hope you are taking notes."

Glyer slurped and brought his palms together, bowing.

"We have to begin planning for a contingency. While we lack the firepower to re-take Home as is, things have begun to develop that may ensure that we can still harvest what is ours."

Glyer perked up at this, watching Umbra pick his goblet back up and begin to pace back and forth along the narrow side of the embedded steam-pool.

"My eyes in Home have shown me that the might of the Republic is already split in half, and furthermore, I have good reason to believe that what's left in the Ziggurat will soon become even weaker than it already is. A storm is brewing in Home. I almost couldn't have planned what is to unfold better myself."

"Sounds promising, my lord," Glyer said.

"Indeed. We will be watching the coming events with great interest. In the meantime, send another volunteer into the Labyrinth. Find me the Hermit. If we can have him, then I may not need the Anvil after all."

"It will be done."

"That is all. Go, do as I commanded and report back when you have finished," Umbra said, finishing his wine. Placing the empty cup back down, he tenderly raised his fingertips to his eyes, feeling them and reflecting on the events that had caused them to grow a second iris and pupil. Glyer began a backward slither, retreating to the safety of the exit and beyond.

"Must I do everything myself? At least Warbak had a spine." Umbra chuckled to himself at the inside joke. The last time Glyer had failed him, he'd had the man's spine literally removed, hence the metal frame the stooge now needed to remain upright and living, even if it was a sort of half-life.

Umbra strode to the opposite wall of the room. A transparent rectangle of glass-like material separated his spa from the cavernous chamber beyond.

He scanned the room on the other side of the transparent panel and felt a hunger stir inside him.

Row after row of glass orbs ran the length of the massive expanse. *They should be filled with souls by now, fuel for the Engine. One of these things needs to work. Either I find the Hermit or the Anvil. Perhaps both?* Umbra smirked at the possibilities that would bring. *Soon.*

Martin awoke from the dream, images of Nguyen's shriveled husk of a face being eaten by that alien starfish lingering in his mind's eye.

Gasping and shivering, he sat up and brought his hands to his face. He rubbed vigorously as if trying to erase the images that haunted him. The room was cold, and he noticed it quickly, due to the large wet patch of cold sweat that stained his gray athletic shirt and covered his back.

"Just a bad dream… just a bad dream…" he mumbled, still rubbing his eyes. Awareness of his situation came to him. One—he was awake and no longer dreaming, and two—that he was in his command tent and not back in the dark copse of trees where he had watched Matiaba sic a demon on his boy. His breathing slowed, his mind calming, but the shivering intensified now that his torso was upright and free from the confines of his mummy-bag.

Glancing around the inside of the tent, which was still dark, with only the very first hint of dawn's gray light sneaking in, he saw that the tell-tale blue light of the gas furnace was missing.

"Heater went out," Martin mumbled. He crossed his arms over his chest and rubbed his hands up and down his arms, trying to stimulate blood flow. "It's freezing in here."

Still shivering, he crawled out of bed, shed the sweat-soaked shirt, and reached for a dry one, followed by his black sweater, the one with the leather shoulder pads.

Squinting against the pre-dawn gloom, he popped the access plate off the back of his tent's heater and frowned. *No fuel.*

Making a mental note to get more before he retired the next night, Martin finished dressing and, pulling away the flap to his tent, stepped out into a miserable early morning.

Freezing rain came down steadily all over his camp. The walking paths between his tents looked like off-road ATV trails. The rain had turned the dirt to mud, and sentries' footsteps had turned that mud into a topographical landscape in miniature, complete with mountain peaks, saddles, and valleys. Then the nightly drop in temperature had frozen both the mud and moisture that sat atop it, creating crystal-like growths of ice that pushed the mud out into strange honeycomb-like formations, as well as puddle-sized lakes of sheer ice. The rain flap of his tent, and the others around it were all decorated with stubby, wet icicles that *drip, drip, dripped* onto the ground, joining their drops with those of the persistent rainfall.

This sucks, Martin thought, and then frowned deeply. His reflexive inner dialogue complaint about the weather—behavior he abhorred in any soldier, especially himself—brought back memories of Nguyen, and the horror-show images from his dream.

He wondered then, and not for the first time since his rendezvous with Matiaba, the Provocateur, if his devil deal, his agreement to work with the former aide, and his use of Invasive Drop-trash would prevent him from seeing a good night's sleep ever again. He shuddered once more, this time not just from the cold.

Shaking off his troublesome musings for the time being, Martin pulled his overcoat tighter around him and made his way to the quartermaster's supply tent.

"Attention!" Quartermaster Irsik announced when he noticed Martin entering the tent.

"At ease, soldier. Cold morning, eh?"

"You got that right, sir," Irsik said, visibly relaxing and going back to what he had previously been occupied with.

"What you got there, Todd? Breakfast?" Martin asked, lifting his chin to better smell the pleasant aroma.

"Yes, sir! Just beans, but you're welcome to some."

"Just beans?" Martin asked, closing the gap and coming up alongside Irsik and the gas stove he manned.

"Yeah, sorry to say. But we are just about out of food. It's going to be a long winter, I fear. What brings you here so early?"

"Tent's heater is out of fuel," Martin reported.

"Oh, uh. Well, you can have what's left of this." Irsik gestured to the small canister plumbed into the side of the small stove.

"What? That's it?" Martin asked.

"Afraid so. I hate to say it, sir. But we didn't bring nearly enough supplies with us from Home."

Martin scowled, and his belly rumbled. Suddenly, he found his reservations about working with Matiaba and his willingness to partner with Drop-trash not quite as unpalatable. *Besides*, he thought, *it's only a means to a greater end.*

"Don't fret, buddy. Things are going to start getting better for us real quick. And we will have plenty to see us through till spring. After that? We will retake the Zigg."

"Sir?" Irsik said, his eyes growing with excitement.

"That's right, soldier, things are now in motion that will all but guarantee our success. As for supplies in the meantime? Hang on."

Martin broke away from the cook and his beans and went to the supply tent's radio table. Picking up the handset with one hand, he punched in the number for Lincoln's forward guard.

"Forney, you got a copy? Forney? This is Martin, do you copy?"

The speakers crackled with static for half a minute then popped to life with another man's voice.

"Loud and clear, sir. Forney here. Good morning, sir."

"Don't lie, soldier. It's a shit morning, but maybe you have some good news for me. Have the eagles come home to roost?"

"Yes, sir, they have! I just received word an hour ago that they are due back in Lincoln by thirteen hundred hours," Forney reported, his voice sounding quite chipper.

"Excellent news, soldier. Carry on, Martin out." Martin sat the handset back into its cradle and faced his quartermaster.

"You're going to have a busy day today, Irsik."

"Sir?"

"Phase one of the plan is done. We have successfully raided the supply caravan from the farmlands that was *en route* to the Ziggurat."

Irsik's eyes grew even wider than before.

"We will have all the food and fuel we require for some time," Martin said.

"But, sir! Won't theft provoke Home into open hostilities with us?" the young quartermaster asked.

"I certainly hope so, Irsik. I certainly hope so."

It wasn't until they had found Carbine alive, bruised and beat up, but alive nonetheless, that they relaxed enough to let the real hurt of their moral defeat sink in.

After walking out the gates of the city, concern weighed heavy on Jon's mind. Carbine's railgun had fallen silent after Fernando had returned fire. It was hard not to fear the worst when hope was in such short supply.

Making their way up the hillside by memory, Jon unslung his hammer and allowed its million pinpricks of swirling blue-white light to serve as a lantern. He held it high above his head, hoping its glow would help his companions as well.

Lucy, not needing light to see, made better time and moved on up ahead, finding Carbine first and calling out to the others.

"Is he okay?" Jon called up the slope.

"Yes, but he's hurt. Get up here quick," she called back.

A long minute later, Jon, Maya, and Ratt approached Lucy and the supine form of Carbine. A chunk of what used to be railgun jutted out of a black mass of scab on his friend's right hip. On the ground lay the scattered remains of both the railgun and its incredible scope.

Although unconscious, Carbine still stubbornly clung to a hand-held torch.

"Oh man, what did you do to yourself?" Jon asked aloud, already knowing the answer. It was clear that Don Luis Fernando's shot had re-traced the exact path of Carbine's last slug, disintegrating the railgun and severely wounding Carbine. "Carbine must have used the torch to cauterize the wound," Jon murmured. The fact that Carbine had finished the painful task before passing out was a testament to the true mettle of a New Breed soldier.

Lucy ordered Ratt to give her the nano-medi injector. Ratt dug around in the pockets of his cargo pants and retrieved a large syringe, identical to the one Jon had seen him use back in the Underground.

"Um, that's the last one," Ratt announced, shoulders drooping.

Seeing that his friend was healing nicely with the application of the last of the nano-machines, Jon turned his head southward and entered the pseudo-meditative trance that would recall the images Wyntr had shown him. A second later, the pillar of golden light appeared on the horizon.

It's going to be tough going from here on out.

"I... I almost didn't... didn't see him... in time." Carbine's voice interrupted the silence. Everyone turned and looked to see the wounded soldier's eyelids flutter open and a grimace, one part pain, one part wry humor, spread across his ruddy face.

"I was covering... Maya and Ratt's escape... but..." He began to sit up, paused and took a deep breath, then let it out. "When they got hit... I lost them in the crowd." His words were sounding clearer now, and the creases of pain that lined his face were slowly smoothing out. His mouth twisted into a sideways half-smile that, paired with his still furrowed brow, made him appear amused with himself. He had been looking at Lucy since regaining consciousness and continued to do so. "I saw that bastard about to do you in." Lucy was a silent statue, listening.

"I missed my mark, but it looks like it was enough." His grin grew twice the size. "You're still alive." Then, half-joking, he added, "No thanks necessary. Saving lives is what I do." He was intentionally hamming it up, taking great pleasure in pointing out to the strong, silent, killer jaguaress—who had at one point wanted to leave him for dead because of his uselessness—that he had, in fact, saved her life.

When the expected insult didn't come, Carbine's grin fell off his face in surprise. A small wet spot on Jon's cheek punctuated the awkward silence. Then another, and another.

Great, rain.

"Can you march?" Jon asked his friend, now sitting up fully.

"Yeah, sure, why not?" Carbine said, chuckling. "Things

already suck, so go ahead and bring on some more suck. Though I could sure go for one of those Puebloan tacos."

A pang of envy stabbed Jon's heart when he recognized Carbine's blissful ignorance for what it was.

Lucky bastard.

Carbine had always been happy-go-lucky, but Jon knew the real reason his friend could manage to stay that way, despite the current events. Carbine hadn't been there when the people of New Puebla had rejected their "liberators." He hadn't had to suffer the verbal attacks, the cries of the survivors who had lost loved ones, nor suffer the killing blow that had been the realization that those people had been happier in slavery; that they didn't *want* to be free. When it had finally sunk in, there up on the stage, that they had been blinded by their own hubris, that they had forced themselves on the people, that they had *done wrong*, a part of Jon had died inside.

Turning now to study Maya, he found her back turned to the group, her gaze on the city down below, where columns of smoke still rose from the central plaza.

A part of her had died down there too.

"Wait, what? We're leaving? Why?" Carbine asked repeatedly.

Jon and the others ignored him, packing up what little supplies they had left on the hillside.

"Come on, it's starting to rain. We need to move. Maybe find some shelter," Jon ordered.

"But why aren't we staying in the city?" Carbine insisted, confused. "They can shelter us! I mean, didn't we just save those people?"

To everyone's surprise, Maya lost it.

"Just shut up about it, okay?" She wheeled on him, fresh tears in her puffy red eyes. "People don't *want* to be saved! Just *shut up*!" She walked off from the rest of the group, who were pulling the essential bits of cargo from their pile and loading up and rearranging their backpacks. She only went about twenty meters and stopped, crying into her cupped hands and falling to her already scraped-up knees. Jon had begun to follow her, when Lucy lay a surprisingly gentle hand on his shoulder and offered, "Give her time, Jon. Space and time." Jon hesitated, but then nodded his understanding.

Several long, quiet hours later, they gave up trying to find shelter, the terrain being flat brush-land as far as the eye could see. Jon and Lucy may have wanted to press on, as it was raining in earnest now, but the others simply were unable. Exhaustion claimed them first, and cold was coming in a close second.

The rain picked up its intensity and Jon hunched his shoulders up, hugging himself. On the other side of the fire they had barely managed to light, now sizzling like cooking bacon with each volley of droplets, Ratt frowned.

"Maybe we should find another place to camp?" the kid suggested, projecting his voice over the sound of the growing deluge. A flash of lightning briefly lit up the soggy companions.

"There is no other place to camp," Lucy growled. It was true. They were in the saddle two small mountains, had in fact only made it a few peaks away from New Puebla. Tired as they had been that night, none of them wanted to sleep in the shadow of that place. Being that close to what they had done and what had been done in return would surely bring troubled dreams. And so they walked until dawn, just over the southern peak of New Puebla's valley, and slept half the day.

They soon found, however, that no matter how far they walked, they couldn't outrun the ghost of their sin.

The party rose at noon and trekked on, deciding that late

evening was as good as a time as any to eat and let Maya, Carbine, and Ratt catch up on their sleep.

The booming roll of thunder came the second Lucy finished her statement of the obvious. There were no trees up in this saddle, or anywhere nearby. No rock ledges, no caves. They would be whipped by wind and rain all night, it seemed.

Jon got up and walked over to Maya. She hadn't spoken all day. She looked like a drowned mouse, or the ghost of a scorned lover—broken in damn near every sense of the word.

"Hey." One word, simple, but the way in which he said it carried more warmth than the fire had been providing before the rains picked up. She sat, feet flat on the ground, with her legs bent before her, cradled by her arms. She peered over her knees at the dying fire and did not seem to sense Jon's presence, word, or intent. He took off his jacket and draped it over her head and shoulders. That got her attention. She peered up at him from under the hood his jacket had made. He couldn't tell the difference between the raindrops and tears on her face. In his characteristic way, Jon sucked his lips into his mouth, inhaling through his nose, then released them along with a long, slow sigh. He knelt down next to her, rain pouring down onto his head and forming two rivers that ran down his face and joined at his chin, to fall off.

"Hey," he repeated. He could see now that she wasn't actively weeping. It was just the rain after all. Nevertheless, he reached out and used the back of his fingers to brush the droplets off her face. His military jacket was doing a decent job of keeping more rain off. He sucked his lips in again, making an apologetic face. "I'm sorry," he tried. She blinked at him and visibly relaxed. She shook her head side to side so subtly that it barely even registered.

"It's fine. It's just…" She looked away to the side as if to imply that she couldn't give power to her thoughts by speaking them as long as she was looking at Jon. That it was too much. The intimacy of eye contact pushing the rising tide of emotion over the breaking point of the levee. "It's just that now I'm questioning everything. Like why are we even doing this?" Now that it was spoken, now that she had said it, some of its power over her subsided.

Jon nodded equally as subtly and breathed another sigh. Her eyes jumped back to Jon's face and locked into his own blue eyes, encircled by the rivulets of water. "Let's say we find the Morning Star. Let's say we get the answers we seek, the tools we need to defeat the Harvesters and can return Earth to how it was. Will we just be hated? Will we be no better than Warbak, pushing what we think is best onto people without their consent?"

Jon gulped. He did not know what to say.

"How can violence be justified if people don't even want to be free?"

Jon felt something stir in him. Something he could not explain. A sense of *déjà vu*. But it was as elusive as those tears had been in this monsoon. He blinked and frowned, prompting Maya to do the same.

Jon noticed the hurt and concern on Maya's face and dismissed the self-inquiry, rushing his words in an attempt to soothe and calm the goddess. "No, no. No. You're right. But hear me out. I mean, yeah, okay, maybe we don't have the right to free people from a situation that we think is deplorable. Maybe it's morally wrong. Okay. I get that. But—"

"No buts," Maya interrupted.

"No. I mean, yes. Listen. We messed up back there, that's obvious now. But we *are* different than Warbak, all right? He knew better. We didn't. I mean, we do *now*! We didn't mean any harm. I know that doesn't help how we feel right now, or the New Puebloans, but we can learn from this. Grow from it somehow. Warbak always knew what he was doing. He *meant* to do evil. His Ministry preached nothing but lies and propaganda. Sure, some nasty things come out of the Drops, like that urchin back there, but he never stopped there. He had everyone believing that everything and everyone who wasn't fully human was a potential threat. Tagged and bagged. Step out of line just a little, and they'd whisk you away to Social Purity, never to be seen again. All the while he himself was Unpure and working with the Harvesters! Does that sound like something we'd do?"

Maya's face sharpened as she listened. Encouraged by the sound of his own voice and the feeling that he was at least halfway making sense, Jon continued.

"And let's look at the Harvesters. These things actively hunt down, capture, and enslave people against their will. Their prisoners don't get the luxury of even the third-world accommodations that the people of Puebla got! They get pulled into a void, a black prison. Who knows what happens to them after that? I don't, but I'm sure it's not good!" Jon stammered a bit. He felt his argument turning into frustration and emotion. Somewhere in there was that elusive teardrop, that nagging green worm of doubt. That feeling that he had had this conversation, this very conflict before, and that he didn't fully believe himself. The Harvesters were evil, of that he was sure.

"And now, thanks to our meddling, New Puebla may fall to them, the Harvesters," Maya said flatly.

Jon started, his words forming a lump in his throat. She was right, of course, and they would have to live with that.

"I just… It's just that—!" Jon floundered, lost in his rage, almost forgetting that he was initially trying to comfort Maya, not soapbox. Maya's gaze drifted down to her folded arms and knees again.

Subconsciously, without even knowing it, Jon switched gears. Somewhere between the paradox that was the fear of defeat and peace that was surrender, and the sheer terror that comes to a man who is impotent to banish whatever or whomever is causing the one he adores to suffer, Jon found himself calming down.

"Look, I don't have all the answers. And maybe there aren't any. But right now, we keep moving forward. We don't think about it. We just do it. One day at a time, one step at a time. I know that sometimes leads to horror. Even if you hadn't shown me all of history, I experienced it for myself yesterday. We all did. I didn't want to kill those people, but at that point, if I hadn't, they would have killed me… or you." She lifted her head back up and stared, somewhat astonished at Jon once more. "And yeah, I know we could have avoided that whole situation if we had just gone around the city. I know we screwed up; I know. We move on. We learn from it. I know what we did was wrong, but I also know that if we don't find whatever it is that you are looking for and find it soon, the Harvesters will rally to Home first, and then the rest of the planet. What we are offering has got to be a whole hell of a lot better than that. We stole New Puebla's protection from them, so we must replace it with something else. It's our duty." Maya said nothing. Jon sighed, exhausted, defeated, and hung his head. He shifted from his squat to a sitting position and crossed his legs. He tossed his hands maybe half an inch into the air and finished with, "I don't know. I give up."

Maya unclasped her hands, stretched her legs out as lithely as a cat, and shifted her weight to one side, bringing herself closer to Jon. He didn't notice. She reached out and placed her small hand on the back of his large one. Jon's head, still down, cocked a bit to the side and he stared at the back of her slender, smooth hand and fingers.

She truly is beautiful. It's so sad that she is so sad. He knew that her sadness went far deeper than the debacle that had been the liberation of New Puebla. He wanted so badly to know what the source of that was, and then to displace it from her life.

"Jon." Her voice, quiet, wove its way through the falling rain and thunder and landed on his ears as soft and warming as the promise of tomorrow's sun that would heat the chilled land and dry away the leftovers of the night's storm.

He lifted his head and peered into her jacket hood. The falling rain looked silver behind her.

"Let's... how do you say? Soldier on?" There was hope in Maya's voice. Jon half chuckled. Then that spark touched some unknown, hidden tinder and began to make a flame. A reluctant, tired smile spread across both their faces.

"Yeah. That's right. Good idea, Maya. Let's."

"I'm hungry!" Wyntr whined, pouting.

"You have to be patient!" To-Kan called from across the room, where she was preparing food for the child.

"But I'm hungry now!" Wyntr said, jumping up and down on the room's luxurious couch.

"Wyntr!" To-Kan yelled back, her voice taking on a serious tone. "Be still, sit down, and stop yelling, or you won't get anything at all!"

"Okay..." Wyntr said, plopping down onto her rump as she finished the last jump. She crossed her arms and frowned.

"Thank you. Now, here you go. Lean over and don't make a mess."

Wyntr watched with anticipatory glee as her elderly caretaker, crossing over the open floor of the suite that had once belonged to the nice Lily Sapphire lady who rescued her, bringing her a steaming bowl of warm curry.

"Yummy!" Wyntr exclaimed, receiving the bowl and digging in.

"I know how much you like my butter chicken," the old

woman said as she smiled down at Wyntr. "Eat up, then it's bath time."

The child didn't have to be told twice and began to devour the food, when a beep came from the door.

"YOU HAVE A VISITOR," the room's limited AI announced. Continuing to inhale her dinner, Wyntr watched To-Kan go to the front door and touch a panel adjacent to it. The door snapped open to reveal a haggard-looking Miller on the other side.

"General Miller!" To-Kan said. "What a pleasant surprise."

"Please, To-Kan, just Miller when we aren't in the council chambers. May I come in? We need to talk."

"Of course, of course. Come on in. Have a seat. Dinner is on if you're hungry."

"Thank you, but that won't be necessary. I won't be staying long," Miller said, stopping just inside the door, which snapped shut behind him.

Taking her bowl in her hands, Wyntr twisted on the couch and peered over the back of it, observing the adults as they conversed by the door.

"I take it you're here about Matiaba?" To-Kan asked.

"You think? How could we let that happen?" Miller replied, quickly becoming agitated.

"You know I trust you, Miller, always have."

"But?" the big man asked.

"But," To-Kan said gently, resting a hand on Miller's thick metal arm, "despite the... slimy nature of that lawyer, Libis, Matiaba has a point. We don't know that he was any guiltier of anything than any other soldier."

"Really? You really gon' doubt the things he put Lucy through?"

"That's not what I'm—"

"That's what it is, To-Kan. By letting him walk, we are completely dismissing Lucy's testimony."

"I know, I know. But she isn't here, Miller. And we could use Matiaba's help getting this city running again."

"That's the other thing," Miller said. "There has been no word from them. Not a peep. We lost contact before the first day was even over, and they've been gone two weeks now! Sooner or later, everyone will know. Even Martin and the Old Guard. I'm worried about what will happen then. You know the supply caravan didn't make it back. I'm gonna have to send troops out east to investigate, and…"

Miller and To-Kan continued their conversation, failing to notice as Wyntr climbed down from the couch and placed her empty bowl down on the squat table next to it.

As quiet as a ghost, Wyntr slipped away from the room and the arguing adults and entered the sleeping chambers. Things were as she had sensed; another window was opening.

She stood off to the side, hiding her small frame behind the raised mattress, and watched as a small window of light grew into existence from nothing, stopping when it reached the size of a dinner plate. Crouching down, she left only part of her face exposed; it wouldn't do to be spotted.

As expected, another object came flying through the tiny portal, landing softly on the room's floor. The third such delivery in two weeks, this one was folded paper, unlike the first two squares of lightweight metal.

A second later, the window blinked shut and was gone. Knowing that she no longer had to hide, Wyntr approached the folded piece of paper and plucked it up off the floor.

Opening it, she read:

To whomever receives this message, To-Kan, or Miller. Things did not go very well in the city we encountered. Low on supplies. Really hoping that you get this message in good order and would like to schedule a face-to-face. Perhaps you could send us some food? We are now making our way to the Morning Star on foot.

Ratt says we are in the same time zone, so we will try this again tomorrow at noon. Please have supplies ready for us, as it is tiring to keep these windows open for very long. If only you had another transport, we could determine our exact location by the stars and you could send someone to pick us up. Might be in for a long walk. Anyway, talk to you tomorrow.

 Love, Maya

Wyntr folded the paper back up and made for the large walk-in closet on the far side of the bedroom. Opening its doors, she beheld the tiny mattress that To-Kan had placed there for her, and the small pile of stuffed animals at its head. She crawled onto her mattress and began moving the toys to one side, revealing a small box that she kept hidden there.

She turned to the bedroom door, her eyes narrowing. She had to make certain that the adults didn't catch her. Not when she was under the spell of her secret compulsion. Soon she would forget about this whole scenario, but for now, she had to—was *commanded* to—exercise caution.

A second later, she opened the box, placing the folded note inside it, right on top of the two squares of metal.

GET 3 BOOKS FREE!

as a thank you for reading *Hostile Genus* book two in Invasive Species.

We hope you enjoyed it as much as we enjoyed bringing it to you. We just wanted to take a moment to encourage you to review the book on Amazon and Goodreads. Every review helps further the author's reach and, ultimately, helps them continue writing fantastic books for us all to enjoy.

If you liked this book, check out the rest of our catalogue at www.aethonbooks.com. To sign up to receive a FREE collection from some of our best authors as well as updates regarding all new releases, visit www.subscribepage.com/AethonReadersGroup.

JOIN THE STREET TEAM! Get advanced copies of all our books, plus other free stuff and help us put out hit after hit.

SEARCH ON FACEBOOK:
AETHON STREET TEAM